Stoc

COPPER PENNY
PUBLISHING

Titles by Donald D. Allan

The New Druids Series
Duilleog, Volume One
Craobh, Volume Two
Stoc, Volume Three
Freamhaigh, Volume Four
Cill Darae, Volume Five
Gaea, Volume Six

Leaf and Branch (The New Druids Vols One & Two)
Stalk and Root (The New Druids Vols Three & Four)
Priestess and Gaea (The New Druids Vols Five and Six)

The New Druids Compendium (Volumes One to Six)

DONALD D. ALLAN

Stoc

A New Druids Novel
Volume Three

STOC: A New Druids Novel, Volume Three
Donald D. Allan

National Library of Canada Cataloguing in Publication Data

ISBN-13: 978-0-9958490-3-7

Cover Design—	*JD&J Book Cover Design. http://www.jdandj.com*
Cover Credits—	*Images and art purchased from http://www.123rf.com/profile_designwest, http://www.123rf.com/profile_1enchik, and http://www.123rf.com/profile_epantha. Use of the triskelion within this novel from http://en.wikipedia.org/wiki/File:Triskel_type_Amfreville.svg. The image is licensed under the Creative Commons Attribution 3.0 Unported license and is attributed to the author Cétautomatix (artéfact), Ec.Domnowall. Title page art: Copyright: http://www.123rf.com/profile_olivier26 from http://www.123RF.com. Part Three Title page art: Copyright: http://www.123rf.com/profile_martm*
Map Credit—	*Stephen Chase*

For James and Katherine.

I'm always so proud of you.

Stoc

A New Druids Novel

Volume Three

Map of North Belkin: Munsten and Cala Counties

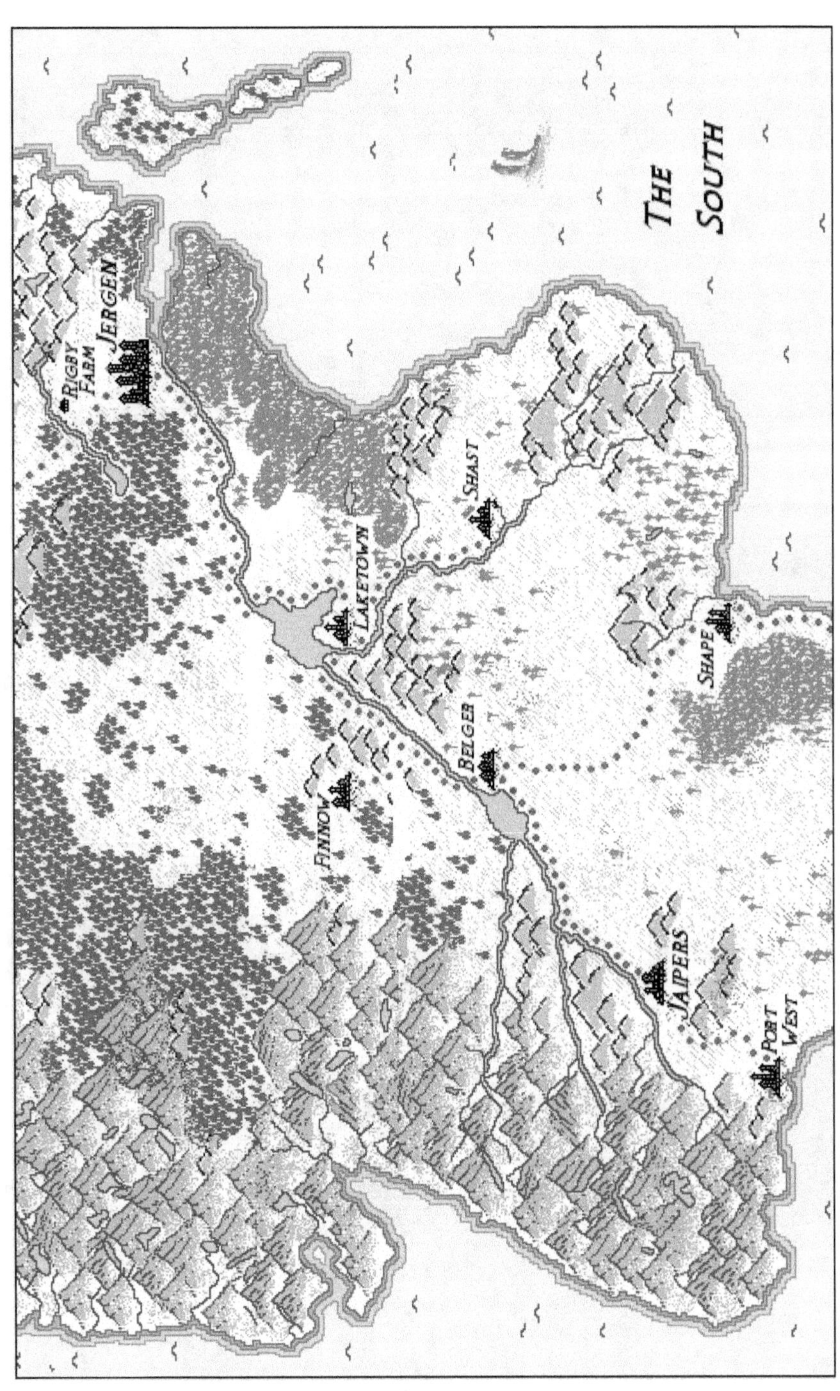

Map of South Belkin: Turgany County

Prologue

Somewhere in Cian-Oirthear, across the ocean east of Belkin, March 901 A.C.

H OT WINDS SWIRLED and gusted and brought sand up to whip past the face of the man standing unfazed by such common things. He was covered from shoulder to feet with a sand coloured *thawb* tied tight to his body with weathered leather straps. He wore a traditional *keffiyeh* around his face and shoulders and had it tied tight to his head with a dark brown *agal*. His light hazel eyes were obscured by tinted goggles and small movements of his head revealed he searched for something or someone atop the densely packed dune on which he stood.

Around him were miles and miles of an endless desert. He knew a mere hundred miles to the west the land changed and grew lush with greenery before the vast western sea appeared. He shuddered at the thought. That much water was unnatural. The sand, palm trees, dried figs and the world on horseback were his domain. The sea was out there and one day he would need to face it. He would depart these lands he held with sweat, blood and determination.

Leave it behind and seize the promised wealth of a new land.

He didn't need to look behind him to see his men hidden and spread out around the waterhole. The horses hidden behind another dune were silent and ready to respond to his men. The soft whisper of sand brushing across the dunes and the hot breath of wind were the only sounds. It was peaceful in its way, but he hated this place. It brought back memories he fought to keep distant.

The sun reached its zenith, and he drew a slow breath. Now was the appointed time and soon his wait would be over. A small trickle of fear ran down his spine and he braced himself. Fear was good, but this fear always threatened to overwhelm him. He could never escape it and it never grew stale or a companion easily suffered.

Seconds crawled past and his fear was replaced by worry. His master demanded punctuality and here he was—on time and his master late. Seconds ran into minutes and he glanced about. This was not normal, and his hand strayed unerringly to the pommel of the great curved blade that hung exposed from his waist.

He thought of ambush and deception and turned to look to his men. His second, dressed as he was, rose from the sand a hundred yards away and stared back at him expecting orders. Sand poured from him only to be swept away by the dry, hot winds. A sense of disquiet descended. The heads of his men rose from the sand to look at one another and time seemed to slow and then stop. The wind died and the hairs on the back of his neck rose with an itch. He watched as his second raised a pointed hand toward him and he spun around, his hand starting to draw his sword.

"You really need to be more observant, Mushir," said the imposing figure who stood before him.

Mushir Adham bowed deeply. "Sahib." When he rose he looked closely at the man who had appeared so suddenly before him. His master was a master of magic. A djinn. He wore the garb of a djinn and beneath the silks his obsidian skin bore a terrible scar.

"Yes, I am damaged. A minor inconvenience," intoned the figure who called himself Kamal Sherwami.

"Sahib, how is this possible? You told me you were impervious to any damage. You are immortal. A djinn."

Kamal stood silent and Adham regretted his words. His master was far from forgiving and quick to anger. He took lives like the wind tore grains of sand from the dunes. The shock of seeing Kamal injured shook him and a kernel of doubt took seed. It proved his master capable of lies and lies always led to deception. Mushir Adham had risen to power in his lands by being careful of men who spread lies. Not for the first time, he considered striking down this creature. He thought of his great scimitar and imagined drawing it forth and taking the head off clean from the shoulders. *It would be pointless*, he knew. *Kamal slew with a thought.*

"Yes," whispered Kamal. The word filled his ears and head like two voices and Mushir shuddered. "Lies. Lies bind us all and make believers of those who would doubt. Try it, Mushir. Strike me down. See what that brings you and your men."

Adham released his thought of attacking. He knew his men would follow him down any path he chose and knew if he tried anything with this creature, they would be slaughtered like goats on the altar. He ground his teeth and nodded. "My apologies, sahib."

"Noted. Worry not. This mark is proof of my continued efforts to provide you with riches beyond your wildest imaginings. I am injured fighting and weakening those forces I would pit you against. They are now ripe for your conquest and rule. The capital is primed for your arrival. The land in disarray. You will head west and board the ships I have provided you. Do not delay. Split your forces as I have told you. The bulk will go south to Jergen. Hold the port. Seize the crossroads. Push south from the capital and crush all who stand in your way. Be ready."

"Yes, sahib" Mushir Adham bowed deeply as he spoke the words. "It shall be as you..." He rose to find Kamal gone. He looked to the sand and found no marks to indicate his master had ever been standing in front of him. He drew a calming breath and turned and gave a shrill whistle.

His men erupted from the sand and turned to leap to horseback as the horses ran clear of the dune. Sand billowed and spread in a massive cloud only to be scattered by the winds. The men quickly formed up and his second led them with Mushir's horse following obediently beside him. As his horse approached, he leapt to the saddle and rode beside y-Mushir Hassim.

"That was interesting," said Adham quietly for Hassim's ears only.

Hassim grunted in reply before speaking. "It always is, Mushir."

"He was wounded."

Adham saw Hassim snap his head toward him. "Injured?"

"Yes, it looked like a burn mark on his chest. Scarred over but recent. It was not there a week ago."

"What does this mean?"

"I'm uncertain. It does not bode well. All the promises of swift victory and sweet rewards across the sea seem to be built on a dune of lies. It is unravelling, my friend. We must be cautious."

"It shall be as you say, Mushir."

"Orders remain unchanged except I want to increase our force to the North. It is a land of apostates. We must strike hard and hold the capital. I will lead this group."

"Mushir?"

"You will lead the southern group. Switch out the men, stay with those you trust. The fight will be hard, but you are capable. I will hold the North and swing south when I can. You must be ready to be entrenched in Jergen. Double the re-supply runs."

Hassim nodded.

Protector Healy rose from his breakfast table and tossed his napkin onto his plate. He looked out the window of his stateroom to the city of Munsten below. Smoke from chimneys rose straight up into the still air and the crisp look of autumn with trees bursting with colour was everywhere. He loved this time of year. Autumn was the decay of the old life and readied the world for the new.

Appropriate, he thought. *I usher in a new era for Belkin. A new rule.*

A soft knock sounded at his door.

"Enter."

The door opened, and a courier stepped in and came over and held out a dispatch. Healy accepted it and the courier stepped away and left, closing the door quietly behind him. Healy turned the dispatch over and saw the wax seal of Jergen. His lips tightened into a straight line and he cracked the seal and opened the letter. As he suspected, it was from Major Gillespie.

The plan failed. Cargo lost. Target escaped. Waiting in Jergen for further orders.

That was it? Nothing else? Healy crumpled the paper in quick anger and tossed it to the breakfast table. *Unacceptable!*

"Captain!" he yelled out to the door. After a moment the door opened, and the captain stationed outside peered in with a questioning look on his face.

"Sir, yes, sir?"

"Send me my Chief of Staff at once."

"Yes, sir. Your Chief of Staff. At once."

Healy ground his teeth. He hated the military with their discipline and haughty airs. He hated how they always repeated every word he said. He would correct that soon and then wipe the world of the Bairstow brothers and rule the entire realm of Belkin with full authority. The past ten years had been building to his final plan. A plan that would allow him dominion over all without question. Without all the rules and laws of bygone days. He had rid the world of that insufferable Archbishop and soon the Church would collapse with him. Nothing stood in his way except those loyal to the Bairstow brothers. And money. He needed the coin Redgrave had stolen. Money bought people and kept them loyal. And now that coin was lost once again.

He turned to demand what was taking his Chief of Staff so long and yelled out in fright. Kamal Sherwami, the emissary from Cian-Oirthear, stood before him and Healy only just managed not to raise his arms to hide his face.

"You disappoint me, Healy," said the man.

Healy knew without asking that Kamal was aware of everything that transpired. He always did. It was unnerving, but he had long learned not to question it. He swallowed and quickly thought. "Kamal, you know, you bade me use that Major when I was against it. I followed your direction. I don't know what has happened, but he is still in place, with his men holed up in Jergen."

"Yes, and there he will stay until Bairstow arrives. He must slay him by whatever means. Strike him down as he enters the city gates. I care not for exposure. Or repercussions. Do it. Do you understand?"

Healy stared in surprise. This was unlike Kamal. He always worked in the background. Silent and deadly in a way Healy admired. This was far too offensive. Too open.

"In view of everyone? That will be difficult to quell. To keep from my rule."

"Assassinate him. I care not what happens to the major. Bairstow must be removed from the game. Am I being clear?"

"It will be as you say," Healy then hesitated. "One thing, the coin Redgrave stole. It has gone missing. Taken by the Sect according to my network. It is needed for the plan to work."

Kamal laughed. The sound was foreign and filled Healy's head in a way that made his bowels want to loosen. "The coin? I care not for coin. That is your affair. The chest in Jaipers was empty of all but pence. Two thousand of them. It seems Redgrave had the last laugh."

Healy stared in disbelief. Kamal had promised him the stolen treasury would be returned to him. It was the deal that pushed him down this latest venture, to where he stood today. Now it was exposed for what it was—a lie—

and he was far too committed to back away. Healy felt doubt form in his thoughts. Lies built on more lies. Healy struggled to keep them sorted in his head. Some days he longed for the time before the Revolution. *I was a simpler man back then.*

The gold was important to his plans. *If all the chest contained had been copper pence, then where were my gold crown coins?* It had taken him years to gather that much gold. His efforts to replace the amount since then paled in comparison. Frederick Bairstow and his brother Brent had forced him to keep his efforts quiet and small. The money he stole from the Realm now trickled in when once it poured.

If the stolen crowns were not in Jaipers where were they? Redgrave had taken all the coin in his vault all those years ago. His quiet investigation into the theft had revealed nothing. His investigator did not understand how Redgrave had found entrance nor how he had absconded with thousands of crowns in one night. There had been no witnesses. Torture had revealed much, but no one admitted to helping with the theft or knowing about it. A window of opportunity of a scant three hours had been identified when the theft had occurred. Healy was certain it was impossible to have moved that much gold in such a short time, but Redgrave had managed it. Healy had long ago suspected the demon druids were behind it. *Their magic could have done it—they probably made his men help them and then wiped their memories*, he thought not for the first time.

The only time he and the Archbishop had agreed on anything was in dealing with the demons. The knowledge of men and women holding vast and powerful magic powers was abhorrent to him. He would wake in a sweat from dreams where he revisited the night of the coup attempt when the woman Belle Arbor revealed her powers and held him helpless. He watched again and again as she slew armed men with so little effort and looked so frighteningly calm while doing so. The air had been filled with a fine mist of blood and she had walked away untouched. He remembered his weakness, too. Once it had sunk in that an assassination had been attempted he had collapsed in front of the Archbishop. Thankful and open to almost anything, the Archbishop persuaded him to hand over the investigation to the Church. He had agreed and then regretted it.

Word came to him over the years of the atrocities committed by the Church Sect. He looked away at the time and was thankful the demons were being eradicated without his hand on it. He now lived with nightmares and they were always the same: his limbs frozen against his will with his sight locked on Belle Arbor's calm visage as she snuffed the life from trained military men. His heart thudding in his chest beating out the time until she would inevitably turn to him. It was the lack of control which frightened him beyond measure. In the months and years later, the Archbishop would tell him tales of what the demons were capable of—what they were doing in the world. He tried drugs to stop the dreams, but they worsened. He had nearly reached the end of his sanity when Kamal had appeared. He promised to remove the nightmares with remedies from his land and helped him regain his authority and mind. Kamal had given him back his control.

It was Kamal who learned that the druid coin had been located and spoke of tracking where it went. That had led to the discovery that Bill Redgrave still lived. Healy remembered the furious anger when he learned that the traitor was in Jaipers sitting with a chest full of his stolen coin. He formulated a plan to get his gold back and remove one of the Bairstow brothers from his life. Then more ruin. His hand-picked men sent to recover the gold had been dismissed by the half-wit Brent Bairstow, his former General of the Lord Protector's Guard. Then he discovered the Church Sect, by orders from the Archbishop, had interfered in Jaipers and seized the chest. Healy had been beside himself for months. And then, as if the last laugh could be his, the gold crowns were not in the chest. In spite, he arranged the removal of the Archbishop through his old drug contact in the Chirurgeons Guild. *Watching that man die, naked and in his own Church, was almost worth the price.* Now he owned the Church and spread the drugs everywhere he could. He was making a tidy profit from the guild. Unexpectedly and fortuitously, the Church was gaining power throughout the Realm. *When hope is gone, the masses turn to their God. And I rule their God. Better yet, I have someone powerful within the Church Sect. There is nothing I don't have my hands in now.*

Healy was furious at the loss of his gold. His deal with Mushir Adham required the gold to keep the man and his army at his beck and call. He needed it back. "If the gold was not in the chest where is it? We have searched everywhere. Tracked all coin in the Realm and large expenses. Nothing ever stood out. It must be somewhere! Surely, with your powers, you can locate it?"

"I care not. The Mushir will land in Belkin in three months' time. Be ready."

Healy gritted his teeth. "I am ready. All is in place. But I need that coin. I need it to secure the realm and the Mushir. You do understand that? For this to work, I need that coin! That was our bargain! You need it as much as I do!"

"Do not tell me what I need! I have planned for a long time. A scant thousand coins will not matter..."

A soft knock at the door announced the Chief of Staff had arrived. Healy glanced at the door and when he looked back Kamal was gone. Healy shuddered and felt vertigo. Kamal seemed worse than the druids. *And yet I made the deal and here I am. Magic is such an evil thing and Kamal wields it like none other*, he thought. *At least that Archbishop was smart enough to wipe the demons out of existence.* The memory of Belle Arbor throwing magic around in this very room flashed through his thoughts and he shook himself. *Everything that has happened goes back to that night.*

Healy tried to compose himself. The loss of the gold was staggering, and his thoughts reeled with it. He felt the world rock under his feet. He held his head in his hands a moment and then centred himself.

"Enter," he called out and watched as his Chief of Staff walked in carrying documents under his arm. "We have much to discuss. Sit, and I will order more refreshments."

Part One: Parry

Stoc

One

Rigby Farm, March 901 A.C.

T HE LAST SIX months passed at a furious pace at the Rigby Farm. We gathered the harvest, and celebrated Mabon Days, although the time was dampened by the mourning for those who had fallen. Crying from the flocks of birds flying south ceased and the winds from the North grew cold and snow soon followed. Samhain, Yule, and Imbolc celebrations came and went in a blink of an eye. When the snow and ice melted with the warmer winds of spring, the cries of birds returning north filled the sky and the fields were turned with ploughs for planting.

The farm, I learned, was self-sufficient, and I wandered about marvelling at the work and chores. Having raised myself in the wild and with little understanding of normal activity I was amazed at the activity I saw daily. Steve Comlin's crew and the farm hands produced everything our small community required. Various buildings supported the storage and manufacture of everything the farm produced, with the work in the forge and the stable central to the effort. The smithy was an exciting but a dangerous place to be. The fiery coals in the hearth would shower sparks all around when using the bellows; which were huge and worked by a long, slim, wooden shaft. The handle was pulled down hard, then released to produce just the right amount of air for the fire.

Often pieces of metal looked harmless but were burning hot to the touch. Once I got caught out when watching as our smithy, Charlie Mearns put the finishing touches to a horseshoe he was making. Using pincers, he placed the shoe on the anvil and with his hammer thinned the metal out until the excess fell off. I shouted as the red-hot fragment sprang from the anvil and got lodged in my boot. He laughed as I plunged my boot and foot into the cold-water tank.

"That wull larn ye!" he said, his face flushed red with heat and effort.

The smithy was strange to my draoi sight. I could sense Charlie, and the effort he exerted. I could see his aura flair with emotion and strain as he forced the metal to his will. But of the metal or even the rocks, I could sense nothing with Gaea's power. It was only life, in all its forms, that filled the world with its bright, vibrant energy. Sometimes I spent hours just watching the surrounding life. We all were quick to identify a draoi caught up in the wonder with their face smiling and eyes unfocused. Those caught were teased, but we all did it. It made us feel that much closer to Gaea and the harmony of nature.

I often watched as Charlie shoed our horses. The most pungent smell of all around the forge was when a newly made horseshoe was embedded in the hoof. Before that happened, the old shoe was removed, and the hoof cut back, pared and cleaned. Charlie would blow out with a hissing noise to prevent his inhaling the acrid smoke from the burning hoof as the shoe was put in place. This noise was very like the sizzling sound made when a red-hot horseshoe was plunged into cold water. Charlie did it all so effortlessly, and I loved to watch him work.

The trickiest moment was when he had to lift a hind leg to look at old, broken shoes. Levering off one of these shoes took both hands, so there was a danger the horse would kick out unhindered, or it could lean its whole weight on our farrier, possibly crushing him against a wall. It infuriated Charlie when an animal thwarted him. My draoi students would work with Charlie and keep the horses calm. They also calmed Charlie. He had struck a horse once. He had yet to repeat the act after Katherine had spent an hour yelling at him.

Once, in Jergen, we had bought a poor red cow that no one else would bid for to augment our dairy production. We had tied it to the back of one of our floats and dragged it home kicking. In time, my draoi had calmed the animal, but it had taken a long time. The poor animal had been horribly abused and it loathed people on sight. At first, the only way to milk her was to tie one of her hind legs up and put a rope on the other. It was a battle of wills. The cow would kick out the stars in the sky when milked. Once calmed, the cow, named Potato by Charlie, was one of our nicest animals. She followed Charlie when she could; which annoyed him no end. Katherine hid her smiles, but we all knew she was behind it. Another cow was welcome on our farm as the added milk improved our diet: milk to drink, butter to spread, and custards and puddings became everyday occurrences from Dempster.

The birth of Anne's baby girl had been a welcomed distraction in November and Nadine had nursed over mother and child incessantly since. Dempster hovered over mother and child much to Anne's annoyance. He figured himself the surrogate father and doted on them. He was always preparing new and strange foods for the baby. Strained and pureed were new words for all of us. He talked about starting a business with it. Anne thought him daft and would pull out a teat and latch the baby to it and point and say that was all she needed. They argued like a married couple but we all could see that Anne wanted little to do with Dempster. I felt sad for my old friend. When we cautioned him, he would smile and nod. He was convinced otherwise.

Steve Comlin had slipped back into his role as leader of his sixty crew and had taken a firm control of the farm and farmhands and had them focus on the land and building the draoi school buildings in the first month. His crew trained daily with sword, bow and plough. The crew and farmhands shared the same building. Steve called it the barracks, but it looked and felt more like a home. We all knew one another, and friendships formed easily. The crew watched in wonder as the draoi practised their skills. It was becoming commonplace to see magic working the land and animals. It made life so much easier for everyone.

For me, it was a little strange to see the bustle of so many people and see the smiles and nods of recognition toward me. It was welcome after a lifetime of solitude but strange, nonetheless. Nadine and I would walk hand-in-hand throughout the farm and help out where we could. I gathered herbs and grew a large garden near the main house for Dempster. He found he had a knack for gardening and was always bent over weeding and tending to the plants.

Steve Comlin was often gone visiting the Baron of Turgany at his country estate leaving Franky in charge. He said he was working with the Baron to train his private army. Baron Andrew Windthrop had pulled together an army of some size despite the laws of the realm forbidding it. They trained in secret for a purpose I could only guess was aimed at the Lord Protector Healy. When he was gone, I often found Franky and Nadine speaking in hushed whispers. Seeing me they would stop and glare at me until I withdrew. They had their secrets, and I was fine with it so long as it didn't involve me.

We all tried to keep an eye on Katherine, but she spent all of her time outdoors with Dog and the horses. She wanted nothing to do with the druid school and she and Nadine often threw heated words between each other.

Katherine was not happy, and it appeared she never would be here on the farm. The death of her parents was in constant reminder and the farm only brought her bad memories. My bond with her was strong and through it, I could feel her pain. She wept most nights holding tight to Dog. I wept silently with her. She had come a long way since that horrible evening. No child should watch her parents die and the way her father had been killed and then rose under Seth Farlow's evil to kill her mother had broken her. Somehow Dog had pulled her back from the brink of whatever insanity she faced. They were now inseparable.

The first students who arrived had been bewildered, scared, and confused. They were happy to have reached the end of a journey of which few could explain other than they had felt a strong irresistible pull to come. They arrived in various emotional states to be greeted by me and Nadine. We would explain to each one what was happening. Explain their powers and help them adjust. But I was not ready to begin the school. I greeted them and then gave them to Steve to find work for them. We had forty draoi students all eager to learn and all I could do was promise the school would begin soon and then weeks passed.

It was Katherine who squared me off one day late in November.

"Start teaching them, Freamhaigh," she told me at the kitchen table.

I looked to Nadine, but she was fussing with Anne's baby and pacing inside the entrance to the kitchen. Franky smirked and told Dempster to serve up the meal. With no one to save me, I turned my full attention to Katherine. "I will," I said.

"When?"

"What do you mean when? Soon."

"Soon is what you always say. You have a building and classrooms set up with tables and chairs. You have everything you need."

"True, I do."

"So?"

"So... what?" I mumbled not wanting to discuss this any further.

Katherine screeched in frustration startling me and she slapped the table with an open palm. "So, start teaching them, that's what! They need you to talk to them. Tell them what's happening. About that black creature. And Gaea. Everything. Teach them how to be druids! They came all this way. More show up every day! There's forty of them now! Women and men, some with their children. Gaea sends them, they arrive, and you ignore them. They are afraid and understand nothing of what is happening to them."

I sat in silence and Dempster dropped steaming bowls of vegetables and a platter of pork chops down on the table and gave me a frown. I glared at him.

"Well?" demanded Katherine.

Nadine chose that moment to sit beside me. Katherine glared at her which Nadine ignored. The baby stared up at her from her arms and pulled her red hair to her mouth to chew. We all watched them for a moment before Nadine looked into my face and I saw her displeasure. *Uh oh.* "You owe her an answer, Will. You know how I feel. They're all here now. Gaea told us."

I pulled the hair out of the baby's firm grip and nodded. I took a deep breath. "Aye, I do know." I turned to Katherine. "Tomorrow. I'll start tomorrow. Promise."

"'Bout time," grunted Katherine and spooned food onto her plate. Dog laid his head on her lap. Katherine grabbed a pork chop and gave it to him and he disappeared under the table. Dempster grunted from the kitchen and when I glanced at him he was scowling at Dog.

The meal passed with no further mention of the school and I thought hard about what I needed to do. The truth was I felt inadequate to the task. *Who was I to teach anyone anything?* I worried I would let them down. But now I had made a promise to Katherine even though I hadn't felt I meant it.

Later that night, I tossed and turned in bed and found myself wide awake when our rooster cried to the rising sun. Nothing seemed clear except one course. I crawled out of bed and splashed water in my eyes to remove the gritty burn from the lack of sleep. I looked in the mirror and saw a young face with no idea what to do looking back at me.

After a light breakfast, I drew strength from the earth to overcome my lack of sleep and Nadine and I called all the draoi students into the classroom. The building was new and the smell of fresh cut wood permeated the air. With the number of students, the room was packed. The children of the druids were also there, and they looked excited. I look out to a sea of expectant faces and swallowed the lump of fear in my throat.

During the night, I had decided that I wouldn't try to be a teacher. I couldn't be something I was not. Instead, I would just talk and let whatever knowledge I had pour from me. If I sucked at it, Gaea would replace me. But she had chosen me and for a reason. It had to be enough. My original fear was diminished with the assurance she was at least a little smarter than me.

I sat on the edge of the desk facing the room, looked to the floor, and spoke. I told them everything that had happened since my mother and the druids were hunted down and killed. I talked to them about finding my power through my herb work. I talked about the Draoi Manuscript page and how it led me to the road to Jergen. I talked about my capture and the fear I felt. I described the hatred the men from the Church of the New Order had for our kind. I told them of the wolf that sacrificed himself for me and felt the loss once again.

I laid out all the horrors that the draoi had lived through for centuries and how the draoi had worked in the shadows and hid their abilities. Once or twice I stopped talking for a little while. The silence in the room was such that I could hear the horses in the barn two buildings over complaining about their oats. When I stopped for too long, Nadine would reach out and grasp my arm or hand and I would resume. The morning passed, and no one stirred or interrupted me. I poured all my doubts and fears into my tale. I told them I doubted myself and what the future held for us. I looked up into those faces and saw the same fear reflected. Many wiped away tears and laughed. I saw people looking back at me who were afraid and uncertain but happy they were together at least. My tension and fear left me and I felt Gaea brush my mind and her happiness for us filled me. We were a family. I smiled then, and the faces of the draoi turned to expressions of surprise. Nadine sucked in her breath and I felt joy fill her. She felt it, too. We were draoi, and we had a purpose in this world. All of nature was waiting for us to step forward and do something about making the world harmonious. We were healers.

I stood up and held my hands high in the air and laughed. "But never forget we have magic!" I shouted to the rafters. A few of the draoi laughed, and I caught the glint in their eyes. *They understand*, I thought, *and it gives me hope.* Smiling, I spoke then of the beauty in the world: the bright life of a plant or a bird in flight. About how we can communicate with nature and heal those who are harmed. I explained Gaea and the roles the druids used to have in the world. I talked about balance and harmony and how it was our role to maintain that harmony. Eyes lit up, and the draoi smiled and nodded along with my words.

Soon all were on their feet and the desks and chairs were pushed to the sides. We gathered in a group and many held hands or shoulders. Nadine and I demonstrated our magic and had our students show us what they could do. We laughed and praised each other and grew stronger for the sharing. In a moment of clarity, I remembered what Daukyns had taught me so many years ago. I had tossed all last night fretting until I recalled the words of a friend. I had asked Daukyns back in Jaipers why he wasn't afraid to teach the Word to so many and he had laughed.

"But I am afraid," Daukyns had answered once his mirth subsided. "I look out into the eyes of the people and see them looking for answers. For direction, and an understanding. I feel the weight of all that hope in the words of my teachings. But I see they have the same doubts and worries I have. Once you understand and accept that then the journey between teacher and student is one of discovery. Then, and only then, can you both learn from the experience."

And this is what I did that morning. I exposed my fears. My worries. And then I embraced the power that Gaea gave me and shared my joy of life. My words found a home with these people. We gathered together, and wet eyes and bright smiles found each other. The sense of joy that followed was something we would never forget.

Each student then told a tale of being lost in a world where they knew they had powers but not how to release or use it. Each told a tale of how they had discovered and opened their magic. How a strong urge to follow their instincts had them travel from all over the realm to the Rigby Farm. They described the trials of those journeys and the constant doubt of their sanity that followed them. They had left family and friends to be here. They said they could no more resist the urge than they could throw themselves off a cliff. It had been too strong.

What we learned that morning, and well into the afternoon, was we all shared a common ability and that brought us together. Trust was gained, and we formed a family. With our senses, we could see our druid bonds were strong and vibrant. We could sense each other and like Gaea, we were one. We were no longer alone, and that gave us strength and hope.

I looked around then and realised that Katherine and Dog had not attended the gathering. She was off on her own sitting in the nearby forest. It was too much for her and I sent her my love. She responded with a shrug and turned her attention elsewhere.

The teachings began the next day. Nadine and I taught them all we knew. Nadine explained the draoi powers and how they worked and the rules that bound us to Gaea. Foremost that we could not use our powers to harm others. Some tried minor things to see if it was true and learned quickly to avoid it. We explained how Gaea shared her power with us and how we borrowed it for our use. Our history was taught, and we all agreed that the future required change. We decided to no longer keep our abilities hidden. Nadine wasn't happy, but she agreed. The draoi would make themselves known to the world. We could no longer hide in the shadows.

Around us, the farm continued to recover and grow. Steve and Franky met with my students and told them they were safe and protected. When I told Steve I was confused, he smiled and clapped my back.

"My crew will always be here for you, Will," he had said. Franky had looked surprised and stormed away. "Never mind her, I can see your people have a need for protection. You have it from me, Will."

I had blinked back tears as my emotions overwhelmed me. I had never considered needing guards but now I had them promised to me and I valued them. The Church and the Sect were still out there and a threat. They had come once to destroy the druids and would do so again. Brent Bairstow and his gift had destroyed the black creature Erebus, but he was long gone with his friend James Dixon and likely back to Munsten by now. His last letter had informed me he was heading there with James. He had asked for my support and I had refused him politely. My draoi had a long way to go before we could be involved in politics and the Church if ever. I had wished him well. For now, my draoi had Comlin's men and women to avoid further persecution by the Church. It let me sleep at night.

In the Draoi School, we learned what each of the students could do with their magic. As I had suspected they each had unique skills. We discovered those strong in healing, those strong with animals or plants. Some demonstrated strength in manufacturing potions and unguents. Some could twist plant and animal parts into wonderful works of art or tools. Each of them had an ability in vision, sense and influence in varying degrees of strength. We taught them how to see the other druids and the ropes of power that tied us together.

They had started as duilleogs, but by the end of March, they were each craobhs ready to become stocs. Nadine told me Gaea was pleased with our progress. In time, the students would become the teachers and the school would grow. It was all happening so fast.

My only disappointment was with Katherine. She refused to take part in the school despite her earnestness that I start it. She stayed away from the farm more and more but always with Dog at her side. Her loss was too much. I had tried to get through to her. To talk about my loss but she wanted nothing to do with it. She argued with Nadine and always found fault with her. Nadine stayed clear of her when she could. Katherine was like a dog fighting another over the same scrap of food. Hackles were raised and a growl always rumbling in the background. Dog even sided with her. They moved as one and it was hard to tell where Katherine ended, and Dog started. For Nadine and I it was too much and so we kept our distance out of respect. We knew it was only a matter of time before she would leave and not come back to the farm.

"She's wild, Will," Nadine said one evening in bed. "Something broke in her that night her parents were killed. No child should ever see that and then the horror of them becoming aos'si. She has gone wild, and she's filled what she's lost with her bond with Dog."

Aos'si was the word we found in the manuscript for the animated dead. *Aos'si* was a use of our power forbidden centuries ago and I had agreed once I read what it was. It was a horror and changed the druid who used it. They became *sluagh sidhe.* This is what we assumed Erebus was and Seth had been. Gaea offered no knowledge, but Nadine and I often spoke of it. Nadine was worried that Katherine would follow down that same path. I knew she would not. She could never become something that could do what had happened to her parents.

"Aye, she is at that," I agreed at last. "Wild. Her bond with Dog has become something more than it should. I fear she has lost a part of her humanity. I lived with wolves for a long time, but never did I want to become one of them. Nor did I have magic that would allow that to happen. She has no such reservations."

I felt Nadine nod her head on my chest before she spoke. "I fear for her. Why she hates me so much I do not understand although I suspect it has everything to do with authority."

"She doesn't hate me."

Nadine smacked me lightly on the chest. "Dummy. You don't use your authority over her. I do. I'm always the one that has to tell her what to do. You don't get involved. If you did, you would fall under her wrath, too."

I thought about that for a time. Nadine fell asleep and snored. I felt a wet spot on my chest and chuckled. I looked down and saw the drool. Nadine was the love of my life but had some most amazing quirks. *Poor Katherine,* I thought before sleep stole me too.

The snows had cleared early, and Ostara Day in March arrived. Nadine surprised me with a birthday party marking my nineteenth year. It was the first birthday party I remembered having, and it was a fun day. The draoi, crew and farmhands all gathered outside, and Gaea made a silent appearance. Everyone gasped and moved aside to give her room. A quiet settled on the gathering. I smiled at Gaea and she smiled back.

"Get out!" came a shocking loud screech from Katherine. We turned and saw her standing with fists clenched at her sides, her face red and furious. "Get out of here, you *cailleach!*" Her spittle flew.

Gaea looked back with a sad face and said nothing. The moment stretched and Katherine growled deep in her chest. Dog whined and looked from

Katherine to Gaea, unsure what to do. Without another word, Katherine turned away and strode off to the house. Dog ran alongside her looking back to us and Gaea.

I moved to follow her, but Gaea stopped me. "Leave her be, Freamhaigh. She blames me for the loss of her parents. And she is correct."

I hung my head. "It pains me to see her like this. Nothing Nadine and I do seems to help. She is lost to us, I fear."

"But not to the earth, Will," replied Gaea, and I looked to her. "She is furious with me, but she is still very much a part of me. Katherine knows this too, and it fuels that anger. She can no more lose that tie than she could sever her own legs and still walk. She will leave soon. Let her go. I will watch over her. Dog will be there for her. Your bond to her grounds her. Believe in that."

"She is family and I would rather she stays with us, but..." I struggled to finish the thought for I knew the words would be final within my heart. "But she can no longer stay here." I looked out to the far distant tree line to the North. "I need her to leave and find herself. Hopefully, she comes back to us." Nadine wrapped an arm around my waist and pulled me tight against her.

"Perhaps. Time will tell. Look what your time in the wilderness did for you."

I snapped my gaze to Gaea and felt an anger simmer.

"See? That anger you feel toward me, it is so much stronger in Katherine. She needs to find peace with it and herself."

Defeated, I released the anger and looked to my students standing nearby with looks of awe on their faces. They stared at Gaea with such adoration it caused me to chuckle. "Look there, Gaea. There is love, no?"

Gaea smiled at the students. "You are all doing so well. You are almost stocs and sure in your abilities. I am proud of you, my children. Enjoy this day where we celebrate the renewal of life."

The students cheered and moved closer to reach out and touch Gaea. A few farmhands joined them. She let them and then turned her face to regard me and I sucked in a breath. Before me stood my mother. Nadine made a soft cry and covered her mouth.

"Happy Birthday, my Will."

I nodded past swimming eyes and with no sound Gaea disappeared and the students laughed and spun around.

Nadine drew me into an embrace. "Happy birthday, Will, my husband and love." Her lips touched mine and then she wiped the wetness from my eyes with gentle fingers. "Enjoy your day."

Later that afternoon, I wandered out past the orchard trees and crossed the fields toward the small wooded high ground that marked the northern border of the farm. I reached out with my senses and felt the awakening of life all around me. Spring was here and with it the chance for a new life and new beginnings. The fields had been planted and for a time the farm focused on fixing up the damage of winter and taking a deep breath before everything changed.

Steve and Franky were drilling the crew every day at daybreak and for most of the afternoons. It was a side of Steve I had never seen, and I admired his leadership with the crew. Franky and he made an excellent pair, and the crew was getting into shape better than Steve had hoped. The draoi joined them when they could as a distraction.

The sounds of the farm faded behind me and I followed the thread that led to Katherine and Dog and I saw them up ahead. Katherine was tossing a stick and an excited Dog was running barking after it and bringing it back. As I approached, I could sense that Katherine was aware of me. There was little draoi could hide from one another. It was a blessing and a curse.

"Hi, Freamhaigh," she said and tossed the stick once more. Dog barked at me in joy and ran after the bouncing piece of wood. "Happy birthday."

"Hmm, thanks," I replied. "I don't feel any older."

Katherine squinted at me. "Nope. You don't look it either."

We looked out across the fields toward the farm buildings and watched smoke rise from the chimneys. We could see people moving about and with our vision, we could track all the draoi as they did one activity or another. I stole a glance at Katherine and caught her stealing one from me. I laughed at her and she punched my arm.

"Ow!" I yelped and rubbed my arm. "What is it with the women in my life always punching me?"

"You ask for it."

"What? How is that possible?"

"You just do with all your weird ways."

"Me? Weird? I don't think so. I'm the head of our kind. Well, me and Nadine. That deserves respect, don't you think?" Katherine smirked back at me and looked out to the woods. Dog ran up and dropped the stick and sat and lolled his tongue from his mouth.

Katherine looked at Dog and nodded at some word between them and then looked at me and I could see the sadness in her eyes.

I reached out and placed a hand on her shoulder. "I know, Katherine. Just ready yourself. Come see me tonight and I will tell you what you need."

A look of fright crossed her face. "You know?"

I used my hand on her shoulder to pull her into an awkward embrace and she started to cry gently, hiding her face in my arm. "Of course. I'm the Freamhaigh. Go. Out there somewhere. You and Dog, both. See me tonight. I can tell you how best to survive. It's easy when you know how, plus you'll have Dog with you."

She nodded her head against my shoulder and then cried a little more. "I can't..." she said, her voice muffled against me. "I can't be around people anymore. Everything about the farm reminds me of my mum and dad. It's too much. Dog agrees and said we should go. I didn't want to at first, but I'm convinced now. It scares me, Will."

I glared at Dog who at least had the common courtesy to look ashamed and lower his head to the ground. "I understand. I do. And I agree with Dog, despite his nefarious ways. Dog knows the land. He can help you hunt. Keep you safe. And you have your powers. You are the strongest of us all I think. Be careful."

Katherine pulled away and hid her face from mine by crouching down to hug Dog. Dog looked over her shoulder at me and winked with both eyes. I glared at Dog. He was becoming a bad influence. But he was right, I'd give him that. I poked his nose for good measure and then wiped my wet finger on Katherine's back.

"You'll have to explain this to your father. Steve needs to hear it from you and not from me."

Katherine wiped her nose dry with her sleeve and then held Dog's face in her hands. "He's not my father. My dad's dead and buried."

"Aye that he is. But Steve Comlin is your da, Katherine. He loves you in his way and he's only just learning how to be someone for you. Don't leave him now without telling him why. He'll take it personally otherwise and run after you. You know that."

"I'll think about it." Dog prodded her with his nose and she laughed and rose to face me. Her eyes were red.

"Steve is like a father to me as well, Katherine. That makes us kin."

"I suppose it does at that. Brother?" she asked testing it out and then laughed and shook her head. "Freamhaigh. That sounds better."

"Fine. See me tonight. After supper, okay?"

"Okay, Freamhaigh. I'll be there."

I turned and started back to the farm. Behind me, Katherine softly called out to me. "Thank you."

I stopped and turned back to her. "Don't thank me. If I had a choice, I would make you stay. We all love you, Katherine. We love you enough to let you go, too."

Katherine chewed her lower lip and nodded.

I turned and waved a hand behind me and kept walking. My feet were heavy on the ground and my heart felt broken. The tilled furrows of the fields let me hurry back to the farmhouse. The sun was sinking fast and the afternoon would soon be over. I saw Nadine step out from behind the orchard trees and cross her arms over her breast and hold herself tight. Through our bond, I could feel her emotions stack on my own. I was not the only one who was suffering and kept my head high as I approached. One of us had to remain strong, and I voted for myself.

Two

Rigby Farm, Early May 901 A.C.

THE DRAOI STUDENT on sentry duty on the southern approach road informed the others that the Baron of Turgany was approaching with a large contingent of armed men and women. It was midday and Nadine ordered Dempster to prepare for a large meal for supper. I bounced down the stairs to the main landing just as Steve emerged out of his bedroom, cinching his belt buckle. As the door to his room swung shut, I spied Franky lying naked on her side on his bed. She caught my stare and winked. She had no shame or inhibitions and smiled when I turned beet red.

"Will," said Steve. He saw my face and glanced back to his door and seemed relieved to see it closed. He checked his sword and then gave me his full attention. "It's true? The Baron is on the road here?"

I nodded. "Yes, he'll be here in an hour. He just passed the outer sentry line."

"By the Word, I wish I had people with those skills when I was working the roads all those years ago."

He often referred to his time as a highwayman as *working the roads*. "Yes, well, the draoi weren't as *helpful* back then, were they?" I chuckled to hide my ire at the thought. I still fought with Nadine over this point. She was the most stubborn woman alive. She even argued with Gaea. A smile flitted across my face thinking about my darling wife.

"No, I suppose not. Still, would have been nice. Now excuse me, I have to round up the troops." Steve moved to go past me, but I stopped him with a touch of a hand.

"Shouldn't Franky be doing that?" I asked and grinned at Steve as colour rose to his cheeks.

"Franky?" He glanced again at his bedroom door. "She, um, she..."

"She's basking on your bed and probably biting her cheek to stop laughing. You forget I'm a druid. I can see all sorts of things. Like when two people are enjoying each other."

Steve stared at me in horror. "What do you sense?"

I laughed. "No, not that. I can sense the love between you. All emotions, actually. You care about each other. Seems wrong to hide that."

Steve looked flustered and then I saw him clench his jaw and a steel look came to his grey eyes. "Yes, well. She's also my second. Not right to fraternise."

A loud laugh from the kitchen came from Nadine. "Sounds like you fraternised all night, *Reeve* Comlin!" shouted my wife with a large amount of satisfaction somehow heard in her tone.

Steve growled and pushed past me and out to the front door. I heard it slam and closed my eyes and watched him jog toward the main barracks building. I heard the bedroom door open and opened them to see Franky leaning against the doorframe, dressed in her leathers and stroking the handle of a long knife sheathed at her waist.

"You're a naughty one, Will Arbor," she purred.

I blinked at her in response.

She leaned forward and gave me a quick peck on my cheek. "Love, you say?" And she sauntered past me and out the front door looking satisfied with herself.

I leaned back against the hallway wall and thought back to what I had said to Steve and then groaned.

"You're an idiot, Will," laughed my wife from the kitchen. "But at least you're my idiot."

I walked into the kitchen to find Nadine drinking tea and picking at the preserved apples in front of her. Dempster waggled his eyebrows at me and then turned back to whatever he was preparing on the stove. I slid into the seat next to Nadine and thumped my head into my arms. Nadine stroked my back for a moment.

"Bealtine Day. An auspicious day for the Baron to arrive, don't you think?" she murmured.

"I wouldn't know. I never followed the calendar days as well you know. It's just another day, love."

Nadine made a tutting sound, the sound always reminding me of her true age of sixty-something-or-other. Her renewed youth gave her advantages beyond just looks. "They're there whether you know it or not. They bring change. Mark my words. Such as the Baron showing up today of all days."

I raised my head and stole a piece of apple. It crunched between my teeth and I sucked in the sweetness. Being draoi allowed us to preserve fruit as fresh as the day we picked them. I spoke around the mouthful. "I suppose Gaea told you he was coming?"

"Course. I knew days ago."

"And you couldn't find the time to tell anyone? Say me, for instance?"

"What's the fun in that?"

"Old woman, you are evil, you know that?"

"Young man, you love it..." and she reached out and grabbed me high on the thigh. I yelped and jumped in my seat. "Now be a good boy and round up the students for me. I want them presentable."

I settled back in my seat. "They're not students any longer. They're almost all stocs now. We have to promote them soon, Nadine. I want a ceremony to mark it. Something special."

"Hmm. Yes, well, we used to have a ceremony for that before. You wouldn't approve, I don't think."

"It's not that. It used to be a private ceremony. Hidden and secretive. I can't have that now. It needs to be in the open. With witnesses. With oaths to the land, animals, people and to Gaea. She better be there."

"She will," Nadine hesitated. "She promised she would be."

I ate another piece of apple and then changed the subject. "Have you asked her about Katherine?"

"Yes, of course. Says she's fine—but we knew that already—but she did say she is watching over her. Says she's glad she's moved on. Has something to do. Typical cryptic stuff. I swear she makes it up as she goes along."

"I think so, too. All right. I'll get the craobhs rounded up and ready for your inspection within the hour."

"Thirty minutes, mister!"

I rose and gave her a smart salute. "Yes, ma'am!"

"You're spending too much time training with the crew, Will. It's going to ruin you."

"Ruin me how?" I replied and kissed her. "It's got me in better shape than ever."

Nadine ran a hand inside my shirt across my chest. "I'll say. It's nice."

I laughed and kissed her again, this time we lingered and sent our love across our bond. I rose and started to leave. Dempster coughed into his hand and I turned to him.

"Yes, Dempster?"

"The wee child, Anne's... why won't she name her?" Dempster twisted a dish towel in his hands.

"She will when she's ready. It's her tradition from the North. They don't name their children until they are one-year-old."

"But that's nonsense! You and Nadine will make sure she's healthy. She should name her."

I opened my senses and examined the auras of Dempster and Anne and I understood at once. He loved her, but she didn't love him. It explained the special treats he kept making for her daughter. I looked back at Nadine and she winced. She knew it, too.

"Dempster, the baby is fine, and she doesn't need a name to be healthy. Anne has her ways. Respect it and leave it be."

Dempster untwisted the dish towel from his hands and tossed it into the double sink. He nodded once and then turned back to his task. *More baby food by the looks of it*, I thought. *As if Anne didn't have enough already.*

I left the kitchen with Nadine looking at me in sympathy. I didn't need it. There was nothing I could do. People are people and love is love. Nothing in my power could change that.

As the sun reached its zenith, the Baron, his retinue, and a portion of his army entered the road circle in front of the main farmhouse. The army continued out past the inner fields. Our sentry had counted over two hundred men including the chirurgeons and supply people. Dust rose from the hooves, feet and wheels, but the brisk wind swept it clear and away.

Lined up in front of the house were Steve Comlin's crew wearing leathers with swords and bows and looking grim and serious. Steve stood out in front of them with Franky by his side. My students stood off to one side and wore their simple grey cloth tunics and pants. Nadine and I stood near them in similar clothes. *We look so boring so near to the crew.* Nadine poked me at the thought.

The Baron rode his horse with years of experience showing. I had never met him before and Steve had said little about him. I was feeling a little excited by all the activity here on our little farm. His back was straight, and he looked important. Nobody like Lord Windthrop had ever graced Jaipers, and I looked on in wonder. His men rode and marched behind him in three long columns about a shoulder-width apart. Carts filled with equipment were in the centre of the column. With them, I could see the black robes of the chirurgeons on their own cart. I was impressed, but I had never seen an army before. Nadine grunted beside me and I felt her laughing at me.

The Baron's horse, I could sense, was proud of its stature and lifted its forelocks higher than a normal horse would. Just then the horse sensed me and faltered for only a moment, but he stumbled, and his eyes grew wide. I laughed and turned to my craobh with the strongest animal sense. Tara nodded, and I looked back to the horse as he settled down with her calming.

Steve yelled out an order, and the crew drew swords and presented them in front of them. It was one large ringing of steel and the sun glinted off the oiled blades. It was a wonderful moment, and I was impressed again. I squeezed Nadine's hand when I felt her mirth roll over me.

The Baron recovered on his horse and stopped in front of Steve. A moment later the entire column stopped more or less as one when one officer behind the Baron yelled out to halt. The Baron swung free of his saddle and drew his own sword and held it before him. Steve stepped forward and brought the sword to his nose and then swept it in front of himself to hold it angled outward from his body, the point to the ground. The Baron lifted his sword to his nose and then lowered it in front of his body with the blade pointing straight up. Steve raised his sword to his nose and then lowered it to the same position as the Baron's. The military had strange customs, and I didn't see the need for any of it. *It looks good though*, I thought.

The Baron sheathed his sword. Steve followed and then stepped up and grasped the man's forearm. Grins split their faces and then Steve beckoned to the crew.

"Do you wish to inspect, Lord Windthrop?"

"They look well turned out, Steve. Well done to you and Franky. I can see from here that I doubt I'll find a single piece of equipment in need of attention. Let them know I appreciate their attention to detail for me. I won't hold them here. Let's forego pageantry, eh?"

"Yes, sir. But if you'll indulge me, I would like to introduce you to Will Arbor and his wife Nadine." Steve raised a hand toward us.

The Baron's eyes lit up, and he strode over to Nadine and I. He towered over most people and was wide of girth with a belly to match. His hair was dark black and mutton chops sprung white and thick from his cheeks. His face was bright red and a large bulbous nose protruded from it. He was an imposing figure. I shook his hand when he offered it and Nadine curtsied; something I had never seen her do before. I gawked at her and she scowled sideways at me.

"Baron," introduced Steve. "This is Nadine Arbor, Cill Darae to the draoi and her husband, Will Arbor, Freamhaigh to the draoi. Gathered are their students, all draoi in training."

"Ah, the draoi," smiled the Baron. He looked about the farm and ignored my students. I frowned, the slight seemed intentional. "Not so long ago we could not have spoken those words out loud in company, eh?" Nadine nodded with her face grown serious. I sensed her dislike of the Baron through our bond. "I've known the draoi my entire life, dear woman, no need for the long face. Steve has told me he explained Peter to you?"

Nadine and I nodded. Peter had been a healer for Steve and his crew during their highway robbery days against the Lord Protector to line the Baron's pockets. "Yes, he had. I suspect he was draoi, sir."

"Yes, indeed he was. He was my childhood friend. Peter Parks. His death tore my world apart. He never kept being draoi secret from me. Not when he discovered he had powers as a child, not during all his training, and not when the Archbishop and the Lord Protector hunted him down and killed him like an animal."

Nadine frowned. "He shouldn't have revealed it. That was not our way."

"Yes, he explained that to me. Some things transcend rules, eh?" The Baron didn't wait for an answer. He turned to Steve. "Shall we retire inside? I feel strained. Major Sibbald will see to my men." He looked over and scowled at the Major until he nodded.

Steve nodded and led the way with Franky walking amicably beside the Baron. Nadine and I took hands and walked behind them. I looked to my students and shrugged. A couple of them smiled and rolled their eyes to the sky. One had the audacity to hold up her middle finger to the back of the Baron.

This should be interesting.

We retired to the large dining room table in the main farmhouse. Nadine sat next to me and the Baron took the head of the table at the far end away from us. Steve settled in next to him and Franky sat next to Nadine with a nod and a smile. Yelling outside was all that could be heard as the Baron's men stabled their horses and established a camp in a fallowed field. For a time and over the din, Steve and the Baron exchanged pleasantries about the road, the weather and the travel. Dempster entered and placed down china cups and small plates.

He returned with a steaming pot of tea, milk and honey, and again with two trays laden with pastries and small fancy sandwiches.

The Baron wasted no time digging in and for a time the only sound at the table was that of fine china, ringing teaspoons, and smacking lips. The outside noise faded, and I found I could hear the large clock ticking in the front hall. Nadine kept feeding me little morsels and laughing at my discomfort under everyone's eyes. Steve glared at her and she pouted back.

"It seems love is not lost at Rigby Farm," boomed the Baron with a brass chuckle when he noticed the look on Steve's face. "It warms my large heart. Don't begrudge the young their exuberance, Steve. Let them enjoy it while it lasts."

"She's over sixty years old, Lord Windthrop," said Steve.

The Baron blinked. "What's that you say? Over sixty? Do you jest?"

"No jest. She's sixty-something-or-other. She was renewed or some sort," intoned Steve while grabbing the last pickled cucumber sandwich. "She drives us all insane." Nadine beamed at Steve.

The Baron looked to Steve to see if he was joking. When Steve refused to look back and sat and chewed his sandwich, the Baron looked back and forth between Nadine and Steve. "You *are* serious! How is that possible?"

"Dunno. Ask her," replied Steve.

The Baron looked at Nadine and scowled. Nadine looked back at him nonplussed and then tucked a stray strand of red hair back behind her right ear.

The Baron grew a little redder in the face. "Well?"

Nadine placed a hand on her breast and faked a look of surprise. "Are you speaking to me?"

"By the Word, woman!" thundered the Baron. "Have you not been listening?"

"Why, yes I have. When you address a woman, you should start by using her name and then phrasing the question in words that have meaning."

The Baron flopped back in his seat and let his hands dangle by his side with his mouth agape. "Why I never...?"

"Why yes, you have, dear Baron. I remember you as a man-child running around the castle in Munsten. Always precocious and always in trouble. Your manners have not changed a whit."

The Baron looked apoplectic. "As a man-child!? That was before your time, young lady. You are insolent." Steve groaned at the words and pleaded with his eyes to her.

Nadine's eyes sparked, and she leaned forward in her seat. "I remember you stealing kisses in the garden behind the bushes. You, me, and the son of an Army sergeant. You were much fitter back then. It was all a game until you stole a kiss from the boy. He fled crying. Remember? You made me promise never to tell a soul or you would have everyone who knew me killed. Do you remember that? The incident got out anyway. That boy wouldn't shut up trying to embarrass you. It caused quite a stir. Your family hushed it up and had the sergeant's entire family exiled to the North. All because of one small kiss."

The Baron sputtered and clasped his chest. His eyes were wide and white. In fear for his health, I reached out with my power to calm his heart, but Nadine was already there and calming the muscle. The Baron relaxed and then hung his head for a moment. Nadine squeezed my leg, and I placed my hand on hers. I doubt the Baron even understood how bad his heart was. It seemed to be a common ailment with the middle-aged. One of my draoi was certain it was a result of bad diet and was working on finding a balance of food that would make people healthier. He was making great progress. His father had been a wordsmith in Salt Lake City in the North and he applied the principals of the Word to everything he did. A gifted draoi that was unfortunately fond of practical jokes.

When the Baron raised his head, he locked eyes with Nadine. "Nadine Brewster. That was her name. We were friends back when I was allowed to play with others beneath my station—as my father often told me. Repeatedly." The Baron squinted at Nadine. "I see similarities in you. But how could I possibly believe you are that same person? You've heard the tale from some gossip. By the Word, I still hear the tale whispered in corners even after all these years."

"Do you remember wearing my dresses? You liked my white one with the embroidered blue rose on the shoulder. It fitted you perfectly."

The Baron turned white. Steve looked at him in shock, his face nearly as white. The room grew quiet. I looked around at everyone and could see the discomfort in all eyes except Nadine's. She was enjoying this. I cleared my throat, and all eyes turned toward me. Steve looked grateful for the interruption.

I laid my hand on Nadine's shoulder. "Lord Windthrop, sir. I assure you this is the same Nadine you knew as a young man," I shifted in my seat not sure what else to say. "Gaea changed her. Stole all her years away so she could be the Cill Darae and serve her for a longer time."

The Baron held my gaze. "Peter often spoke of his magic. About how he could speed the healing of others. Bring the flesh back together. Is that of what you speak? Surely your magic cannot turn back the years."

Nadine and I shared a glance. "No," I said simply. "That is not in our power. There is much we can do, but that is beyond us."

"Then I simply won't believe it. Enough of this charade, Will," said the Baron, leaning forward in his chair until he loomed over the edge of the table. "I'm here for only one reason. And that is to discuss my plan. Steve and I have talked at length about your druids and we believe we have a role for them. If you will listen."

I was surprised and grew angry at once. *How dare they talk about my draoi and not include Nadine and I.* My thoughts must've been visible because Steve looked embarrassed. I was about to speak when Steve raised a hand to quell my protest.

"Will, I'm sorry," he began. "It started innocently as a series of what ifs and it spun into something more substantial. Over the last few months, we have come to believe you are a crucial part of what we do next..."

"But..." I tried to interject, my anger growing stronger.

"Just listen, please. I can see you're angry. Please, the decision will be yours. You and Nadine's. There's a war coming, Will. A war to end the Lord Protector's tyranny, and finish what the Revolution started, and maybe return a king to the throne. Belkin has suffered long enough. The realm is divided, and the Baron seeks to unite us. That's why he is here today. To enlist us to his cause. He will need the druids beside him. He saw what Peter could do. Imagine what dozens of druids could do to turn the battle! It would give us the edge we need.

"I've been fighting the Lord Protector my entire life. Except for my years in Jaipers, I have always fought the enemy. I have worked with the Baron for years and been in countless fights and I have seen men and women close to death saved by Peter Parks. I thought him merely an exceptional chirurgeon. I can see now the truth of it and I've seen your druids practising their arts. Your magic is powerful and will give us the edge we need. You can slow the advance of the enemy. Heal our wounded. By the Word, your druids have picked up using weapons like no one else I have ever seen. Such speed and accuracy. You would be unstoppable. A force for good to unite Belkin and restore order."

"You want to put my draoi in harm's way?" The words come out of me in a dry, low hiss. "To put them into battle? Draoi do not fight, Comlin. Draoi protect the land and provide harmony to the world. We don't march with swords in hand to kill those who we would protect."

"No one is suggesting you do, far from it, young man," interjected the Baron. "Peter never marched into battle. He tended to the wounded. Had them up on their feet and back on the line faster than any of my best chirurgeons ever managed on their best days. No, I see your druids filling a support role. Healing the wounded and what not. Working safely in the Red Tents, behind the line."

I looked to Nadine for support and stopped when I was surprised to see a gleam in her eyes. *She approved?*

"Nadine, no," I pleaded.

"I think he is right, Will. Listen to him. You weren't there during the Revolution and the Purge. You didn't see so many innocents struck down and lying bleeding on the streets. So many died and the draoi could do nothing to stem it. Here's our chance! A chance to step forward and show the world the good we can do. They'll accept us then. They'd have to."

"No, Nadine," I shook my head. "This is too much to ask. You and I cannot decide here and now, and I won't without speaking to the others first. This is their choice, too."

Nadine looked a little startled but recovered and took my hands. "I would expect nothing less from you, love. It's why I adore you. You are right. The others have a say. Forgive me."

The Baron coughed politely into his hand. "My dear boy, take what time you need. This is a decision that history will look back on. Make sure it's the right one. Perhaps you should understand what else is happening in the world first. It will affect your choice."

Just then a knock at the entranceway to the dining room turned our heads to see a captain in the colours of Turgany standing politely in the opening.

"Beg your pardon, sir. You asked me to report once the men were settled. I've set up the map table in the barn as you ordered."

"Ah, thank you Captain Tibert. We'll be over momentarily. You are dismissed."

The captain came to attention, saluted, and turned and left. The Baron turned back to me.

"Tell me, young man. Do you trust your people?" he asked.

Nadine growled and lurched to her feet. "Listen to me, Andrew Windthrop. That's thrice you've belittled Will to his face. He is not a dear boy or a young man. Now you question the loyalty of the draoi? He is the Freamhaigh of the Tree and the draoi. Selected by Gaea herself. He has been charged to return this world to a state of harmony and protect all life. I dare say he outranks you or anyone else in Belkin. He is the Freamhaigh of the entire world, you smug bastard. Do you ken me?"

The Baron rose to his feet and planted his fists on the table and leaned over. He glared at Nadine and I. "I've had enough of this charade. The druids are nothing but a group of healers and plant sowers. They will heal my people. I require their obedience. You are my vassals and you will talk to me with respect!"

Nadine screamed in rage, but I remained calmly sitting. I cared nothing for politics. Nadine hated people who took on airs and found a target in the Baron. "You insolent child! You were a peevish little brat when you were twelve and you've not grown to be anything more than a blustering entitled fool. You've been told again and again what the draoi are. Why won't you believe?"

The Baron looked furious and Steve rose beside him ready to intervene. Franky stood up beside Nadine, but I remained seated and waited. I was strangely calm inside. I had come through my anger to a realisation that none of this mattered. My knowledge of my powers was enough that I knew Nadine and I could easily keep anyone from being hurt. We could stop them from moving if we wanted to. I realised unlike the faith of the Church of the New Order, people would always require substantiation of our power. Soon the world would know what the draoi were capable of and proof would always be needed.

I snorted, and Steve shot me a look. "Sorry, it's just that everyone always asks that we prove ourselves with demonstrations. That's what's pissing Nadine off more than anything. Trust me. It's not enough for us to say who we are. Always there will come demands of proof. I can see that now. But that's the idiocy I need to change in this world. When a draoi says he or she can do something people should believe it." I looked up at the Baron and saw the confusion in his eyes. "You want proof? I will show you, but I want to be clear. I do this because the draoi believe that all should benefit from our power. Regardless of whether we like them or not. But in this case, I will undo what we change. I want you to remember this. You come here with no respect for my draoi and yell at my wife in our home. You sit at the head of our table and make demands of my people when you have no right. I will never forget that Baron Andrew Windthrop. Are you ready?"

The Baron looked about for support but found none.

"Your eyes are weak are they not?"

The Baron looked surprised but nodded. "Yes. And getting worse. A common ailment for men my age. I can't see very far, and my men need to read my documents to me. I have spectacles, but I always seem to misplace them."

"Then we'll fix that," I clasped Nadine's hand for show and drew our combined power. In a moment, we corrected his eyes.

The Baron blinked and looked around at all the faces in the room. He rubbed his eyes and then looked around at all the chairs, tables and ornamentation in the room. "It's a miracle! By the Word! I can see so clearly. All your faces, I can see every little mark. By the Word!"

I drew my power and braced myself. I focused on his eyes and undid the corrections. I tensed waiting for the pain to descend. When it did it was so slight as to be barely noticeable. I looked to Nadine in confusion and saw hers reflected back. Gaea should have punished us for using her power to harm. *Perhaps this time she approved?*

"What did you do?" cried the Baron. "Bring it back! Bring back my vision!"

"I don't think so. You have your proof. Enough of this, Lord Windthrop. We've heard your demands. Made from ignorance of what we are. You demand obedience or what, death? What you must come to realise is Nadine and I are rebuilding the draoi. We have craobhs, students still that you saw outside and refused to register. We are bringing them back from a slaughter. The Purge. Once they are ready, we will send most of them out into the world, with some remaining behind to teach others.

"The time has come for the draoi to be known in the world. To take a more direct role and work with all the people of the land and teach them how to nurture the land and each other. I hope they will cherish us. Welcome us. More importantly, they will learn not to fear us. The Purge can never be allowed to happen again. Too many lives were lost. Like Peter. And my mother.

"The draoi answer to no one but Gaea. We are outside the political games of the realm. We have a higher and more important role to play. Nadine says I outrank you. That's not true. This is not about rank, it's about roles and my role is to answer to the demands of the land. All the land. Not Turgany, but all of Belkin. Then more, perhaps. You can play kingmaker and I wish you luck. The draoi are not your tools."

The Baron shook his head. "You are part of Belkin whether you like it or not. You have to pick a side because the future hinges on that. If the Lord Protector is allowed to continue his tyranny, many people will suffer. If you are so determined to heal the land then surely that means preventative measures. You are naïve, Will Arbor. You can't just come out and declare yourself to the world. People aren't ready to see magic. Once people see what you can do, they will fear you. Panic will set in. Then distrust. They will strike you down by that same fear and justify doing it in the name of anything that suits them. The last time it was the Church. This time they may not need something to name."

I absorbed the words. There was a ring of truth in them and it spoke to the doubts I carried. Nadine and I had spent months debating what it was the draoi should do to announce ourselves. Nadine understood what it was I wanted, but she remembered the Purge and horror. She was caught between wanting to have the draoi remain as they once were and embracing the vision of the future I painted. She was uncertain and if she wasn't sure then I would continue to doubt myself.

In the silence that followed the words of the Baron, Nadine sat back down and took a sip of her tea. It was cold, and she grimaced. "I've been saying that but he won't listen. I've been fighting Gaea on this very issue as well. She wants it all at once, but she agrees with Will."

Some of the tension in the room evaporated, and the Baron sat but did not look happy. Steve and Franky sat as well and looked uncomfortable. The Baron pursed his lips and then seemed to deflate a little. "Will and Nadine, I apologise for my words. Steve warned me to treat you with respect, but I didn't listen." I could see by his aura he was not being sincere, and I gave him a wry look. I sensed a layer of deceit about him. He was being duplicitous. "I admit that you have powers. I formally acknowledge you two are the Freamhaigh and the Cill Darae of the druids, but that doesn't hold power over me, my men, or this country."

"I beg to differ," said a feminine voice behind me and I knew without looking that Gaea had appeared.

I sighed. "Hi Gaea," I said by way of introduction. She ignored me.

The Baron backed up in fright and knocked his chair clattering to the floor. He gasped for breath and pointed at her. He tried to speak but nothing escaped his large mouth. I could see the others were taking Gaea's appearance rather well, and I was pleased with that. Steve and Franky's eyes were a little wide, but they remained calm. *She needs to get out more.* I turned to look at her and she shot me a dirty look.

Gaea stepped between Nadine and I and placed a hand on each of our shoulders. "These two people represent me in this world and have my full authority. They are tasked with restoring the harmony of the world. Belkin is but a tiny island in this world, Andrew Windthrop. Your grievance with the Lord Protector is petty in comparison.

"Nadine speaks correctly, and perhaps a little rudely. The Freamhaigh and the Cill Darae are my vassals, not yours. They answer to no one but I. I can see how you would have difficulty with this. Nonetheless, rest assured they seek no position of authority in this realm. Nor do they voice that despite your fears. But I see you still do not believe, you stubborn little man."

Gaea stepped away from us and moved toward the Baron. Between one step and the next, she transformed into a simple dressed man with mousy hair shot with grey.

Steve gasped. "Peter!"

The Baron whimpered and stared at the apparition of his old friend.

"Andy, relax," said the figure of Peter.

"It can't be," whispered the Baron.

"It's me, love."

"No!"

Peter stepped up to the Baron and pulled him into an embrace. He whispered in his ear and the Baron's whole demeanour changed in a heartbeat. The strength left his legs, and he nearly collapsed, but Peter held him upright.

"I love you, Andy. Now stop being an overbearing ass and listen. If you want Will's help—and you will need it—then work with him, not against him."

The Baron twisted his face to stare up into Peter's. "How Peter? How can you be here?"

"I am part of Gaea now. I am part of a whole you cannot imagine. You trusted me once. Now trust Will. He doesn't know it yet, but he knows the way to what you seek."

"I-I don't understand," he stammered. "But I trust you, Peter."

"Good man. Do you still have the stone?"

"Of course. It's always with me."

"Like our love, enduring. Timeless. I miss you, Andy."

Peter leaned his head down and kissed the Baron. The Baron froze for a second and then melted into the embrace.

Nadine and I shared a knowing look. I could see that Steve was looking away disgusted. Franky looked oddly interested and looked from Steve to the couple and tapped her lower lip in thought. The kiss went on for a long time until they separated.

"They hurt you, didn't they?" asked the Baron.

"Yes. Very much so. But it was my thoughts of you that kept me strong until the end. Thank you, my love. I'm sorry I left you so soon."

"I miss you, Peter. Don't go. Don't leave me again."

"I have to Andy. I'm part of the world now and I have work to do."

Peter stepped back and nodded to Steve. Steve hesitated and nodded back.

"Hi, Franky. Looking good as usual," he said to her and winked.

"Don't I always?" replied Franky.

"Got to go," said Peter and then vanished.

Three

Rigby Farm, Early May 901 A.C.

THE BARON REQUIRED several minutes alone to recover. We moved to the kitchen to give him some privacy and stared at one another. No one knew what to say. Dempster ignored us and washed dishes in the sink. When the Baron emerged, he had composed himself but looked a little ashamed. For a moment, I thought I had seen and felt a flash of anger from him. He stopped in front of Nadine and then hesitantly gave her a brief hug. He then shook my hand and apologised for his behaviour. I could sense he still didn't mean it. He shook Steve's hand and Steve seemed to relax and even smiled at Franky with some amusement.

Steve then got our attention and spoke. "Okay, folks. I think I understand your position, but I would like to show you our plan first. Perhaps you'll see things differently. We've set up a command centre in the barn. Shall we head over?"

The Baron smiled. "Capital idea! The table should be set up by now."

Nadine beamed at him. "Why not?" With that, she grabbed my hand, stuck her tongue out at the Baron, and pulled me out of the house and outside. The others followed behind with Franky laughing out loud.

I sent orders to the draoi to return to their studies, and I sensed their joy at being released. I had them waiting nearby to meet with the Baron should he decide to be civil. That was clearly not going to happen. Nadine stopped pulling me and we walked over to the barn. We looked around and gawked at the changes made to the farm grounds. Military tents now stood on the fallow field in varying states of assembly. The Baron's people were running about pulling guide wires and lifting canvass. It looked like chaos, but I could sense a well-practised pattern to it. We approached the wide doorway to the barn and the guard standing there moved aside only when he sighted the Baron behind us. I scowled at the man.

We entered the gloom from the bright late afternoon sun and immediately spotted a new large table established central to the building. A wide beam of sunlight streamed down from the overhead open bale doors. We could see right away that the table was covered with a raised feature map of Belkin. It was beautiful and made to scale with mountains rising high off the surface. It was a replica of the land and it appeared accurate. Franky whistled in appreciation and reached out to touch a mountain.

"Don't touch," demanded the Baron, and he walked around to stand to the south side of the map. "It's fragile. Gather round, everyone."

Steve moved beside the Baron and Franky took the south-east corner not far from him. Nadine and I stood beside West Port and I looked longingly down at Jaipers. It was just a small circle beside the river, but I knew it was more than that. I looked out over the entire rectangular table. It was made of four tables pushed together and measured a total of twenty by thirty feet. I felt like a bird looking down at the world and I admired it. All the towns, cities and rivers were painted in exquisite details. Forests, ranges, and plains could be made out. It was a work of art.

"It's beautiful," I said in admiration.

"Thank you," replied the Baron and looked pleased. "It took me years to make."

"You made this?"

"Yes, a hobby of mine. I have models of all the major cities, too. I haven't brought them out yet. They're still being unpacked. They fill two carts."

"Why make this?" asked Nadine.

"Why for war, dear woman," The Baron spread his arms out over the table in a sweeping gesture. "Information is power. The more I have the better chance of success. What the enemy doesn't know is to my advantage. This map is one, small part of that advantage. I study it and plan."

He reached under the table and pulled open a wide shallow drawer. I looked over and saw it was filled with miniature soldiers and horses. "In here I have pieces that represent the military forces." He started pulling them out and setting them on the table. I saw that they were different colours and styles.

"Help me out, Steve," he ordered. Steve opened another drawer and pulled out more carved miniatures. Little men with bows, little crossbows on wheels, ships, horses, men on horses, soldiers, and other strange shapes. They pulled them out and began the process of sorting them by type and colour. All the while they discussed where they should be placing them on the map. The Baron produced a long pincer tool to place some of them beyond his reach. It looked like they would be at it for a long time.

I sensed one of the craobhs enter the barn and Nadine and I excused ourselves and walked over to meet her.

"Freamhaigh, Cill Darae," she said beaming a smile.

"Hi, Heather," I replied, grateful for the interruption. "What's up?"

"I would like to administer to the Baron's injured men and women. They are in the red tent the chirurgeons have set up. We can sense their pain."

"Of course, why ask?"

Heather looked down shyly. "I wasn't sure you would approve."

I took her hands, and she looked up at me. "Heather, we are draoi. It is what we do, surely you remember the teachings. We help all who require aide regardless of who that may be."

Heather bit her lip. "It's just... it's just that this will be the first time, won't it? The first time we openly use our magic and expose what we can do. I didn't want to be the first one. I thought you or Nadine would like that honour."

I looked at Nadine and she appeared a little surprised. I felt the same. I nodded to Heather. "I see, take us over."

I looked back to the others busy at the table. "Baron, Steve, Franky. We are going over to tend to your people, Baron. We'll be right back."

The Baron lifted a hand and waved dismissively, lost in his work. I doubt he heard us. Franky was now helping, but she was stealing pieces from Steve, much to his annoyance. We left them and walked out of the barn.

Outside, Heather guided us over to where the tents were being set up. The Baron's men scurried everywhere doing one task or another. Heather led us directly to the large red tent, and we ducked to pass inside the opening. I wasn't surprised to see our two other draoi, Chris and Joshua, standing to the side and looking around unhappily. They were a family each strong in healing like Heather. I nodded to them and they looked relieved to see us.

"Hi," I said. "What's wrong?"

Chris pointed his chin toward the back of the tent at the two chirurgeons making noises with a patient lying on a cot who was clearly in a lot of pain. The smell of alcohol and burning incense was very strong in the tent and my eyes burned. I looked around and identified a dozen or so other patients sitting or lying down throughout the large tent. The sunlight through the canvass painted everything with a red, bloody hue. I shuddered despite myself. I moved closer to where the chirurgeons were working and saw a snapped femur extending through the thigh of the poor man lying on the cot. He was in agony and the second chirurgeon was holding him down with force. I quickly used my senses and scanned the room and examined each patient. I grimaced. These two were working on a man with a broken leg, with little to no bleeding while the poor woman in the back corner needed immediate attention.

I moved next to the chirurgeons. "Afternoon, gentlemen, I am Will Arbor, Freamhaigh to the draoi. I have Nadine Arbor, my wife, and Cill Darae to the draoi. With us is Heather, Chris and Joshua, all craobhs and highly skilled in healing. We are here to help your people."

The chirurgeon holding the man down scowled up at me. The other one who I assumed was the head chirurgeon, looked up in surprise from where he was pushing the flesh around the exposed bone with dirty, bloody fingers. "What's that? Who are you?"

"As I said, I am the head draoi. Or druid if you prefer. Through Gaea, the Earth Mother, we have been granted the power to heal. I am here with my healers to offer our services. We have a duty to see to their injuries that we cannot ignore."

"Healers? Power to heal? You must all be daft. You aren't chirurgeons. Get out." The man turned back to the fractured femur and started poking it again.

I glanced at Nadine and she gave me a wry look. I reached out and tapped the man on the shoulder. He scowled up at me.

"Can't you see I'm busy? This man is in pain and needs our attention."

"Yes, he is and does. I can help you with that. Have you not determined who needs help first? That woman over there..."

"You are interfering with our work and are to leave at once! You can't possibly understand the complexities of the human body. It takes years..."

While he spoke, I reached out to the poor man writhing on the cot and blocked the pain from his leg. He froze for a moment and then collapsed in relief on the cot and stopped struggling.

The chirurgeon stopped talking and looked up at the other chirurgeon. "What happened? What did you do?"

The other just shook his head and shrugged his shoulders.

The man stirred in the cot. "I'm fine. The pain just disappeared. Such a relief. I feel so exhausted. I'm parched. Is there any water?"

I glanced over to Joshua while I spoke. "I stopped the pain." Joshua nodded and moved over to the water jug and filled a goblet. He brought it over to the injured man and lifted his head up to let him drink from the cup. The man gulped at the water and then let his head drop back to the cot.

"Thank you. I needed that."

The head chirurgeon who had watched all this was growing angrier by the second. He stood up and pointed at me. "That's enough! You will no longer be permitted to interfere here. Leave at once, or I will summon the guards!"

I ignored him. I'd had enough of him. I beckoned my healers forward, and they lined up in front of me. "Right folks. Here's the test. Tell me, who needs help first. Talk me through it."

Heather spoke up first. "The woman in the corner is first. Her appendix is about to burst. It's septic. Without immediate help, she will die."

Chris nodded in agreement. "Yes, and second is the ginger boy sitting there. He has a bad sliver deep in his right foot. It's badly infected and turned to blood poisoning. It's spreading up his calf."

They all nodded. Joshua spoke next. "Then this poor fellow with the broken femur. The others in the tent simply have sprains, cuts and torn muscles."

Nadine and I smiled. "Correct. See to it, please."

My healers moved out into the tent. Heather and Chris went to the woman in the corner. The chirurgeons stood gawking not sure what was happening and watched my healers move to the cots. Joshua knelt in front of the red-haired boy sitting with his eyes wide open listening and watching everything going on. So were the rest of them.

"Blood poisoning? How'd you even know that? How'd you know I had a sliver?"

Joshua hushed the man and lifted his pant leg. Black veins coursed up his lower leg.

"By the Word!" said the man in fright. "Help me!"

The head chirurgeon moved forward and thrust his face in front of mine. His face was all screwed up with dislike and venom. "That's it. I'm getting the guards." He pointed a finger at the other chirurgeon and flicked it toward the tent opening. He smiled and rushed out of the tent calling loudly for guards. "Now you've had it. You should have listened. No one interferes with guild work."

I pushed past the man and knelt beside the broken leg. Nadine sat on the cot by the man's head and looked down at his alarmed face.

"Easy," she soothed. "We're going to fix your leg and you'll soon be walking out of here. You won't feel a thing."

"What? That's crazy!" shouted the head chirurgeon. "Leave that man alone!"

"Wh-what are you going to do?" asked the man on the cot. "What are you... oh!"

I relaxed the muscles in the man's thigh, strengthened myself, and pulled the leg out straight. The exposed bone disappeared back inside the thigh and I concentrated on lining the bone up perfectly. Once in place, I rejoiced when I felt Nadine join me and together we knitted the bone back together, fused the torn flesh and muscles, and removed the contamination. We pulled power from the land and let it flow through us. Time passed until finally, it was done, and I opened my eyes to find evening had fallen. Lanterns lit up the tent and shadows cast against the red canvass.

Nadine and I blinked and looked around. Steve, Franky and the Baron were sitting at a table and eating their supper. My healers were gone and so were their patients. All the wounded were gone, and I smiled. They were healed, and the draoi had shown their power. I looked around the tent and spotted the two chirurgeons standing together by the entrance whispering together and glancing over at us.

"Ah, Freamhaigh," said the Baron. "Come join us at the table. Your man Dempster has prepared the most amazing meal at my request. We've only just started eating. No sense letting it get cold, eh? Come, come!"

The man on the cot stirred and woke up. Nadine had put him to sleep soon after we started. Now he was awake, and he reached out to his leg and wiggled his foot. "Wh-what? How is this possible?" He looked from Nadine to me. "What did you do?"

"We healed your broken leg. It was a compound fracture but a good clean break. Your veins and arteries were all missed. We fixed the break and closed your thigh up. Good as new. You can get up and go if you like."

The man then noticed his Baron sitting nearby. "Sir, my apologies, I didn't see you there. What's happening, sir?"

The Baron continued chewing for a moment and looked pensive. "You've been healed, my boy. You are among the first to be openly healed by the druids of the land. Now out you go. Go tell your mates. Let them know what the druids can do. The others from in here are already speaking the tale of the miracles. Have fun."

The man hesitated to see if his Baron was making a mockery of him. When the Baron continued eating in silence, he tentatively swung his legs out from the cot. I could see he waited to feel the pain return and when it didn't he grew bolder and struggled to get to his feet. He wobbled a moment and then found his balance. Feeling more confident he took a step forward with his previously injured leg and then another. "Haha! This is amazing!" he cried out. "Thank you!"

He laughed again and then shook my hand and Nadine's. He moved to leave and then stopped by the chirurgeons. "Why couldn't you do that? I lay for hours in excruciating pain." He shook his head and then disappeared into the night without waiting for a reply. The chirurgeons glared at me as if this was somehow my fault.

"Come and sit you two," ordered the Baron.

Nadine and I shared a look and then sat at the table and found two plates of food laid out for us. Pork chops and applesauce. I smiled to myself and remembered this very meal in the Woven Bail Inn in Jaipers. It was my favourite. Thick cut pork chops with fresh-made applesauce. I found myself sucking back my own spit in anticipation. I dug in and within minutes found myself staring at an empty plate. I met the eyes of Franky and she mouthed the word *wow* to me.

I felt Nadine's look and glanced over at her.

"Pig," she said and went back to cutting her pork chop into small pieces on her plate. Most of her meal remained. I wanted it. "Nope," she said. "Mine."

I sat back and burped into my hand. The Baron smiled at me and took a sip of his wine.

"So, Freamhaigh. You've made quite an impression in here with your healers. It's all the word of the camp. The man whose leg you healed will milk drinks out of his tale for weeks, no doubt."

I nodded, not sure how to respond. I looked to the chirurgeons and wondered how they felt about it. Probably not good and I was sure I had made enemies of their guild.

"Ah, I see you looking to my chirurgeons. In my experience, there are many ways to make an impression. For the longest lasting impression make sure to embarrass someone publicly. Equally, you can heap praise on someone—again publicly. Everything in between has varying degrees of effect. So, what do you think you managed here, eh?"

The Baron looked a little smug to me and I felt my anger rise. "Well, Baron. First, you would need to ask yourself whether you actually care about what the other person thought. Second, you would need to ask yourself what you were trying to achieve and why you take the path you chose. For example, let's say you enter a tent and find injured people. One of which has an injury that looks bad and another who's injury is direr but ignored. Then let's suppose you confront those who are tasked to treating those injuries. You are polite but insistent.

"Then you get treated like a criminal. Belittled. How would you respond? Now, before you answer me, you must understand that behind all this lay your duty to do what is right. You have no option but to treat those who require treatment. Yet you are blocked. What say you then, Lord Windthrop? Do you tuck your tail between your legs and leave or do you ignore the insufferable sons of *bitseachaigh* and correct the problem and damn them to whatever hell awaits them?

"So, there you sit smug in your seat eating food from my larder that was prepared by my good friend. I have no doubt you ordered this because you felt it was your due and then had it set up in this tent for effect. Now you try to have me second guess my decisions. You can sit there for all eternity for all I care. Your opinion matters naught. I am the Freamhaigh of the Tree. My duty is to the land. I do not seek permission from anyone to allow my draoi to do what it is that they *must* do. We are sworn to Gaea. You've met her. She explained this to you and yet you still feel you can question and lecture me. No longer. I am not your vassal. Your opinion matters little to me. Think long and hard how you next approach me or question my intentions. The next lecture from you on my business will see me walking away from the likes of you."

I rose, and Nadine rose with me. Inside I was shaking. I had never spoken to anyone like that before. Nadine gave me strength.

"Steve, Franky, have a good evening."

Nadine and I walked to the tent opening. We stopped at the chirurgeons and I glared at them. "Never come between my people and those who require medical care. I will not be so kind the next time."

The head chirurgeon shot me a look of such hatred it honestly surprised me. His aura flickered black and grey. This was a man capable of many harms in the world.

I looked back to the table to see Steve holding the Baron down in his seat. He was red-faced and angry. I didn't care. "This man here? This chirurgeon? He should never be permitted to treat people. There is something wrong with him. He seeks to administer pain, not treat it."

Nadine and I disappeared into the night. As we walked slowly to the house, she hugged me across the waist. "I'm so proud of you, hon."

After thanking Dempster for the lovely meal and seeing to Anne and her baby, Nadine and I retired to our bed. It was the same bed the Rigby's had assigned to us so many months ago. Steve had asked me why we hadn't moved into the master bedroom and our answer had been simple: it wasn't our house. It was Katherine's.

Thoughts of her had me following our thread to find her and Dog well to the north and travelling along a high road pass. She was heading to Salt Lake City. She had covered a remarkable amount of ground in a short time. I was proud of her. I could sense she was fine, hale and fit. Then I saw that the bond between her and Dog shone bright white and it startled me.

"Nadine, her bond is white with Dog," I said.

"Yes," she replied softly. "It is."

"What does that mean?"

"They are in love."

"Human and dog? But white is more than just love. It's so much stronger."

"Yes, love, it is."

"What do we do?"

Nadine sighed and slipped naked under the covers of the bed. She was wearing me out, and I looked at her with a weary expression. She patted the space beside her. "Hurry up. I'm hungry and I didn't get to finish my supper before you went after the Baron."

I paced the room and drew off my shirt and tossed it in the corner. "I'm worried about her. How can she love Dog like that?"

"I asked Gaea about it. She said not to worry. She said all things on earth are her. I hate it when she says things like that. Hurts my brain. Let it go, hon. Katherine is happy and so is Dog."

I nodded. "I'll try. How's she managing?"

"Really good. She took your advice, and she's gathering herbs. Oh, I never told you, she has my sickle with her."

"Really? That's the symbol of your position, hon. Why'd you give it to her?"

"You carried it for years. It's not a symbol. It's a tool. Anyway, Gaea told me to. I handed it to her, and she took it without a word. Seemed to think it belonged to her, and I was returning it."

"Hmm. Well, I'm worried about her." I sat on the bed and pulled my pants off. The night air was still chill and so I ducked under the covers. No sooner had I slipped under than Nadine slid over and ran her hand down my chest and crept it lower.

"I'm proud of our healers today," I said and squirmed a little. "They did well."

"Yes, they did. In my days, the talent they used would make them stocs on the spot."

"I was thinking the same thing. It was interesting, giving them a test like that. I think that all our craobhs should be tested for competency. Our students now all have it in spades. Honestly, I think they are all stocs already. The next group may not have the same strengths. We need to test them."

"Well, we used to assign stocs to craobhs. The assigned stoc assessed them over a period and announced when they were ready. It was a good way and I think we should do that again. But I will admit this bunch is different. Like you. Highly skilled without an apprenticeship or master to guide them."

Her hand had stopped, and I found I could focus. "We don't have stocs for that. We'll need to find another way."

We grew silent in thought. Nadine stirred and slipped her arm over my chest and snuggled in tight against me. I loved the feel of her against me and I closed my eyes relishing it. *Maybe she will let me sleep tonight.*

"I don't trust the Baron," she said after a moment.

"No kidding," I snorted. I opened my eyes and stared at the ceiling. "He's an ass. Who does he think he is? Coming here to our school and throwing his weight around and making demands?"

"He's the Baron. This is his land. That's who he thinks he is. He's been living his whole life bossing people around. He thinks his actions are the correct ones and doesn't question them. Take tonight for example. He saw you challenging his people and sided with them. He never questioned whether they were in the wrong or not. To him, you were wrong—automatically. He ignored all the surrounding evidence. He sees what he wants to see. He's a fool."

"So, what do we do about it?"

"Honestly? Nothing. Let Steve worry about him. Time for him to step up and lay down the law on our dear Baron."

"Why would the Baron listen to him?"

"Because the Baron is attracted to Steve Comlin."

"What! Whatever makes you think that?"

Nadine laughed. "Trust a woman to know. Franky sees it."

I mulled that over. "Okay, say it's true. How does that help us?"

"Once Franky convinces Steve—and she will—and then she explains what he needs to do with that—and she will—Steve will start manipulating the good Baron over to seeing our way of things."

"You sure?"

Nadine rose and kissed me. "Baby, of course I'm sure. I'm the Cill Darae and I always get what I want. Like this..."

I yelped and then the Baron was soon forgotten.

The next day we gathered around the map table in the barn. The Baron refused to make eye contact with me and even had Steve place himself between us. Nadine and Franky stood to the right side of the table and we studied what we were looking at.

The table had clusters of miniatures placed in the cities and towns. Little ships sat off the harbours at Munsten, Portsmouth and Jergen. I spotted the small garrison at Jaipers. The county of Turgany miniatures were coloured blue and the others, those of the Lord Protector, were red apart from some green ones in Munsten. I figured out those probably represented the Lord Protector's guard—a small army in its own right. What we were looking at were the positions of all the military units in Belkin in advance of a civil war. The south against the north. I felt sick, and I looked up to see the same disgust and fear I felt in Nadine's eyes. Franky looked bored, the Baron was clearly excited, and Steve stood quietly and kept his emotions withdrawn.

"As you can see here," began the Baron. "We have placed all the units under my Command and those at the disposal of Healy on the map. The information is up-to-date. I have it under good authority that the Fleet Admiral of the Realm and some of his ships have already defected to our side. They are here in Portsmouth and Jergen. The rest of the navy is Healy's, but this will be a land war and the navy does not concern us.

"We have two main objectives, Jergen and Munsten. This is where the bulk of the units are located and represents the greatest strategic gains for whoever holds them. The cities are well-defended and can withstand a siege for far too long to be permitted. We own Jergen. It is my capital here in Turgany. But that does not mean we will hold it. To win this war, we must hold both the cities.

"Unfortunately, we do not have the strength to hold both cities simultaneously. For this reason, we will hold Jergen and close the south off from the north at the Crossroads. I will divide the realm and force the Lord Protector into a parley. My goal is clear: return the land to a monarchy. Enough of this revolution nonsense. The realm has seen enough turmoil. But there will need to be changes. We need a king on the throne. But no longer will a king have absolute powers. A cabinet of representatives of the people will provide guidance and veto bad decisions. It will be a time of prosperity. Peace will be allowed to return to the realm."

Peace? I thought aghast. *There has been peace.* The Baron would start a war to bring terror and fear into the people in the name of peace. He frightened me. I didn't see the need for any violence at all.

"Who will be king?" I asked.

Steve and the Baron glanced at one another. The Baron answered me. "Me."

"You? Who decides that?"

"Will, Lord Windthrop is the only noble with bloodlines to the old King. He is next in line. The succession is clear."

"Is that what this is all about? Making him the King?" I glared at the Baron. "Why not just declare yourself king now and ask the Lord Protector to step aside?" I asked.

"Because that won't work, Will," answered Steve for the Baron. "The Lord Protector would never willingly give up his power. He would respond with his armies and navy. He would kill Lord Windthrop and execute anyone involved, no matter how remotely. We've looked at many courses of action over the past months. Of all of them, this plan, the one that secures our position in the south and places Lord Windthrop on the throne, protects the people and produces the least risk, with the greatest chance for success, and the least loss of life.

"There are other factors you should be aware of. One, Frederick Bairstow, is on our side already and he's in the castle and watching the Lord Protector. He has been corresponding with our good Baron here. It seems Healy has been embezzling heavily from the realm coffers for years. He wants to arrest Healy but fears the power and reach of Healy. The entire cabinet is under his thumb and he says the military of the realm is no longer truly under his direct Command. Two, his brother Brent, who we met here months ago, was the head of the Lord Protector's Guard and could have secured Munsten in a heartbeat and made this simple for us. No longer. The new head of the Guard has moved out those loyal to Brent. Munsten will not fall to us and the Lord Protector is now far too protected.

"We need to show strength in the south and then make our demands from that position. The north could rally and attack the south but that would prove too costly. The Army of the Realm is not large enough to contain the south. This is a simple plan. We make use of our strengths and then get what we want. Healy doesn't have the forces to push us out and once we make it clear Lord Windthrop intends to take the throne, we hope to erode his base support. The south feeds the north. If necessary, we will force an embargo. Starve them out if need be. In time Healy will have to step aside. It is a good plan, Will."

I had neither the knowledge of military planning nor the insight to make a comment. Nadine looked troubled and I could sense her disquiet.

"I see. You've included Nadine and me in this discussion. I presume you think we are your allies in this?"

Steve blinked in a moment of surprise. "Of course we think you as an ally. Why wouldn't you be? The Lord Protector enforced the Purge, did he not? He is not your friend."

"True. I admit to a rather large dislike for the man. He is responsible for the death of my mother and father. The Sect even more so. But my personal issues with him are just that—personal. I am the Freamhaigh and Nadine the Cill Darae of the Tree. Our task is simple, Steve. We must bring harmony to the world. That is not the harmony between South and North Belkin, or between Healy and the Baron, or even placing a king on the throne. It is about the harmony of the earth and nature. I am more concerned with what people do to the earth than what they do on the earth. When you starve the north, you will kill people while the Lord Protector eats and gluts himself in Munsten.

"I cannot take sides in this. There are no sides for me or the draoi. I represent both the people of the north and the south. Both will require our aide."

The Baron smashed his fist to the table and roared startling us all. The miniatures on the table bounced and landed in a clatter. "Treason! You openly admit you would aid the enemy! Steve, you promised me these druids would help us. I see now your judgement was clouded with your emotions and a false sense of loyalty. I see nothing but children before me all imagining a world of peace and beauty."

Steve looked apologetically at me. "I'm sorry, Will. I shouldn't have spoken for you. I should have discussed this with you first. But honestly, you surprise me with your words. I know your past. How could you possible side with Healy?"

"I am not taking sides, Steve. And I am no longer the boy you knew in Jaipers. The Lord Protector is not my worry other than the effect he may have on the harmony and even the balance of the world. The plants, insects, animals and people interact continuously. It is a beautiful dance and I wish you could see it as we do. You speak to me of war. I care not except for easing the pain of it. War is inevitable. Animals war. Insects war. Trees war for sunlight. My task is to reduce the damage and ease the return of harmony. It is not an easy task and my numbers are few."

"Guards!" cried out the Baron. Steve whirled toward him.

"What are you doing?" demanded Steve.

"Doing what I must," declared the Baron.

A moment later five guards rushed in with weapons drawn. Two positioned behind myself and two behind Nadine. The fifth stepped in front of the Baron and saluted.

"Sir, the druids have been rounded up and detained as per your orders."

Steve stepped forward, but Franky held him back with her one arm. "Leave Will alone!" he demanded.

The Baron ignored him. "Excellent, Captain Tibert. Take these two to the others and restrain them. I'll have further orders shortly. Get them out of my sight. They sicken me. Steve, don't interfere."

Steve and Franky looked stricken as they watched the guards grab Nadine's arms and mine. It was good to know they hadn't known or been involved. Nadine glanced at me and I could sense she was upset that I had been right.

I turned my head to look the Baron in the eye. "You are to leave this farm immediately. You are no longer welcome here."

The Baron laughed. "Excuse me? You insolent bastard. You are nothing. A treasonous son-of-a-*bitseachaigh*. Guards take them away."

The guards tried to move us but found they were unable. They tried again, and Nadine and I looked serenely across the table at one another.

"Windthrop," said Nadine with a sigh. "Perhaps you didn't hear my husband. Leave at once."

"Guards, what's going on? Remove them!" yelled the Baron.

"Sir, we can't budge them."

"What? Try harder!"

The guards grunted with strain as they tried once again to move us. This continued for several seconds with the Baron yelling at his guards to try harder. Steve and Franky moved aside and looked on with wonder.

"Freamhaigh," said Heather who had entered the barn quietly behind us. "The farm is secure."

"Thanks, Heather. Time to go, Lord Windthrop."

Nadine and I shrugged past the guards and strolled out of the barn holding hands. The farm was deathly quiet. We could see that the Baron's men were clustered together on the lawn in a large group. Surrounding them were hundreds of animals. Dogs, cats, deer, wolves, bears and even the Baron's horses quietly stood or sat in a circle surrounding the soldiers. Insects of all kinds swarmed in a large circle around the men. The soldiers cowered in fear and glanced upward to the hundreds of birds circling overhead.

The Baron emerged from the barn shielding his eyes from the morning sun. "What is this? What's happening here?" He cried out in fright once his eyes adjusted and he saw his men surrounded by wild animals. "What in the Word? Why are my men surrounded by animals? Steve, get out here!" A hint of panic touched the voice of the Baron and Nadine and I smiled at one another. We saw our draoi standing nearby with their hands clasped in front of them. *Non-threatening, just like I wanted,* I thought happily.

Nadine and I watched the Baron stumble past and approach his encircled soldiers. He fumbled for his sword but couldn't seem to find the pommel. A black bear turned toward him and roared, and the Baron slid down onto his backside and then scrambled to distance himself; his sword forgotten.

"Steve! Steve!" he cried.

Steve and Franky ran out of the barn and stopped to survey the scene. I caught a quick frown on Steve's face toward me before he composed himself. His aura was lit up with conflict and so was Franky's. That was not good, I needed them to remain with the draoi. I was worried about that. Nadine had assured me last night not to worry after we worked out this response. She didn't think it would be necessary but once the Baron had called the guards on us she had known that I was right. I had argued the Baron would do anything to secure our aide and that we should be prepared.

Steve ran to the Baron's side and helped him to his feet. I watched as the Baron's aura sparked with anger and hatred. Franky drew her sword and surveyed the area. The men and women from Steve's crew were standing in the shade of the main house and laughter burst from them at intervals. Franky relaxed a little and then, like Steve, threw a frown our way.

"They won't be harmed, Baron," I said, once he focused on me. His face was scarlet, and I could see he was about to start screaming at me. Nadine moved to stand by Franky. Steve stood next to the Baron, and it was to him I spoke next. "Nothing would have happened if the Baron had left my draoi alone, Steve. The moment they rounded them up all bets were off."

I could see Steve's jaw clench. He looked out over the surrounded men and the calm animals that circled them. The occasional cry from a bird being the only sound. The Baron struggled to speak but Nadine kept his throat constricted just enough to stop that. We had heard enough from him.

"How?" asked Steve, and he glanced at the Baron and then back to me.

I looked at Franky and stared meaningfully at her sword. She shook her head a minuscule amount and that small gesture broke my heart. Nadine looked sorrowful and hung her head a moment before looking up and speaking. "It only took the draoi a matter of minutes to bring in the waiting animals to circle the Baron's troops. Then they silenced your men and stood calmly over there asking the animals to act as they did. No harm will come to your men so long as they behave and leave peacefully."

I stepped in front of the Baron. "You, sir, came into my home and thought to take possession of my people. We welcomed you, healed your injured, and remained civil despite your constant attempts to belittle those efforts. We listened respectably to you. We heard your plans for domination in the south and lead the land into civil war and your intention to take the throne. Those plans will not and cannot involve my draoi." I left the circle and walked over to my people. They smiled at me, with their trust in me and Nadine absolute, and our trust in them more so. They were warriors of a different kind. Warriors for the world.

What the Baron and the others were not seeing was the tremendous effort my draoi were exerting. It was taking all of them to control the animals, insects, and the soldiers. They had lent Nadine and I the strength to remain rooted in the barn. If they had thought to simply pick us up, we would have had to use other means. As it was, we were simply so very much stronger than the guards. It was taxing, but we felt the power of Gaea supporting us and drew satisfaction that she agreed with us in this. I turned back to regard the enraged face of the Baron. Nadine eased his heart somewhat, but he was very close to a full heart attack. The man simply had no idea who or what he was dealing with, despite our best efforts to educate him. Ignorance is bliss, my old friend Daukyns used to say.

"You disappoint me greatly, Baron. Steve spoke so fondly of you and so I had expected a better man. You are a man who had known the draoi. Even loved one dearly. Yet you chose ignorance instead. You are a small minded, petty tyrant. You would take when someone offers. You would condescend rather than listen. You are heading into a war, Lord Windthrop, of your own making. Gaea, whom you met I might remind you, tells us a greater conflict is coming. Your worldly desires pale in comparison.

"My draoi are the strongest the world has ever seen. It would take much more than a couple of hundred soldiers to contain us. It bodes well for our future, but I'll be honest with you: this use of power in this way does not sit well with me. Or Nadine. Our purpose is to restore the harmony of the land. Not force others to our will.

"You've insulted us. Ignored us. Then opted to grab us for your own selfish ends. We are done. You are to leave the farm and never return. You are no longer welcome here."

I had never spoken to anyone in this manner and I fought to control my limbs from shaking. Nadine helped keep me calm. I looked out at the soldiers of the Baron and saw nothing but fear. This was how the draoi would be remembered. Not as healers, but as people who could control strange magic.

There was no helping it. I was confident we were stepping out on the right path. The Baron thought to use us as part of his power base. Last night my draoi discussed the future and agreed our path was elsewhere. Something was coming to Belkin. Something far more serious than an uprising to overthrow a start-up petty dictator like Healy. Those last words had been Nadine's, and I smiled remembering her acceptance.

In time we would find a way to show the world the good we could accomplish. For now, our first open use of magic would follow with tales of fear and horror. It was not the way we wanted this. But we couldn't be a tool for anyone's dreams of conquest.

I walked over to Nadine and we clasped hands. I nodded to the draoi, and the animals turned and fled into the surrounding fields and woods. The birds cried out and flew off in every direction. The insects spread out and disappeared into the grass. The Baron's men slowly drew apart and looked to the Baron for orders. He was a sight to behold. His face was beyond furious. This was a man who did not accept humility or defeat. The draoi had made an enemy this day but it could not be helped. He had forced this on us with his arrogance.

Steve shook his head and then took the Baron by the arm and gently pulled him away, whispering soothing words to him. Franky shot Nadine and me a baleful look and then strode over to the Baron's men yelling out orders to pack up and move out. Nadine released the Baron's voice, and he started cursing and yelling.

The next few hours were uneventful but ultimately sorrowful. My draoi and I remained outside where we were and watched the Baron's men pack up and then ride out in silence. He said nothing to us as he left. He didn't even spare us a glance, and I was thankful for that. A moment later Steve and the crew emerged with their belongings and a large piece of me shattered. Steve stopped his horse next to me and looked down at me. He looked angry, disappointed and sorrowful all at the same time. His aura was shot with so many colours I couldn't make it out.

"It didn't have to be this way, you could have helped. Why, Will?"

I swallowed the grief that threatened to consume me. I had expected Steve to understand. He had vowed to be our protectors in the world. He was breaking that vow and not seeming to care. This man who had protected me as a child would now leave and follow the hollow promises of a petty, angry man instead. I didn't know him anymore. The months on the farm had changed him back to who he had been before. I didn't like this former highwayman. I think perhaps Reeve Comlin would agree with me.

Nadine squeezed my hand and answered for me. "Shame, Stephen Comlin. Shame! You follow that arse of a man down that road and abandon those here who protected you and cared for you. Off you go. You know why this is wrong. You just won't admit it to your heart. When you figure it out, come back and apologise to me. Until then, off on your merry way with your merry band."

Steve looked startled and started to speak. Franky reached out from her horse and grabbed his forearm with her one hand. "Leave it. We must follow, you know why. There's nothing you can do or say here. They don't see the greater calling. Come on."

Steve hesitated and then nodded. "Farewell, Will. Good fortune."

I didn't answer and watched Steve Comlin and his crew until they disappeared down the road. They were heading south toward Jergen. In the direction Brent and James had gone six months ago. It was there that the conflict would begin. We had only a few months and then it would start.

I embraced Nadine and the other draoi broke apart to tend to chores and the farm animals. Life on the farm would resume. It always would. Despite all the grief and betrayal, I still felt hope. The time of the draoi remaining hidden in the world was over. I felt a sense of purpose in what Gaea was doing. I trusted her. I knew that I needn't worry that the people would always fear us. We would be the calm before the storm and smooth the way for the true hardship that was on the horizon. It was us against the world.

Four

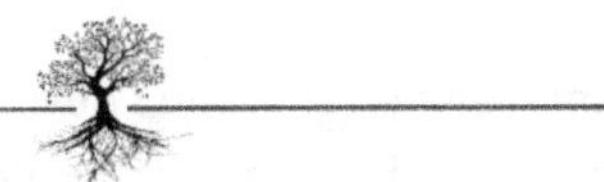

SIX MONTHS AGO

Heading to Jergen - November 900 A.C.

BRENT AND JAMES dismounted to walk alongside their horses. They balanced the ride transitioning from a walk, trot, and canter, and every two hours they walked for fifteen minutes to give the horses a break. Since leaving the Rigby Farm they had made good time. They had been on the road for only a week and the occasional flurry of snow reminded them to make haste to the city of Jergen. They rode in silence and slept well off the road at night and kept warm by a small fire. They were on a constant vigil for any sign of Major Gillespie and his men. *They were somewhere between the farm and Munsten, that's for sure,* mused Brent. *I wish to Hell I knew where he was.*

While walking the horses they often brought up the night at Rigby Farm. Brent expressed confidence he knew what had happened, but James still had his doubts. They recounted the race upriver, urged to go faster by Steve Comlin, and dragging a complaining Dempster along with them. They discussed stumbling into the horror of the farm and finding men without life walking upright and killing. Later, the young man Will Arbor had named them *aos'si,* or the *sluagh sidhe.* Names from fairy tales designed to frighten children. But Brent had seen them and believed.

"So you're saying God came to our side and slew Erebus, the demon figure?" asked James rhetorically.

"Yes. What's so hard to believe about that?" asked Brent. "Holy light shot out of my forehead—and the amulet—and pierced the creature from Hell. We all witnessed it. I'm surprised you still doubt it."

"Will seemed to think it was something else."

"Yes, well, Will is not an expert on religion, is he? He follows the Word and Gaea. Plus he's only eighteen. What does he know?"

"Well, we all saw Gaea. She's real."

"I don't need to see God to believe, you heathen. Have a little faith!"

"Pft," snorted James. "I have faith in my sword, sir, I'll have you know. Will could do some pretty remarkable things, you have to admit. His wife and the others, too. I can't get it out of my head. Who has powers like that, anyway?" James thought for a second and then grinned sideways at Brent. "'Cept maybe you, I suppose."

"Shut up! I liked you better when I outranked you."

"Well, we all pine for the days of yore, don't we? When everything was wine and fine women all the time." James heaved an exaggerated sigh. "The heady days. Back when you were sufferable."

"I'll knock you back into yesterday if you like. Just keep talking."

James laughed, and his horse ducked his head at the bright sound. The weather looked promising. The snows of November had only produced a light dusting. They were making fast time on the road. They would reach Jergen in two days' time. Nadine had told them to stay at her house along the coast and had written a note introducing them to the woman currently staying there. The prospect of a warm house drove them forward.

For a time, they walked in silence. Each chasing their own deep thoughts. James looked out across the field to their right and watched a murder of crows take flight at some sound. He kept his eyes on the tree line and then coughed slightly. Brent turned his head to observe, and they slowed to a halt. After several minutes, they shook their heads and resumed their walk.

"Nothing. Keep an eye anyway, James."

"'Course."

"I know you have your doubts, James. I can see it in your eyes. But I also know you trust me, so thanks. I don't understand why God would use me in this way, but I live to serve His will."

"Humph. What else am I to do? You've ruined my military career along with yours. So I guess I'm stuck with you," James chuckled to take any bite out of his words. "I can't imagine a better person to spiral into certain death and doom with. Truth be told, I'm curious to see where this all goes."

"Me, too. It's just... it's just I feel a draw. A certainty to my step, James. I am on the right path. I just need to see it to its end. We have a purpose. I won't say trust me, but I will say I am glad to have you by my side. Hopefully with a happy ending for both of us, eh?"

"T'would be nice, I admit. Beautiful women, wine, and large beds. That's a perfect ending for me."

Brent laughed. "You and me, my friend. Growing old and still chasing women."

"There are those two in Jergen. Think they'll remember us?"

"Hopefully they stay up at night with a candle in the window for us."

"We'll see. We'll see."

Their arrival in Jergen was as uneventful as the journey. Brent and James passed through the northern gate around midday without so much as a glance from the guards. They rode in silence until they reached Nadine's single-level weathered house standing quietly along the coast. The sun was high in the sky and the shadows of seagulls darting and crying in the cold air swam across the ground. The small house was surrounded by a whitewashed picket fence that enclosed a once-sprawling garden, with fruit trees picked clean of their bounty. The house needed work. It was battered by winds, rains, and now the cold of winter with the freeze and thaw cycle.

They glanced at one another, their breaths clouding in the cold air, and dismounted and stood still for a moment. James chuckled and pulled off his riding gloves. "Well, here we are."

Brent grunted and blew a cloud of breath out.

James tucked his gloves into his waistband. "So how do you want to do this?"

"What do you mean?"

"Well, we can't very well just march up and tell the poor woman inside that we are moving in, can we?"

"Hmm. No. I suppose not."

"You should do it."

"Why?"

"You're older. More trustworthy."

"Bugger."

"'Tis true and you know it. Plus, you outrank me. Rank has privilege, no?"

"If that were true I would be ordering you to do it."

James laughed and waited. His horse reached out with his head to nuzzle his tunic pocket. James reached in and pulled out a dried piece of apple and gave it to the horse. He rubbed the horse's nose and pushed the horse's lips away from his face.

"Alright, off I go. Wish me luck." Brent handed James the reins to his horse.

"Luck."

Brent walked up to the small gate in the fence, opened it, and passed through letting it swing shut behind him. His boots crunched on the seashell path leading up to the door. "Hello inside! I beg your pardon, ma'am, I'm a friend of Nadine. She bade us come and introduce ourselves. We mean no harm. I've got a note from her announcing us."

Brent paused on the path a few feet from the front door and waited.

After a long moment, the voice of a woman called out. "Who are ye?"

"My name is Brent Bairstow and my companion outside the gate is James Dixon."

"You've got a military look about ya. I don't like military types. They always take and leave nothin' but grief behind 'em."

"I assure you, fine lady, that we promise to do neither. We are here in Jergen for the winter, but we aren't without means. Nadine asked us to care for you and we mean to. Hopefully, from inside the house before the winter storms blast in from the sea."

Silence greeted this remark and Brent looked back at James who shrugged and watched the seagulls wheel overhead.

"Leave the note under the door and back up to the gate."

"As you wish, my lady."

"I'm no lady, stop calling me that. Now hurry up."

Brent walked to the door and drew the sealed letter from inside his tunic and slid it into the bottom gap of the door. He walked unhurriedly back to the gate and joined James.

"What do you think?"

"I think we need to prepare ourselves for a bloody cold winter. What's Plan B? Camp on her doorstep, or find an inn?"

Brent growled and stood staring at the door.

"What do you think she wrote in the note?"

"Knowing Nadine, nothing good, I suspect. She has the devil in her."

James laughed. "Sounds like this woman is of the same ilk."

The front door of the house opened and standing in the doorway appeared a woman of perhaps thirty years. Her long brown hair was tied up loosely on her head. She wore a patched dress with an apron around her waist. She was barefoot and dirt smudged her cheekbones. She looked worn down and tired and annoyed. Pressed up tight behind her cowered her three young ones, peering around her legs and blinking in the sunlight. A large hairy dog pushed past her legs and woofed gently.

"Alright," she said after a moment. "Come up to my door and let me see you. Leave the horses outside the gate. I won't have them *caccing* in my yard."

James and Brent tied the horses to a fence post and came through the gate and up the path. The dog raced toward them, and they held out their hands for the dog to smell. The dog barked once and trotted happily alongside them.

James whispered to Brent. "Well, one down, one to go. Which do you think has the worst bite?"

Brent ignored James and stopped a few feet short of the door. Through the doorway, he could make out a boy with bright red hair and a heavily freckled face. He was maybe twelve years of age. Beside him was a smaller boy of maybe eight years with the same red hair and freckles. Beside him was a little brown-haired girl of no more than four years with her thumb stuck firmly in her mouth. A small, stuffed animal that looked like an elk hung limply from her other hand. Brent smiled at the girl and then looked at the woman. She was thin, and her dress was too cold for the weather inside or out. Her bare feet were callused and cracked. The children looked in better shape and dressed well enough for the coming winter. Brent nodded to her.

"Nadine says in this note that I'm to trust you and let you in," she shook the note in her hand for emphasis. "Now that I'm looking at you I think her more than a wee bit daft. How'd you meet her and where?"

Brent coughed politely into his hand to hide his smile. "Let me introduce ourselves again, dear lady. I am Brent Bairstow, and this is James Dixon. We're originally from Munsten and both ex-military. We've come south from a farm some days' ride to the north-west of Jergen. Nadine's there with her husband and the others."

"What's that? Husband? She's sixty-eight years old, ya daft git. Don't be spreading *cac* on my doorway."

"I'm afraid it's quite true. She's a druid, dear lady. The Earth Mother, as she is called, brought back her youth."

"By the Word! Then what she says in the note is true then? Dammit. What are ye doing standing out there? Get in out of the cold. I've no idea what you can do with them horses, but you can bring them out back out of the wind. I've no stables for them. And I'm no lady. Stop calling me that. You're pissing me off. My name's Ness. Short for Vanessa."

Ness moved into the house and pushed her children out from underfoot.

"That one there's my oldest. Named Joshua Junior after his da. Don't need the junior no more. He went and got himself drowned at sea. Idiot went fishing straight into a storm. Left me these lot. The middle one is Willy. The youngest is Fiona. Watch her, she'll have you doing whatever she wants, if you let her. Don't let them big weepy eyes draw you in. Everything is a drama to her.

"I've nought for supper so I hope you brought your own fare. I've tea left behind by that young man who stole Nadine away from me. Good stuff, though. Clears the aches right outta ya. Come in, come in, yer letting the cold in."

James looked apprehensively at Brent who raised a hand and gently patted the air and whispered. "No worries. Go see to the horses and bring in the packs. I'll rub the horses down later. We'll have to find a stable for hire tomorrow." James nodded and ducked outside.

Brent closed the door and looked around. It was a spacious, single room dwelling with an earth floor. The winds outside whistled in the cracks in the walls. Herbs of all kinds hung from the rafters and support beams. The smell in the house was intoxicating, earthy, and rich. He felt immediately at peace and better understood why Will had expressed a longing to return. In one corner was a thin mattress on a cot and in the opposite corner were three straw mattresses on the floor. Two cats sat on the dining table and flashed their tails back and forth at him. The dog came in close and nosed his groin. Brent pushed him away and then walked over to look out the back window placed over the kitchen sink. Beyond he spotted a swing chair, cliffs, more seagulls, and the sea.

The wind blew outside, and Brent felt it across his skin. *Draughty place and cold unless the fire is kept well stoked*, he thought. He glanced at the small supply of wood by the stove. Ness was standing next to it and rubbing her upper arms. Brent reached into his waist pouch and pulled out a groat.

"Can your eldest be trusted to fetch food at a fair price?" he said holding up the coin.

The woman looked surprised and then pressed her lips together. Her eyes stared at the coin and after a moment she nodded once.

Brent tossed the coin to the lad who snatched it out of the air. "Get some food, Joshua. As much as you can carry. Meat and grains. Sweets for you and the other two. Hurry back."

The boy Joshua looked to his mother and when she smiled a little and nodded, he took off at a run. He flung the door open to find a startled James standing on the other side. The boy looked up at him, murmured something, and then squeezed past and out the door.

"Where's he off to in such a hurry?" asked James closing the door behind him with a foot and dropping the saddlebags and bedrolls he carried.

"Food," replied Brent. "Don't get relaxed yet. We need wood. Check out back."

James nodded, "Horses first." James went back outside.

The woman scowled. "D'ya think to buy our trust, do ye?"

Brent ignored the woman and went over and picked up the saddlebags and bedrolls. He carried them over to where the cot was set out.

"You won't be sleeping wit me!"

Brent picked up the cot and the thin mattress and carried it over to the other mattresses on the floor. "Warmer over here I think. You'll sleep with your children, ma'am. You'll feel safer."

"Safe? You come here and you're already taking over? In my home? Who says ye can stay here? I won't have it!"

Brent went back to the saddlebags and started pulling out supplies and laying them down on the earth floor. A whiny from his horse carried from out back. Brent noticed he could still see his breath in the home.

"Answer me!" declared the woman.

Brent looked over at her. She had her two remaining children behind her and she looked a little scared of him. He stood up with a package wrapped in cloth. He went over to the kitchen table and laid it down. "For you, from Nadine."

Brent went back to unroll the sleeping rolls. He took out his personal items and laid them out with military precision. Whetstone, shaving kit, utensils all in their right spot. He heard a soft cry from behind him and looked over his shoulder to see Ness looking down at the contents of the cloth. Brent knew what it contained. He had watched Nadine wrap it up.

Ness called her two children over and gave them each one of the cookies. Brent stood and his knees cracked. "Dempster, our cook back at the farm, he made them special at Nadine's request." The children squealed with joy and quickly started to eat the rare treat. "The cloth though. That's the real treat."

The woman looked confused for a moment and then reached out to pick up the cloth that wrapped the paper covered cookies. She held it out and gasped. It was a beautiful needlepoint.

"Nadine said it was a fair likeness of your husband. Said you would enjoy it."

The woman drew in a stuttered breath and clutched the cloth to her chest.

Brent waited a moment before speaking. "Nadine told me to tell you that this is still your home. She won't ever ask you to leave here. We are guests, nothing more. Be at peace, ma'am. God be with you."

The woman snapped her head to stare at Brent in shock. "God?"

"Yes, ma'am. I am a man of God."

"And you openly admit that?"

"Yes, ma'am. I'm tired of hiding it. I'm here with a calling from God. The Cathedral calls me even now."

Ness remained silent and stared at Brent. Her eyes searched his face. The wind picked up outside with a low howl and he heard the first chop of wood outside. After a moment, she looked away and placed the needlepoint down on the table and smoothed it out. The fine needlepoint outlined the face of a man with strong features but with a smile to the eyes. *Nadine's a true artist*, thought Brent. He had told Nadine, and she had just patted his arm and smiled.

Ness wiped an eye. "When Joshua—senior that is—when he died that night, I was lost. I chased him as a wee lass. Drove him batty. He was always trying to hide from me but I always found him. As we grew older, we grew to love each other. He was my life. My everything." Tears fell free from her eyes and she wiped them with the heel of her hands. "I hated God for so long. Hated Him with everything I had. I still do. He took my husband... my..." A sob shook her, and she stuffed a hand in her mouth and a cry escaped her.

Brent crossed the room and held her. She froze for a moment and then collapsed into him. She cried for a long time and Brent held her. The front door opened and James stepped in with a load of wood in both arms and froze when he saw them together. Brent rolled his eyes toward the stove and James nodded. He mumbled an "excuse me" as he strode past and laid the wood down. He went back outside for another load.

Ness pulled free and smoothed her dress down. She turned away from Brent to face her children who were standing nearby looking a little anxious. "Away, go get your wee toys out and play. Chores are done for the day. Go."

William and Fiona ran into the corner by their mattresses and opened a small wooden chest. They pulled out some wooden toys and started playing with them. Ness looked back at Brent and then looked away to watch out the window.

"God didn't take your husband from you, ma'am. The sea and weather did. He was a fisherman."

"Call me Ness. Ma'am makes me feel old."

"Alright, Ness then. I'm Brent and my companion is James."

"I know that. You've told me."

"I apologise."

"Don't apologise, makes you look weak," Ness threw her head back and looked up at the ceiling. "I blame God." She lowered her head and blew out an exasperated breath. "I've always wanted to say that out loud. Being a believer is so hard sometimes. I want to scream it out loud."

"Then do. Nothing's stopping you."

"Sure, there is, men and women of faith don't expose themselves. We all know that for truth. Exposing yourself only brings ridicule and pain. When my husband died, I had to sneak into the Cathedral to pray. Not that it did any good. I sat in that place and prayed until my knees bled out on that cursed place. My husband and I, we believed. Like our mums and dads. We were raised in the church. God took him away and left me nothing." She reached out to the needlepoint and touched her husband's image. "It's so hard sometimes. Gah, listen to me rambling like some old woman."

"I hear you, Ness. It was much the same for me. When my father passed my brother, and I each grieved in our own ways. For me, I turned to the church. The Church helped me through it. You shouldn't be ashamed of that. Faith is personal but sometimes you need to reach out to others to reaffirm it. I can help you if you want."

Ness looked up at Brent searching for something. "And who are ye to offer me help with my faith? Eh? Such cheek."

Brent went to answer but then shut his mouth and thought for a moment. "I really don't know. No one, I suppose. But I believe. Maybe I can't help you. God will guide us both."

Ness looked at her children and shook her head. "Unlikely. He's done nothing for me."

Brent smiled. "Nothing? You've a roof over your head for your children. Wood piled by the stove to push the cold out. And food on its way to fill your bellies. I would say he's done plenty for you. He rewards those that fend for themselves, Ness. I believe that truly. Plus, He sent James and I. You have the former General of the Lord Protector's Guard and a former captain of the Army guarding you. You couldn't be safer."

Five

Jergen Cathedral - November 900 A.C.

BRENT AND JAMES stood outside Jergen Cathedral and admired the architecture. The Belkin National Cathedral was hand carved from blocks of pure white limestone; which shone dully despite the grey and overcast morning. The high outer walls rose to pointed arches and flying buttresses. Soaring above the city, massive framed stained-glass windows looked out over a nation that had long abandoned the pursuit of religion. Central to the building was the main tower, inside of which were two sets of bells, silent since the Revolution. Wide marble steps gleamed and rose to the main entrance and the narthex and provided seats for many who stopped to rest.

Jergen Cathedral stood on the top of one of the highest hills in Jergen and towered over the city. Where the two stood they could see far out to sea and a good way inland to the west. Brent wondered if he could see Munsten to the north if he climbed atop one of the four towers at the corners of the building. On the south side of the building they could see the massive attached library.

The last time he had been here Brent had never stopped to admire the artistry of the building. This time James had asked to stop and now he stood with his neck craned back trying to figure out all the intricate carvings in the stonework of the facade. Animals and gargoyles—and who knew what else—

covered every inch of exposed stonework. It was an architectural wonder. James was calling out what he was seeing, and people were giving them a wide berth on the sidewalk and Brent smiled at them as they passed.

"Seen enough?"

"Amazing. Look at that wolf there. It's a wolf, right? Not a dog?"

Brent glanced at where James seemed to be looking and spotted the carving. "Yes, a grey wolf. When we were here before you never thought to admire it, why now?"

"Didn't care then. I do now."

"We should head in."

"What do you expect to happen inside?"

"I'm not certain, to be honest. The worst most likely. The Church is rotten from within. This Sect. Never heard of them and now it seems they are everywhere. What Seth and the demon Erebus said in Jaipers. It haunts me."

"Will said the Sect wiped out the druids. With the Lord Protector and Archbishop's blessing. Killed them all. Hunted them like animals. Tortured them. Wiped out families. Bloodlines, he said. No one knew. All covert. Secret and right under our noses. What could lead men to do something like that? War, I understand. But killing your own people? Women and children? Seth, he was a right crazed fool. Frightening that someone's faith in God could lead to that."

"Which is why I am here, James."

"To kill them? Is that why we are here? Armed and about to enter a building we assume will be hostile?"

"Perhaps. We are military men and manage violence. Prepare for the worst and expect everything to go south as soon as we engage the enemy."

"Your brother introduced those teachings at Tactics."

"He wrote the class."

"He's brilliant. You would have thought it would run in the family, eh?"

"Bugger off."

James rubbed the back of his neck, strained from looking up for so long. He gathered his long cloak around him. Underneath, like Brent, he wore his armour and short sword. The past week at the house had been a boon to Ness and her children. James had chopped the entire woodpile, and they now had more than enough wood stacked for winter. Brent had patched the outer walls and removed most of the draughts. Brent and James had hammered together a wooden floor where the children and Ness slept to get them off the dirt floor. Leaks in the roof had been sealed tight and already the house was warm and comfortable within. The children had rosy cheeks, and laughter—combined with full bellies—filled the house. Ness had stopped complaining as much and was ordering the two of them about like vassals. She handed out chores whenever one occurred to her. It was madness. James was glad to be finally clear and doing something else.

"Rules of engagement?"

Brent looked around to make sure no one was near enough to overhear. "As discussed. They attack, we respond. We will not instigate anything."

"You won't mind spilling blood in your church?"

"No. It's a building, James. Faith is between you and God. A church is a building. Nothing more. The actions of these men must be stopped. Their judgement is coming. It is why we are here. If it comes to blows, so be it."

"Alright. Lead on, my general. I have your back."

They climbed the steps two at a time and Brent moved to the small inset door within the large double doors of the entrance. James turned to watch the street. No one paid them any notice. "Clear," whispered James.

Brent pushed the door open and entered the narthex. James swept in behind him and they moved apart to allow themselves room to draw swords if needed. The sudden quiet from the noise of the street was in complete contrast. The air was much warmer than outside, but their breath still clouded the air. They looked out over the nave and crossing. The cathedral appeared deserted. The raised dais high up on the faraway apse held a large cleared table. High above the apse was a large ornate dome. Light streamed through the stained-glass and gave the entire worship area an ethereal quality.

Brent strode down the centre aisle of the nave and heard James fall in behind him a good fifteen feet away. He scanned the right side of the nave. "Clear to the right."

"Clear to the left," replied James.

Brent stopped at the crossing and heard James stop to keep his distance. He looked left and then right into the transepts off the crossing. There was an opening at the back of the right transept that led to inner offices of the cathedral. They had discussed how to best search the building and agreed to remain together and head downwards. If the Sect was headquartered here, they reasoned they would be located in the basement.

James came closer to Brent with his back to him and looked into the dark transept to the left. "What's in there?"

Brent followed his gaze. "The transept. We're standing on the crossing. The left transept represents Preservation, the right Destruction. The crossing here represents Creation. It is the triad of the faith of the Church of the New Order."

"Three seems common."

"It is. Sometimes it is referred to as mother, father and child. Or past, present and future."

"Did you know the druids call it life, death and rebirth?"

"What? No. Who told you that?"

"Nadine. I was asking about that weird symbol on your amulet. She explained it represented life, death and rebirth. Sounds a lot like your Church. Is that why it's on your amulet?"

Brent said nothing and headed to the opening at the back of the transept and peered around the corner. A large room lay beyond with chairs and tables. Additional worship icons covered the walls. Brent ignored all this and moved to the hallway that led from the room deeper into the building. The hallway had many smaller rooms it fed into. Large openings ornately cut into the Cathedral walls allowed the daylight to brighten the rooms. They stopped at each door and opened them to peer inside. They advanced down the corridor until they found the offices of the Dean.

Brent paused here and looked at the name in gold gilt on the door. He reached up and touched it. He looked back at James who arched an eyebrow back at him. Brent shook his head and opened the door, peered inside, and then closed the door and moved on. James paused by the door and glanced at the name: Dean Andrew Strong.

A large opening provided access to a stairwell leading up and down. The staircase was enormous. Four men could climb the stairs shoulder to shoulder. Brent peered up then down the stairwell.

"No one," he said.

"It's too quiet. How is a building this size this empty?"

"No one goes to church anymore, James."

"Yes, well, someone has to run this place. Clean it and the like."

"True. It is odd."

"Who is Dean Strong?"

"What?"

"Dean Strong, the name on the door back there. Who is he?"

"The Dean, I suspect."

"You know him?"

"No. Never heard of him. Look, I know we said we would head straight down but I am thinking we should check upstairs first. Make sure no one is above us."

"Fair. After you."

Brent moved to the stairs and climbed the stairs two at a time. They wore soft leather shoes and made no noise. They kept their armour covered but one hand remained on their sword hilts.

Over the next hour, they scoured the upper floors. Large rooms filled with ornate furniture spread out from floor to floor. A large balcony overlooked the choir area forward of the apse. All-in-all, the cathedral towered four stories high. Rising above the cathedral, they climbed each corner tower and paused at the top of each to admire the view and to catch their breath. In time, they returned to the stairs leading down to the sub-levels.

"I'm knackered," wheezed James, his breath boiling out thick clouds in the cold air. "Maybe we should have gone straight down. Too tired to fight now."

"Poor baby," panted Brent. He looked about and then glanced down the stairwell. "This is crazy. Where is everyone?"

"I know, right? Can I remind you I said the exact same thing an hour ago?"

"Shut up. Let's catch our breath. Did you bring any water?"

"No."

"Damn."

They stood in silence, each keeping an eye on the corridors. After a time, Brent moved to the stairs and made his way down. James waited until Brent reached the landing below before starting down.

The first sub-level stairwell landing was lit with two torches. The rest of the floor was pitch black. They grabbed extra torches from the supply basket placed beside the wall and lit two and explored the darkened level. The rooms they found proved the floor to be more of a living space. Large rooms with empty beds, offices, and a massive kitchen dominated the floor. The beds had no sheets and the kitchen and pantry were empty. They returned to the stairwell.

"Stranger still," said Brent.

"Torches were lit here though," replied James.

"Yes, someone is here. Empty beds and an empty larder though. If the Sect is here, I would have thought to see signs of occupancy."

"I'm thinking they aren't here in the Cathedral."

"Same," agreed Brent. "Let's keep moving. Someone has to be here."

They carried their torches and moved to the next sub-level. Torches lit only the immediate area. Beyond was more dark corridors. They paused and listened for any sound.

James looked down the stairs. "Nothing here. Skip this floor and keep moving down?"

"Agreed. Torches will light the way I am thinking."

They descended two more levels before the stairwell ended at the start of a massive long corridor. The end of the corridor could not be seen as it disappeared into the darkness. They exchanged torches for newer ones and started down the hallway. The air was now warm and damp and carried a faint scent of mustiness. A faint dripping sound echoed from somewhere up ahead. They walked for about a hundred feet before stopping. Their torches let them see no more than fifty feet or so in front and behind them. The walls were damp and the stonework rough. The dripping sound was louder.

"What do you think?" asked James in a whisper.

"Not sure, we keep going obviously. You notice the floor slants down slightly?"

"Now you mention it, yes. I am pretty sure we are out from under the Cathedral, too."

"Yes, under the Library now I think."

"Hidden passage between them?"

"No, not hidden. Perhaps just a servant corridor or something," mused Brent.

"Perhaps. Never seen anything like this. This place is huge. Bigger than the castle in Munsten."

"No, not bigger. You don't know the castle like I do."

"Right, who am I to question the General of the Lord Protector's Guard? Must be nice to only have to guard one thing."

"Have you always been this much of an ass?"

"Yes."

"'Nuff talk." Brent started down the hallway toward the sound of dripping. After a few feet, their torches lit up a bend in the corridor. They rounded the corner and found the hall ended with a set of narrow stone stairs leading up. Without a word, they climbed the steps and found themselves in a small room with an opening on the far side. A cistern was inset in the right stone wall, water from above it dripped and was producing the sound they heard.

"Shall we?" asked Brent.

"After you."

Brent moved toward the far opening when a grating sound reverberated through the stone. An iron portcullis slammed down in the opening ahead of them at the same time one slammed down behind them sealing them in. James cried out and rushed to the portcullis behind them. He threw his torch to the floor and grabbed the gate with both hands and heaved. It held fast. Brent moved cautiously to the portcullis ahead of them and peered through the bars.

"A light approaches," he said.

James rushed over and put his back to the wall next to the right side of the barred opening. He drew his sword and held it in front of him.

"We appear to be trapped, James."

"Appears so."

In a moment, the light showed that the corridor beyond the opening turned sharply to the right. The light stopped moving just around the bend and a voice called out.

"Hello."

Brent looked at James and raised an eyebrow. James made a wry grin. "Answer him, Brent. They know we're here."

"Um, hello there. Can you let us out, please?"

"Who are you?"

"Worshipers. Enjoying the church."

"Worshipers normally stay up in the nave and don't go wandering down in areas they don't belong," replied the voice. It was a man's voice and confident sounding.

"Can you come out into the light so we can see you?" asked Brent.

"In time, first I need to understand why you are here. What are you looking for?"

Brent looked at James and whispered. "What do I tell him?"

"The truth?"

"So you suggest I say, 'Hi, we killed your leader and now we want to sort you lot out?'"

"Well, not exactly in those words, but sure. Get us out of here, Brent, say whatever you like. Convince them."

"Just so you know," said the voice around the corner. "We can hear everything you say. We've been monitoring you since you came into the Cathedral. I think it's time we had a talk. I need you to take out your swords and your knives and throw them down the corridor toward me. Then I will ask you to lie face down on the floor with your hands behind your head. Only then will the grate open. Several of my men will come in and tie your hands together. You will then be escorted elsewhere, and we will talk. In case you were wondering, I have absolutely no problem just letting the two of you rot in there. Your choices are compliance or a long slow death. You have one minute to decide. This offer will be made only once."

Brent looked long and hard at James. "Sorry, James."

"Nothing to be sorry about." James sheathed his sword and undid the belt.

He pulled out his waist dagger and then passed both through the bars of the portcullis and tossed them down the corridor toward the voice. Brent hesitated a moment and did the same.

"Boot knives too please," said the voice.

James and Brent pulled out their boot knives and added them to the other weapons.

"Anything else?" asked the voice. "If we find other weapons on you, it will not go favourably for you."

James looked at Brent and then pulled another knife from his tunic and added it to the other. He hesitated for a moment and then pulled a wire garrotte from a pocket and threw that down the corridor.

"A garrotte?"

"You never know."

"Hmm. True."

"Shall we?"

"By all means."

Brent and James moved to the centre of the room and lay down on their stomachs and placed their hands behind their heads. The portcullis was slowing cranked up by some mechanism behind the walls. The loud clanking of metal on a gear vibrated through the floor. In time, it stopped and without a sound Brent and James were suddenly looking at black leather boots. Brent tried to raise his head to comment when a hard rap on the back of his head stole his consciousness.

Brent woke to hooded blackness and a pounding headache. He could feel the cloth over his head. He was on a hard chair with his hands tied behind his back and his feet secured to the chair legs. Thankfully, his mouth was free, and he licked his lips to moisten them. "James?"

"He's here. Beside you. Still unconscious, I'm afraid. Softer skull than you. He's fine for now," replied the same voice from the corridor. The voice was just in front of him and close by.

Brent struggled briefly and felt the ropes binding him tighten in response. It felt like they were alive, and fear stabbed through him. He felt the wrongness of the ropes like he might smell smoke from a fire.

"The more you struggle the more they tighten. I've seen men lose their hands and feet. I would relax. Good advice and freely given."

"You ask me to relax when you have us restrained and threaten us."

"Yes, I do, Brent Bairstow. You and James Dixon. Late from Munsten.

Former military men. Sent on a task to fetch a chest of gold in Jaipers."

Brent sat still and said nothing.

"We know all about you, Brent Bairstow. We saw what happened in Jaipers. We were there. We have been following you since you escaped. Trailed you along the river until you stepped ashore. Followed you to that farm and watched you kill our leader, Seth."

Brent remained silent and thought furiously.

"So now we find you here in the Cathedral. What are you looking for here, Brent Bairstow?"

"God."

A laugh came from the voice. "God? What makes you think that God is here, or that He expects you?"

"My faith. God calls me. I have answered. He brought me here."

Brent waited for a reply but there was only silence. Brent strained to hear breathing but heard nothing other than James next to him. He breathed normally. *Asleep, most likely,* thought Brent. *And alive, thank God.*

"What happened at the farm?" asked the voice.

"Were you there?"

"Yes."

"Then you know what happened. Why ask me?"

"What happened in Jaipers?"

"Were you not there, too?"

"I was not present. It was reported to me. Something happened in Jaipers. What was it?"

"Your men were there. They would have told you."

"Enough!" said the voice. Brent could hear the anger in the tone. "Answer!"

"Or what? Will you start to remove my fingers again? Threaten to kill me?"

"No, we will harm your friend instead."

Brent paused. James had discussed this with him at the house. He had told him this could happen and how he wanted him to respond. Brent sighed. "You cannot use my friend against me. I have sworn to him I would not allow his life to come between me and my God. I have sworn to God that I will honour that. Harm him and know my vengeance will be swift. I will strike you all down."

The voice laughed. "And we are to believe that? Are we to leave him alone based on your word alone? Do you take us for fools?"

"Yes. I do. You believed you were following God. You killed and tortured hundreds. Families. Children. You followed a man so corrupt he raised men from the dead to do his bidding. You heard about the creature at the farm. The demon from Hell. Erebus. Why do you not speak of it? You have been led by demons. It is you who are the abomination. You are evil."

Brent waited for an answer. Moments later he heard a door open and then softly close. Whoever they are, they move with no sound. He waited, and an hour passed. He called out, but no one answered. He hung his head and prayed for a time.

A little later he heard James stirring. When his breath quickened, he spoke fast. "Relax, James. Don't struggle. The bonds tighten as if alive. We are tied up and being interrogated."

"Oh, is that all?" slurred James.

"Are you okay? You have been out much longer than I."

"No. They hit me pretty hard. I think I taste blood. I put up a good fight after they clubbed you. Ha-ha. Took one down. He won't walk anytime soon. His nuts are up in his mouth."

Brent smiled. "You are probably concussed. Anything broke?"

"Just my pride."

"They threatened to harm you to get me to talk."

"Did they? See? Told you. Who's the smart one now?"

"You, my friend. I owe you ten groats."

"You better pay up."

"I will."

"Hmm. So, what are they asking you?"

"About what happened in Jaipers and at the farm. They followed us from Jaipers. Seems like we led them straight to the farm."

"Maybe so. They also had the note from Steve. It was only a matter of time. Still, we won there."

"Won? I suppose. Not sure what we won exactly."

"The right to..." James was interrupted by the sound of the door opening.

A chair scrapped on the floor and someone cleared their throat. "Tell me what happened at Jaipers." It was the same voice as before.

"Who are you? Give us your name at least."

"I am Kevin Balfour. I am the new Head of the Sect of the Church of the New Order. I have replaced Seth Farlow, the man you murdered at the farm."

"I have murdered no one in my life. He was evil and attacking innocents. He razed Jaipers and slaughtered my men. I was fulfilling my duty to the Realm. I declare your Sect unlawful and I will arrest you once I get free of this confinement."

"What happened at Jaipers?"

"You know what happened at Jaipers."

"Tell me!"

"Tell you what? That God worked through me? Allowed me and my friends to escape? Why do you need me to tell you what you already know to be the truth? Where is your faith?"

"Do not lecture me on faith. I must hear from your mouth what transpired."

"Why? You know the truth. Why must I voice it?"

"Humour me. I will ask you: please."

"Now you feign politeness? You keep us tied up, hooded, and expect us to cooperate? Now pleasantries?"

"One moment," said Balfour. He heard him rise and then his hood was lifted. Brent blinked at the brightness and watched the man remove the hood from James. He sat back down on the chair and looked back at Brent. He was completely bald, and his head looked polished and gleamed in the lamplight. He wore a simple robe of thick-spun brown wool and wore black boots on his feet. He lacked eyebrows, but bright intelligent blue eyes stared calmly back at Brent. Brent couldn't help but notice that this was a man of exceptional fitness.

Brent glanced at James and saw that dried blood ran from a cut on his forehead down his face. His face was bruised, and numerous cuts were across his chin and cheeks. His left eye was swollen shut. It looked like he had put up a good fight. James caught his eye with his one good one, and they nodded to one another. Brent looked around the room and it was empty except for the three chairs they sat on. The one door out was behind Balfour and was solid with iron supports. A lamp sat on the floor beside Balfour and gave the only light.

"Our ways are set," said Balfour. "We have been this way since we were first created by the Archbishop, God rest his soul. Our way has always been one of violence. It has survived the years and proven highly successful in the task that God himself gave us."

"Violence should be used as a last resort. It is a means to an end and seldom a good one. Men of true strength find other ways."

"We were faced by demons. We were directed by God to wipe the earth of their presence."

"It was not God who led you. It was a demon."

"This cannot be true."

"You were at the farm?"

"Yes."

"You saw the creature that appeared. The creature that spoke to your leader?"

Balfour clenched his jaw and nodded once.

"Then you know the truth. You have been doing the work of Hell. Spreading fear and death in God's name. Torturing and killing innocent women and children."

"You have seen the power they wield. It is unholy. God cannot abide such evil."

"That is not so. I have lived with these people. Call them for what they truly are: druids. They work the earth, nurture it, and heal people. They cannot use their powers to harm others."

"Many of my brethren have been slain by these demons."

"Not demons: druids. They defended themselves. Never did they strike out at you first, correct?"

Balfour hesitated and then nodded.

"I am bound here with ropes that writhe and squirm with an unholy life to them. You use such tools? Surely you can sense the evil that they are?"

Balfour blinked and looked quickly at the ropes binding Brent's feet to the chair. "These tools were provided by Seth. Created by God."

"Wrong. They were created by Seth using blood magic. Will Arbor explained it to me. He studied what your people left behind at the farm. The red rubies, the ropes and the boots. All infused with Seth's blood magic."

Balfour rose suddenly and left the room.

James looked surprised and stared at Brent. "What the... ?"

"No idea. Crazy people. How can they not see the horrible things they have done for what they are?"

James shook his head in response and winced in pain.

"How's the head? Your face is covered in blood, bruises and what not. You look worse than normal."

"Pounding headache. Pretty bad actually. Hard to focus. Harder with one eye swollen shut. I'll survive though."

"Wonderful."

James forced a smile. "So what's the plan?"

Brent pondered the question for a moment. He had no plan. "I have no idea. I only know I have to be here."

"That's comforting. Thanks. I appreciate it. This God of yours sounds wonderful. Why not just appear and say 'Here's what you need to do'. Why all this whatever this is? Gaea has it right. Show up. Say something. Disappear. Nice and clean that is. I like it."

"It doesn't work that way."

"Why not? Who says it has to be the way you think it is?"

"Faith is rewarded. Without Faith, there is no path to God."

"And if you fail to have Faith?"

"Then you are not rewarded."

"Rewarded with what?"

"Eternal life in the afterlife. Heaven. Or if you lead an evil life, Hell. Eternal damnation."

"Seems harsh. Kind of a 'believe or else' kind of scenario."

Brent grew quiet. He had wrestled with his demons long ago and was confident in his faith. He heard from James all those same doubts he once had. It was always trying when he heard them again. He calmed himself and focused. He had faith. He had enough for a lifetime.

He looked up when the door opened, and Balfour strode in. He was not alone this time. Another man followed him in and looked like he would rather be elsewhere. The man had black hair and a broad white moustache. Balfour looked from James to Brent and then seated himself. The other man stood behind him.

"This man is Martin Jordan. He is a vicar and the senior clergy in Jergen. The Lord Protector pulled back everyone above vicar to the capital. Please. Explain to us what occurred at Jaipers. In your own words."

Brent looked to James, and he shrugged. "You fellows had wiped out my men. Ambushed and slaughtered us in the streets. Set fire to the barracks. I've no idea how many you murdered. Civilians were killed. It was madness. I was struck down and woke in the common room tied to James and the Reeve of the town, Steve Comlin.

"Seth came in and started to torture me. He cut off my pinkie. Repeatedly. Taking great pleasure in it, I might add. Then a light came out of my forehead. Our bonds fell to the ground. We rose. They ran. And we left."

The vicar spoke for the first time. "What do you mean by 'repeatedly'?" His voice had a rough quality to it. His accent placed him from Munsten.

"It was cut off. Seth took pride in measuring the distance it flew. Then a new one would grow back."

"You have a pinkie on both hands."

"Yes. They grew back. Vicar, why do you associate with the Sect?"

The vicar looked startled. Balfour shifted in his seat and glanced quickly at the vicar to silence him. "And the light that came from your forehead. Describe that."

"It was bright. Wouldn't you say, James?"

"Yes. Very bright," James nodded his head. "And it was the symbol of your church. Shouldn't forget that."

"You blaspheme," stated Balfour, the words flat.

"If you say so," replied Brent.

"The farm. What happened?"

"I arrived with James, Steve and Dempster just in time to find Seth on a horse that should have been dead. Surrounded by men who also should have been dead. Seth was in the process of attacking a young man, William Arbor. I came to his aide. Then a demon called Erebus appeared. Remember him? All black? Evil? My forehead lit up again and struck the demon and it was destroyed. Along with Seth, too. Such a shame."

"I see," said Balfour.

"Don't forget the amulet," added James. "It lit up too."

"Amulet?"

"Ah, yes," said Brent. "My amulet. It bears the symbol of the Church of the New Order. If you haven't removed it already, it is around my neck."

The vicar came forward and pulled the amulet out from Brent's tunic. He gazed at it and then turned it over to see the symbol of the Tree on the reverse. "This is the symbol of our church, but on the back is the symbol for the heathens."

"Turns out the druids worked closely with the church. A long time ago that is."

"This cannot be. This is not what we were told," sputtered the vicar.

Brent felt sorrow for the man. The man and most likely the entire Sect had been misled by the Archbishop and Seth. He was certain that these were not men of evil. Just misguided. He wondered if that was why he was here. To correct them. Set them back on the correct path.

"Your Archbishop has much to answer for."

Balfour stirred. "Our Archbishop is dead. He was struck down by the Lord Protector's men."

The vicar let the amulet fall free and moved to stand beside Balfour.

"What? When was this?" asked Brent.

"Some time ago. The Archbishop had become addicted to a drug. A drug that has made its way into the Church members and runs rampant. The Archbishop reportedly attacked the Lord Protector. Naked and in the church. The drug is insidious. A lot of the senior clergy are now addicts."

"But not the Sect."

"No. We use something else, life salt. It focuses us and is not addictive. It is enough."

"I'm sorry for your loss. I knew the Archbishop in the castle. A strange man, but decent enough."

Balfour bowed his head. "You are kind to say so."

"Who runs the Church now?"

"The Lord Protector," answered Martin.

Brent blinked. *Plots within plots. That man has no end to his greed for power,* he thought. *The church cannot be run by the likes of Healey. That is unacceptable.* Options opened up before him. His experiences in recent months laid out before him like a map. He lowered his head and gave thanks before looking up at Balfour and Martin. "Untie me. I must return to Munsten and put the church in order."

Balfour looked surprised and laughed. "I do not think that will be possible. We have only begun to question you. There is much we need to understand."

Brent felt his bonds fall free, and he stood. "I don't think so. I'm here to guide the Church back on the path. To return you from evil. There is much to do." Balfour stared in shock at Brent and looked to the floor by the chair where the ropes lay smoking. He struggled to his feet and his chair fell over backwards. Martin made a high cry and backed away. James stood when he realised his bonds were also gone.

Balfour moved to back away, but Brent reached out and clasped him on the shoulder, halting him. "Come. Introduce me to your brothers and sisters."

Six

Munsten Castle - May 901 A.C.

LORD PROTECTOR JOHN Healy sat in front of the Chamber of Representatives with his arms folded in his lap. The full Chamber was composed of representatives from each county and city in Belkin. It had been expanded to include towns with a large population in recent years and the ranks had swelled. Sitting with the Chamber were the members of the Privy Council, the Military Council and the Judicial Council. A gathering of all the representatives was uncommon. A gathering that included the three councils was unheard of. The time was late in the evening and the chamber had been in closed session for most of the day. Reports of unrest were flooding in from all over the Realm and the representatives and council members wanted answers.

Healy had been moving the conversation to the climax of his finest hour. The chamber was tired, and many looked toward the chamber doors and Healy could see they were exhausted. Healy felt energised and stared out at all the people in front of him. Healy had dirt on all of them and had them all in the palms of his hands. These meetings and decisions were all for show. As the Lord Protector, he had an unwavering control and authority over all the decisions in Belkin. He gave them the illusion of power and let them think they still had a choice in the matters of the policy and it let them go home and sleep with a clearer conscience.

Lanterns and candles lit the room now that night had fallen. Torches were lit around the outer perimeter. Flickering shadows bathed the room from all the carvings in the stonework. It gave the room an eerie feel. A few members were asleep in the back row. Healy had watched their heads bounce up and down in an effort to stave off sleep but they each succumbed to the fatigue.

Healy could see many heads turning toward the exit. The head of the Judicial Council Robert Ghent was still speaking, but no one was listening. He was describing the increase in crime in the realm. His magistrates were reporting a rise in religiously motivated vandalism. Common houses that were used as gatherings for the Word were being torched. The realm was in turmoil and the sharp rise in religious fanatics was causing the land to divide. The Chancery was hard pressed to issue legal orders and was gaining little support from the Church of the New Order.

The demise of the Archbishop and Healy then taking over the Church of the New Order was not being well received by the people. People were demanding a new Archbishop be named. In response, Healy had pulled all the bishops back to Munsten and had them sequestered. *They believe they are determining who will be the next Archbishop. I will never give up the Church now that I have it,* smiled Healy. *I am the King in all but name.*

Healy looked down to his head of the Privy Council, Advisor Robert Hargrave, who sat near him on his right and recorded all the conversations. He had three scribes behind him and later they would compare notes for the official record. It would only be official after Healy edited the words. Hargrave and his scribes were the only ones listening to what was being said this day. Sensing eyes on him, Hargrave looked up to Healy and smiled briefly before returning to his scribbling. Healy looked out over the chamber and put on his most charming smile and tried not to frown when several of the council members looked frightened at seeing it.

"Enough, Chancellor Ghent. I fear you have lost your audience. The Judicial Council has the power over the Chancery to administer necessary new laws to better support our magistrates and reeves. As the interim head of the Church, I have ordered the deans and vicars to police their followers and urge calm and stop the violence. I have asked the Military Council to increase the garrisons and I ask that the Judicial Council consider allowing the reeves to bring in more deputies and arm them accordingly." The floor buzzed with conversation at the words. The ones asleep in the back snorted awake and looked blearily around. Chancellor Ghent gave a weak smile and sat back down in his seat. He leaned in toward his second and they discussed something in private. Healy ignored them.

"I think we can all agree Belkin is in a state of turmoil. The Military Council has reported unrest in all the villages and towns. The Church has stepped in to assist as you well know. Wordsmiths are gathering the people in the common halls and asking for calm. People are listening, but they are still afraid. Echoes of the Revolution haunt their imaginings and drives their fears. We need greater security in the Realm but already our Army is spread so thin they manage little."

The representative from Turgany, frowned, and raised a hand. Healy ignored him.

"Your votes throughout the day have already been tallied and no longer up for debate. Previous matters are closed. Turgany, lower your hand, enough. We have discussed internal security measures far too long already. I need your attention on a more important matter. Attention, everyone." Healy rose from his seat and waited for murmurs to subside.

"Martial law was imposed on the land by this chamber as a result of continued unrest after the Revolution. Belkin is a country which has faced the realities of post-Revolution reconstruction. We possess a government under martial law which does not shrink from the consequences of facts and has maintained the courage to impose remedies required to secure and to stabilise our national recovery.

"I remind you we cannot forget the significant threat from the land of Cian-Oirthear to the east. Years ago, our spies reported a surge of activity to the east that was rapidly pushing west to the Belkin Sea. We had reports they looked with longing to our land and craved our riches. We heard the forces of Cian-Oirthear were led by a man named Mushir Adham with a military skill and tactics unparalleled in Belkin. Today I report I have been in contact with Cian-Oirthear and this Mushir. I am pleased to announce that the overseas threat is no longer. I wish to table a motion to remove the edicts of martial law."

The chamber exploded with shouts. Council members and representatives looked at one another in shock at the words and looked to Hargrave for confirmation. All tried to talk at once and many called out to Healy for an explanation. The man from Turgany being the loudest.

"Silence!" shouted Healy. When no one paid him any heed he picked up his gavel and slammed it repeatedly on the table in front of him. "Silence!" After a moment, the chatter concluded until all eyes were once again upon him.

"I assure you there is no threat of war from overseas. The threat is from within our Realm. Years ago, I spoke of it. I had thought the Archbishop, and the Church, had it all in hand and indeed they did for these many years. With his death, I have taken over the Church and I now have intelligence that tells me that the evil that lay just beneath the surface of our civilisation has not been wiped clean. It has grown in power and threatens us all. But I will get to that in a moment."

The council member from Turgany spoke up. "How is the threat from overseas no longer a threat? What proof do you have?"

Healy suppressed a desire to laugh, Turgany was playing right into his hands. *I had never offered proof all those years ago of an overseas threat and the chamber accepted my words without hesitation and now they want proof it was gone?* "I'll do better than proof." Healy turned to the exit and nodded to the guard positioned there. The man turned and opened the door and called out.

The chamber looked questioningly at one another and at Healy. Conversations rose. They looked toward the doors and many leaned forward to get a better look. Footsteps could be heard and then a man emerged into the torchlight. The man strode with confidence into the hall looking straight ahead. He wore a strange garb: loose black cloth wrapped around his form and was held in place with brown leather straps. He was adorned with heavy gold jewellery encrusted with precious stones and gems. A naked and glimmering great curved sword hung from his belt. He sported a pointed black beard and his head was covered with a cloth ring hat from which scarves hung and wrapped around his head to disappear behind him.

Healy beamed at the chamber. "I have the honour to present the emissary from Cian-Oirthear. Sirs, I present the honourable Kamal Sherwami, advisor to Mushir Adham."

The man bowed deep at the waist to the gasps from the chamber and righted himself. He bowed his head to Healy. "My thanks, Lord Protector, you humble and honour me." He turned to the chamber. "Sirs, I am here as an emissary from the great Mushir Adham himself, leader of our great and vast realm of Cian-Oirthear—a land of rolling sand, sweet figs, beautiful women, and riches beyond imagining. He bade me present myself to you and tell you that we are allies and friends. We do not look upon your land with hunger and greed. I am here to tell you that an agreement of friendship and mutual support is to be signed by my hand at his behest.

"Mushir Adham is an honourable man. Yet he knows men of power must protect their land and have sworn oaths to defend that land and cannot trust words alone. For this reason, we bring a great gift."

Kamal turned to the exit and beckoned. The chamber watched as two guards struggled to carry in a large wooden chest. They carried it across the hall, sweat pouring down their faces from the strain. After a time, they halted near the Lord Protector and lowered the chest to the stone floor with a thud that could be felt throughout the chamber. The guards stood and looked to Healy. Healy nodded, and the men removed the large clasp and lifted the hinged lid. Gasps from the chamber filled the hall, and many rose from their seats to look closer. The chest was filled with gold bars, stacked within and gleaming in the flickering light. It was a fortune in gold, enough to fund the country for decades.

Kamal waved a hand over the chest. "This gift from Mushir Adham is proof that any threat from our land is no longer. We present the gift of peace."

Healy stepped forward and stood beside Kamal and placed his arm around his shoulders. "There is more. Kamal has a tale from his land that will strike fear into your hearts. I tell you that on hearing this tale you will understand the need for this alliance. Kamal, if you please."

Kamal looked out at the council members. "My friends, my tale is a horror and I ask your forgiveness for raising such stories of evil in this respected house of your government. Many decades ago, my land faced a threat unlike any we had ever faced. From within, demons rose throughout our land to strike at us. They tore into the very heart of our people. Fear ruled our land. We were vanquished at every turn. Nothing we could do could stop their insipid advances. Our armies were powerless against them. They used the powers of magic to take us down and render us defenceless. Friends turned into enemies. Wives and children rose with evil in their hearts and eyes.

"Over many years we fought. We looked once to cross to your lands to escape the threat but then Mushir Adham found the way forward. A way to thwart the evil they represented. I am here to tell you that thanks to Mushir Adham my land has eradicated this threat from within. My people are trained in recognising and defeating this magic and wiping the evil from the land."

Healy stepped forward and swept his arms out to his sides. "The Revolution revealed this threat to Belkin many years ago. I advised this very chamber of that threat. It revealed itself attempting to take my life and seize control of our government. Thankfully, the Archbishop thwarted it and revealed the demons that lived amongst us. We fought long and hard that night eradicating the threat. Munsten burned for a week. Do you remember?"

Many of the council nodded their heads in unison. They sat forward in their seats, eyes glancing to the chest of gold. Healy shook his head in sadness.

"Men, women, and children you knew as friends and family were users of this magic. They could enter your minds and steal your ability to defend yourself. The very same demons that Cian-Oirthear fought for decades are here present in Belkin. I myself witnessed this great horror. I still wake from nightmares. But I tell you, from the ashes grew a great strength. From within the Church a group was established with the skills to defeat this enemy. They have defended this realm for years in humble obedience to the Church. Until today we had thought they had won." Healy looked around the chamber and saw he had the complete attention of everyone. Many sat on the edge of their seats, horror and fear on many of the faces.

"But there is more," Healy paused and the two guards moved suddenly toward the council member from Turgany. They seized him and carried him forward despite his cries and struggles. The nearby council members moved to distance themselves. "Silence, Turgany!" One of the guards wrapped the crook of his arm over the mouth of the council member. His eyes were wide and afraid, and he cried out muffled against the arm. In a moment, he seized his struggles when it became clear he could not escape. His eyes darted fearfully to the other council members pleading for help.

Many in the chamber looked uncomfortable and Healy noted them all before continuing. "Turgany has raised an army that seeks to strike at the heart of our government. They are assisted by the very threat the Church hoped to eradicate. The Church has failed, and the number and strength of these demons are greater now than ever."

Many in the chamber cried out in alarm at these words. Healy waited for calm to return.

"Sadly, I must also report that the threat has infected our Army and Guard. Many within, despite their oaths, now side with the evil and threaten to conduct such treason it almost takes my heart away. For this reason, I must sentence those treasonous members of the Army and Guard to the dungeons to await trial. As we speak, loyal members of the military are moving against them. Arrests are occurring across our great land. This will leave us in a much weaker state against the threat, I'm afraid, but it cannot be helped. We find ourselves far too weak. Coupled with the insurgency across the realm, I fear for our future.

"I have; therefore, asked Cian-Oirthear for assistance. My request was answered immediately. The emissary, Kamal, has not only brought us gold to fund this war but sends us troops trained in striking down this evil and its magic. They arrive within weeks here in Munsten and Jergen. With our loyal remaining Army, we will strike down this uprising and secure the port of Jergen from Turgany's treason and secure our capital from this great threat."

The hall erupted in shouts from the council. Guards poured in from the wings and positioned themselves around the hall. Healy stood in silence and waited in patience. In time, the cries calmed, and the council looked worryingly at the guards. The representative from Turgany was trying to be heard through the arm that covered his mouth. Healy looked at him and shook his head.

"This is a time of strife and turmoil. We must stand united at this terrible period of our history. We can no longer tolerate weakness or petty politics. You are the sworn representatives from the counties and people of Belkin. This is a land under a terror threat from within. We can no longer abide those intolerant to change. We are a house divided and I can no longer tolerate it. I am going to call out names of members of the council. When your name is called, you will stand and quietly leave this great hall, never to return."

The chamber looked from one to another. Fear filled the faces of many. When the first name was called, the man leapt to his feet and pleaded for mercy. Healy ignored him and when he wouldn't move to the exit, he nodded to a guard who stood along the wall. He moved up and led the man, still protesting his innocence, out of the hall at sword point.

Over the next several minutes sixteen council members were removed. Some fought and were struck down and dragged unconscious out of the room. Most accepted their fate and chose to leave the hall with dignity. Some chose that moment to start laying down lies of collusion. They shouted and screamed to be heard until they were dragged out of the hall. In time, the hall grew quiet. Those that remained looked relieved and looked to Healy with hope. He stood calmly and then he gestured to the council member from Turgany still held by the guards.

"This man from Turgany is the worst of them all. He knowingly came to these hallowed chambers while the Baron of Turgany, his liege, formed an illegal army and marched against the Realm. I sentence him to death for high treason. Kamal, you may have the honours."

The guards holding the council member released the man's head and pushed him over a desk until his neck and head were exposed. They held him still despite his aggressive struggles to escape.

"Healy! You won't get away with this! It's you who is treasonous! There is no internal threat, just..."

Kamal moved like the wind. He whirled and drew his sword and in one smooth motion, he cleanly separated the council member's head from his shoulders. The head landed with a heavy thud and a great arc of blood fountained from the neck, once, twice, and then three times. Each time reaching less and less far until it abruptly stopped. Those seated in the front row of the chamber looked down in horror at the blood covering their clothes. A few council members were violently ill and threw up the contents of their stomachs.

Healy looked out to the council members and the Chamber of Representatives. "In these times of great strife, we can no longer hold on to the ways of old. Decisive decisions will need to be made. For these reasons, I declare Belkin the New Republic of Belkin and me, its President. I will bring order to the realm. I have spoken."

A spattering of applause started within the chamber and in moments it rose to a thundering noise. The name Healy chanted over and over.

Much later that evening, President Healy sat at his table in his private chambers and beckoned to the chair opposite him. Kamal Sherwami bowed his head and sat. On the table was a modest spread of wines and fine cheeses. Healy took a small knife and cut off small pieces and laid them on his side plate. He handed the knife to Kamal, and he took his time to select his own choices. Once the wine was poured Healy sat back and smiled.

"A good beginning, wouldn't you say?"

"Yes, most promising. The land is prepared for the arrival of Mushir Adham and his army. Glory be to his name."

"The gold was a nice touch," Smiling Healy turned and indicated the chest of gold his men had left with him to enjoy before it was deposited in the vault.

Kamal coughed into his hand. "It is but a ruse, surely you know this?"

Healy jerked his head to stare at Kamal. "What do you mean a ruse? You promised me gold!"

"And it is coming, my friend, it comes with Mushir. It rides safe with his army. Fear not!"

Healy rose and strode over to the chest and yanked the lid open. He reached in and pulled out one of the gleaming bars and straining carried it over to the table. He dropped it next to his plate of cheese and grabbed the knife. With the knife clutched tight in his hand he scored the top of the gold. He stood panting and then collapsed into his seat and draped his arms over the armrests of the chair. He stared morosely at the bar before him. Beneath the deep scratch on the surface the dull shine of lead was revealed.

"Lead," he said with little strength. "You give me lead painted with gold."

"Of course, John. What did you expect? You failed to deliver your own gold and so we prepared this for you instead."

Healy sat staring at the gold for a time before reaching out and grabbing his wine glass. He downed his wine in shuddering gulps and then filled it again. He stared at the full glass and then with a cry threw it across the room. It shattered against the far wall and a bright wet stain of red wine covered the wall, floor and drapes.

"No, no, no! I will not have it! We had an agreement you and I! A deal! I have risked everything for this venture. You promised me gold, power, men at my disposal and access to the eastern trade routes. Already the deception your country is known to be so capable of rears its ugly head. What do you offer me but lies and treachery?"

Healy strode over and stood before his fireplace and stared at the burning coals. His left hand rested on the mantle near where his sword hung mounted on the wall. He heard Kamal rise behind him, heard the scrape of the lead bar from the table, and he turned to watch Kamal place the bar back in the chest. Kamal kept his back to Healy.

"Mushir Adham is a tolerant man, John Healy. He has waited patiently for you to prepare this land for his presence. You would best remember the aid our land has provided you in the past."

"Aid? You have offered little in the way of support. We had agreements between your country and mine."

"And that has not changed. We left you alone for all those years. Now you must be patient. The troop ships arrive here in Munsten and in Jergen in one of your fortnights. I trust their landings will be welcomed?"

Healy glanced at the sword on the wall and then returned to the table. He selected a piece of blue marbled cheese and popped it into his mouth. He grabbed the decanter of wine and poured another glass. "Yes, of course. All will be prepared."

"And Bairstow? What of him? I have heard he escaped your net."

"It's true. The former Knight General of my Army, Frederick Bairstow, caught wind of the seizures and fled into hiding within the city with some of his men. The men loyal to me are searching house-to-house for him now. He can't have gotten far. His remaining men loyal to him have been rounded up and culled. He is alone out there and an old man. Fear not. He offers little in the way of threat. I know him. I understand what makes that man tick. His honour will be his undoing. I have someone he wants."

"So you say, but I have seen men like him achieve great things with less."

"Such as?" Healy turned to stare at Kamal and found him looking lost in thought. For a moment Healy was sure the image of Kamal had blurred. Healy rubbed his tired eyes. Kamal felt the eyes on him and smiled back.

"No matter. History has a way of repeating itself, no? We should be celebrating you and I! You are the self-appointed President of the New Republic of Belkin! Never has one man achieved such power in this realm. You are a force to be reckoned with, my friend!"

Healy smiled and took a large sip of wine. "True. This will be a night of much celebration. This republic nonsense seems ideal. Tell me, where did..."

A knock sounded at his outer chamber door.

Healy called out to the other room. "Enter!"

The outer door opened, and female voices could be heard murmuring. In a moment, four women entered the private room dressed in little than silks. They were frightened and looked about the room and stared at the shattered wine glass and spilt wine. They refused to make eye contact.

"Come in, come in! Nothing to fear!" intoned Healy with a smile spread across his face. "You're with the President. All is well."

The man known as Kamal Sherwami rose from the bed in his chamber. He glanced for a moment at the still figures of the two women who lay huddled under the covers of his bed. Kamal gave them no thought and rose to head over to the chamber next to his. He peered inside and saw Healy passed out with the other two women lying unconscious across the bed.

Whether they were beaten or worse, Kamal could not tell and didn't care.

Healy is becoming too unpredictable. Too fast to anger. Unstable. But for now still valuable.

Kamal shimmered in the room and for a moment a figure made of solid black stood in his place. His body absorbed all light so much that no visible features could be discerned. One of the women on the bed looked up for a moment and her gaze swept past him without focus.

The creature known as Erebus smiled and shimmered back into the figure of Kamal. Soon Healy would no longer matter. Belkin was the last significant land that continued to resist him. Once it was his he would own this world at long last. The millenniums of fighting were almost over.

Seven

Jergen - Cathedral - February 901 A.C.

BRENT BAIRSTOW CLASPED the extended hand of James Dixon and pulled the man up to his feet. They stood in the back courtyard of the Cathedral. Brent had the tables and chairs removed and converted the area into a small sparring pit. Winter was upon them, but only a light dusting of snow covered the ground. The weather so close to the sea was often mild of temperature but could often become fierce with gales and sleet. So far, the winter had been mild.

Brent had insisted the members of the Sect learn new skills other than those of thieves—as he had called them. They had formed an uneasy truce here in Jergen. Over the past few months, Brent had met with all the remaining Sect members in the region and with the vicar in Jergen. Brent knew they were all men and women of faith, but they were stubborn. Years of isolation from the tenets of the Church had changed them. They chose violence as the first course of action and were far removed from teachings of the Church as they could be. Brent pitied them. Especially the vicar Martin Jordan. He was a good man who had suffered with the burden of knowledge of what the Sect had done in God's name. He had believed the druids to be evil with all his heart and was having a hard time believing Brent and James when they related the tales of healing from the druids. Brent met with them frequently and had become a leader of sorts.

The events in Jaipers and at the farm had given them enough doubt to accept him. Martin had confided he had a good feeling about him at least.

Kevin Balfour had insisted that Brent leave for Munsten and take key Sect members and those of the clergy with him. Brent was happy the Sect leader was coming around to understanding the need to mend the Church. Theirs would be a mission of peace. They would plead with the bishops and take back the Church for the people. The Lord Protector as the head of the Church could not remain. Brent meant to take it from him. James thought him crazy and urged him to stay in Jergen.

He had sent word to his brother where he was and that he was well, and they now exchanged letters weekly. Fast courier boats ran the coast routinely. After word from his brother that the evidence on Healy was now overwhelming Brent felt more at peace than he had in years. He would ride to Munsten and take back the capital. Frederick would rule until elections could be held.

It was all so thin, but Frederick felt he had enough men loyal to him to secure the castle and take Healy under arrest. Brent's arrival would cause enough confusion to make the coup that much swifter. For now, until they left next week, they would train and prepare for the sail up the coast. One of the many benefits of the Sect was that they had resources few people could imagine. Having their own fast boats was one of them.

James slapped Brent on the shoulder. "Not bad. I let you best me that time. To boost your confidence."

"You did, did you? How come you're doing that every time? My confidence is boosted about as high as it can go."

"Perhaps. Perhaps." James turned at the sound of someone clearing their throat nearby. He spotted Kevin Balfour standing a respectful distance away. "I see your new shadow is ready for more talking. I'm out. Speak later at the house?"

Brent nodded and watched James leave. He beckoned for Balfour to join him. "Do you wish to spar?"

"No, I'm here for other reasons. Vicar Jordan waits for us in his rectory. Do you wish to join us?"

"Surely. No time like the present."

They walked in silence to the rectory. The small building lay behind the Cathedral but faced the Belkin Sea. It was a modest building and Vicar Martin rarely left it. He was a troubled man coming to grips with doubts about his faith and what he knew to be true. Brent entered and spotted the vicar sitting at his usual spot at the kitchen table. Fresh water, cheese and bread had been laid out for all to share.

Brent sat and poured water for Balfour and himself. "What do we discuss today, my new friends?"

Martin tore a heel from one loaf and placed it in front of him. "I've more news from the towns and villages. The church continues to report to the Cathedral in hopes we can do something. They know the bishops are sequestered in Munsten, but they have no communication to the outside world. It all falls on me now, I'm afraid to say. I am reading more and more disturbing reports from much of the Realm. Mostly in the northern cities of Munsten, Salt Lake City, Curachan, and Cala. Men from the Army of the Realm are deploying into the towns and villages. They are stirring up the residents and causing dissent. They overrule the magistrates and reeves and are getting the more devout and fanatic to speak out more against the Wordsmiths. It is the same everywhere. The realm is unbalanced. I do not understand the goal. Or why. But it is happening with malicious intent.

"Elsewhere, the Sect members have read the notice we put out about the demons. Sorry, the druids. They do not accept your tale. They dismiss it as fantasy. They answer only to the Archbishop and with the Lord Protector assuming the role they listen to no one. You must realise it is hard to dismiss decades of knowledge overnight. We have discussed this. You know it to be true."

"Yes, yes. The problem is not the towns and villages. It is the evil bastard in Munsten. I told you what he did. How he corrupted the government. Replaced the council with his own men. And within the Army and Guard. He has a spider web of corruption spread out across the land. We need to strike at the spider: Healy himself. Only then can we begin to heal the land and the Church."

Martin looked at Kevin before responding. "The Church cannot take a position of opposing the lawful head of government. That is not our role in this land, Brent. We must remain impartial."

"Yes. I understand your position. I merely need you to get me to Munsten and be present to witness."

"Witness what?"

"I'm not sure. I only know God wants me there and I need you there. Isn't that enough?"

"It would be easier if you gave us more. And these druids? What have they said?"

Brent growled. "They have said no. Their Freamhaigh says their calling is larger than the Realm. We are on our own, I'm afraid."

"These dem... sorry druids. I am not convinced they can be trusted. I know you vouch for them, but what have they ever done for the Realm?"

Brent swallowed a bite of cheese. "They would say they have done everything. All from hiding and fear of persecution. They claim to have protected the land itself from the ravages of man. That their purpose is to protect the earth itself. Will would claim no allegiance to anyone save his own purpose. I admit I admire that in him. He is a pretty remarkable young man. Reminds me of myself when I was his age." Brent grinned a broad smile at Martin.

Martin chuffed. "It does not sound like they can be trusted. They are only out for themselves! That is not God's way!"

Brent lost his smile. "Will would say the same thing about the Church, I suspect. You did murder his mother."

Kevin had the good sense to look away for a moment. "We did as God bid us do. While I do not doubt that evil had corrupted Seth, I have faith that we followed God's path. The Lord Protector seems to be doing his best to force a country to open rebellion."

Brent raised an eyebrow. "I've told you he has been stealing from the Realm for decades. He fabricated lies and murdered families to keep it hidden. He is the evil in the land. The worst we can do is to do nothing."

Kevin looked down at the table. "Stories have many sides. He faced the evil of the demons. He likely did what he thought he needed to do."

Martin saw a flush spread across Brent's cheeks and interrupted before the two started yelling at each other again. "Gentlemen now is not the time to bring up this old argument. Brent was the General of the Lord Protector's Guard and was privy to many things we simply cannot dispute. There is much to atone for in our history. The Church, the Sect, the government. All have had a hand in making the world what it is today. But that is not what I wish to speak about today."

Brent leaned back and nodded to Martin. Kevin scowled, but sat back and listened.

"I understand that God drives you to Munsten. You believe in your heart that this is your purpose and that you must confront Healy. But, my son, even if you did all these things, surely you understand that the Church comes from the King. It is only through the King that an Archbishop can be named. To see a King on the throne, you would need to find the next in line. Place him on the throne and then see the Church led once again by a true believer."

"I understand all that, Martin. I won't dispute it. God led me here and now leads me to Munsten. How this is supposed to happen I have no idea. I put my trust in God."

Martin looked grim. "Even men of the cloth have plans, my son. God gave us eyes to see. Not to blindly run off hoping He will save the day. We have free will. Choice. God will help but He cannot take direct action."

Brent smiled. "I once thought that. I know differently now. I leave in a week by the fastest boat. The winter storms will have passed, and we will make record time. Have faith, my friends. God watches over us."

James patted Brent's back as he heaved one more time. He had long since stopped throwing anything up but the urge to vomit still kept returning. He kept trying to get him to eat the dry crackers the sailors urged him to eat, but he refused. The very thought of food, he said, made him want to vomit more.

They had left Jergen only two days ago on the *Azure Tip*. Brent had been sick since the moment they stepped on board. With two weeks of sailing ahead of them, James worried for his friend. James argued that chronic seasickness was serious, and they should land and seek another path to Munsten.

"You can't keep this up, Brent. You've no strength left." The bow of the ship plunged deep into the bottom of a swell and then lifted shuddering. A light spray misted across the upper decks. The ship was a two-masted royal schooner and beautiful in design. She was used for running precious cargo and mail items—previously for the King. The ship had started her career fishing but once her speeds were known she became a royal courier ship and was now known as the fastest ship on the coast. She had won many the race in her day and remained undefeated for seventeen years. The captain bragged of her whenever he had the chance.

Brent retched in reply.

"Captain Walters said to eat the ginger root. Says it helps. Will you not try it?"

Brent shook his head.

"You're a big baby you know that? Ness was right. She said sailing to Munsten was a daft thing to do. Well, here we are. Miles offshore. Wind pushing us like a banshee across the moors. And you spending the entire time tied to the railing up here in front. Or bow, or whatever this is. Bloody glad I joined the Army and not the Navy. Daft gits."

Brent raised his head. "The Admiral always..." He swallowed feverishly for a moment to keep down his puke. "Always said there was no life like it. Thinkin' he was right."

"Aye, no life like it all right." James watched two sailors fly up the main mast like gymnasts. "It's insane leaving the safe hard ground for this. You've no control out here. It's all wind and water."

Brent kept his eyes on the horizon as the captain had instructed him to do. "How're the others?"

"Martin and Kevin? Fine as rain. They're up with the captain. Kevin insists we stop en route for a day. Martin has agreed, and they've decided on Portsmouth. Four days at this speed, they say."

Brent nodded. He was past caring and the lure of standing on dry, unmoving land was overwhelming.

"Ness and the kids will be fine," stated James for no reason and Brent looked up at him. "I know. I just can't stop worrying about them. They're in better shape because of us, right? They're fed and warm. Money in their pockets."

"You... you know they are." Brent swallowed hard. "Why bring them up?"

"I just feel I won't see them again. Something about all this seems wrong."

Brent carefully made his way ashore at Portsmouth across the thin gangplank from *Azure Tip* and fell to his knees on the dock. Five days without food and little water had stripped him of strength. He had been unable to keep anything down and had wasted away and it had happened far too quickly. The captain had said he had never seen such a terrible case of seasickness. He had set course for Portsmouth and they had only just lowered the gangplank before Brent rushed to quit the ship. James reached his side and helped him to his feet. Brent swayed unsteadily, and James lent him a shoulder.

"We'll find an inn and get you rested and recovered. I know Portsmouth. Home of the Belkin Navy. BN folks everywhere. We'll need to stay hidden. Remember? We talked about this?" Brent nodded after a moment.

James looked up as Kevin and Martin joined them. Behind them on the ship were several other members of the Sect and Church who had accompanied them. They were to stay with the ship and arrange things in Munsten for their arrival. It would take three weeks to reach Munsten by road. The ship would be there in a week if the winds continued.

Brent grunted and stood up swaying slightly. "Feeling better already. Except. Except, why does it feel like I'm still on board? Everything is still swaying."

"Sea legs means more than legs on board apparently," muttered James. He could still feel the motion of the ship as well. "Let's be off. I know an Inn near the docks that we can stay at for a few days."

Martin took the other side of Brent and helped carry him. Together James and Martin carried Brent to the end of the dock. Kevin waved goodbye to the captain and the others and hurried to catch up. He paused at the end of the dock and looked around. A man over by some cargo crates nodded once and Kevin gave the signal.

Kevin reached James' side and moved in to take Brent from him. "Let me. I've done this before."

"My thanks, Kevin," said James. "The whole world is heaving up and down." He paused a moment to wipe his brow. He heard a boot scuff behind him and started to turn. He never saw who hit him and went out like a candle and collapsed on the street without a sound.

Kevin and Martin continued to struggle with Brent and moved up the street. Martin tried to look around. "Where is James?" he asked.

"He's coming," replied Kevin. "Let's rest in that alcove there and let him catch up."

They moved between two buildings and caught their breath.

"I'm sorry Martin," said Kevin.

"For what my son?"

"They promised me you would be well taken care of."

"What are you talking about?"

Just then armoured men wielding swords surrounded them. They wore the livery of the Army. One man stepped forward and spoke. "Brent Bairstow, you are under arrest by order of the Lord Protector."

Brent struggled to raise his head and looked up at the man. "Ah, Major Gillespie. How good to see you again."

"Wish I could say the same, Bairstow. You are looking a bit worse for wear." He turned to Kevin. "It appears the drug to make him seasick worked. Well, done, Kevin. Your plan worked. You got him to me."

"I told you I would. You have your man. Let the vicar go. You promised no harm to the others."

"Aye, we will. First, we need to get this man under lock and key. Men, take him."

The men moved to the side of Brent and shackled him at the wrists and ankles. Martin protested, but at sword point they had him moving down between the buildings and into the back alleyway. Kevin waited a moment to see if anyone noticed, but no one had, or no one cared. Kevin smiled and joined the others.

"What happened to James?" asked Kevin.

"Sleeping face down in the harbour," smiled Gillespie.

Martin gasped. "That is murder!"

"Murder, Vicar? No. Justice. He had it coming."

Kevin looked suspicious. "You're sure he's dead?"

"Yes. Did it myself. Knocked him out and held him underwater until he drowned. I'm sure."

Brent cried out in anger.

Kevin looked relieved.

"What, you worried?"

"No, I just don't like loose ends. There are too many here. I have a mission I must complete, and I need to get to Munsten. This is only a convenience, Major. You and I will be done as soon as we arrive in the city."

"Understood. No qualms from me. This man here is my salvation. You have yours. What about this vicar?"

Kevin looked at Martin who was now rather white and frightened looking. "Leave him be. He is a man of the cloth. He is lost right now. He's been swayed to the side of demons. But I will correct that. He stays with me."

Eight

PRESENT DAY

Rigby Farm - June 901 A.C.

THE DEPARTURE OF Steve and his crew stopped all work on the farm for a time. I suspended all draoi training and retreated to the farmhouse with Nadine. I noticed the others staying clear of me and I tried to shrug off the depression I was feeling. Nothing seemed to help. Not even Dempster's attempts to fill my loss with food could lift my spirits. After two weeks, Nadine convinced me to go on a picnic with her in a clearing by the stream not far from the farm. She practically dragged me the entire way.

Nadine carried a small food basket, and we settled down on the grass by the bank and watched the water streaming by. The wings of dragonflies sparkled in the sunlight as they darted here and there. I felt nature focus on us and I gently pushed it away, so I could think. Nadine smiled at me and emptied the contents of the basket. Sandwiches, pickled onions and a large piece of our oldest aged cheese were laid out and for a time we were lost to the simple joy of eating.

"Time to think about what happens next, Will," she said once we had filled our bellies. The remains of the picnic were packed back in the basket and we had thrown the bread heels into the stream for the birds and brook trout.

I was lying back looking at the clouds passing overhead and merely grunted in reply. Nadine smacked my belly, and I cried out and sat up rubbing the sore spot.

"What was that for?"

"That's for feeling sorry for yourself."

"Can you blame me?"

"No, but the others are counting on you. Time to focus on the future. What do we do next?"

I had thought of little else after watching the clouds of dust raised by the Baron and Steve's crew departure dissipate and disappear. Steve had broken his promise to me. The lure of the Baron's cry for vengeance in the land outweighed the need of the draoi. He had failed to understand the greater picture, and I blamed myself for not getting him to understand what the future held for Belkin.

I felt the pull of Gaea and the need to respond to the land. Something terrible was coming, and I felt that Steve was heading into danger. I feared for him but knew the draoi could not help what the Baron was attempting. When Steve had to choose between me and the Baron he had chosen the Baron. I felt abandoned and knew my pain was rooted in my past. Knowing something and feeling another were two different things, and I was struggling. I had to let go and wasn't able.

I laid back down and Nadine settled next to me with our heads together. She lifted a hand, and I grasped it and held it against my chest. "I'm not ready to let go," I said, voicing my last thought.

"I know, love," she murmured. "But you have to. Our work with the draoi is almost complete. We will need to move. Gaea demands it now. She's annoyed with us. Which seems to be a constant state with her these days."

"Humph."

"I want to revisit the basics again."

"The basics? Again? Why?"

"I need to understand it better, Will. I feel it to be true. Gaea has confirmed more or less what you say. I need to believe it more, I suppose. I want to hold a special session tonight. Go over it again. Then talk about how we make the craobhs full stocs."

I twisted on to my side to see her face better. She glanced sideways at me. "So you think I'm right?" I asked.

I watched her chew her lip for a moment and then nod once.

I flopped back down on my back and smiled at the sky. "Okay, tonight."

The large fire crackled and sparked into the midnight air and all around the fire, I looked at the expectant faces of my seated draoi students. We had placed large logs around the fire and we were somewhat comfortable. Some had blankets spread out on the ground and were leaning back against the wood. The sky was star-filled and cloudless. Only a whisper of a wind could be felt.

The draoi had received what training Nadine and I could provide. They were craobhs of varying skills and were ready to move to the next level. Nadine had spoken to Gaea, and she had confirmed that they should be stocs. Full druids with all the responsibilities that entailed. Nadine and I had differences about what should happen next. She spoke of ceremonies of which we had no time for.

Dempster sat on the porch of the farmhouse in a rocking chair. He had his hands folded over his large stomach with his eyes closed pretending to be asleep. When he truly slept his snoring could be heard for miles. Anne sat next to him with one ear to her baby sleeping inside. Our blacksmith, Charlie, was absent and asleep. The farmhands sat nearby at the edge of the firelight and talked quietly. The summer night was cool but comfortable and welcomed after the heat of the day. Nadine hummed a quiet tune, and I smiled at the serenity of the scene.

I used my senses to probe the night and was marginally surprised to find several dozen animals gathered outside the light of the fire. They were waiting and excited. I looked around the fire and found the two draoi who communed with animals. Chris and Tara Whitby smiled when they caught my glance.

"I see we are not alone tonight."

"No, Freamhaigh. They insisted they be present," replied Chris.

"That's well and good. My apologies to them for the large fire. I hope it doesn't frighten them too much."

Tara laughed a little and shook her head. "No, they are quite content where they are."

Chris held her hand and nodded.

I looked at Nadine beside me. "Ready, Cill Darae?"

"Yes, Freamhaigh. It is time."

I stood from our log and looked down at the eager, smiling faces. "You have all come a long way, my friends. I apologise for how I have been these past few days."

The draoi all spoke at once telling me not to worry about it. I held up my hands, and they quieted. "Thank you, but I was miserable, and you know it.

Nadine has convinced me to get past it and move on and I agree."

I heard Dempster mutter "about time" under his breath and several draoi laughed out loud.

"Yes, yes. About time. I agree. You will have to indulge me for a moment. Nadine has asked me to go over our powers once more. Back to the basics, she said. Change is coming and with it your skills will be required. Soon we must travel. And I want to be sure you understand your strengths and what they mean to this world and Gaea. So, bear with me please."

The draoi looked at one another and then settled onto their logs. Some slipped off to sit on the ground and put their backs to the wood. As they settled I smirked, it was surely a sign that I would be talking for some time and they knew it.

"I will try to keep this short."

More laughter erupted, and Nadine shushed them. Some had the sense to try to look guilty. Some grinned openly back at her. "Such cheek," she scowled.

"Alright, I see you've settled in. So, what have we learned this winter? A lot, I suspect. We have learned from each other and grown stronger for the experience. Nadine and I have only a cursory understanding of the powers of the draoi. Nadine with her years of experience from the draoi who came before us taught us much of our history and the beliefs of those who fell to the sword and worse.

"I have challenged those teachings. The *Draoi Manuscript* gave a lot of detail, but I felt it was flawed as you know. It gave all draoi the same powers and abilities. We know now that each draoi is gifted differently by Gaea. Those differences give us strengths when we work together. As the carpenter works wood, and the blacksmith tempers iron, so do the draoi work nature and the earth we stand on.

"Please humour me while I explain those powers in some detail. You know me and what I have been able to do. I can see all of nature around me and determine its desire. I can take the damage to nature and heal it. I have communed with Dog. I have caused flowers and plants to thrive.

"You know all this because each of you has similar powers. Some only have one. Each is different. But tonight, let us re-examine those powers and discuss their use." A few groans came in response to my last words.

"Ha-ha! Humour me. Healing seems to most of us as the most useful, but I must disagree. I'll explain that in a moment. Healing is important for obvious reasons. We use it to heal people, animals, insects, and plants. All living creatures. With another draoi, they can lend their power, or use their own healing skills to increase how much we can heal. Agnes, Katherine's mum, was an example of that strength. We healed her of a terrible wasting disease, but it took Nadine and I both to do that. We both have healing powers and together we bonded and healed that poor woman."

I looked down at Nadine and she smiled sadly at the memory. A few made the sign of the Word. Agnes had been healed only to die soon after at the hands of her murdered husband, risen by Seth, the monster who had killed my own mother all those years ago.

"We can manipulate all living things. This power has a price. We can cause no harm or that power is reflected back to you. This is our bond to Gaea. She nurtures life. She causes no direct harm. For that reason, her powers, which she grants us, can only be used as she can use it. But why would we harm others? That is not our purpose. I hope you can all see that."

A young draoi named Olivia, strong with healing, stood. "Freamhaigh, can we not help the war? Take down the enemy?" Her brother, Nathan, also a healer, sitting beside her nodded his head in agreement. Heather and Chris, the other healers, looked up in interest.

I shook my head. "No, Olivia and Nathan. That's not our purpose although many would hope so, like Lord Windthrop. The war is not our concern. We are focused on the world around us and making sure that nature survives. The old draoi felt they had to maintain a balance. That was not fully correct. We are here to ensure that harmony is maintained."

"But is there nothing we can do to help?" asked Chris. "Surely, Freamhaigh, stopping the war would help nature? War destroys, not much else."

"Perhaps. Perhaps we will be involved. There is much we can do that is certain. I just don't see it at the moment. Part of me would run to help. Another part of me, the part that Gaea pleads with, says no. I can see the same desire in all of you. We can heal the wounded. Ease their pain. That you know. But we would need to heal both sides. All who are injured deserve our healing regardless of their side in a war. Can you see that need?"

Olivia hesitated and then shook her head. A look of fright crossed her face and I could sense she was afraid she gave insult. Olivia behaved in a fashion that made people around her socially uncomfortable. She was completely unaware and uncaring of how others perceived her. She could be picking her nose while others talked around her. It was her way, and we all accepted it. She had a heart of gold and we all loved her. "Fear not, dearest Olivia. It will take time to understand that, perhaps. We all have much to learn and the art of healing is a powerful skill and one that we cannot be selective about who benefits. We'll talk more on this on the morrow. For now think on it. It is not intuitive, but once you see the reason, you will understand. Gaea led you here and I believe that we share a common sense of value. Think on it then come see me. With your brother."

She nodded quickly and sat back down next to Nathan. They glanced at one another and then back to the fire.

"Plants are next, I suppose. I started with plants myself without knowing it. A gift from my mother, the former Cill Darae from a bygone day. I lived on my own in the wild and I harvested herbs outside Jaipers for years. I knew I had a talent, but never guessed that my draoi powers were leaking through."

A few laughed, and I watched Ethan jab an elbow in Warren's ribs across from me and smile at one another. The brothers had a special gift for plants. They were almost my equal in gathering herbs and fruits and vegetables. The flowers growing in the beds around the farm were bursting with life and their aroma filled the air. They worked the fields and Dempster was making the richest bread anyone could remember enjoying.

Sitting near them were Elisabeth and Jolene, their equals in the plant skills, if not perhaps a little better. They wove vines around the trestles of the farm. Their use of the magic was subtler and lacking the brute force of the brothers. The young ladies coaxed and asked the plants to do their bidding. It left a stronger sense of harmony than the brothers were capable of. As a result, the fields they tended were bursting with grain. The grass fields grew thick and lush. The fields of the boys were impressive, but I could sense a small amount of resentment by the plants.

"Working with plants is a gentle art. They speak to us if we listen. A gentle hand goes a longer way than a rough push or twist." I smiled at the brothers to soften the words. "We are here for the long term. Nothing is so pressing with plants that we can't take the time to ask rather than demand. This is the way to harmony although it can create a sense of balance."

Warren looked up at me and smirked. "Yes, Freamhaigh. I will say that we have twice as many fields soon ready for harvesting than the two lovely ladies." A few laughed at the words and Warren glanced worried at Elisabeth who scrunched up her nose and made a face back at him.

"Yes, and this is well and good. Just close your eyes for a moment and feel the field nearest us. Sense the wheat. Tell me what you feel."

I watched the draoi close their eyes and concentrate. I glanced at Nadine and she grinned up at me. When I looked back to the others, I could see those with the power to sense plants nodding in understanding. Warren started and snapped his eyes open to look at me.

"I'm sorry, Freamhaigh. I see now." He looked at Elisabeth and she had the sense to release him from her teasing. She reached out and took his hand. Ethan opened his eyes and looked confused.

"The field is healthy and growing strong, you can see that and sense that. But underneath is a feeling of disquiet, isn't there?" Ethan nodded his head slowly. Warren looked down at the ground and held Elisabeth's hand a little tighter. "It has been pushed. Coerced. It comes close to breaking our rules. We do not force life to go against its own nature. We can ask, plead, and beg if we must. Your fields are growing strong and tall. But the plants are angry. You can sense that, no?"

Warren nodded his head and Ethan finally seemed to understand. He looked from me to the field and then stared at Jolene sitting beside him. She grimaced and nodded. She took his face in her hands. "Told you, you big stupid head," she said and then kissed him to soften the words.

Ethan kissed her back, and we all watched as he struggled to find words. "Will you show me how to gentle my hand?" he asked her.

"Of course, ya big dunderhead. That's what I've been telling you for months!" She smacked his leg for good measure and the draoi laughed. A couple of draoi leaned over and thumped Ethan on the back.

"Alright settle down, folks!" I called out laughing and in time they settled down. "Next is our *Vision*. We can all do this. This is our most important power. Some find it easier than others, but all with some talent. This magic allows us to see the life within all things. We can see how interconnected all life is. The relationships. The dependencies. We could be blind and still see the world for the life that fills it. It is the strength behind all that we do. We can see the balance and affect the harmony of all life.

"This is the power behind healing. We can look deep into a life and see the damage there. We can see how it should work and correct what has gone wrong. I have shown you how to go so deep that blood vessels seem as large as you and I. There is power here. A mother in difficulty birthing her child can be helped by our powers. We can ease the functions of the body and remove pain when necessary. We could, if Gaea did not forbid it, stop a heart, or cause brain function to cease. Such power! But that is not our purpose. Our power is not ours to wield in this way.

"There is so much power in life. You can all sense nature and have learned to draw that strength to your benefit. We could walk from one end of the realm to the other and never stop. Nature grants us this power. We do not take it. We are gifted it. Gaea would tell you that all life is one, and she is all life. I believe her. You and I are one. We always have been and always will be. When we pass our life energy returns to the whole. Gaea never forgets her parts. The enemy of the Baron is the Baron, do you see?"

A few draoi shook their heads, and I smiled.

"You will understand in time and I won't force you to that understanding. Best you come to terms with it on your own. And here comes the difficult part to understand. For this reason, we cannot choose sides. All life is life. I tell you that should you have a murderer before you dying of some injury you must heal him as you would the mother of a child giving birth. We do not care what a person has done—only that we can heal them. If we were to join the Baron, he would expect that we heal his people and not the enemy. That we cannot do. I would heal the enemy for they are not my enemy, nor yours. They are life and we treat life.

"Erebus is different. I wish you had seen him, but I am glad you didn't. He is not life and yet he lives. Gaea could not sense him. Could not control him. He was like the rocks and minerals of the earth. We cannot sense or manipulate the rocks of the world. The inorganic is blind to us. The earth that we till with our magic is saturated with plant matter and organisms. But the soil, the soil is different, just like rocks. Erebus is perhaps something similar to this. We don't know. Erebus was defeated here on this farm and at great cost. He had changed people, stripped them of their ties to this world. It was unnatural and what we would call evil.

"We cannot change the natural processes of the world. All live to die someday. We can ease that passing, but we cannot stop what must come. We are called to heal and heal we must. The Baron didn't understand that and thought to own and control us. Sadly, Steve and his crew left with him and I blame myself for that. I didn't take the time to explain what we are to him. I thought he understood. I was wrong, and he left."

I looked around the circle and saw concern reflected back with the firelight. These people had faced their own demons and crossed the realm to find Nadine and I. Gaea had merely pushed them along their path, but they knew nothing other than they had a calling to come here to the farm. They arrived not knowing what to think, and I, as their teacher, gave them little of my time and understanding. I felt I had failed them. I could not form the words to explain my sense of disappointment in myself and instead, I opened myself up and pushed my feelings to them across our bonds.

I had toyed with the idea of empathy for weeks now. We communed with animals and plants, but no words passed. We knew what was being said despite the absence of language. It was a form of empathy. I could sense all of nature around me at all times. Pulsing and breathing. The power of life so unimaginably strong. I opened my emotions and poured it to my draoi. It engulfed them and swam through them. They gasped as a whole and stood with heads thrown back and teeth exposed with the strength of the emotions. I fed them my sorrow, my happiness, my pride in their abilities, and my fear and hope for the future. I showed them a world where everyone was in harmony and working toward a better world. I showed them the role we would play and how we would do the work for Gaea.

It all happened in a few heartbeats, and then I released them. Many gasped for breath and dropped down to sit hard on the logs and ground. Nadine reached up with a trembling hand and took mine. I pulled her up into an embrace and she whispered in my ear. "Never do that again! It was too much. Too much emotion! I lost myself and I was you. I was you, Will!"

I held her and looked out over her shoulders at the others. They all stared back at me in shock. "Now you understand?"

They nodded.

"I'm sorry that was so intense. I knew no other way to express myself." Nadine thumped my chest. "We are leaving the farm soon. We are called to the north. Something will happen there, and we need to be there. Together you know we are stronger. Nadine and I can heal far better together than apart. Elisabeth and Jolene have already discovered how they can work the farm almost in isolation. What took twenty farm hands they can do almost solely together. Imagine what we can do once we head out into the world.

"We will be leaving Ethan, Warren, Elisabeth and Jolene here with Dempster, Anne and her child. Plus, the farmhands. Oh, Charlie, too. We leave in a week."

Chris stood up, and I nodded to him. "We don't doubt your words, Freamhaigh. But I question whether or not a few craobhs can affect that much change?"

I smiled at Chris. "No, you are correct. Craobhs aren't up to the task, are they? But you aren't craobhs are you? You've all known that you have your full power. We understand as much as we can about our powers and wield them to the best of our abilities. Harmony and balance. Preserve life whatever the cost. This is our mantra.

"In times long past, Nadine told me that the draoi had specialised ceremonies to promote craobhs to stocs. Special moonlight ceremonies.

Running around naked in the woods. Wild orgies, and who knew what else."

A few laughed out loud and Nadine smacked my bum and muttered: "Did not".

"Not my style, people. Perhaps in time, we will find a way to make the transition more meaningful. For now, I can merely just state 'Congratulations, you're all stocs.'" I beamed at them and the draoi looked to one another. *Dammit*, I thought, *I could have done that better.*

The draoi in front of me drew in a breath and looked behind me. I turned to find Gaea standing there with a frown on her face.

"That's it?" she said accusingly.

"Afraid so," I replied. I looked at Nadine, but she looked away and frowned.

"A friend of mine used to say, *'Not on my watch'*. Now, I think I understand him," she intoned. She motioned toward her with her hands. "Gather round. Come."

The draoi hesitated and then moved to surround Gaea. A few reached out to touch her, and she smiled.

"Close your eyes," she ordered and when we did she hit us with her magic. It filled every pore and crevice of our being. With it came the faces of the many draoi who came before us. Faces beamed at us and smiled their encouragement for what we were. Stoc after stoc greeted us and smiled at us and welcomed us to the fold. Ceremonies played out. Quiet settings in moonlit glades. Animals from far and wide gave tribute and acknowledged the new stocs. Tears of joy streamed down our faces, and we clasped hands and basked in the memories.

The images slowed and then stopped with the last of the draoi, my mother. She was the last to appear and smile her welcome and I sucked in a breath of sorrow at seeing her again. We opened our eyes and looked to Gaea. She was surrounded by light and the night was lit up like daytime.

"Welcome my friends. I've waited a long time for draoi stocs such as you. You have your work cut out for you. Follow the words of the Freamhaigh closely. In time, you will fully understand. We are all one. The world is in danger. Head to the crossroads. You will know what to do."

With a flash of light, she disappeared, and we blinked in the sudden darkness with the image of Gaea burned into our retinas.

Nadine coughed. "That was much better than a simple congratulation."

Laughter filled the night.

Nine

FOUR MONTHS AGO

Portsmouth - February 901 A.C.

JAMES SLOWLY ROSE from mental darkness to feel a weight pressing on his chest and a deep burning sensation in his lungs. He coughed uncontrollably and felt water gush from his lungs and out his mouth in a torrent. Little air remained to cough again, and he struggled to draw in a breath. The burning grew worse, and he felt his abdomen clench painfully of its own violation and more water was forced out. He drew in a small shuddering breath and used it to immediately cough up more water.

His head pounded in time with his heart and he felt as weak as a newborn lamb. He tried to open his eyes, but the pain that racked his body kept them squeezed shut. He heard a voice speaking to him, but it sounded too far away to understand, and he ignored it. He cared only about the pain. He was on his side and could feel someone rubbing his back in a circular motion. He thought feverishly to remember what had happened to him. *I had just left the boat, hadn't I? I was walking with Brent. Glad to be ashore. Then what? I drowned, but how?* He tried to remember, but memories eluded him.

For now, it was enough to just draw in a breath and force water out of his lungs. The weight in his chest was almost gone and the burning sensation was greatly reduced. He managed to crack open his eyes and found himself looking into the concerned face of a stranger leaning over him. He was a man well into middle age with thick startling red curly hair clinging wetly to his face. More notably he wore the black of a chirurgeon. The man was on one knee in front of him and holding him on his side while rubbing his back across his body. The man was soaked through. James could see he was lying in the mud in the shadows between docks right beside the water. The tide was out and the smell of who knew what invaded his sense of smell and he gagged at the odour of rotten fish.

"Easy, sir," said the man. "Take it easy. You're out of the woods but you'll need to lie there a spell until you can breathe with ease."

James nodded and drew in another breath. Before he could cough his stomach twisted violently and vomit and water gushed out in a powerful torrent. Immediately the pressure on his chest cleared, and he almost passed out in relief. His chest felt like it had been smashed, but it felt better than before. A coughing fit took him, and water continued to force its way up and out of him in a trickle. *That can't be normal.*

"Easy, there," soothed the man. "Vomit is good. It will ease the pressure on your diaphragm. Make it easier to draw in a breath. It will be awhile before you clear all the water in your lungs. Just relax and let your body do the work. Don't force it."

James rolled his eyes toward the man and tried to think of something witty to say before his stomach clenched again and he vomited. The man was in a position to remain clear of it, he noted. *Too bad I hate chirurgeons, or I might admire him*, thought James. He tried to laugh but his lungs would only let him cough.

I was hit from behind, he suddenly remembered. *I was walking behind Brent and heard a noise behind me. I turned to look, but before I could see who it was, I was struck on the head.* With the memory came a shooting pain at the back of his head.

James drew in a ragged breath and fought the urge to cough. "Wuh-what...?"

"What happened?" asked the man. "I saw you attacked while your companions carried the sick man away. You were struck down and then held in a barrel of rainwater before being thrown into the harbour between the docks. I saw it happen and rushed over to save you. Just in time, I might add. I've some experience with drownings. I wasn't certain I could revive you. I'm pleased I was. It was a close thing. The coldness of the water helped, I'm sure of that."

James nodded once more. *Attacked and then drowned. Clean work. But whoever attacked me should have knifed me,* he smirked to himself. *Make sure the job was done.*

"M-my friends...?" he asked fighting a cough to speak.

"They were taken away. The vicar went willingly. Very strange behaviour even for Portsmouth. One of your companions was a Sect brother, did you know that?"

James shot a look at the chirurgeon. *Bloody smart fellow,* he realised. *He has an air of familiarity about him. That red hair is something.* He forced air into his lungs and spoke quickly. "The sick man is my friend. I must find him."

"I've no idea where he went, I'm afraid. Bad news though, just before I jumped into the water I am sure I saw military men meet your companions in the alleyway. Are you in some kind of trouble?"

James shook his head and then coughed for a while until his strength left him. "No, well, yes actually. But not what you think. Depends on your side of things, I suppose."

"Side of things? I'm on no one's side. I'm a chirurgeon. Nothing more. I save people."

James smiled at the words. "You sound like a person I know. A young man who aims to save the world." He winced as the pain in his chest stabbed at him.

"Is he a chirurgeon, too?"

"No, no, never that I think. He's a different kind of healer."

"I would very much like to meet him, then. I am a little, um, unorthodox when it comes to my craft. I am always looking for new medicines and techniques. I've several theories I worked out. Using the Word that is. So true theories, not just some crackpot ideas. Speaking of which, can I leave you for a moment? I dropped my bag before I jumped in the water."

When James nodded, he quickly left slogging through the mud. He was barefoot, and he squelched his way clear. James focused on his breathing and was starting to wish he was lying anywhere else but next to the offal that fouled the harbour shoreline. He heard the chirurgeon cursing as he picked his way back to James. He dropped next to him and carefully placed a large satchel on top of discarded old netting.

"By the Word, you are starting to look much better! Your colour is coming back at least." The man grabbed one of James' hands and squeezed the fingertips and watched them a moment. "That's a positive sign. You are, I should mention, only the second person I've managed to revive from a full drowning. I worked on you for at least a quarter of an hour. Hard to tell time when you're all excited, but I think I am correct in that."

"Thank you for saving me."

"You are quite welcome. You won't thank me for the cracked ribs though. I had to manually restart your heart, you see. You apply pressure like a heartbeat to the rib cage right near the heart. It keeps the blood moving in your veins. And I forced air into your lungs. Repeatedly. The last person I revived was bedridden for a month afterwards. Do you have anyone I should contact? A place to stay?"

James tried to follow what the man was telling him but couldn't fathom the meaning. He understood now why his chest was spearing him from the inside. James had suffered many broken ribs in the past from sparring and fighting, but this felt different. He felt as if someone had smashed his breastbone with a sledgehammer. Each breath was tearing his insides. He looked at the vomit and water swirling in the mud in front of him and was glad to see no blood.

"You died, you know. When I got you clear of the water your heart was stopped. According, to my craft that's it. No heartbeat, no service. I disagree with my fellow chirurgeons you'll be glad to know! Haha. Yes, well. I was lucky I didn't drown myself. I jumped in with my robes. Nearly pulled me down. Thankfully the tide was out. The water's only up to my waist. Fortunate that was. By the Word."

The chirurgeon grasped James' hand and pressed two fingertips to his wrist and closed his eyes for a moment. He pressed the back of his hand to James' forehead and then looked into his eyes for a moment. James thought of Brent and struggled to rise.

"No, sir. Stay still. You've only just returned from the dead. You need a moment. Did you see anything when you were dead?"

James glared at the chirurgeon to see if he was serious and found him waiting for an answer. James shook his head.

"Pity, I've a hypothesis about that. Life after death and all that nonsense. Just you rest for now. At least an hour I think. Then I'll see about getting help to move you somewhere. An inn perhaps? Do you have money?"

James nodded. He had a purse stashed inside his tunic and could feel the bulge.

"Good, good. Just rest. I'm Edward Hitchens, by the way. Pleased to meet you."

Five weeks later, James was finally sitting up in bed and able to make it to the chamber pot by himself. The innkeeper had put them in a basement back room. Edward stayed with him and brought James food and cared for his return to health. The small fortune in coin James carried on him assured their privacy and the innkeeper could be trusted according to Edward.

James fought to leave and race after Brent, but Edward refused to let him leave. His chest had been flailed around the breastbone. Fluid in his lungs continued to need to be aspirated and Edward worried about a condition he called *water in the lungs.* The condition claimed the young and the elderly. He said it was an infection of the blood that attacked the lungs. Despite James desire to leave, he found he had no strength to do so. He convalesced and griped instead.

Edward had described the men he had seen carry off Brent. It hadn't taken much detail for James to recognise Major Gillespie had finally found them. James would never have given Gillespie the brains to figure out how to intercept them. Edward believed the member of the Sect who had accompanied them had been to blame for the capture of Brent.

"The Sect is well known in Portsmouth and the land, I would hazard a guess. They believe to be hidden, but they are not. They have spent too many years bringing terror to the populace. Rumours here and a sighting there and it all adds up. People are not as daft as the Church would believe. That led to the Revolution in many ways, don't you know? The Sect was always more than a myth or legend. The man with you, with his black boots, and with the vicar you befriended. He was behind your capture I would suspect and well, honestly, your murder as it might have been."

They spoke of many things in the small basement room in the inn. James found he genuinely liked the fellow, even for a chirurgeon and told him so. Edward had laughed hard at the announcement.

"My mother hated the chirurgeons, too. Said they practised in deception. Oils and watered herbs. Knowing nothing and saving no one except the money that goes in their pockets. Charging to heal people! That's the real crime if you ask me. We should only be paid enough to let us continue to do our work. Instead, the chirurgeons prey on the invalid. Hold them hostage to their pain and suffering and offer little in return until money passes hands."

Edward explained he had been a chirurgeon for twenty of his forty-two years. His mother had been a healer of sorts. A midwife mostly, as the realm allowed, but in private she practised the craft of chirurgeons. "A punishable offence if caught, but no one would dare turn her in," Edward had said with a laugh. He said half of Portsmouth had relied on her. Her rates had undercut the actual chirurgeons. As her son, he had helped and learned along the way. His mother, he had informed James, was exceptional in her skills and had followed a logic not normally seen today. She had discovered many truths about healing and her successes had been very high. Her success had, unfortunately, at long last, caught the attention of the Chirurgeons Guild.

When they came for them, to Edward's surprise, it was him they were interested in. He had methodically catalogued all their developments. His journals contained numerous recipes for medicines and techniques for curing common and uncommon illnesses. Edward told James the guild had informed him, during one of their many long talks in a gaol cell, to join the guild, or be punished. It was then, he admitted, that he realised he knew more than them. He had accepted at once and soon found himself discussing much of what he and his mother had practised with others. They scoffed at much of what he said but he had shown them his journals. All his research and findings recorded in detail. They had taken the books and returned them two months later. They awarded him the robes of a chirurgeon, released him from gaol with his mother, and charged him a joining fee.

"That simple?" asked James in disbelief.

Edward laughed. "No, not really. Much worse than that actually. Mother and I were gaoled for a long time. Only the promise of letting them see my journals got us out. It was too late for mum though. She caught an illness in that cold and wet gaol cell. Water of the lung. Something you and I are concerned about, no? Nothing we could do about it. She died soon after. She died peacefully at least. I saw to that."

"So you are a rather special chirurgeon, Edward. How fortunate for me that you found me floating face down in the harbour."

Edward had been standing in the doorway when he said this, and he smiled back at him. James lying on the bed looked up at him and his red curly hair and the feeling of recognition returned. "Do I know you, Edward? Have you been to Munsten?"

Edward looked surprised and then struck a pose in the doorway. He placed his fists on his sides and looked up and away to the left. Framed by the doorway he looked like a painting for a moment. "Just your friendly town chirurgeon, I'm afraid!"

James gasped in sudden recognition. "The King! By the Word, you look just like the King!"

Edward looked startled and rushed to the bed. "Shush! Quiet!"

James shook his head refusing to be quiet. "Edward, you look exactly like a picture of the King that hangs in the Church in Munsten! The same hair! The same eyes and chin!"

Edward sat on the bed edge and shook his head. "You mustn't say anything! By the Word! What are the chances?"

"What do you mean? What chances? You're the King's bastard, aren't you?"

"My mother told me I was. So yes, probably. Maybe. I don't know. How could I know for sure?"

"I've seen the painting. He looks just like you. Or you like him. Whatever. Few would know or remember what he looked like. Blue eyes and curly red hair. That's rarer than you think. Almost all gingers are green-eyed."

Edward looked sad and hung his head.

"You knew, didn't you?"

"Yes, my mum told me when I turned of age. Thought I should know, *just in case*, she said. After the Revolution, she realised she must keep it hidden. She told no one. She birthed me herself. Used to colour my hair. I stopped that years ago. Too much bother and who could possibly link me to the mad King now? Except you, of course. Bloody hell."

"How? How did it happen I mean?"

"The usual way, I suppose."

"You know what I mean."

Edward smiled and looked down at the floor and away from James. "The King came into Portsmouth aboard his flagship a couple of years before the Revolution. He was in the market with his entourage. My mum was there buying herbs for her medicines. The King fell. Badly. Sprained his wrist or something. My mum was right there and rushed to help him. That was her way, you see. No common sense, or anything. She would see someone hurt and then rush to their side."

"Kind of like you, jumping in the water after me."

Edward glanced at James for a moment and then away again. "I suppose so. Anyway, the way she tells it, the guards went to strike her down for touching the King when two of the people with him, his advisor Benjamin Erwin and a learned woman, Anelise Bracewell, stopped the guards and let the woman tend to the King. She helped him and was invited to the King's residence in Portsmouth for dinner. And nine months later along came me."

"*The* Benjamin Erwin?"

"Yes, from the Great Debate. None other. What are the chances? Anelise was important back then too although many don't know her tale. She is attributed to the Word as it is today. Only the Wordsmiths seem to know what she did. I admire her and follow her teachings."

James had never heard of her. From his dealings with Will Arbor and knowing what he knew now, he had no doubt Benjamin Erwin and Anelise Bracewell were the Freamhaigh and Cill Darae of their time. And now Edward was here taking care of him after a chance encounter with the King over forty years ago. *Curse Gaea and her conniving ways*, he thought furiously. *What am I to do now?* He looked up at Edward and knew at least he had to keep him close.

"You are coming with me to Munsten. I have to free Brent if he still lives. I'm not sure what your role in all this will be, but I mean to strike down the Lord Protector. Brent means to bring the Church back to its former glory. And now the heir to the throne of Belkin is hiding in chirurgeon robes in Portsmouth with the only man that can hope to get him inside the castle. If we strike down the Protector and Brent brings the Church back, both the realm and church will need a King. I'm yours to command, your Majesty."

Edward stared at James in shock, his mouth hanging open. "Are you daft?" he sputtered.

Ten

Munsten Castle - Dungeon - June 901 A.C.

BRENT STRUGGLED TO keep his wits about him. He had been held in the dungeon cell for months with no interaction with anyone other than his gaolers who he saw only once per day. He marked the passage of time with scratches on the stone wall and was sure he had kept a pretty good track of how long he had been held. He had been captured in February and it was now at least June by his reckoning. *Good enough*, he thought as he pushed through another series of push-ups and deep knee bends. He had barely any strength left to exercise. He longed to be able to move freely in the small cell but resigned himself to pacing the small six by six square feet his world had been reduced to.

He wore a simple thin covering. He no longer felt the chill and damp and the meagre food he received barely kept his strength up. His muscle mass had greatly reduced and the act of completing a set of push-ups kept him winded and he strained to stay fit. It was a losing battle, but he forced himself to continue.

He prayed several times a day and knew his faith was being tested again. The hallway outside his cell was quiet and empty of guards. Over the weeks he had called out to the others in nearby cells and they had established the other cells were filled with men and women of the Guard and Army all loyal to his brother Frederick and himself. There were over a hundred of them. All of them told the same story of being grabbed and thrown in gaol with no court or appeal.

He had pieced together what had happened since he had left for Jaipers. It had not gone well for his brother. Over a period of hours, a mere month after he had left, the officers and men of the Guard had been slowly replaced with those loyal to the Lord Protector. Men disappeared overnight with their whereabouts remaining a mystery. Those who had not been killed had ended up here, deep in the dungeon. Healy now owned the Army, the Navy and the Guard. The men feared for the Realm and what would happen next.

As for his brother Frederick, no one knew where he had gone, and it was feared he was dead and his body thrown out to sea. Brent despaired for his older sibling and although he assumed the worst he couldn't believe he was dead. He prayed for his brother and for his men. He prayed they would be saved and released, but in his heart, he knew that nothing good would come of this. Every day men and women would be pulled from their cells and often no one returned. His faith was tested daily. He knew the day would come when he would be dragged out of the cell, but he held firm to his belief that God had a greater purpose for him.

He talked to the men and women nearest him and his words were relayed to the others. He told them the tale of what had happened since he had left for Jaipers and many refused to believe in the druids and their magic. He spoke of his faith and his desire to see the realm returned to its former glory. He told jokes and told them whatever he needed to in order to keep their spirits up.

Today was like any other. He had been fed a thin soup hours ago and his bowl had been returned. He collapsed on his pallet and grunted against the burning pain in his arms and legs from his short workout. He flexed his right arm and shook his head at the little muscle mass that remained. *Picking up a sword will be difficult.* He wondered when his gaolers would come for him when he heard the door at the far end of the corridor bang open and heard the voice of Major Sean Gillespie call out.

"Bairstow!" shouted Gillespie. "It's time we talked." The gloating in the voice was unmistakable and Brent scowled. Several of the men in the adjoining cells yelled out comments about Gillespie's mother and Brent grinned.

Brent listened to armoured feet striking the stone floor draw closer and then stop outside his cell. A foot scuffed across the floor and a key turned loudly in the lock and the door was pushed open. The head gaoler stood a moment in the opening and then backed away to be replaced by Gillespie. Brent continued to lay on his pallet and looked up at the uniform his brother once wore. Gillespie had been made the head of the Army of the Realm. Bile rose in the back of his throat and he coughed to clear it.

"Stand up in front of your superior!" ordered Gillespie. A glint of hatred was there in his eyes for all to see but it was aimed at Brent.

"Piss off," replied Brent.

Gillespie strode forward and struck Brent across the head with his gauntleted right hand. Brent tried to block it but his reflexes were not what they once were. The back of his head struck the wall of the cell.

"Ouch!" he cried and lifted a hand to rub his head. "Bastard. This how you show your strength? Striking an unarmed superior?"

"Superior? Do you not see the uniform I wear? I am your Commander. The General of the Army of the Realm! Stand up!"

"I see an arse dressed up like a child on Samhain. You are no more the head of the army than I am the head of Women's Guild. Now get out. I want my privacy."

Gillespie stepped aside, and two army sergeants stepped quickly forward. Brent recognised them as the two who had travelled with him to Jaipers. He forgot their names but not their faces. *Their eyes are too close together,* he thought and chuckled as they grabbed him under the armpits and roughly handled him up onto his feet. Brent staggered and felt light-headed. His vision swam, and he blinked.

"Follow orders, swine!" one of them yelled in his face and the other one punched him hard in the stomach.

Brent bent over double and retched. The sergeants hoisted him higher and Gillespie moved forward to stand over Brent as he slowly found his feet. He tried to straighten but his legs had no strength. He hung limply from the arms of the sergeants. *This is disgraceful*, he thought.

"You'll answer our questions if you know what's good for you," he said and spun and strode out of the cell. The sergeants dragged Brent out into the corridor. Brent swallowed the bile that rose in his gorge and looked blearily around. With his bare feet dragging on the stone floor he was pulled down the corridor. The scraping of his toes was a far-away pain compared to his stomach.

"Hullo, soldiers!" called out Brent struggling to put strength behind his voice. "I'll be back in a moment. Don't start the party without me!"

Laughter could be heard coming out of the cells and a few called out for Brent to remain strong.

"If someone could save me a glass of wine I'd be appreciative!" he answered back to the cheering.

The sergeant holding him on his right punched the back of his neck. Brent gargled and fought to remain conscious. His vision swam, and he blinked only to find himself seated in a small cell with his feet chained to a chair and his hands shackled to a ring embedded in a solid oak table. An empty chair sat across from him and he was alone. He looked around and blinked back tears caused by the smoking torch on the wall. The floor was covered in straw and he could see dried blood pooled in areas. *Torture,* he surmised. *I wondered when it would start.*

The door banged open and Gillespie strode in and sat in the empty chair. He stared at Brent for a long time and Brent gave him no satisfaction and merely looked back at him without expression.

"Where's the gold?" asked Gillespie.

The question surprised Brent, and he ran through the many replies he could give and then shrugged instead. The chains holding him rattled with the effort. "Gone if it was ever there."

"What do you mean?"

"The chest was full of copper pence."

"Liar! It was full of gold. Where'd it go?"

"There was gold on top. Underneath it was all coppers. Redgrave had the last laugh."

Gillespie stood quickly, reached across the table and punched Brent in the face. Brent was surprised by the speed of the strike. It hit him square in the nose and he felt the cartilage shatter and his nose spread across his face. *I'm in terrible shape, I should have been able to dodge that. I'm weaker than I thought.*

Pain suddenly blossomed across his face and he cried out at the intensity of it. Gillespie sat back down and then slowly pulled off his gauntlets while watching Brent recover. Blood poured from his nose and chained as he was Brent couldn't stop it. He held his head down and let the blood pour out. He swallowed the blood running down the inside of his throat and thought perhaps he might drown. This brought a quick laugh, and he groaned at the increased pain.

"What happened in Jaipers? You were attacked. Your men killed. You escaped. What happened?"

Brent coughed and tried to blow blood out his nostrils, but they were now swollen shut. He raised his head a little and looked over at Gillespie. The man had a smug look on his face and was clearly enjoying this. "The Sect ambushed us. Struck us down in the streets of Jaipers. Ask them where the gold is. I saw them dump the chest out before I was struck down."

"The Sect? What Sect?"

"The Sect of the Church of the New Order, that's who," said Brent and hated the sound of his voice. He sounded drunk. Brent watched Gillespie and realised he had no idea who the Sect was. *Strange, I was brought here by the head of the Sect and he doesn't know that. Seems Healy isn't telling Gillespie all he should know.*

Gillespie opened his mouth to speak when the door behind him opened. Gillespie looked annoyed and rose to berate whoever had opened it when he spied Healy standing there. "President!" he exclaimed.

Healy tore his eyes from Brent and glanced at Gillespie and then frowned. "I told you no one was to speak to him alone."

"Yes, sir, I thought I might get the details you wanted from him."

"You thought wrong," Healy turned to the door and called out to the other side. "Kevin, come in."

Brent watched Kevin stroll in. His bald head continued to shine in the torchlight. Kevin kept his eyes on Brent and smiled as he moved over to stand by the table.

"What's he doing here?" asked Gillespie.

"He's the head of the Sect you know nothing about, you moron," replied Brent. "He's here to torture me."

"Leave," said Healy and Gillespie looked surprised. He opened his mouth to reply then thought better of it and quietly left the room and closed the door behind him.

Kevin sat in the vacated chair and crossed his legs under his robe. He placed one arm over the raised knee and placed the other arm over it. "Hello, Brent. Good to see you again."

"Likewise."

"You look like *cac*. Your nose is shattered, did you know that? Sorry about Gillespie. I've only just gotten to know the man. I agree with your assessment. He is a moron. Speaking of which, the President and I have been speaking about you."

"President? Who's that?"

"I'm the President of the newly formed Republic of Belkin. There's been a regime change," replied Healy.

Brent tried to focus on Healy, but his eyes betrayed him. He looked at the table instead. "I didn't vote for you."

"Ha-ha! No one voted for me, Brent Bairstow. I have to admit to a great deal of pleasure seeing you here in my dungeon. When Kevin let me know you had arrived on his doorstep in Jergen, I could scarcely believe the words! You really are an interesting fellow."

"Really? I didn't think I was that interesting."

"Ha-ha! I assure you that you are," replied Healy. "Kevin, he's yours."

Kevin nodded and reached into his robe and pulled out a leather bundle which he laid on the table. He started to unroll it as he spoke. "There were some things I wanted to ask you in Jergen and wasn't able to. There are some truths we need to get to, don't you think?"

Brent watched the leather bundle unroll and spied the gleaming tools he had seen in Jaipers when Seth tortured him. "Oh goody, time for pinkie shearing again?"

"No, not this time, I'm afraid. I'm curious to see if your ears, nose and eyes will come back as quickly as your pinkie did. What do you think? Is God going to save you again?"

"Couldn't tell you. Hey Healy, you cac," replied Brent looking over to Healy where he leaned against the wall looking amused. "Where's my brother?"

Healy blinked at the affront. "How dare you...!"

"Oh, I dare. Where is my brother?"

"He's not here to save your sorry ass, I'll have you know that!"

Brent smiled and then spat a thick wad of blood to the side. "So, he's alive then. Good."

Healy spluttered. Kevin raised a hand to silence him and Brent was surprised when Healy closed his mouth. "Tut-tut, none of that. We need to focus. I've questions for you. Answer truthfully and perhaps you save the lives of some of your men and women in here."

Brent hung his head a moment and when he lifted it Healy was surprised by the smile he wore. "Go ahead. Those men and women swore an oath to defend this realm with their lives. Do you seek to threaten me with their lives? I never owned them. This man, this President did. You will be killing his own people."

Healy laughed. "They were never mine. They swore allegiance to the realm but in reality, they swore it to you and your brother. I know what your brother was investigating. Nothing happens in the capital without my eyes and ears on it. You thought you were so careful."

Brent looked at Kevin and squinted. "What is that you want? Can you not see the evil that lies in this man? You are a man of God. Show some moral compass."

Kevin grinned. "I think you will find that I am not so blinded as our former leader Seth Farlow. Our President has had me spying on the Sect for decades.

Ever since the Revolution, really. He never trusted the Archbishop. Too religious. Zealotry will get you nowhere."

Brent closed his mouth and then opened it again to breathe. His head swam with pain and he tried to stay focused. The edges of his vision grew dark, and he fought to remain conscious and to speak clearly. "Wuh-what is it you want?"

"You know what we want," said Kevin with little emotion. "Time you told us, eh?"

Brent awoke an indeterminate time later. Every part of his body was in agony. Kevin had tortured him for hours. He was sure it had been hours. *That little knife...* Brent shuddered and wept a little in fear. It had cut and left no pain at first. He watched it part his flesh and wondered at the lack of feeling and thought maybe God was protecting him again. Then a cold burn started along the cut and then excruciating pain followed. His throat was still raw from screaming. Cut after cut followed. He had lost count.

He lay on his back on the pallet and could feel that his back had bled long into the straw and was stuck fast to him. He could feel it tearing at his back with his breathing. Tears streamed from the corner of his eyes and filled his ears. He lifted his left hand to the light and stared at the single finger and thumb that remained. The blackened burned stubs along his knuckles showed where his three smaller fingers had been.

"Tomorrow will be the right hand," Kevin had said as he wrapped up his tools. "Be thankful your ears, nose and eyes remain. Include that in your prayers."

They had only asked one question over and over. *Where was the gold? Where was the gold? Where was the gold?*

Brent choked back a laugh that threatened to escape him. He knew if he let that laugh out he wouldn't be able to stop. *Not ever.* He forced the wrist of his maimed hand into his mouth and bit down to stop the laughter that bubbled up inside him.

He told them he didn't know where the gold was. He had hung on to the thread of that truth. It was true—he didn't know where the gold was.

But he was pretty sure he could guess. *Oh yes, I'm sure I could guess.*

He heard the lock of his cell door unlock quietly and he rolled his eyes toward the door.

It opened a crack, and he heard a soft whisper. "Brent? Brent is that you?"

Fear struck Brent when he recognised the voice. *No, it can't be. Not here. Not now.*

"Brent, damn you. Answer me!" said the voice.

There was no mistaking the voice and Brent whimpered. He kept his eyes on the crack of the door as it widened, and he saw his brother's face peering in from the hallway.

"Go away!" he hissed. "Run!"

Frederick opened the door further and crept into the cell until he was crouched over Brent's lying form. "Run? I'm here to get you out, you daft fool! What's the matter with you?"

Frederick was dressed in common garb. A simple shirt and roughspun pants. On his feet, he wore cheap sandals, and he wore fingerless knit gloves. His face was smeared with dirt to hide his face from the light, but it was an unmistakable face. Frederick gasped a deep breath when he saw the injuries to his brother. "By the Word! What have they done to you?"

"Nothing. Nothing. Get out. You have to get out. They will expect you. You have to know that."

"Yes, yes. I've been careful."

Brent wept and tried to push his brother with his maimed hand. His right arm was broken in three places and wouldn't move the way he wanted. "No. Go... please, for the love of God..."

The hallway beyond the door lit up with torchlight and Frederick whirled toward the door. The door swung open all the way and Gillespie stood in the doorway framed by his two sergeants.

"Well, well, well. Who do we have here?" chided Gillespie.

"Gillespie, you traitor. You won't get away with this," replied Frederick. He reached into his shirt, but the two sergeants were quicker and reached in and grabbed hold of him and disarmed him.

"No, no, no..." moaned Brent.

Gillespie took the dagger from his men and held it up to the torchlight where it gleamed brightly. "Lovely blade, General. Here. Have it back." Gillespie drove the point of the knife deep into the abdomen of Frederick.

Frederick gasped and then cried out.

Gillespie looked into Frederick's eyes and then twisted the blade one way and then the other. Frederick cried out and tried to grab the dagger to stop it. The sergeants held his arms to his side and grinned.

"I always hated you, General," whispered Gillespie and then with a twisted grin sliced the dagger out through his side and eviscerated him. The sound of the entrails hitting the stone floor was wet and sickening.

"Frederick!" cried out Brent and tried to reach toward him but he was too weak.

The sergeants let go of his brother and he fell to his knees and grabbed his stomach. He then reached out with a trembling hand toward his guts on the floor. Gillespie loomed over him and with one quick stroke, he cut deep into his throat. Blood fountained through the air and Frederick fell to his side and reached up to his throat.

Brent found his brother's eyes looking at him. Frederick's eyes shone with fear and desperation. He tried to breathe but was unable and his mouth gaped open. Brent wept and called out his brother's name as he watched the light of his eyes dim until there was nothing left.

Gillespie reached down and wiped the dagger blade on his brother's shirt. He looked down at Brent and grinned. "You're a sorry sight. Enjoy the company of your brother. Get some rest. Looks like you could use it."

Gillespie and the sergeants left the cell laughing and locked the cell door leaving Frederick's sightless eyes staring back at Brent.

Part Two: Thrust

Eleven

Jergen - Outside the main northern gate - June 901 A.C.

THE BARON OF Turgany, Lord Andrew Windthrop, led the long train of men and women soldiers on the final mile of approach to the main northern gate of Jergen. The high stone wall with its wide rampart was clearly visible with the flags of the realm, Turgany and the city, flapping briskly in the stiff onshore wind. He could see the gatehouse and the wall tower that overlooked the entrance. His train was spread out for at least a mile. The Baron had picked up his main host once they left Rigby Farm and now, combined with Steve Comlin's sixty men and women, he had an army numbering nearly seven hundred. He smiled to himself. He had amassed his army in secret and with Steve's help had trained them hidden from the eyes of the Lord Protector. *It wouldn't do to have an army this size, now would it?* he thought and chuckled.

The journey from the farm to Jergen had been uneventful, but slow going. Steve Comlin had insisted on keeping his men and women separate from the Baron's army. The Baron had agreed if for no other reason than to keep the bickering down. It was not Steve's crew he worried about, but his own soldiers. He admitted that his men were not as well-disciplined as Steve's and they resented their skills. He had often admired Steve's crew in the past, and now they were even more seasoned and all the more professional. If not for Steve's crew, they would still be days away from the city gates. Steve's senior crew had kept the discipline and kept the carts and wagons moving down the road. Camps at night were established in a way the Baron's men had never seen and they were quick to set up and equally quick to strike down. The only time the Baron had stepped in was once when Steve had tried to discipline a couple of his senior officers. It was not his place to admonish his soldiers. *That is my right.* He still didn't understand what Steve had seen wrong with his officers, but he had yelled at them, anyway. Major Sibbald and Captain Tibert had the decency to look chastised.

He regretted in some small way how he had treated that insufferable Will Arbor. Still, after the fiasco at the farm he needed to find a release. A release only Jergen could provide him. What grated him the most was he had never been spoken to by a commoner in that manner. *The slight will not be forgotten,* he vowed for the hundredth time. *Once I am King, I will bring these druids under my thumb.*

The astonishment of seeing Peter, his long-dead lover, had shaken him to his core. Afterwards, he had realised the trickery of it and decided then that Will Arbor and his lot would be ruled by him for his purpose. His attempt had been thwarted and the image of his men encircled by wild animals had almost loosened his bowels. Their trickery had robbed him of his voice and he would never forgive the slight. Or the condescending words that young pup and his *bitseachaigh* had said to him. *I had the last laugh though,* he chuckled to himself. *I took away his Steve Comlin.*

The journey along the main road approaching the city had been beautiful to admire. The road hit the coast north of the city and allowed an unobstructed view of the ocean. An onshore breeze was cooling and the Baron's relished the break from the oppressive heat of summer. Jergen was nestled on the coast around a deep bay and could be seen from miles around. He was proud of his capital city. He visited as often as he could. From here he could see the white stone of the Cathedral rising above all other buildings and the thick city wall. The city was built around the cliffs rising from the sea and wrapped around a large natural bay. It was a naturally defended bay, one the Admiral of the Fleet often bragged about.

The Baron smiled as he thought of the Admiral. He enjoyed his company. He hadn't wanted to be with anyone after Peter had died. Then the Admiral and he had discovered each other at one of the many galas the Baron held in his mansion. They were like-minded people and they bonded immediately. Now, the Admiral often came south from Munsten and Portsmouth to engage in Navy manoeuvres in the broad bay as often as he could. The Baron had sent word to the Admiral he would be in Jergen this month and he hoped the man would soon be in port. He longed to see the Admirals great big ship sail into the harbour with its red sails snapping in anticipation.

The Baron's messenger had recently returned with the word the mayor of the city and the garrison commander, Colonel John Masters, were pleased to receive him and that his staff at his mansion would be informed at once. Room in the barracks would be arranged and stables for the horses. He worried that an army this size would raise the alarm in the city. *It's not every day these many armed men stroll up to a major city, even if it's mine.*

He admitted to himself that he was anxious to return to his home in Jergen and the comforts it would bring. He preferred it to his country estates. *There is immediate access to the pleasures in life I can't get in the country. I won't be here long so I best make the most of it.* He smiled to himself.

The gate was much closer now, and he smiled wider knowing he would be soon be surrounded by people who owed him allegiance. He liked the mayor of the city. An affable man and quick to please. The man owed his rise to mayor to him and the Baron never let him forget it. *Colonel Masters, on the other hand, is a pompous ass.* He was too proud of his heritage and equestrian skills. And he was favoured by the Lord Protector.

Colonel Masters had the privilege of leading a garrison of over three hundred men and women. He and Steve had discussed the garrison at length. They were uncertain how they would be received. It would bring conflict, but Steve was certain they could gain access to the city under the Turgany flag. The city owed allegiance to Turgany, but it also held allegiance to the capital and the realm. Only the fact that Turgany had long fought the tyranny of the Lord Protector gave them hope for a quick resolution to where the city's loyalties lay. Colonel Masters was the unknown element. Steve said he would need to be replaced immediately, and the garrison sworn over to Turgany. The Baron could see the need. *My position as Baron of Turgany, and next in line as King, should assure their loyalty.*

The Baron knew he would be expected to review the garrison and dreaded doing so. He hated military things despite the army at his back. *Insufferable bunch the lot of them,* he thought miserably. *Still, they will serve me in seizing back control of the Realm. All tools should be used for their purpose. And I will use mine for great gain. I will strike down Healy and take the throne.* He hated John Healy to the core of his being. The incident in the past between his family and the Healy family could never be resolved. They were first cousins on their mother's side. When the King was imprisoned, Healy had his father, the former

Baron Windthrop, thrown in gaol in Munsten. His father died in the dungeon, and his mother soon after with grief. The Baron wanted his revenge. *Soon*, he thought to console himself. *Soon, I will have Healy's head sitting on my dining table in Munsten watching me eat*

His claim to the throne was weak at best and he knew it. *Those who conquer get to write the history*, he thought. *My claim is the strongest one. By proximity of blood on my father's side. Which is why Healy had him killed.*

He was pleased to see the numerous caravans and travellers on the road move to the side to permit unimpeded transit of his soldiers. They swung in behind his train for safety and that was fine with him so long as they stayed back and enjoyed the dust he was kicking up. He was glad to provide a small amount of protection for his people. It was his duty. The road traffic was heavy in both directions this time of the year and his scouts were doing an admirable job keeping the road clear. Plus, the weather was perfect for travel. Which also meant it was perfect for highwaymen such as Steve Comlin used to be. The Baron smiled to himself and glanced at Steve who rode slightly behind him to his right.

"Lovely weather," said the Baron.

"It is, Lord Windthrop, perfect for travelling," replied Steve and watched the Baron blink at the words. He heard Franky snort behind him but ignored her.

"When we get inside the city, I want your crew taking the entrance area of the barracks. Watch my men. They still require discipline."

"Sir, you have your own senior officers to administer discipline."

"Yes, I do. But I also have you, don't I?"

Steve remained silent as they continued along their way until the wall of the city loomed high and the gate could be clearly seen. They watched as a small band of men on horseback emerged from the gate and trotted toward them. Three carried flags raised high; one for the realm of Belkin, one for the county of Turgany, and the last, the city flag of Jergen. The Baron grunted and signalled to his flag bearer. The man lifted his standard and the flag of Turgany snapped in the wind.

Central to the troop was the Mayor of Jergen, Robert Oldfield, and flanked to his right was Colonel John Masters. The mayor had donned his mayoral robes with a large golden chalice hanging from thick gold chains around his neck. Masters wore his finest uniform and displayed his expertise in horsemanship with a flair. His horse pranced next to the mayor's, and the Baron thought him foppish; however, they looked a magnificent pair as they exited the shadow of the wall. The noon sun glinted brightly off their uniforms.

The Baron halted his train with a bellow and allowed his horse to advance a few paces before halting himself. Steve and Franky stayed back with the front line. The army train jostled, and the carts and wagons slowed to a staggered halt. The mayor and the Colonel waited for the noise to settle before riding up to halt in front of the Baron. The colonel saluted and then raised a gauntlet in greeting. Baron Windthrop flapped a hand in response.

Mayor Oldfield bowed a little in his saddle and looked aside at Colonel Masters. "Lord Windthrop, it is my privilege and honour to welcome you to Jergen. Our gates are open to you and your men. Your men have been given accommodations in the barracks and Colonel Masters will see to their comfort and needs. Your officers have been given rooms in the officer quarters. Plus, I have taken pains to ensure that your mansion staff know of your arrival. Your home should be ready for your arrival if not sooner.

"My Lord, my family would be most honoured if we could open our home to you and your senior officers for a meal once you are settled. You merely need to have your men send word to my deputy and it will be arranged. With regrets, I must inform you that the Castellan of Jergen could not attend your arrival, and he sends his apologies. He was called away to Munsten unexpectedly. He left by ship yesterday morning."

Steve listened in to the conversation and pondered that piece of news. He found it odd that the representative of the Realm in Turgany saw fit to leave the city right before the arrival of the Baron of Turgany. He caught Franky frowning at the news. The mayor was fidgeting on his horse and stealing looks at the Colonel. He focused on the Colonel as the Baron responded.

"My dear mayor, thank you for this honour of being greeted in such formal attire outside our city gates. My men will be here only for a fortnight. We have business elsewhere. Nothing elaborate is required. Dinner tomorrow evening will be wonderful. I accept and will bring only four officers with me." The Baron turned in his saddle and gestured at Steve. "I introduce Stephen Comlin, the Reeve of Jaipers and now my trusted advisor. He has accepted a senior officer position with me. Beside him is his second Franky... er..." The Baron hesitated when he realised he didn't know Franky's last name. "Just Franky," he finished after a moment.

Steve had watched the Colonel feign pleasure at seeing him with the Baron. *He knew somehow*, he thought. *He knew we were coming. This does not bode well.* The Baron continued to exchange pleasantries with the mayor. He caught a fleeting amusement in the eyes of the Colonel before his eyes fell firmly on

Steve and appraised him. One eyebrow lifted, and he turned his attention to Franky. Steve watched him frown as he noticed her missing arm and a slight smirk appear. He immediately disliked the man. *He can ride a horse better than anyone I have met, but his attitude needs adjusting.* The Colonel looked at the sun to mark its position and the look of amusement crossed his eyes once more. The Colonel's horse turned slightly, and Steve spied a war hammer strapped to the saddle.

Franky moved her horse up beside Steve and looked at the hammer and gave him a meaningful look. *She knows something is wrong, too. No one would ride out to greet the Baron and carry a war hammer. Unless...* He looked above the gatehouse to the battlements and saw archers silhouetted by the sun looking down at them. *Far more than required if at all.* The guards outside the gatehouse were glancing at one another repeatedly. He nodded to Franky, and she moved back to warn the crew. Steve nudged his horse with a knee and it moved forward to stop beside the Baron.

"A word, Lord Windthrop, if I may?"

The Baron looked annoyed and opened his mouth to chastise Steve when Steve frowned at him and beckoned sharply with his head. The Baron clenched his teeth and turned to the mayor. "One moment, please. My man wants a quick—and no doubt terribly important—word with me."

"Oh, of course, Lord Windthrop. Please, we are at your mercy." The mayor inclined his head and shot a worried look over to the Colonel who ignored him and continued to watch Steve with interest. Steve moved his horse out of earshot and the Baron followed. "This better be good, Steve."

"It is, this is a trap of some kind. They were expecting us."

The Baron opened his mouth and kept it open, staring at Steve. "A what? A trap? Are you out of your mind? I have close to seven hundred men!"

"Shh! Keep your voice down!" Steve looked to the Colonel who was blatantly staring at them. "Yes, a trap. The Colonel has something going on. The mayor knows something and is being watched by the Colonel. Once we enter the city streets, our people will be pinned. They know nothing of fighting in a city. Plus, it's no coincidence the Castellan has left the city. Something is up."

"Yes, well, sometimes that ass of a Lord Protector makes unreasonable demands. Have you nothing more to go on?"

"No, just my instincts. And Franky's too. She knows."

"Your instincts."

"Yes."

"You want me to leave Jergen, my capital city, right in front of its gates because of your instincts?"

Steve pursed his lips. "Yes."

"Not on your life. This is foolish. Stop wasting my time. Follow." The Baron urged his horse back to the mayor. "My apologies, mayor. It was nothing. Please lead on."

The mayor grimaced and nodded before turning his horse toward the gatehouse. The Colonel hesitated a moment and then nodded to Steve with a smile.

Asshole, thought Steve.

Steve let Franky ride up beside him. He leaned toward her and whispered. "Warn Sibbald and Tibert. Quietly. I want the crew up front. Be ready to retreat. This is a cluster." Franky nodded and slowed her horse to fall in beside Sibbald. He saw her whispering to Sibbald and urged his horse forward to take a position behind the Baron, the mayor and the colonel.

They passed through the gates with Steve nervously looking for an immediate attack. The Baron's men made slow progress through the streets of Jergen. The mayor had ordered the streets cleared to speed their way but the Baron's men and horses were not disciplined enough to march in an orderly fashion. They bunched up and spread out repeatedly and movement often ground to a halt. The windows of the tall buildings pressing in on the narrow streets held many citizens gazing down at the men and Steve tried to determine threats from every location. He wasn't comfortable in large cities. There were too many places where danger could come from.

Now they were inside the city walls Steve could smell the rich scent of the ocean carried on the strong onshore wind. The harbour was obscured for the moment by the buildings and Steve was eager to set eyes on it. On the road along the coast, he had spied the sails of merchant ships heading in and out of port. It had been years since he had seen the sea and he had loved to watch the ships make their way through the water. Seeing the ships had raised a longing inside him to be elsewhere.

What am I doing here? he thought for the hundredth time since leaving the farm. *I left Will at that farm. I broke my promise to him and never explained why. I was too much the coward.* He looked ahead to the Baron swaying on his saddle and engaged in some discussion of some kind with the mayor. *Did my oath to the Baron all those years ago truly come before my promise to Will? I thought I had left that behind. The oath should have died with it. But he brought it up, didn't he? He never forgot.*

Steve broke his thoughts when he caught a movement out of the corner of his eye down a side street. He looked, but the street was deserted. Franky cleared her throat and Steve slowly turned his head to his left to catch her in his peripheral vision. She was tilting her head toward another side street on the opposite side. *We are being encircled.*

Steve and his crew had a series of hand signals they had used for years as highwaymen to communicate. He lifted his right hand and gave the signal for ambush and could almost feel his crew react silently to the signal. Lowering his hand to the pommel of his sword he raised it an inch from the scabbard to make sure it was free. The Baron was too far ahead and talking much too loudly with the mayor. The Colonel was looking from side to side and glancing back at Steve. *He is checking on his men. Making sure they aren't seen. But it's too late for that, we've seen them, and we know. What now? Curse the Baron for moving so far out of position ahead.*

Just then the front of the train rounded a street corner into a large open park with a large statue in the middle. The harbour was exposed below them down the steep city streets. Ships ploughed the large bay across wave tops foaming white with the brisk wind. Steve's eyes were immediately drawn to six large dark foreign ships racing for the docks. Even from up in the city Steve could see that the people on the jetties were bunching together and pointing at the speeding ships. Stevedores stopped their work and turned to stare.

The black ships were ignoring all other shipping and moving at a reckless rate of knots for the inner bay and harbour. Although the distance was great, Steve spied armed men covering the upper decks, crouching down, and avoiding the heavy bow spray. It was then his eyes truly saw the scene in front of him. He spied the red sails of two Navy frigates and one massive ship-of-the-line giving high pursuit. He recognised the centre ship-of-the-line by reputation as the *BNS Munsten*, the Admiral of the Fleet's flagship.

Strangely, black and white plumes of smoke erupted from the bows of the Navy ships and the ships raced through the thick clouds. All was silent and then a thunderous blast echoed up from the harbour and the cliffs. Screams were heard throughout the city at the sudden and unfamiliar noise. The main mast of the dark ship farthest behind had large pieces blown off by some impact. The high winds sheared off what remained of the mast and it took most of the men arrayed on her deck with it into the water. The ship heaved around to the right out of control.

Steve was about to shout a warning when armed men in Jergen battalion uniforms swarmed the front of the Baron's train from the alleyways and side streets. Crossbows were lowered and pointed at the Baron. The Colonel halted and pulled his gaze from the harbour battle to face the Baron. He looked a little shocked but then a huge smile spread across his face.

"Lord Andrew Windthrop, you are accused of high treason by the President of the Republic of Belkin. You are under arrest. You are to follow me to the gaol where you will be imprisoned until you can be transported to Munsten for trial," the Colonel declared in a loud booming voice.

The mayor looked from the Colonel to the ships in the harbour and opened and closed his mouth. He raised an arm to point at the ships fighting in the harbour and then dropped it. "What is going on? Colonel? What is going on?" he pleaded with a high-pitched break in his voice.

Mesmerised, Steve watched the dark ships turn hard to starboard to drive their port sides into the piers. Wood splintered, and screams could be heard faintly rising from the harbour as people were smashed against the hulls. The men on the ships leapt from the decks and Steve wondered what it was they wore. They were dressed in sand coloured wraps with gleaming curved swords. Jergen was under attack. The Colonel looked down at the harbour at the sound of splintering wood and faint screams and smiled. "Our friends from the East have arrived." Steve saw his smile turn into a frown when the Navy ships turned in the harbour to present their sides.

The sides of the Navy ships disappeared in more black and white smoke. A massive booming sound echoed up from the harbour and the dark ship floundering in the harbour exploded in splintering wood. The air around the ship turned red as the men on the deck were decimated by unknown projectiles. The ship's upper deck was wiped clean of men and rigging. Screams then cheers were heard throughout the city in response. Whatever the Navy was using was having a great effect on the enemy ships. Plume after plume of smoke erupted from the Navy ships followed by massive rolling booms. The dark ships along the jetty were vulnerable and wood splinters and bodies sprayed across the harbour. Many citizens of Jergen were caught in the same blasts and Steve winced at the sight. Dozens of armed men and people were wiped out. The Navy was decimating the enemy forces with some unknown weapon of destruction.

Steve spied several of the enemy in the harbour stop and cluster around some strange device they pulled off one of their ships. Others pulled out longbows and flames sparked on arrows bristling along their line. Steve watched several men pull back on the strange device and watched a small round container arc through the air toward one of the Navy frigates. *That's a little like an arbalest*, thought Steve. The container struck a ship's side and shattered, spraying some kind of liquid across the wood. Several flaming arrows followed, and one struck the liquid. The moment the arrow struck the liquid it burst into flame. *Oil!* thought Steve.

Container after container was launched into the air and both frigates were struck. Arrows followed and soon both frigates were aflame. Sails were burning freely and sailors on fire leapt into the water. The flagship veered hard to starboard and made for the safety of the bay. Two containers smashed on her stern, but the following flaming arrows fell short in the bay. What remained of the enemy on shore turned and ran into the city. The flagship continued her turn and beat against the wind to escape the flames. Steve watched as she struggled to lower longboats to the water.

Steve tore his gaze from the harbour and observed that everyone; including the garrison soldiers, had eyes only for the harbour. He gave a hand-signal and as one his crew drew swords and hacked into the nearest men. The Baron's horse whinnied and reared back in fright at the smell and sight of blood. The Baron fell from his saddle yelling in fright. The front hooves of his horse thrust wildly through the air and one smacked into the Colonel and knocked him clear of his horse. The Colonel landed straight on his back and gaped for air with the wind knocked out of him.

The Baron's horse, now in full panic, ran screaming into the open square up the road spilling garrison men as they dove to the side. Steve smiled at the sight and plunged his sword into the nearest man. As the horse left the square it was replaced by at least two platoons of garrison soldiers who ran in and stopped to form up. They carried swords, spears, and crossbows. They eyed the train, and a leader stepped in front and brandished a sabre. He drew breath to give an order and then hesitated when he saw the Colonel between his men and the Baron's army.

"Retreat!" ordered Steve and then signalled his crew to clear the way. He drove his horse forward and swung clear of the saddle to land beside the Baron. He grabbed him by the waist and hoisted him off the ground. Grunting with the strain, he forced him up into his saddle. The Baron rolled his eyes wildly and locked onto Steve's. The sclera of his eyes was bright white and wide. He gaped to draw breath.

Steve grunted. "No time, Lord Windthrop, get your ass and your men out of the city."

The Baron shook his head.

"Retreat! Now! You will be wiped out in the city." Steve hesitated and then decided. "My crew will stay and hide. We'll strike from within. When the gates open, you attack, understand?"

The Baron hesitated and then nodded once. Steve released his saddlebags from the saddle and grabbed his bow and quiver. "Get out of Jergen as quickly as you can and camp out of bow range." He slapped the horse on the ass and it bolted back down the road after the Baron's fleeing army. He heard the Baron's weak cry to retreat, and the train turned as one and rode and ran back the way they had come in. *Figures they can manage a retreat rather than a rout.* Steve could see they had abandoned the carts and wagons on the streets. *Nothing to be done about that.*

Steve turned to appraise his crew. They were all standing over slain garrison soldiers and holding their personal weapons and saddle bags. His crew and the garrison seemed frozen for a moment in time. Steve gave the signal and his crew smiled and melted into side streets and alleys. He glanced once at the Colonel now getting to his feet but still labouring to breathe. Steve gave a mock salute and sprinted down a side street and into an alley. In moments, the crew had disappeared.

The men in the square shouted out in alarm and ran forward and spread out to search the nearby streets. The Colonel drew a staggered breath and began barking out orders. He ordered an attack on the retreating army of the Baron and coordinated a street-by-street sweep for Steve's crew. Minutes went by then hours. Steve and the crew harried the attackers on the Baron and suppressed their ability to engage. When night fell, the garrison was ordered back to the barracks and debriefed by the majors. Two dozen of the garrison were missing and presumed dead. Curfew was imposed, and martial law declared. Colonel Masters was not pleased and was observed by many yelling in public at his officers and staff sergeants.

Citizens hid in their homes and watched through curtained windows as the garrison patrolled the city streets. The enemy then joined with the garrison, shocking the city. The leader of these strange clad men had been met with the Colonel and they had clasped forearms in friendship. The gentry and merchants were in turmoil: Jergen had been invaded by a foreign army and then been embraced by the Colonel. The citizens of Jergen eyed one another and hid to weather the storm.

The citizens took heart seeing the flagship of the Navy had escaped the oil and fire attack and limp out of the harbour to stand guard at the bay's entrance. Her scarlet sails were a beacon of hope for the city. Her longboats ploughed the harbour waters recovering sailors who had leapt to safety in the water and helping those who were badly burned. All eyes were on the dark ships decimated on the docks with bodies strewn about like discarded husks. Four of the ships had floundered and lay fully on their sides in the water. The other two were hard up on the jetties and would not sail again without repairs. The Navy had dealt a severe blow to the enemy, and the city was thankful.

Outside the walls, the army of the Baron set up camp. Campfires were lit and the city could see the hundreds of men of the Turgany army staring at the braced gates and they wondered how they would get through to take the city back. Fighting on the streets continued throughout the night and garrison soldiers were found with their throats cut and with eyes looking unfocused to the night sky.

Every citizen understood one thing looking as the ship-of-the-line in the harbour mouth went to anchor for the night and the army camped outside the main gate settled in: whoever this invading army was they were stranded here. They were not leaving any time soon.

Colonel Masters stood in front of the large bay window in his office overlooking the harbour and watched the clean-up of the harbour jetties. To his right, pinned to the wall, was a scaled map of the city he had just left examining. He had placed markers with flags on areas cleared by his men. They couldn't find Steve's crew anywhere in the city. Reports of his patrols being ambushed continued to arrive at his desk. His men now searched in half-squads of eight and that seemed to have lessened the attacks. His men were being hunted in the streets by this band of highwaymen. *Like a flea you can't seem to find,* he growled. *It keeps biting and biting.*

The Colonel had heard rumours of a band of highwaymen working under the graces of the Baron of Turgany before he was posted to Jergen. Several officers in the wardroom at Munsten had talked about events from years ago. Their leader had been cunning and frequented with a fighter woman with only one arm. Seeing Steve Comlin outside the gate with a woman with one arm had confirmed those rumours. He had requested all paperwork on the subject and was still waiting for archives to produce anything. Steve Comlin was good. He could admit that. Estimates placed about fifty of his crew loose in the city. Hidden like rats. The garrison was searching door-to-door and making little progress in a city the size of Jergen. *It will take weeks, and weeks I do not have.*

He was furious Lord Windthrop's illegal army had escaped unbloodied and worse; the Baron was not behind bars. The Lord Protector had been adamant the Baron be arrested and brought to Munsten for a public execution. Now the Baron sat camped just outside bow range and showed no sign of moving. *Not my problem though,* he thought. *It's that foreigner that will have to march out and deal with him provided he still has the men for it.* Down below in the harbour, he watched as a sand coloured body was tossed high into the back of a cart with dozens of others.

This is a right mess, he thought. The timing of events had been atrocious. The Baron had arrived just as the Easterners had sailed in. *Damn the Admiral and his luck at catching them at sea!* The flagship still sat at the entrance to his harbour. He could see it now strutting back and forth at the bay entrance. His infamous powder guns had decimated Hassim's men. The losses to y-Mushir's men were staggering, and he felt a twinge of doubt the plan would survive. He cursed to himself instead. *I had only to arrest that buffoon of a Baron and then welcome the Easterners. But it all fell apart. It was to be so simple and now...* He clenched his fist and struck his thigh, using the pain to focus on the tasks before him.

A soft knock on his door turned him back to his desk. He sat and composed his face. *I have to appear stronger than I feel to these foreigners.* The President had assured him that all would be well, provided he remained respectful. He had briefly met the foreigners at the docks and then led them to the barracks and left them to settle. He had more pressing issues with Steve Comlin loose in the city. Now, he was formally meeting the second-in-command and he was worried despite the assurances of the President.

"They are not invaders," Healy had said all those months ago. "They are assisting in the establishment of my rightful rule and by joining us they assure fair and equitable trade for generations. This is a business transaction, nothing more."

The Colonel shook his head to clear past doubts. He was beyond that now. "Enter," he said simply, and his door was pushed open by his batman. Colonel Masters stood when y-Mushir Hassim strolled in to his office looking to the left and right and ignoring him. Colonel Masters clenched his teeth at the slight. Hassim was over six feet tall and sported a trim beard shot with grey and gleaming with oils. His eyes were the colour of flint and piercing. Hassim had a nasty cut high across his left cheekbone, but otherwise, he appeared hale. He was soon flanked by two of his men of equal height. They wore the strange clothing of their land. Beige robes held tight to their forms with leather bindings. No markings were visible, but they looked like uniforms. Gleaming exposed scimitars hung from their waists. Daggers were strapped to their calves. The men standing next to Hassim stared intently at the Colonel and he felt a small bead of sweat trickle down the small of his back.

A small, balding man with a sparse beard, and wearing a loose-spun and dirty robe, stepped out from behind Hassim and looked to the floor grasping his two hands in front of him. The robe was too large for his frame and he looked like he had been beaten. Bruises surrounded his head, and a dried line of blood had escaped his left ear.

Colonel Masters held out a hand. Hassim merely stared at it, until embarrassed, the Colonel lowered it. "Sir, welcome to Belkin and the city of Jergen."

Hassim grunted and reached out to the small man and grabbed him by the back of the neck and dragged him close beside him. He said something quick and unintelligible to the man. The man looked up and said something in return. Hassim responded, and the man looked up to the Colonel.

"y-Mushir Hassim say thank you for welcome. He charge. Make men come together," mumbled the man.

The Colonel could barely make out the words for the accent. "I don't understand. What do you mean?"

The man flinched and repeated the same line. The Colonel shook his head, still unclear. Hassim looked from the man to the Colonel and then struck the man hard on the back of the head. The man cried out and exclaimed something in his language and cowered. Hassim barked something else, and the man looked up at the Colonel, pleading with his eyes for him to understand. "y-Mushir Hassim say get men together."

The Colonel blinked in confusion and then understood. "He wants my men gathered?"

The man looked relieved and then nodded once.

Colonel Masters frowned and studied Hassim. The man sweated arrogance. He stood in his office with his arms folded across his chest and staring at the Colonel like he was beneath him. The President had said to be respectful, but he struggled to keep to that advice. He glared back at the man. "Tell e-Mush Hassum first I need to know how many of his men survived."

The man looked fearful and said nothing. The Colonel repeated what he had said and pointed at Hassim. The men alongside Hassim placed their hands on the handles of their swords and growled. Colonel Masters raised one eyebrow at them and then barked at the small man. "Tell him!"

The man turned to Hassim and took a small step backwards and away. He spoke quietly. Hassim stood with his arms folded and said nothing. He glared at the Colonel and then looked thoughtful for a moment. The Colonel noticed that Hassim's men still had their hands on their swords. He thought to call out to his men waiting outside but dismissed the idea. *Things would escalate too quickly.*

Hassim's face suddenly broke into a tight smile and he spoke quickly. The little man seemed to sink in relief and turned to the Colonel. "He say enough." Hassim barked a quick laugh.

The Colonel raised an eyebrow in disbelief. He had ordered the bodies counted as they were pulled out of the harbour. The Admiral of the Fleet had decimated the foreigners. He had lost at least half of his men. "Bullshit. How many?" he repeated to the man.

The man translated and Hassim smiled broader and showed his teeth and said something in reply. "y-Mushir Hassim say count self. Gather."

Frustrated, the Colonel glared at Hassim for a moment and then called out to his batman without breaking eye contact. The man stuck his head in the doorway.

"Sir?"

"Order a full parade. Thirty minutes past sunrise tomorrow."

The translator whispered to Hassim. Hassim grinned and then walked around the desk and brushed past the Colonel to look out the window. Colonel Masters watched him. Hassim then moved over to the map and stared at it for a moment. He picked a paperweight off the desk, looked at it, and then tossed it back down. He laughed once and strolled out of the office. His two men followed in his wake. The Colonel sat heavily and leaned back in his chair. That could have gone better. *What did he mean by 'he charge'? Surely, he doesn't think he's in charge? That would be preposterous. They're allies, not invaders*

In a moment, his batman poked his head in the office door and announced his two senior officers wished to see him to report on the search. He nodded and put his paperweight back in place. Colonel Masters swivelled his chair to look out the window once more. *My entire career has led to this point. A little decision here and there and now I am deep into this. I feel the traitor and I probably am.* He heard a throat clear, and he turned to his two majors, at attention and saluting in front of his desk.

"Report," he ordered.

Twelve

Munsten - Reviewing Pavilion - June 901 A.C.

PRESIDENT HEALY ROSE from his chair and yelled out for silence. He called out twice more before the Chamber of Representatives, and the three Councils quietened and returned to their seats. They were all seated looking out toward the sea in the reviewing pavilion. It was here that the King had received sail-pasts from his Navy and returned his salute. The massive pavilion thrust out over the harbour with a central dais raised to give the harbour an unobstructed view for the reviewing King and Admiral of the Fleet. Healy had rarely used the pavilion but enjoyed it now. He had Kamal Sherwami seated next to him and the Councils placed directly below him in seats placed to either side of the dais. The representatives were arrayed out by the railing with awnings providing shelter from the noonday sun. A stiff breeze blew in from the water, but the skies were blue and cloudless. It was a gorgeous summer day.

A small group of minstrels played quietly behind them, and servants circled and manoeuvred through the gathering with silver trays laden with meats, drink, and sweets. The wine was flowing, and the alcohol was allowing cooler heads to become more vocal. The announcement that allies to the Realm were about to arrive at Munsten and Jergen had taken the representatives by some surprise and despite their better judgement to not contradict Healy openly they had talked amongst themselves. Healy scowled inwardly. *The idiots knew the ships were coming but now that they are arriving suddenly they feel the need to squawk like the gulls turning about on the wind. Time to be done with the lot of them. Once Mushir enforces my rule, I will revert this republic back to a monarchy and take the throne.*

Kamal coughed politely into a hand and pointed toward the island chain sitting just off the harbour. "Which direction did you say?" he inquired politely.

Healy chewed his inner cheek for a moment. Kamal knew exactly where the ships would appear. A few of the council members tried to hide it but they were waiting for his response and so he pointed with his goblet toward the larger island to their right. "They should appear just to the right of that large island there. Coats Island."

"How soon?"

Healy growled in annoyance and then stopped himself. Kamal could be touchy. He forced a fake smile to his lips and took a sip of wine. He swallowed and beckoned a servant forward with a tray full of little lemon tarts covered in toasted meringue. He grabbed one and stuffed it fully into his mouth. "Mmm," he exclaimed once he swallowed. "Delicious." He patted his lips with a silk napkin. "My dear Kamal, they will be here when they get here. Today is the day Mushir Adham said he would arrive when the sun is at its zenith. Soon, I would wager, soon he will be sighted."

As soon as the words left his mouth, he spotted the first glimpse of a ship breaking free of the edge of Coats Island. He laughed at the timing and stood and pointed. "There!" he exclaimed. His audience followed his finger, and many spotted the ship right away and helped others find it. Soon other ships could be seen trailing behind the first.

Healy turned to Kamal and found him smiling. "You knew, didn't you?"

Kamal nodded and drank his wine. "Of course! Of course! Mushir will be here within an hour. The wind brings them quickly. Is all prepared?"

Healy twisted in his seat and found General Gillespie standing behind him. He beckoned him over. Gillespie hurried over and leaned in. Healy spoke quietly. "All is in order I trust, General?"

"Yes, sir. The Army is gathered down by the docks to receive our allies and escort them to the barracks. Translators are divided up amongst the platoons. We'll merge the Army with these others. It will be as you directed."

"Excellent, and the Navy?"

"The Fleet Admiral sailed with two frigates and a barque a week ago. Word is he received a message from Turgany and took off at once. He left two ships guarding Portsmouth."

"And the rest of the Navy?"

"Tied up alongside in Portsmouth. Doing whatever the Navy does. They won't sail with the Admiral's ships blocking the harbour."

"Too convenient. I'm afraid we might have lost the Navy support."

"Humph, well, it's not that they added too much to our need."

Healy leaned back to get a good look at Gillespie. "Are you that stupid, or are you simply trying to be funny?"

Gillespie had the common sense to look confused. "Sir?"

"Without the Navy, we are landlocked. The Realm is nothing more than a large island. The Navy ensures our shores are safe and trade continues. This is not good, Gillespie. For now, I can ignore our Admiral, but in time he must meet the same fate as Frederick."

"T'would be my pleasure, sir."

"No doubt. See to the arrival. Make it smooth and problem free. Mushir Adham will be a touchy guest here. I suggest you treat him with the most respect you can muster."

"Aye, sir. Will do. Is there anything else?"

"Yes, I want Brent Bairstow executed at dawn. I plan to invite our guests to witness. It should make for a grand start to our relationship."

Gillespie grinned. "Aye, sir. At dawn."

"Dismissed," ordered Healy and Gillespie saluted, turned about and marched quickly away. Healy watched the man leave and then rotated around to find Kamal smiling at him. "That man is an ass. Again, why did you want him?" he whispered to him.

"He amuses me. Chaos is such a wonderful tool, and that man causes so much of it. He does nothing right. He tries so hard and continues to fail. It's quite funny," whispered back Kamal.

Healy glared at Kamal. "Not really. Too much rides on so little. I want this army merged with mine. Together we'll control the land and wipe out all resistance. These demons for example. I thought them gone already."

Kamal's face grew dark. "No, not gone. Like an infestation of lice, you miss one and they come back stronger than ever. They live. This army will wipe them out. And soon."

As they were speaking a cry of alarm was heard on the far-left side of the pavilion area. Healy lifted his head to get a better look and saw that the councillors were eyeing a strange woman who walked slowly along the front of the seated members. Kamal snapped his head toward the woman and stood up.

The woman ignored everyone and walked toward Kamal. Her eyes roamed and didn't seem to focus on Kamal. Healy looked her over and didn't like what he saw. He gestured to his guards nearby, and they strode forward drawing their swords. The woman ignored them and stopped in front of the dais looking up.

"I cannot see you. Just an emptiness where life should be," she said to Kamal. "Why do you come here? What need have you of this land? You have so much already. When will it be enough?"

Kamal hissed. "When I say it is enough. You know my purpose. Why must you fight me?"

"Your purpose is in error. You know this. It has been explained. Leave. This is all that is left. It must be protected."

"My task is almost complete."

"Your task is in error."

"Enough, if you won't leave I will," Kamal whirled and left the dais and disappeared into the back hallways of the castle.

Healy watched him go and turned back to the woman. He was amazed Kamal had fled like that. *What is there about this woman that would cause him to flee?* He studied the woman and couldn't quite determine what she wore. *A robe, certainly.* It was hard to describe, and he struggled to grasp what he was seeing.

The woman stared intently back at him and made no sounds. The council members had cleared an area around her and watched in confusion. Some laughed openly at her and others scowled. Healy felt something around this woman. *A sense of disquiet. Guilt perhaps.* The guards arrived and stood on either side of her and reached out to her. "Leave her a moment," he ordered, and the guards stepped back a pace. "Who are you?"

"Gaea."

"Who?"

"Mother Earth is what the draoi call me."

"Mother...? Are you serious?" Healy laughed. "You? A simple woman?"

"There is nothing simple about me, John Healy. I have watched you for years now. Watched your thirst for power and avarice for gold consume you."

Healy took a closer look at the woman. Her face looked almost familiar and while he watched it morphed and changed. Suddenly Belle Arbor was looking back at him. Healy cried out and lurched back out of his chair and away from her. The guards reacted quickly and reached forward and grabbed the woman. They held her firm by the arms and looked up to Healy for orders.

"It can't be you," he said with a hiss.

"Belle Arbor? My Cill Darae you chased out of Munsten so many years ago? I am her and she is me. But I am not her. I am Gaea. Did you know the Archbishop had tried to kill you that night? It was Belle who stopped him on my orders. She saved your life."

"What are you talking about? She led the coup. She tried to take my life."

"You need to listen better, John Healy. I tell you: she saved your life and protected you from an attack by the Church. You blamed her and allowed the Archbishop to take power and wipe out my draoi."

"They were demons!"

"Demons? No, never that. I would give that title to the members of the Sect of the Church. Do you believe in God, John Healy?"

Healy looked around quickly at the council members listening in. To admit to believing in the Church was suicide. Word would get out and he would be hard-pressed to keep control. He shook his head. "Never. I am merely their head for now. I follow the Word. Now leave. Guards, escort her out of the city."

The guards pulled the woman away. Healy was relieved she went willingly. As the guards walked her to the exit from the pavilion, the woman turned her head back to Healy. "Pity you don't believe in something. Here's something you should believe: you are a puppet to him," she said.

"Wait," he ordered, and the guards stopped and looked back to him. "What do you mean? A puppet to who?"

"Erebus. The man you think is Kamal. He is not a man. He is Erebus. He uses you. He uses everyone. Whispers promises. Sees weakness and exploits it. It is what he is and what he does. You think to gain more power and more wealth. You believe him because you want to. But, in the end, you will be dead along with everyone else in Belkin."

Healy felt his face grow hot, and he gripped the back of a chair to steady himself. "Why should I believe you?"

"Time is short. Talk with Brent Bairstow. He will explain if you will listen."

Healy stared at this woman who wore the face of Belle Arbor and repeated the conversation over again in his head. "What task did you speak to Kamal about? Explain."

The woman looked sad. "An old task. Older than you can imagine. He will purge the world."

"Purge the world? Purge it of what?"

"Life."

"Why should he want that? Men crave power and money. Not the death of all. Nothing is to be gained by that."

"He is not a man, John Healy, you know that. Speak to Brent Bairstow.

Perhaps his answers will resonate better from a man who believes in an almighty being rather than a simple being such as I."

"Simple? You are nothing of the sort..." Healy cried out as the woman vanished in front of him. The guards yelled in fright and turned to search for the woman, but she was gone. The council members stood nearby with frightened faces and hands over their mouths. Healy composed himself and stepped back.

He looked toward Coats Island and saw that the ships were halfway to the port. They were making excellent time. Soon the army from the Eastern land would merge with his own and sweep across the Realm and put order back. He noticed the council members had yet to return to their seats, and he allowed his anger to replace his troubled thoughts.

"Music! Continue! My council, please return to your seats. Trickery seems to be that crazy woman's skill! Now sit, talk and enjoy the fine foods. Our allies soon arrive and a new greater age descends upon us! Today we witness history in the making and you are all a part of that! Eat, drink, laugh! Please!"

There was a moment of stillness and then the musicians started up a clumsy tune and then grew stronger and more confident. As the music surged, the council members seemed to relax and smiled weakly to one another and reached for their wine goblets.

Healy returned to his seat and sat heavily into it and then gulped down his wine. He saw that several council members notice and look worried. *Let them. I care not.* He shook his head to clear it. *Erebus? Speak to Brent Bairstow? I've only a few hours left before that will be impossible.* John Healy forced a chuckle and the members closest to him relaxed on hearing it. *Who is this Erebus?*

As the ships docked in the harbour, Healy was already there waiting. As they came ashore, Healy welcomed Mushir Adham with a large crowd gathered to watch. It was a quick affair. They clasped hands and publicly agreed to the alliance between the lands in front of the Judicial, Military and Privy Council members. Smiles were passed all around. The crowd cheered.

Healy made introductions. "Mushir Adham, I present the General of the Republic Sean Gillespie. He will see to your men and make sure you are accommodated. He will work with you to determine how to best work together. We can meet in the morrow to discuss further details. I imagine after the long sea voyage you will wish to refresh yourself."

Adham looked to Kamal. Kamal spoke rapidly in a strange language and Adham nodded and replied. Kamal turned to Healy. "Mushir Adham thanks you for your generous hospitality. Despite feeling the cold of this land, he is eager to begin working with your army and fighting the demons. He agrees to meet on the morrow at your convenience."

Healy smiled. "Please invite Adham to a public execution tomorrow morning at dawn. We are executing a leader of the rebellion. One of the men who worked closely with the demons."

Kamal relayed the information. "Mushir Adham says it will be his pleasure and accepts."

Healy beamed a smile and thanked Adham. He turned to Gillespie. "See to it, General. And on our best behaviour. I do not want reports of fighting. Keep our people polite. Bring him around tomorrow."

"Aye, sir," replied Gillespie. He beckoned with his hand and led Adham away and over to where his officers were discussing logistics with his. Translators were talking quickly, and Healy could see the frustration between the two groups already. In the background, wooden cranes were already raising large black horses from the cargo holds of the ships. The horses kicked their legs and *cac* and piss rained down on the stevedores. It was a noisy place to be and Healy was eager to be gone.

Healy turned to Kamal. "He called you *sah-heeb*. What is that word?"

"It is nothing, a word of respect. Come, we should retire."

Healy smiled and waved to the gathered crowd and excused himself. Kamal walked beside him, and they made their way back up to Healy's private chambers with a guard escort.

As soon as they entered, Healy went to the liquor cabinet and filled a tumbler with a large amount of his finest aged Cala whiskey. He gulped down half and then sat in his large leather couch. Kamal stood by the window and watched him with amusement on his face.

Healy scowled and pointed at the space on the couch. "Sit. I want to talk."

"Of course," Kamal walked over and sat on the couch as directed. He watched Healy take another gulp and grimace as he swallowed. "What do you wish to talk about?"

"What happened out there?"

"Out where?"

Healy slammed the empty glass down on the low table in front of the couch. "Don't play games! Answer me!"

Kamal leaned back on the couch and crossed his legs. "Ah, you mean Gaea?"

"Gaea? You know her? What is she? What was that?"

"An unexpected visit. We rarely meet in public like that. Normally we dance from a distance. Never in person. That's the second time in over two thousand years. I admit she unnerved me."

"Two thous—? What are you talking about?"

"Dear John, you are involved in something so much larger than you can hope to imagine."

"She called you Erebus. Who is Erebus?"

"I am Erebus. Not a name I chose, but it was given to me a long time ago. I admit I like it now. It has grown on me."

"Who are you? Kamal or Erebus?"

"I am both. But mostly I am Erebus."

"What?"

"Haha! Yes, exactly. A what. I am Erebus. But it does not matter. What matters is what you and I are doing. We are unifying two lands. Together we will fight the demons. They are very real. You have seen their power. Gaea is their leader. She controls them. Gives them her power. It is she we must defeat. We start by wiping her demons from the world. She can only influence the world through her bond with her demons. It is a constraint she operates under. A constraint she willingly accepted. I am not so constrained."

"Constrained? You speak in riddles. What am I involved in here? I don't understand. Speak clearly!"

Kamal sighed and uncrossed his legs. He rose and brought the decanter of whiskey over to the table and refilled Healy's glass. "Don't take this the wrong way, but I have no intention of explaining myself. Be at peace. You will get what you desire. Power. Wealth. Is that not enough?"

"She says you lie. Dangles gifts but you don't deliver. How am I to believe you?"

"How can you not? You are too far down this path with me and Adham. You've taken one small step for man."

"Small step?"

"Excuse me, an expression from a long time ago. Trust me, John Healy." Kamal picked up the glass and placed it in Healy's hand. "Drink."

Healy glared defiantly at Kamal, fury on his face. Kamal reached out and placed a hand on Healy's forehead. "Sleep," he said and deftly took the glass from Healy's relaxed hand as he slumped back into the couch asleep.

Thirteen

Jergen - Parade Grounds - June 901 A.C.

COLONEL MASTERS HEARD the drill orders being yelled outside on the parade grounds from within the vestibule. He always loved drill and the precision of it. Direct orders, never questioned, obeyed immediately and with exactly the intended outcome. Outside were the combined armies of the Realm and Cian-Oirthear. The Colonel was worried. y-Mushir Hassim was not a stable man. *I can't read him and by the Word, I can't understand him!*

He would have to deal with him. The plan had been in place for years and now that the other land was here he could scarcely believe it. His future in the Army was assured and promotion and a higher social standing were his for the taking. The army would march north and crush the enemy. The President had laid the plan out in excruciating detail to a select few. He had been fortunate to have been one of those few. He still recalled that long meeting with others in the military in Munsten. All hand selected by Healy. The man's knowledge of military matters had seemed unreal. His attention to supply details, marching times, medical care, horse care, attrition and all manner of military matters had been awe-inspiring. The President had detailed political changes that would occur over the years and that too had come unerringly correct. He had painted a picture of a bright future and they had all been enthralled and glad to be part of it. Now it was happening.

"I place my future in your hands," he muttered and rose on hearing the drill orders that marked the time when he would be required to march out and take charge of the parade.

His batman stood nearby and handed him his ceremonial sabre. The Colonel drew the sword and saluted with it and lowered it to the rest position, the blade balanced straight up with the guard of the sword resting on top of the side of his clasped hand. The scabbard hung free at his waist. It would flop about when he walked, but that was the way. Tradition demanded it, and he would never shirk from tradition. He lived for it.

He paused for a moment in the hallway, took a breath and marched out briskly to take his position in front of his parade commander. Years of drill guided his steps and the assurance that drill was drill and would never change eased the butterflies that flew across his stomach.

Steve Comlin and Franky huddled at the edge of the flat rooftop that overlooked the parade square. It had taken them hours to get into position. They were exhausted but determined. The night had been without sleep or rest with the crew moving from building to building, staying hidden, or exposed in plain sight when need be.

The crew were highly trained in how to blend in and hide. And when to strike when the opportunity presented itself. They also knew the city better than the citizens. Overnight they had executed nearly two dozen garrison soldiers. Some were questioned, and this is why Steve and Franky found themselves on the rooftop. They wanted to see this merging of the two armies. Steve didn't believe it would happen. Franky refused to leave his side and now they lay side by side. It was made easier with Franky's missing arm—there was nothing between them and Steve had his arm over her back. Franky squirmed a little closer.

"Stop that," he hissed.

Franky turned her head toward him and stuck out her tongue. Steve admired her looks for a moment. Her skin was always a deep tanned colour. Her hair was cut short, and it looked messy but on her, it brought out the heart shape of her face. She smiled at his scrutiny and his eyes were drawn to the one eye-tooth that stuck out a little. He liked that little tooth for some reason. He leaned in and gave her a quick kiss and her smile grew broader under his lips.

"Pay attention now," he breathed. "We're too exposed here. The Colonel should have posted rooftop guards. They never look up. Never see us leaping from roof to roof. Idiots. But you never know. At some point, someone will get smart."

"Perhaps, my lover. Perhaps." Franky peered out at the square through the mesh woodwork. The owner of the building had built a small patio on the roof with a little garden. It had a wooden trellis and a wall built up to protect the roof from the onshore gales. The chances of someone spotting them from the parade square was remote, and they felt safe and secure with the square over two hundred yards away. Their escape route was already worked out.

Franky spotted the Colonel emerging from the main building and stride with authority over to stand in front of the parade commander. "There he is, the traitor," she said, and Steve nodded.

Swords flashed in the morning light as they saluted. The parade commander strode to the side and barked more orders. Parade captains saluted, and the Colonel returned it. The entire garrison, minus those who patrolled the streets looking for Steve's crew, were formed up in perfect squares of platoons. There were about three hundred men on parade. Next to them and gathered in a gaggle were the soldiers of the foreign army. They were watching everything and talking openly to one another. Steve counted them and figured they numbered about one hundred in strength. They had lost two hundred to the Navy ships according to what they could determine. A significant blow and one Steve would reward the Admiral with at least one fine bottle of malt spirit from the city of Cala.

For a time, all was quiet. Steve shook his head at the pomp. The Colonel had men being killed in the streets and here he was on parade. *Priorities*, he thought, *are skewed.* He watched the Colonel step forward and bark orders. The parade went to a position of rest and then back to attention. The Colonel turned and raised a hand to the foreign army commander. Steve had been unable to determine his name. The man was imposing. He was at least a head taller than the Colonel. He wore a strange garb that wrapped tight against his body. What Steve noticed most was the large curved blade at his waist. He had heard of these scimitars but had never seen one. The grip seemed small on the blade. *It almost looks fragile*, he mused.

The man strode forward and stopped in front of the Colonel. He drew his scimitar and held it loose at his hip. The Colonel lifted his sword up to his face to salute and then swept it down and away from his body. It was a perfectly executed salute and gave honour to the foreign commander. In a blur of motion, the foreign commander lifted his scimitar up high and swept it out and across. It took the Colonel at the neck and effortlessly separated his head from his body. The head rolled off the neck and landed behind the Colonel at his heels. His body collapsed straight down and blood fountained high in the air.

Everything was still for the briefest of time before the foreign army drew their swords and turned on the garrison. With only ceremonial swords, the air was soon filled with screams and shouts. Franky squeezed Steve's hand and murmured something. They watched the foreign army dance as they fought. They spun and leapt, scimitars flashing and swirling. Steve could barely follow the swords. Neither could the garrison. They fought back but were cut down so quick that Steve doubted he had taken more than twenty breaths. Thankfully the garrison realised their fate and threw down their weapons and surrendered. Less than two hundred and sixty remained.

"By the Word, Steve! Such treachery! Those poor men!"

Steve nodded. He watched the foreign commander issue orders and several of his men jogged out of the parade square. The commander issued more orders and then pointed up to the rooftops of the nearest buildings. Others rounded up the garrison survivors and directed them to the barracks.

"Oops, time we changed tactics, my dear," he whispered to Franky and pushed himself back from the edge of the rooftop.

"Ya think?"

Two days later Steve met with his crew. He had sixty men and women under his command and he looked at them all and knew who each one of them was. He knew what they loved and what they hated. He knew how they used their weapons and what motivated them. They were loyal to the Realm and loyal to him. If he asked, they would lay down their lives. He was proud of them.

They huddled in the main room of an abandoned warehouse along the cliffs where a hand crane once lifted goods from the pier fifty feet below them on the cliff. It was an old location but one where they had agreed to meet should anything go wrong in the city. Steve took in the serious looks on their faces. He could see fatigue, but their determination shone through.

"My friends, we find ourselves so quickly returned to our old ways, fighting for the Realm."

A few of the crew softly called out their battle cry "For the Realm!" Others smiled and smacked them.

"The garrison commander is dead. Executed by the leader of the invading army. He has taken control of the garrison and has them secured in the barracks. I'm not sure what deal has been struck but Healy has gone too far. He has invited these men into our country and they now threaten us from within. Munsten probably faces the same threat. But for now, we have Jergen to think of. The Baron sits comfortably outside the city walls. It is time to open the gatehouse and let his men flood this city and wipe out this threat. The citizens of this fine city need our strength. That's my goal. Our goal. Open the gates and wipe out this threat. Are you with me?"

All around the crew nodded their heads.

"This will be tough fighting. We have the benefit of knowing this city. I'll warn you, they fight like nothing we've seen before. Keep your distance. They have a lot of flair. A lot of movement. Look for tells before you engage. Strike hard and true and back off. This is street fighting folks. No mercy and no leniency. I want everyone back here alive for a celebratory drink. Any questions?"

One of the men in the back raised a hand. Steve pointed to him. "Dae ye think mibbie we shuid hae stayed at th' farm?"

This raised a low laugh from the crew. They looked at one another and clasped shoulders into a large hug of sorts. They were seasoned, and the farm work had put muscle mass on many of them. Steve knew they were up to the task

"Perhaps. We'll come back to that question once this is over. Franky and I counted at least a hundred of the bastards. So easy work, eh? The garrison is down to two hundred and fifty. I want to reduce damage to them if they fight us, too. We might need them in the end. So target the enemy and avoid the garrison if you can. If not, do what you have to.

"The Baron is the unknown factor. Once he's in the city, there is no telling what he will do. He's a hot head, so I think he'll drive straight for the garrison headquarters. Our job is to make that easier for him. I need two volunteers to head to the Admiral's boat in the harbour. Tell him that he could lend a hand with those black powder cannons of his.

"Lastly, I need a volunteer to go out the back door and let our good Baron know what the plan is. That person has to get that sorry lot in line and ready to run for the gate by the morrow. Who's game?"

Franky raised her hand, and many nodded at the choice. Franky had a way with the Baron that had him listen. She was the best bet and Steve knew it.

"I'll be honest, Franky, I'll be glad to see you out of harm's way," said Steve, and many looked surprised including Franky.

"What? Have you gone soft?" she said.

"What? No. I'm worried you'll take more heads than me."

The room erupted in soft laughter.

"We've been together through good times and bad, my friends. We miss Ben and Agnes, but I think they are with us tonight. We've said this often and this time we get to do it right. For the Realm!"

"For the Realm!" returned the crew.

"Let's be about this."

Steve sent Franky out the secret postern gate on the north side of the city to inform the Baron. An hour before sunrise the crew snuck into the gatehouse and took out the foreign guards with bow shots. Sentries along the wall were taken out moments later, and the gate was soon opened wide. Steve smiled and waited. One of the crew called down that the Baron was running hard for the gate with his men. *A good start*, thought Steve.

Steve positioned himself inside the gate and called out to the Baron as he passed inside. "Lord Windthrop, over here."

The Baron jogged over, and his heavy breathing could be heard throughout the courtyard. "St-Steve. By the Word, I can't breathe. Good man. Franky explained everything. I'm going to push the army to the waterfront. Let the Admiral pound them, eh what?"

"Lovely plan, sir. I'll sweep the approaches and clear the city of patrols. The last thing we want is hostages."

The Baron looked strangely at Steve. "The least of our worries are hostages. We have an invading army in our city."

Steve nodded and then turned to talk to one of his crew who rushed up. "Words out. The army is mobilising in the city. We have to move. Have your flank push hard. Push them to the sea." The man nodded with a grin and ran to join the others.

The Baron nodded and called out to his officers to follow him and ordered the army formed up in the gate yard. The noise was far too loud for Steve's liking. He watched a moment as the army continued to pour in through the gate. Satisfied, he signalled his crew, and they disappeared down the side streets. Franky sidled up to Steve.

"Good job, Franky. Any problems?"

"Just the lump between his ears. This is not going to end well. He's all bluster with images of glory. We'll have our job cut out for us."

"Dammit, okay. You have the right flank. I have the left. Take care," Steve started to give her a light kiss, but she reached up with her one hand and pulled him in tight.

"Stay alive, or I'll kill you," she whispered and planted her mouth over his and sucked his breath from him. The kiss went on and Steve leaned into it. She let go and shoved him away. "Get to work!" she laughed and danced away into the night.

Steve stood in stunned silence and then bolted down a side street.

In thirty minutes the Baron engaged the enemy. The enemy raced down a side street to strike at the head of the Baron's line. It was coordinated, but something about it struck Steve as strange. The enemy seemed a little uncertain on the cobblestones. Their dance not as artful as he had seen before. *Perhaps the city is too strange for them, perhaps we can use this to our advantage.*

Despite this, the enemy hacked down the first men. Screams and cries filled the air. Steve directed his crew to lay down fire and arrows whistled through the early morning light and rained down on the enemy. The Baron called out orders and unbelievably he split his forces. Steve cursed and stayed with the Baron. Franky would follow the others.

The enemy engaged again, and the Baron directed the fight successfully and drove them away and high into the city heights. Lord Windthrop called out for Steve and he materialised next to him. "Sir?"

"Take your men and chase down that lot. No mercy. Wipe them clear. Understood?"

Steve hesitated.

"Is that clear?" thundered the Baron. Steve could see that bloodlust was consuming the Baron. He could only nod and order his men in pursuit. *We can't be away from the Baron for too long. We must make this quick.*

In moments, Steve had his men fanned out and searching. This enemy was on street level and not looking up. *Cities are foreign to them. We strike from up high.* He gave the signal, and they commenced a methodical clearing of the enemy. His men and women moved from rooftop to rooftop. Arrows and throwing daggers filled the night air. There was a stillness to the high city. His crew were silent and deadly. He heard screams in the night down in the lower city and near the harbour. A flash of light caught his eye, and he turned to see a whole city block ablaze. Smoke billowed black into the morning air and Steve could hear the screaming from those trapped inside.

This is going badly. Why would the enemy burn outbuildings? They gain nothing by that. Steve grimaced when he realised he knew the answer.

Steve reached the street level to recover his last thrown dagger and just as he sheathed it he heard a noise and threw himself violently to the side. The whistle of a blade crossed where his neck once was but still cut him. He rolled over and leapt to his feet. His sword was in his hand and he turned to see one of the enemy standing near him twirling his scimitar.

Steve sought his centre and looked quickly about to determine his options. He was alone. His crew had moved well ahead of him. But there was plenty of light with no real shadows. *Just me and this asshole*, he smiled.

"Hey, asshole. Go home," he taunted.

The man swirled his sword once more but this time he erupted in an elaborate dance. He leapt and turned, always with the sword circling unpredictably. Steve tried to watch it and failed. He stepped back to give him room and then leapt sideways to avoid a sudden violent thrust.

"Sneaky little bugger, aren't you?" said Steve. He ignored the sword and concentrated on the centre of mass of the man. *There*, he spotted it. The tell— the movement that gave away intent. He moved away, and the sword slashed out where he had been standing. Steve waited and kept his eye on the enemy. He spotted the tell, twisted and struck down with his sword. His blade met the bone at the elbow and neatly severed the sword arm off the enemy. The man screeched and fell to his knees holding the stub of his spurting arm with his other hand. The screech cut off when Steve took the man's head off at the shoulder.

He glanced around quickly and ran after his men.

In short order, Steve's crew cleared the enemy from the high city. He raced down toward the flames and found the Baron standing proud amongst dozens of dead. Citizens lay everywhere with the enemy amongst them. The row of buildings burned hot and acrid. Steve rushed to the side of the Baron.

"Ah, Steve, good man. You were successful?"

Steve nodded.

"Good, good. We just finished mopping up this bunch. Tough bastards. All swirly and what not. Nothing a good bow shot can't handle though, eh?"

"What happened to the people here?"

"They got in the way. Simple as that. Get between me and the enemy and that's the price. We had to burn a lot out over there." The Baron pointed with his sword toward the buildings burning brightly. A bucket brigade was formed up and trying to contain the fire.

"You started the fire?" asked Steve.

"Why yes, you have to break a few eggs, eh?"

"Eggs?"

"Yes, eggs. But no time for that. Franky is out there pushing her lot toward the harbour. I need you to push in from over at the side streets. The Admiral will see them and crush them."

Steve was furious, but the Baron was oblivious. Lord Windthrop had decimated the very people he was sworn to protect. He reached out and pushed the man back and grabbed the front of his tunic. "You killed your own people, you sick *oineach*?" he roared in the man's face. Citizens nearby looked over in fright.

The Baron looked startled. "Wh-what?"

"You just told me that you killed your own people!"

"Well, yes. I had to, don't you see? The enemy was harbouring in the building. I had to flush them out. It was the quickest means, surely you see that?"

"Are you insane!?"

The Baron frowned and reached up and forcibly pulled Steve's hand from his tunic. "Unhand me. I am your King. Now get to work. You have your orders."

Steve could see several of the Baron's men and citizens looking over at them. He shook his head and then signalled to his men. They moved out to the right flank and helped drive the enemy down to the harbour.

The Admiral was ready for them and opened fire. In moments, the main fight was over. Steve looked up at the sun and determined it had only been three hours of fighting. Franky stopped by and they talked quickly. Franky had seen what the Baron had done. They agreed to finish the job and meet up before nightfall.

Hours later the Baron had full control of the city. The few enemy that remained had been flushed out and dealt with. Bodies were piled high in the city common and carts were lined up to carry them clear of the city to dump them into the sea. Citizens were grieving and pulling their loved ones out of the mass of bodies. Soldiers from the Baron's army were helping them as best they could. Their guilt was evident and oftentimes anger would erupt into words and skirmishes. Steve had his crew standing by to break up the fights and tension was thick in the air.

The garrison survivors had been released and sworn allegiance to the Baron. Now they patrolled the streets and manned the gates. They had thought themselves doomed and thankfully returned to their duty. All the officers but one and the senior rates had been killed in the parade square. The more seasoned had received field promotions by the Baron's officers and put in charge of cleaning up the streets.

The Baron sent a messenger asking for Steve to present himself down at the harbour and he grabbed Franky and made his way down the steep streets. As they approached, the docks they spotted the Admiral standing talking to the Baron. The mayor of Jergen was seated nearby and seemed to be overwhelmed with all the activity and destruction. A longboat was moored nearby, and sailors held it ready to depart. The Admiral was in his working uniform with his hat cocked at an angle on his head. He saw them approaching and his wild pointed beard turned up in a smile.

The Baron spotted them approaching. "Ah, Steve and Franky. I would like to introduce you to my good friend, Admiral Charles Kingsmill."

Steve shook his hand with enthusiasm. "Thank you, Admiral, for the timely cannon fire. You cut down the numbers and saved us a great deal of combat in the streets," he said and let Franky move up to shake his hand with her right hand. The Admiral smiled at her and accommodated her awkward shake.

"It was my pleasure," he replied. "I've heard from the Baron's men all about your crew here in Jergen. You've saved a great many lives. Sadly, I lost a great many sailors and two of my fastest frigates. Good men and women, all of them. They will be missed."

"You have my condolences, sir," answered Franky.

"Thank you, miss," he said and turned to the Baron. "Tell me, Andrew, how many did you lose in all this?" Steve looked askance at the familiar tone.

The Baron looked embarrassed. "I'm not sure, to tell the truth."

Steve scowled and beckoned to one of the Baron's senior officers who came over uncertain. "Major Sibbald, how many did you lose?"

The major stepped forward and looked to his Lord for forgiveness before he spoke. "Combined with the garrison we lost ninety-six men, sir. Another eighty-five are wounded. Fifteen are not expected to survive the night. The chirurgeons are tending to them now. We have set up a triage in the common."

Steve thanked the major, and the man saluted the Baron and Admiral and left. "There you have it, Admiral. The enemy was formidable. Their style is not like anything I've ever seen. I lost twelve of my men and women. These men and women were some of my most skilled in sword work. With this battle, we have information that will help—we know their fighting style. I've passed that detail over to the Baron's senior officers. They will ensure your people receive training." Franky looked strangely at Steve.

The Admiral looked long and hard at the Baron who seemed to wilt under the scrutiny. "This is serious business, Andrew. I've just received word from a courier ship that Munsten has welcomed more of the enemy. They are embedded with the Army and Guard. Our self-proclaimed president has handed the capital to the enemy."

The Baron spluttered. "President?"

"Yes, it seems our Lord Protector has declared Belkin a republic and named himself President."

"That's ludicrous!"

"That's Healy. Nothing he does should surprise anyone anymore."

Steve cleared his throat. "How is it, Admiral that you are not fighting alongside this enemy?"

The Baron went red in the face. "How Dare You!"

The Admiral laid a hand on the Baron's arm to calm him. "Relax, Andrew. It is a fair question. I have never sided with Healy. I have been a close friend of Knight General Frederick Bairstow for many, many years. He had been investigating Healy for the past little while. Not a very good secret, I'm afraid. Healy moved to arrest all those associated with the Bairstow brothers. He placed a lowly major as the head of the military. A cousin or some such nonsense. A Major Gillespie.

"I was at sea on manoeuvres when it happened. The timing was fortuitous. I've intelligent men in my Navy, sir. The ships with me chose not to return to port. I've been on manoeuvres for months now. Ha! The rest of the ships were seized alongside in Munsten. No idea about the crews or officers. I fear the worst.

"Andrew here has been kind enough to allow me to re-provision here. My fleet is just outside Portsmouth. I came here to meet with the Baron. He asked me to come, you see. We sighted the enemy ships some leagues out to sea. I sent in a small brig, the *BNS Crescent*, to see what they were about. They boarded her, killed everyone and left her to drift. I've been following them ever since. Chased them under high pursuit all the way here to Jergen. I was losing the race until this morning. That wind favoured us. Plus, I don't think the men who sailed those ships were very experienced.

"A terrible thing losing *BNS Swift* and *BNS Sure*. They were captained by two good friends of mine. Seasoned men. Losing their ships and their lives to fire... that was terrible."

The Admiral grew quiet. Steve grew annoyed at the expression on the Baron's face. He had no empathy for the man's grief. His eyes darted, and it was clear he wanted to be elsewhere.

"How many ships do you Command, sir?" asked Franky seeing Steve glaring at the Baron.

"I had five yesterday. Now only three remain. I have two barques remaining outside Portsmouth. *BNS Invincible* and *BNS Illustrious*. No cannons though. We never had time to refit those ships. Wonderful inventions these cannons. Changes sea warfare. Devastating when used properly. I trust you saw the exchange?"

Franky nodded.

The Admiral looked where her arm should be. "If I may, miss. How did you lose the arm?"

Franky looked surprised. Steve knew that no one ever openly mentioned it to her. Franky spared a glance at Steve before answering. "I lost a sword fight. Took the arm clean off above the elbow. Lost the rest up to the shoulder due to infection and what-not."

"Good for you keeping up the profession," replied the Admiral with respect in his voice. "Don't look so surprised. Sailors lose all sorts of limbs in duty to the sea. I imagine it's worse for you land lot. Nothing wrong with someone with one arm."

"Thank you, sir," murmured Franky and Steve was surprised to see some colour in her cheeks.

"What now, Andrew?" said the Admiral, turning to the Baron.

"I'm not certain. I have most of my men. I still mean to march on Munsten, but I don't think I have the strength of arms."

"Conscript the battalion. They don't care who they fight for. Give them weapons, surround them with your own men and force the march. That will bring your numbers up to about six hundred. You are next in line for the throne, right? Ha! Order them!"

Steve found himself nodding. "Great idea. You'll leave the city undefended though. I'd spend time here first. Build up the garrison with willing city folk. Train them. Then march."

The Admiral turned his attention to Steve. "Hmm. That has merit. I don't think Healy will leave Munsten anytime soon. Some risk acceptance there to sit here though. Still, the best course of action, I think. We need to strike at their centre of gravity and that's Munsten. Not many options here and I believe all roads lead to Munsten, pardon the pun. But to attack Munsten you will need strength. You don't have that, Andrew. Not sure what you plan once you get there."

"The Baron will need able officers to control the garrison conscripts. It will be a tough army to coordinate."

"Are you not going with him?" asked the Admiral raising one of his shaggy eyebrows.

"No, I most certainly am not," replied Steve.

The Baron jerked as if struck. "What? You cannot. You have an oath to me."

"Null and void as far as I am concerned. I cannot fight for a man that kills women and children in his lust to strike at an enemy. You have no honour. You broke the oath." Steve was visibly shaking with fury now that he addressed what was eating him. He forced the words out one at a time. With each word, the Baron grew redder and angrier. "I swore all those years ago to defend Belkin against those that would cause it harm. You have demonstrated today that you are not only capable but willing to do harm. I am done. I am returning to the farm. Will needs me."

Steve turned and took Franky's hand. He nodded to the Admiral. "Good day, sir. It was my pleasure."

The Admiral gave Steve an appraising look before nodding and touching his hat. "Good luck, Steve. If Andrew won't say it, I will: well done here. Jergen owes you a debt."

Steve smiled and strolled away with Franky humming happily beside him. They continued to hear the bellows from the Baron until they turned the first corner. Behind him, his crew filled in the ranks. They marched through the streets and word spread ahead of them. The streets were soon lined with the citizens of Jergen. They reached out and touched the crew as they walked past giving thanks.

"That felt good," whispered Steve.

"About time, you idiot," chastised Franky.

Fourteen

Munsten - The Dungeons - June 901 A.C.

VICAR MARTIN JORDAN waited outside the gaol cell and thanked the turnkey when he unlocked the door. The dungeon was an affront to his senses, and he fought to keep down his supper. He kept his head lowered and ignored the jeering from the adjoining cells. He carried a small bucket of water and a clean cloth. It was all he was allowed. He knew who occupied the cells on this floor and the two others above it. The castle in Munsten was talking of nothing else. The rounding up of all the former General's trusted men had been swift and brutal. Those loyal to the President were now in positions of authority within the Army and the Guard. The arrival of Mushir Adham from the strange lands to the East did not bode well for the Realm and his men were now dispersed throughout the city.

Of immediate concern to Martin was that the Church was in disarray. To add insult, Martin had been placed in a position far above his comfort levels. The President had asked him to advise him on matters of the Church and this had not gone over well with the bishops. Martin had asked that an advisor be nominated from the bishops, but the President had laughed and refused. Martin knew better than to swim against the current and had accepted and then met with the sequestered bishops. They were not happy but understood the awkward position he found himself in. They found a truce of sorts and now a vicar was to advise the President on the souls of the Realm. He prayed daily for guidance but so far God was not answering.

Now he was tasked with giving dire news to the occupant of the cell in front of him. The President thought it fitting that a man of the cloth tell one of his believers that his time was up. The President had laughed and reminded him he was one of those who had led to his capture and that he should be cautious.

The door to the cell swung inward. The turnkey stepped away and spoke to Martin. "A'm ainlie suppose tae gie ye five minutes. Bit vicar, ah will nae mynd th' time. In ye gang. Shout whin ye'r guin tae leave. He's a guid man. Pity aboot this."

Martin struggled to understand the thick brogue and then nodded and entered the cell. The door was pulled closed behind him and he heard the key turn in the lock. The turnkey called in. "Ah will juist be doon th' hall a wee bit."

He looked around the cell and noticed at once the dried blood on the floor at his feet. He heard a moan and looked toward the source on the thin pallet. Brent Bairstow was curled up on his side in the shadow holding his stomach. He was naked and covered in cuts and bruises. There wasn't a part of his exposed skin that was not sliced. Puss leaked from the wounds and his skin was an angry red. An infection had set in badly and the smell hinted at gangrene.

The man no longer controlled his bowels, and he lay in urine and excrement. The strength of it burned Martin's eyes and they watered.

Martin moved to Brent's side, careful where he placed his sandaled feet and put the bucket down beside him. He dipped the cloth in the water and started to wipe gently at the crusted blood and puss from the arm closest to him. He heard a hiss from Brent and stopped a moment before continuing.

"You are in bad shape, my son," said Martin. He saw his cloth was already soaked in blood and pus and he squeezed it out onto the floor and dipped it back in the bucket. "I've news for you."

Brent moved a little on the pallet and tilted his head to the side to peer up at him with eyes that were yellow and caked with blood and dirt. "Vicar Martin. What news?"

"News, yes, none of it good I'm afraid," he paused a moment and used a clean corner of the cloth to wipe the blood from Brent's eyes. Brent blinked and focused on him. "You are to be executed at dawn."

"And when is that?"

Martin didn't understand for a moment and then realised Brent had lost track of time. "Tomorrow morning. It is just past seven at night. Eleven hours from now."

"I see. I should probably get dressed."

Martin heard the quaver in Brent's voice. It was not fear but sickness. He was wracked with illness. "You look terrible. I think what you wear is the least of your worries."

"Depends on the audience."

"Your execution will be witnessed by all. Including the Army of Mushir Adham."

"Who?"

"The Realm has been joined by the leader and an army from the land far to the East. The castle gossip say Jergen has seen a second army join their forces."

"What are you talking about?"

"President Healy has opened the Realm to a foreign army. He says it is to secure the land from enemy forces from within. Including those loyal to your brother. And you. You've been declared a traitor. Posters are up all over the city announcing your execution."

Brent lay silent.

"He also mentioned the druids. Painted them as demons using evil magic to sway the will of man away from good and justice."

"You know that isn't true. Any of it."

"It seems your brother was investigating the President while he was the Lord Protector. Making up evidence. He was about to attempt a coup and seize control of the capital."

"Well, that much is true except he didn't make up anything. The man's a tyrant."

Martin continued to clean the wounds. His bucket of water was now red, and he felt he was painting Brent's body with it. It was a futile act, but this small act of kindness was all he had to offer. "Perhaps. It is not my place to question the authority of the man. My work lies with God."

Brent laughed softly and then winced. "Would you believe me if I told you that this was my work as well?"

Martin stopped and gazed down at Brent. "Do you pray?"

"I never stop."

"Ah, yes. Good. So do I. I pray for guidance. To be shown the way to greater salvation for all. What do you pray for?"

"Not my release, if that is what you mean. I pray for justice. I pray that God delivers to me the means to avenge the deaths that lay at that man's feet."

"Do you think that a wise use of prayer?"

"Yes, I do. God is not kind, Martin. He has never been. He is vindictive and swift in his judgement. I ask to merely be his tool."

Martin sighed. "I can find no words to that. God is loving. Not vindictive."

"We will need to disagree on that," Brent paused. "My men, how are they?"

"You mean the others in the cells? Far better than you. They have been left alone. Mostly it is a lack of food that ails them. Their spirits are shattered. It is only you that the President punishes."

"Hmm. This is the work of that new Sect leader, Kevin Balfour, not Healy. At least not directly. It is his blade that leaves my skin so. Do you think he asks for me to beg forgiveness from God?"

Martin said nothing. He had not known that the Sect leader had done this damage. The torture was evil. No man deserved this treatment.

"They ask me the same thing over and over. Where's the gold?" Brent laughed softly. "Where's the gold?"

"What gold?"

"The gold that Bill Redgrave stole from Healy after he had his wife and children killed in front of him. Bill had been investigating Healy, too."

"Gold? All this for gold?"

"Of course, what else drives the hearts of men to do the things they do? Power and wealth. Gold is power."

Martin sighed and continued to administer to the wounds.

"Any word from James?"

"I'm sorry, Brent. He was killed in Portsmouth. Drowned by Gillespie."

Brent choked back a sob and threw an arm up and over his eyes. Martin was shocked to see only the forefingers and thumbs remained on the hands. Martin saw his lips moving and leaned down to hear Brent praying. Knowing not what else to do he joined him and prayed for a swift end to the man's pain.

After a moment, Brent withdrew his arm and glared up at him. "Gillespie is twice damned. He killed my brother in front of me right here in my cell. And he has killed my best friend. I am God's sword and I will be his justice. Thank you, Martin, for your compassion. I will right these wrongs and see the Church returned to its rightful glory in the hearts of men and women. Munsten is rotten to its core. It needs someone to exorcise its demons."

For a moment, Martin could see the righteous truth in Brent's eyes. He spoke from a conviction of faith that he had searched for his entire life. He felt a surge of awe in the strength of this man. He lay broken, dying, and facing an execution in mere hours. And yet, he still held true to his beliefs. Martin envied him at that moment and then felt the crushing sense of defeat knowing this man could accomplish nothing.

"Perhaps, my son. If God wills it."

It was after midnight when Martin was called before the President. He was rushed past the President's guards outside his chambers and found himself standing before the President. He was in his cups at his table and his cheeks were flushed with wine. Remnants of his supper still lay strewn across the table and he picked absently at it. Martin looked around the room and recognised he was alone.

"You summoned me, Lord Healy?"

"President Healy."

"My apologies, President Healy."

"Of course, I did. You met with Brent. What did you speak about?"

"His execution, as you ordered."

"How'd he take it?"

"As well as can be expected. He is close to death already. He is wracked with infection. His execution will be a mercy."

Healy laughed and took a large swig of wine. He swallowed and wiped his red-stained mouth angrily with his sleeve. "Mercy? Do you think so? Perhaps. What else did you talk about?"

"Nothing, we..."

"Bullshit. You were in there for over fifteen minutes. You talked about more than his execution. What did he ask and what did he say?"

Martin fumbled mentally for a response. "He asked after his friend, James."

"Yes, yes. Captain James Dixon. Killed by Gillespie, he tells me. Drowned in Portsmouth."

"He was upset to hear the news. More so than word of his execution."

"Really? How interesting. We should have kept James alive to use against him. Gillespie was always short-sighted. Not too smart that boy."

Martin stayed silent.

"What else?"

"He told me he had been tortured by Kevin Balfour. Is this true?"

"Yes. He has information we need."

"Information?"

"Yes, about the demons. About Lord Windthrop."

"I see," said Martin. *He doesn't speak of the gold. How interesting.*

Healy grew quiet and then rose to pace the room. "How is the Church?"

Martin was caught off guard by the new direction of questions. "As I said before, I am merely a vicar. The bishops would be better..."

"I don't want to hear about the bishops. They were all complicit in the machinations of the Archbishop. I can't trust them. You, I trust. As if I could ever trust the Church. Answer my question, what is happening with the church?"

"The people are worried. They see a foreign army on our land and question what it is God has in store for them. The villages and towns have become more open to the Church and they gather to discuss what is happening. They look to you, our President, to provide guidance as the head of the Church."

"And now I am asking you for that guidance."

Martin did not respond.

Healy returned to the table and refilled his goblet and then held Martin with a long look. "Keep them in line. I need the people passive as sheep. We are on the verge of greatness in the Realm. A land away from Kings and other nonsense. A land free of druids and their evil. I started this with the former Archbishop and I mean to end it. Faith would have you agree."

"Sir, I do not think you are a man understanding of what faith is."

"I'm not. Foolishness, all of it," Healy moved away from the table and stopped by the great fireplace and stared at the cold hearth. "I wish we could return to yesterday sometimes. Simpler times when I was a mere council member. Then I recall the idiocy of the King and the terrors of his rule. He had no clue. He tore the land apart. Allowed religion to openly compete with the Word. It had no chance to survive. Then the horrors of the Revolution. The attack against me by demons. Insanity. All of it."

Martin kept his mouth closed. He had heard the alternate tale of events from Brent back in Portsmouth. It could be true that the druids had tried to protect the President from an attack from the Archbishop, but Martin could find no truth in the words. It was not possible that the Church could commit such acts.

"I'm a puppet."

Martin blinked at the words. Alcohol was letting Healy talk freely. *Was this what is meant to be the Church advisor? To hear the confessions of those in power?* Martin had no idea but nodded his head at the words. Healy was not even looking at him and paced further through the room waving his goblet.

"I've invited Mushir Adham into our land and I think I may have kicked a hornet's nest. There are powers. Powers beyond my understanding that forces my hand. We may need this God of yours in the end. I need to know I can count on you."

"Count on me?"

"Are you loyal? Are you loyal to me, Vicar Martin? I need to know you have my back. I need the people to side with me."

"I am loyal to God first, my Lord. I answer his call. I am sworn to this and to protect the souls of the people. But I will always give you honest council."

Healy stopped his pacing and turned to stare at Martin. "Not good enough. I need men loyal to me and my cause. I will burn this land to the ground if I must. There can be no weakness."

"My Lord, I am with the Church. My compass is the Tenets of Morality. I urge you to follow them, if not through faith, then through the compassion, they are intended to bestow. I tell you the people are uncertain. They are scared for their lives and livelihood. Strange armies patrol the streets and people wonder what will happen next. They look to you for guidance. The churches are crowded with people looking for answers. The Word can't provide answers to these problems. Only faith can."

Healy stared at Martin for a long time. The silence grew uncomfortable and Martin feared for his life knowing that he had perhaps said too much. Healy growled. "Get out."

Martin bowed once and fled the chambers, knees shaking.

At two in the morning, Martin found himself talking quietly with the turnkey in his small room by the entrance to the dungeons. He had spent the last few hours in the Church praying for guidance. The silence that followed his prayer had led to his thoughts wandering, and an idea had occurred to him. At first, he had dismissed the idea as insane, but it soon grew in him and took hold. His thoughts had turned again and again to Brent in the dungeon. A man guilty only of wanting to bring justice to a land that needed it. A land that he could see was hurting deeply.

Religion was rising fast in the small villages. The Word could not provide comfort to those lying huddled in their homes while armed military men walked the streets and grabbed anyone thought capable of working against the President and the Realm. The Church did not have the leadership required to keep the people calm and fear was running rampant throughout the Realm. Having Healy as head of the Church was not sitting well with anyone. The bishops in Munsten felt helpless. The loss of the Archbishop had hurt them greatly.

Martin had prayed for guidance on the Sect. Over the last few days, he had spoken to the bishops, and they had refused to discuss the Sect. Martin recognised the Church knew what atrocities had been committed in its name and still chose to suppress the information and do nothing about it. He felt betrayed. More so, Kevin Balfour was known and openly ignored as he moved freely through the castle and church. He was seen entering Healy's chambers many times, and the castle knew he had replaced Seth Farlow. He had claimed the old office of the Archbishop and would disappear for days. Martin hated the man and prayed for forgiveness for the strength of his hatred.

He thought again of Brent and knew he felt no such hatred. There was something about the man. A calm that caused Martin to seek his side as a ship might seek the safety of a cove from a storm. Brent had such open conviction of faith that Martin felt small and inadequate beside him. He spoke to the bishops about him but again they turned their backs on the subject. They were afraid: afraid to see more change, afraid to right the wrongs that piled up around them, afraid to fight for the souls of the Realm.

After all these worries, he had asked in prayer for guidance and the silence of response led him to think of something he normally would not do. Something that made him very afraid. *Is this the answer to my prayers? Is this how God responds to me?* He didn't know and instead listened to his heart and tried to push the fear away to better hear the answer. In truth, he knew there was little he could do, but he knew in his heart there was one thing he could do. Something that would assuage his heart and conscience. And perhaps allow him to return to his faith. He had so little left.

His steps had taken him to where he now sat with the troubled gaoler. Martin had seen the man routinely enter the Church to pray, and they had spoken on occasion. This was how Martin came to realise the gaoler was a man torn. He was pulled between his sense of duty and the injustice of the men and women gaoled in the cells who did not deserve their fate.

The single thought that had occurred to Martin during prayer was to convince this poor man to go against his duty and release the prisoners. The gaoler was now muttering non-stop trying to find reasons to do as he was being asked and Martin let him talk.

Martin felt sick to his stomach. His fear rose bile in his throat. His guilt threatened to overwhelm him and force him to flee. The fate of this gaoler was in his hands. Once the deed was done, the President would not be kind to the man. He was sentencing this man to death, and he knew it. So did the gaoler. *This moment in this small chamber will haunt me the rest of my life*, he thought. *Please God, forgive me.*

"Jergins, in cell four?" the gaoler said and looked up to Martin to confirm this as true and Martin, who had no idea who Jergins was merely nodded. "He haes a guidwife 'n' three wee ones. He's a God-fearing man lik' me, vicar. He's ne'er dane an ill thing in his life, he hasn't. A've known him fur years. Shared food 'n' dram wi' him. He spoke tae me o' th' hings he wanted fur his family. A better life fur thaim. He spoke o' th' Bairstows, he did. We a' did. Th' Bairstow brothers! Thay teuk care o' us. Real kind lik'. General Brent, th' younger one, him thats in th' cells now, he dane gie Jergins a gold crown once. A full crown! Fur his youngest wha teuk a sickness awfy ill. Paid fur th' chirurgeons 'n' medicines. Ne'er asked fur it back. A month's wages. Handed it ower lik' 'twas nuttin'. We a' stared at that shiny coin. Passed it round 'n' held it tae feel th' weight o' it. Whit man wha does that deserves tae be murdurred fur it? A dinnae ken, vicar. A dinnae ken whit tae dae."

Martin swallowed. "Release them, my son."

"Vicar! Ah can't dae that! Ye ken whit that means!"

"You must, your heart tells you it is the right thing to do. Doesn't it? God speaks to me in my thoughts. Tells me through my heart that these men and women are honest and God-fearing. Release them."

The man hung his head and sobbed. "Vicar, I'm nae tough enough fur that. I'm frightened! Please don't ask me tae dae this!"

"Give me the keys then. I'll do it. Just hand them over."

The man doubled over and cried for a moment and Martin lowered his head in shame. He looked up when he heard the jangling of keys. The gaoler held the keys up over his head but wouldn't look at him and stayed the way he was. His hand shook, and the keys rattled. Martin took a quiet breath and took the keys and then clasped the man's hand before he could pull it away. "God forgives you for breaking your oath to your duty. Your duty to God and the tenets come first and you are true to them, my son. If you can, flee. You needn't stay. God has demanded all he will from you."

"Ah won't leave mah post, vicar. Thanks fur yer wurds. Please, dae it quickly 'n' quietly. Mah replacement is due in two hours. Ye mist be lang gaen by then."

Martin promised and let go of the man's hand. The gaoler sat there bent over and rocked back and forth. He opened his mouth to speak again but changed his mind and hurried down the stairs to the lower level. His heart thudded hard and painful in his chest as he opened the first cell door and spoke quickly to the occupant. The woman nodded in surprise, but quickly took the keys and started working her way down the hallway unlocking the cells. The released men and women emerged blinking but silent into the hallway and gathered together and hugged and some quietly wept. Martin told them to stay quiet and rushed over to Brent's door. The woman turned the lock and pushed the door open.

"We'll need a litter. He's in bad shape and..." Martin stammered to a halt, backed away, and fell to his knees in a cry. The others sucked air in sharply and grasped one another.

Brent strode out of the cell, naked, and hale of body. The cuts on his skin were nothing but faint scars that gleamed red in the torchlight. His muscles rippled with strength and his eyes gleamed with joy. "Vicar Martin! Well done!" He strode over and pulled the man to his feet and embraced him.

The men and women in the hallway looked at one another. The former head of the Guard, naked as the day he was born, was on his feet and healthy and hugging a vicar. They could see the faint scars but could not explain the healing. They had seen him dragged to his cell and the state he had been in. "General Bairstow, sir? How are you all right?" one asked.

Brent released the dumbfounded vicar and laughed. "I'm right as rain, Corporal Kingsbury. Right as rain, thanks be to God. I need armour, a sword, and a bloody way out of this *cac* hole!"

"Where to, sir?"

"South, we join the army of the Baron of Turgany. Free and gather the rest of our men and women."

"But, sir. How will we get out of Munsten? They won't just let us leave."

"They will with the General leading us out."

"What?"

The sound of boots on the stairs leading to their floor had the released prisoners spinning toward the sound. Two men dressed in hooded dark clothes burst through the door. The nearest prisoner to the door reached out to grab the first through. The man intercepted the lunge and threw him to the floor. He looked up and saw the prisoners all standing still and watching, poised for action. The man behind him was clearly a chirurgeon, and this caused a pause. The man straightened and threw back his hood. "It appears I'm a little late to this party. Where's the wine?"

"James?" shouted an incredulous Brent, and he pushed forward through his soldiers to stand in front James. "You're supposed to be dead!"

"Exaggerations, I'm sure," said James before being engulfed in a breath-stealing embrace. "Do you know you're naked?"

Less than an hour later, General Sean Gillespie woke to the cold of a blade pressed against his throat. His eyes snapped open, and he lay as still as he could. He glanced to his right but the bitch he had been sleeping with was being held to the side with a hand over her mouth by a soldier he knew should be in cells.

He looked up and was shocked to see a healthy Brent Bairstow grinning down at him.

"Morning, Major Gillespie. Time to rise and shine. We have a full day ahead of us. Time to get dressed."

What followed for Gillespie was a nightmare. He was forced to lead the escaped hundred and fifty men and women out the side gate and into the late dark of the early morning. His orders were never questioned once by his own men and he cursed their stupidity. *How could they not sense that I am being forced out of the city by men who should be in gaol?* He promised mentally to have them drawn and quartered once he got out of this mess.

Brent did not speak to him other than to tell him what to say and when. Brent rode beside him with a drawn but hidden sword and he kept his face hidden from the sentries. On all sides, he was hemmed in by more of Brent's men and women. Escape was impossible. The threat of a sword through his heart kept him silent. He could raise the alarm, but he would die in the process. *That was not an option*, he thought with anger.

They rode through the dark until the sun rose slowly in the east. Gillespie tried on numerous occasions to get Brent to talk. How had he healed of his wounds? Where was he going? What did he hope to achieve? But Brent answered each time with a cut across his cheek and so he stopped asking. He hung his head and cursed his luck.

They crossed a couple of small bridges and in time they approached what looked like the burnt-out ruins of a mansion. Recognition flickered at the edges of Gillespie's memory. As they pulled up and stopped outside the remains of a wall and gate, he recognised where they were.

"This is Bill Redgrave's old house!" he exclaimed.

Brent grinned at him. "Yes, it is. Fancy that."

Gillespie was confused. *What did Brent want with this old place?* It had stood vacant for decades. People in the area believed the site haunted by the ghosts of Redgrave and his family and stayed clear. "There's nothing here. It's abandoned."

"Perhaps," replied Brent and told Gillespie to dismount. Brent told four of his men to accompany him and asked James, the chirurgeon Edward, and the vicar Martin to join them. Martin looked bewildered but agreed. James grinned and let Edward go before him. They walked carefully through the overgrown lawn, thick with weeds and small trees. Buried throughout the overgrowth was the charred remains of wooden beams and flooring. Rains and weather had long since removed the soot and burnt ends, but the evidence of fire damage was everywhere.

The mansion was fully collapsed. Little of what remained was recognisable as a house other than the stone and mortar foundation. Brent led the way past the house and then continued down to a small stream that ran behind the building.

James spoke quietly to Brent. "Redgrave survived this?"

Brent nodded.

"Do you mean to drown me like James?" challenged Gillespie. He hated the sound of fear in his voice but hoped to get a rise out of Brent. "Do you?"

Brent refused to take the bait, but Gillespie saw his shoulders tightened and he smiled at the small victory. "He didn't even put up a fight, he didn't. Out like a light." Edward scowled at him and Gillespie grinned back.

Brent said nothing but stopped beside a small rise next to the water's edge. He turned, and Gillespie could see the anger on his face. He smirked, but Brent ignored him.

"Gents, right there," he pointed at the rise. "You'll find a grating behind the tall grass. Pull it free, would you, please?"

Two of the men moved forward and Martin joined Brent and looked toward the rise. The other men kept their short swords at Gillespie's back and turned him to face the rise.

Gillespie was sweating now despite the cool breeze. "What is this? Eh? What are we doing at this traitor's place? It's a ruin. Wasting our time. Give me a sword and let me fight you, you bastard. Give me an honourable end."

Brent kept his eyes to the men pushing through the long grass and said a few quiet words to guide them. Vicar Martin looked from Brent to Gillespie and he could see the worry there. One of the men cried out and Gillespie heard a scraping sound followed by the squeal of rusted metal. Brent motioned for the other men to bring Gillespie up.

"Kneel here, Gillespie. I want you to see this. You two, help the others."

Gillespie fell to his knees and watched the men move forward to the rise. The grass had been pulled back and he could see a dark tunnel on the other side. One of the men crawled in and he heard a shout. Something heavy was passed back to the others and the one nearest Gillespie turned with a large leather bag in his hands. It was aged and cracked, and the man held it carefully but with difficulty. It was heavy.

"Cut it open, Jergins," ordered Brent.

Jergins pulled out a dagger and cut into the tough leather. He strained to hold the bag with one hand, but he forced the point into a crack and drove it in and sliced down. The sack split open and a stream of gold crowns poured out glinting brightly in the morning sun. Hundreds of gold coins rained down and spilt out onto the grass. Gillespie stared in awe, his mouth open and slack.

"Redgrave's gold," he whispered.

He felt a dagger press up against his throat and as it drew across he felt nothing but a thin fiery line. He saw his blood fountain up into the air and he reached up desperately to stop his blood from leaving his body and cried out with a gurgle. His hands were slick on his throat and he squeezed to stop the flow. Horror and fear flooded his body, and he fought to remain standing as his head grew light and dizzy. He felt his hands weaken in strength and he struggled to stay alive. He watched the ground reach up and pull him down and his eyes grew black with the last sight being that of gold coins covered in his blood.

Fifteen

Rigby Farm – mid-July 901 A.C.

S TEVE COMLIN AND his crew reached the top of the ridge that circled the valley the Rigby Farm was nestled in. The cartwheel design of the farm was clear to see from this location. The fields were bursting with crops and here and there the small figure of a druid or farmhand could be seen working the fields or tending to the livestock. Steve had passed Emily, the draoi lookout, and had noticed the smile of joy on the woman's face. He had smiled back and waved and saw Franky do the same. His crew called out to her and a sense of excitement rippled down the line.

As he looked down toward the farm, he watched the draoi turn as one to look up toward them; the farmhands following a moment later. He could see the front of the main farmhouse and spotted Will Arbor come rushing out and stop in the lane in front of the house and look, it seemed, directly at Steve. Nadine came bursting out behind Will and hugged him from behind with such force that Will was nearly knocked over. She let go, and they took each other's hands and danced a small circle for a turn.

Franky brushed her bangs away from her eyes with her hand. "It seems our arrival will be well received."

"Aye, it appears so," said Steve and inwardly breathed a sigh of relief. He had been worried about how they would be received. Their departure had not been a pleasant one. He dreaded his words with Nadine that would come. He was ready to be chastised, but he didn't look forward to it.

"He *will* forgive you, my love."

"I know that, but it's not Will I'm worried about."

"Nadine. Yes, she'll make boots with your backside."

"I doubt that will be all."

"Perhaps a nice pair of gloves? I could use a pair. One glove, anyway. Maybe two right-handed?"

Steve snorted. Since the Admiral in Jergen had openly mentioned Franky's lost arm, she seemed intent to get everyone to notice. "I know where I could stuff one of the gloves."

Franky feigned a hurt expression. "I'm wounded!"

"You haven't shut up since we left Jergen."

"I've plenty to say. Important things, too."

"So you keep saying. Franky, we need to take this slow. Will is touchy about getting involved in the Realm. We need his help and that of his people. Many will die. He has to see reason."

"If you'd been listening, you would know I agree with you. Except, I don't think this will be difficult. Will follows that ghostly-Gaea-woman. Does whatever she says. She's who we need to convince."

"And?"

"She talks to Nadine."

"And?"

"Men," sighed Franky. "Give me strength. We convince Nadine. She convinces Gaea. Gaea tells Will. Done and dusted."

Steve shook his head. "Women."

I was sitting in the kitchen with a cup of tea when Emily Cassels called out to all the draoi from her watch station up the ridge. *Steve Comlin returns!*

I sat in stunned silence and lowered my cup to the table. I reached out with my senses and felt his presence approaching. Behind him, the bright colours of his crew and horses were a sight to behold, and I held it for a moment. Upstairs I heard Nadine's feet thump on the floorboards. She was waking up from an afternoon nap. Her habits of being an old woman remained with her and I teased her about it often.

I rose from the table and rushed out to the front of the house. I looked up and spotted the crew starting down the hill to the farm. I could sense the great joy in the hearts of my draoi and farmhands. Steve and his crew were family, and they were coming home. I hoped it would be permanent but schooled my emotions to expect the worst. It might be temporary.

I thought of the Baron and reached out to *sense* him, but he was nowhere near. I frowned and wondered what had happened that would allow Steve to return. I heard the front screen door bang hard on the frame and before I could turn Nadine jumped me from behind and wrapped her legs around me and squeezed as hard as she could.

"By the Word, Nadine! Let go!"

"He's back! He's back!" she shouted and released me only to grab my hands and force me to spin around with her. Sometimes Nadine was just a little girl, and I smiled. According to her, women acting like little girls was cute and adorable. When men acted like little boys, it was annoying and pretentious. I allowed her this exceptional moment of joy and stayed quiet smiling.

When Steve had left, she had scolded him rather openly. Afterwards, she said she regretted it. She had worried she had made certain he would never return. And now here he was. Through our bond, I could sense her joy and her trepidation.

"Do you think he'll stay?" I asked as we settled down and watched the slow procession down the road. It would be half-an-hour before he arrived—we had time to chat.

"I hope so, love," she said and squeezed my hand.

I sensed Nadine call out to the draoi to gather. They should be present for the arrival of the crew. Steve's people had run this farm for years with Ben and Agnes Rigby. We often felt we took it from them. If Steve was going to stay we wanted to be certain he understood that the farm would always be theirs, too.

The beautiful thing about being draoi was that we were all interconnected. Our bonds were visible to us. Bands of colour connected us no matter where we were in the Realm. I looked at two such ribbons disappearing over the hills to the north. It followed Katherine and Dog. I sensed well-being and contentment through the bond and sent my love to them. We were fortunate. We always felt welcomed and supported. We sensed all life around us and encouraged it to thrive. We soared with the birds or burrowed with the field mice. We stalked with the cat and felt the quick pain of death of the rat. Every living thing was a force, bright in our sight, and humming with potential.

One-by-one, the draoi and farmhands entered the front lawn of the farmhouse. We stood in silence watching Steve and his crew approach. Someone had the sense to warn Dempster to prepare more food and then we waited. Charlie Mearns stepped out from the smith, scowled at the ridge at the approaching crew, cursed, and disappeared back inside. We heard the forge bellow being pumped soon after. Many smiled and there were quick hugs in anticipation. The crew was family. We may not always agree, but we were family.

Steve led the group with Franky riding beside him. Emily had sent us the numbers, and we were dismayed to learn that of the sixty of the crew who had left with Steve, twelve had not returned. I could see now they were closer to us that most carried injuries with mild infections and complications. The draoi shared looks and those with the power to heal took small steps forward, eager to administer aid. Nadine bade them wait, and we watched the crew enter and swing off their horses. They formed up in a cluster and moved forward with Steve and Franky at their front. Nadine and I stepped up and I could see a glimmer of worry in Steve's eyes.

Nadine stepped up and thrust her fists into her hips with her elbows cocked. "Well?" she demanded.

Steve took a quick look at Franky and then stepped forward. "Nadine, I owe you an apology. You told me when I came back I would owe you one and here I am. Apologising. You were right. I was wrong. Please forgive me."

Nadine stood in silence glaring at Steve. I kept my face neutral. I could sense her emotions and knew what she held back. Inside she was shouting for joy, dancing a whirlwind, and running through fields with her arms and head thrown back.

Instead, she nodded once. "Good enough. Accepted. Get your people to tend to their things. Accommodations remain unchanged. Supper's still at six."

Steve looked at Nadine and then back to me. I shrugged.

"Welcome back," I said.

"Thanks."

"You're staying this time?"

"Mean to, if you'll have us."

"The farm was always yours."

"Ah, I see. Good."

Franky blew out an exasperated blast of air. "Men! By the Word!" She whistled at the crew and made a hand signal and the crew raced out to greet the draoi and farmhands. There was hugging and crying, and a few were spun around in hugs, laughing all the while.

Steve lifted an arm toward me, thought better of it, and dropped it. Franky snorted.

"Where's the Baron?" I asked watching everyone pitching in to unpack the horses. Dempster chose that moment to stick his head out the door to the farmhouse and bellow he had sandwiches for everyone out back. He waved to Steve and disappeared back to his kitchen.

Steve smiled at the interruption and then answered me. "Lord Windthrop is still back in Jergen. He's an ass, did you know that?"

"I might have noticed."

"He'll make a terrible king. Still, we took back Jergen from an invading army."

Nadine and I exchanged a look. "An invading army? You're joking."

"No, the Lord Protector, now the President of the Republic of Belkin, invited a foreign host to help quell a rebellion in the land. He says there are demons come back from the dead who want to take over the country."

I gaped at his words. "Demons? He means the draoi, doesn't he?"

Steve nodded, and Franky wrapped her arm around his waist before speaking. "He's out for you, Will. He's brought fighters in from Cian-Oirthear. Ever heard of it?"

I shook my head, but Nadine nodded. "Yes," she said. "To the east. Gaea fought there for a long time but lost. Or so she has told me."

I was surprised. Nadine hadn't said a word about a land to the east and my angst flooded our bond. She shrugged at me. "Sorry, Will. It was never important enough to bring up. Gaea mentioned it in passing months ago. I thought it odd at the time, now I see she was letting slip details." She looked up at Franky and then scrutinised the crew. "What happened in Jergen? We count twelve less of your people. You lost so many!"

Franky and Steve's face grew grim. The crew looked to one another and we could sense the mourning. "Aye," replied Steve. "We lost a good many men and women. This army from the east fights in a weird style. Vicious and mean, the lot of them. It took us a little while to find a counter. We left our fallen in Jergen with those from the city who fell defending her streets. They honoured us. They won't be forgotten."

Nadine wiped her eyes. I felt the misery of the crew and the draoi. Friends had been lost. I felt a strong sense of responsibility envelop me. If we had been there, we could have saved lives. Nadine sensed my emotions and pulled my hand to her cheek. "Don't, love. Don't blame yourself."

"She's right, Will," said Steve. "Not your fault. The crew has fought for years together and we have lost many brothers and sisters. The blame lies at the feet of Healy. Not you."

I heard the words, but I couldn't accept them. There was blame at my feet, too. This was going to be hard to figure out. I was torn between two worlds and I wanted to be in both.

"Thanks for welcoming us back," said Steve when I didn't respond.

I raised both eyebrows at the words and then focused on him. "You belong here, Steve."

"You tried to tell me that once. I had a problem though, one I couldn't get past."

"What's that?"

"I made a vow to the Baron long ago. He held me to it. I should have explained, but there was no time. I-I..." Steve was at a loss for words.

"Uh-huh, and the anger you felt when I didn't join you?"

Steve looked to the ground. "That was real. I wanted you there to help. The power of the draoi is something to behold. We lost men and women as you know. The Baron lost many more. There will be more conflict. You could make a difference. Save lives."

I felt the words slap my doubts and anger rose within me. "You can't lay that on me, Steve. I'll remind you my draoi were not asked to join the fight. We were being forced to join. Not the same thing. The Baron had a lust for power that would see the world burn. People were always going to die."

Steve opened his mouth to say something, but Franky grunted a negative and stopped him. He sighed. "True. I see that now. Still hard to accept fully."

Franky looked from me to Steve and then shook her head. "I'm going inside once I get our horses settled. You two keep having your little discussion. It's so helpful."

Just then the front door squeaked open and Anne with her baby in her arms came strolling out both squealing; the baby, I think, from fright at seeing all the people and horses. Franky smiled and stepped up to her to embrace them both. "Anne! You are looking wonderful!"

"I'm so glad to see you alive! I worried so," said Anne, rocking her baby to quiet her.

"How's Dempster?" asked Franky, turning to the baby and making soothing sounds,

Anne winced with one side of her mouth. "Same as always."

"He's still chasing after you?"

Anne looked back at the farmhouse to make sure Dempster was still inside. "More or less."

"Poor you!" laughed Franky. "We'll catch up soon as we stable the horses and settle them down. See you inside in a little while, alright?"

Anne nodded, gave Franky another hug and skipped back up to the house, the baby stopped crying at once and we all looked at one another.

Steve looked at me and I laughed. "Same, we'll catch up at the house once you settle."

My healers stepped forward and glanced at me. "I think the draoi need to heal your people, Steve. They can sense the pain and it's driving us all a little crazy."

Steve rubbed the cut on his neck and nodded. "We were hoping you'd say that."

Two hours later, Steve and Franky settled with a sigh at the kitchen table. They had embraced Dempster and exchanged small talk before Dempster called a stop to plunk a large pitcher of sweetened cold tea on the table. A few large goblets followed and then a plate of oatmeal cookies, fresh from the oven. Steve thanked Dempster and took an admiring bite out of one of the cookies. As he chewed blissfully, Franky snatched up the remaining cookie in his hand and crammed it into her mouth laughing and spilling crumbs.

"Hey!" cried Steve and reached out to her. Franky tried to move away and fell from the edge of the bench seat to land on her behind with a shocked expression on her face. She froze a moment and then burst out laughing. It was contagious and Nadine and I soon joined in. Franky wiped a tear from her eye and sat back down on the bench. Anne poked her head in to admonish us for waking her child and that got us laughing again.

In time, we settled in and ate and drank our fill. Nadine leaned against me and I wrapped my arm around her. Franky caught Steve's eye and nodded toward us and Steve sighed and lifted up an arm. Franky grinned and snuggled in against Steve.

A comfortable silence filled the kitchen. Outside we could hear the crew yelling back and forth with the others. We could hear laughter and with my senses, I noticed an odd contentment in the farm. It wasn't just the people and animals. It was the entire farm as a whole. *Was it because I wished it so or because they made it so?* I wondered. I watched Anne walk in quietly and pull Dempster out of the kitchen to give us time alone.

Steve rubbed the end of Franky's missing arm and I noticed then just how much more together they were now. Steve seemed to have accepted her in a way I doubt she ever imagined or hoped for. She seemed softer than before, but she still wore the hard fighter image on the outside. I admired that in her. And in him for accepting the change. They were in harmony and it was beautiful.

Nadine sensed my mood and tilted her head back only to miss and kiss my jaw.

Franky saw and raised an eyebrow. "What was that for, I wonder?" she asked.

Nadine pushed herself into me a little more. "A gift for being so smart," she laughed to make light of it.

"Smart at what?"

"Figuring people out. It's easy for me. Him? Not so easy. He's too young."

I snorted and looked at Steve for support, but he was smiling at me in an odd way. "It's the harmony I see," I offered as a way of explanation. Steve looked quizzically at me. "Harmony. Different things working together for the better of each other. You and Franky have that now. I was just admiring it and Nadine caught my thoughts."

Franky furrowed her eyebrows. "What do we have?"

"Harmony," I repeated.

"It's not contagious, is it?" she asked smirking.

"I sure hope so!" roared Nadine in laughter.

We spent the next little while laughing and enjoying our company. Steve kept glancing at me and I didn't lose the intent.

"Relax, Steve. We are good you and I."

"Truly?"

"Yes, I think so. You made me very angry when you left. I'm over it now."

"Me, too," added Nadine. Steve nodded and apologised once again. Nadine stopped him. "Enough, you've explained yourself, but why you would hold yourself to a promise made so many years ago is beyond my ken. Franky should have talked you out of it."

"I didn't even try," murmured Franky. "I wanted to go."

"That's because you crave that life, my dear," said Nadine. People forgot she was much older than them and Franky frowned a little. Her words sometimes sounded strange coming from a lass of her visual youth. Steve stroked her arm stub, and she relaxed. "Don't deny it! You lived too long on the farm. You were itching for a fight and along comes Baron Stupid-Arse with a way to it. Of course, you jumped on the chance. It's in your blood. You're just like him, except Steve fights to avoid violence. You are drawn to it. For justice, same as him, but for different reasons, eh?"

Franky chewed her lip for a moment and didn't respond. In time, she nodded, and that was it. She was tough as nails and if she took offence at the truth, she hid it.

"Any word from Brent and James?" I asked. "Did you hear anything about them in Jergen?"

"No. Nothing. We never had time. There was too much going on."

"Last word we had from him was that he was heading to Munsten. He had met with the Church." I grew quiet and worried a little about Brent. I had liked him. He had stopped Seth and Erebus and I felt a debt to him. The power he had wielded all those months ago intrigued me. We had examined his amulet in detail before he had left. He had even allowed me to examine his forehead with my senses. He was a normal man with nothing extraordinary about him. We talked a little about Gaea and his God. He was convinced they were the same thing. I had felt Gaea's amusement at the concept but withheld that fact from Brent. He was consumed with his faith. He had a journey to follow and I would not be the one to seed doubt in his mind. I changed topics. "The Baron is still alive?" I asked.

Steve nodded. "Aye, when we left he was. Our Lord Andrew Windthrop showed his true colours in Jergen. He would strike down anything and anyone in his path. He was a madman. No discipline. No respect. It filtered down through his men. Unruly lot. Franky and the crew had a time of it taking them down to Jergen."

I sensed Steve's heart rate speed up a little at the words. I watched his colours swirl blue and white and spike with red. "What happened there?"

"In Jergen? That was a mess. I tried to warn the Baron to stay clear, but he would hear nothing of it. He wanted a bath at his mansion, I suppose. Dismissed my warning as if it were nothing."

Franky stirred. "It worked out in the end. Had we stayed clear, the city would have been under siege even now instead of free. We wouldn't have seen what he was capable of. Now we know."

"True," replied Steve, if a bit grudgingly. "Well, we entered the city, then the Colonel of the garrison tried to arrest the Baron. Ass of a man—now missing a head. Just as that happened a foreign army sailed into the city pursued by the Admiral, still loyal to the Realm. We took the opportunity to have the Baron hightail it out of Jergen. The crew and I merged into the city and started to chip away."

"Who were these men that attacked the city?"

"They come from the land to the east called Cian-Oirthear. The same land the Lord Protector used to establish martial law decades ago. They always were a threat to the Realm. Pushing west and ready to cross the Belkin Sea. A land of sand.

"What is disturbing is that Healy is in cahoots with them. Munsten accepted a host at the same time along with their leader, a man named Mushir Adham. Healy invited them to join the Realm to help push down the rebellion. He said he needs them to fight the demons. You. It's a stupid thing to do. It's like opening your house to a bear for lunch. They'll never leave now that they have a foothold. At least they're out of Jergen. We killed their leader—a man called Hassim. Killed with an arrow in the throat. We left Jergen with the Baron. He's bringing the garrison into his army to recover his losses. They'll train together there before heading to Munsten. That leaves us with one threat and that's the army in Munsten. The Admiral had word that they were training together and getting ready to move out into the Realm.

"I worry that we are too few. There is great unrest throughout the Realm. Rumours only but villages and towns are rebelling. The Church and the Word are competing again. It's the Revolution all over again. Many will die. That is certain. I tell you, the draoi can make a difference. Surely you see that?"

I became quiet dwelling on what he suggested. I had known not to follow the Baron to Jergen. And at the moment I felt no stirring need to head to Munsten. Nadine had the benefit of being able to talk to Gaea when she wanted. She ignored me.

I needed more information. I needed to understand better what was happening throughout the realm and until my stocs moved out to cover the land, I was blind. On an impulse, I threw out my senses and asked the draoi to assist me. They responded at once and poured their power into me. Within moments, my sensory range extended out miles and miles. I felt Nadine stiffen beside me as my mind soared following life along the route to Jergen. I kept a thread back to my body and leapt from tree to tree pushing faster and faster. I had never attempted this before but knew I could do it as soon as I started.

Nadine stumbled in her conversation at the small table before resuming. I felt her commune with Gaea and then relax after glancing at me a moment. She turned her attention to Steve. "You are asking the draoi to help you again?" asked Nadine. "Are ye daft, son?"

Steve smiled. "No, Nadine, I'm not. I'm asking for help, yes. The people of Jergen were caught in the fighting. Those horrible cannons of the Navy decimated them. Tore people apart like they were nothing. We needed healing. I lost three people who would have survived if Will and the draoi had been there. Alive now to enjoy their life. But they're gone. I can't lose more. I know I will continue to lose more until this war is over, but I'm not willing to lose them if I can do something about it."

"I hear ye, Steve Comlin. But it's not that simple. It's not pride or any other such nonsense. The draoi are of the land, not the people. Do you ken?"

"I'm trying, Nadine, you know I am. Will has no bigger supporter than I. Surely, he can understand he can help stop the suffering. You have to see that at least."

"We would heal both sides, Steve. We can't take sides. Priority goes to those worse off. People aren't too important to Gaea. It's nature that is important. People are just a small part of that."

Steve looked frustrated and gritted his teeth. Franky sat up and leaned on her one elbow on the table. She spoke softly. "I don't understand why you would hesitate. Our crew are Will's people again. Steve is bound by his oath to you. He renounced the old oath with the Baron in Jergen. Publicly, I should add. No one disputed that right, and we walked away clean. He's here now to help you! Why would you not help him? Us?"

Nadine pulled herself upright. "Will did not require an oath and never asked for one. That oath is between Steve and Will, not between Will and Steve."

"What!" cried out Franky. "How can you say that?"

"Calm, Franky, I'm not trying to cause insult," said Nadine. "The draoi can utter no oath other than the pledge they have to the land."

"So, Steve is bound, and Will is not?"

"Yes. Steve bound himself to Will. Will is bound to the land."

Franky stared at Nadine in surprise with her mouth held open. "That's nae the way it works, lass!"

"I'm not a lass and don't tell me what is what!"

"Ladies, ladies, calm yourselves!" soothed Steve. "I have no problem with my oath. I never asked Will for one and I won't."

Meanwhile, I was farther away than I had ever been—the combined power of the draoi gave me wings. I didn't fly so much as join the land farther and farther out. I could sense my body miles away and hear the conversation around the table, but my sight and senses were well south of the farm and almost at Jergen.

I spied the city and found the Baron soon enough. It took moments. I thought of him and found him amongst the bright lights of the individuals in the city. He was lounging by an indoor pool in a massive home. Lying near him was an unknown man with a pointed beard. They were drinking and eating. I looked out over the city and saw the damage down by the harbour and throughout the city. The fighting had been fierce, and I found many people with injuries. Their pain radiated out into the air in waves. I quickly checked Nadine's house on the cliff and was relieved to find Ness and her children safe and sound. The house was in better repair and the family looked well fed. The belongings of Brent and James was gone and of the two men there was no sign. They must be in Munsten and I turned my gaze to the north.

I left Jergen and headed north as fast as I could. I travelled beside a well-used road and quickly came across a large crossroad with inns and shops. I paused to look it over. It was almost a town but without organisation. Buildings were built here and there beside the roads. Inns, stores and places dark and mysterious clustered in the centre and competed for coin. Beyond the crossroad was a massive area with large open fields and flat land everywhere for miles around. I felt Gaea's interest in the area and then she was gone.

I felt a pull and raced north and saw what I was drawn to. A band of military men were riding south hard on horses. They were well north of the city of Curachan. As I came closer, I recognised Brent Bairstow and James Dixon riding up front. Beside him rode a vicar of the church, looking sore and flustered trying to remain seated on his destrier. Beside them was another man I did not know but recognised his chirurgeon robes.

Following behind were more military men and women on horseback. They looked sore, tired, and weak. Many teetered on the edge of exhaustion. Signs of abuse marked them all except Brent. He looked whole and invigorated. He drove south with abandon. He would kill them in his zeal. He couldn't see the pain he was causing but sensed the chirurgeon did. I circled his horse concerned for his followers. I had to slow him down and so I calmed the horses and asked them to stop and rest.

As one the horses obeyed, and they stopped with sides heaving and foam blowing. Brent looked confused and angry and kicked his horse's flanks and yelled. The men and women looked about in wonder and the vicar mopped his sweating brow thankful for the break.

I urged the horses toward a small stream that fed a tiny lake near the road. I watched in mirth as several of the men and women leapt from their horses and tried to get them to change direction. The horses could now smell the clear and cool water and broke into a trot leaving many behind. The soldiers still riding slid from their horses and followed on foot to the water's edge. Brent looked even more furious and tried to pull his horse's head from the water.

It was then that Brent finally took notice of his people. Many had collapsed on the ground and could move no more. Brent dismounted and ran forward calling on others to help. Finally, he stood and backed away while others stepped forward to help. He moved to his horse and looked her over. He looked around at the state of his soldiers and fell to his knees. I could see him praying and smiled. I fled farther north on the same road Brent had followed.

Munsten grew larger and a small part of me recognised the city. The waterways and bays to the east had beautiful islands dotted here and there. It spoke to me at some level. My vision swam with memories. This is where I had grown up as a young child before I had been forced to flee with my mother. The massive castle rose high up in the centre and blocked and dwarfed everything else around it. It was huge and spread out to consume a third of the city. The smoke from thousands of cooking fires gave the city a cloud-like look and I swept around to the upwind part of the city down by the harbour. I spotted the invaders right away dressed in a sand coloured cloth that wrapped around their bodies. They stood out like white daisies on a field of green. I reached out with my senses and felt... nothing. They were there but were not tied to Gaea.

I recoiled in fright. I saw those nearest me stiffen and draw their strange curved swords. They turned and looked around searching for a threat. Several citizens moved clear in fright of the sudden drawing of steel. I backed away and retreated further when one man nearest me seemed to focus right on me. I fled the harbour and flew up into the castle. My link to myself back at the farm seemed stretched thin. I could feel that my draoi were straining now, but I had to see the Lord Protector who now called himself President. By some memory, I flew where I thought he should be. I flew faster and found him in elaborate chambers. He sat at a table with two other men dressed in the same garb as the invaders, one in sand and the other in black.

As I entered the one in black rose and turned to stare straight at me. Despite how he looked I recognised him for what he was—Erebus! He stood there wrapped in illusion. As before, I sensed nothing of him. Just an emptiness compared to all the surrounding life. Through the illusion, I saw a scar across his chest where Brent had struck him with his light. The Lord Protector stood up and looked where Erebus was focused. He said something to Erebus. This was my first time seeing Healy, and he looked older than I thought he would. His hair was thinning and grey and he looked gaunt and drained. This was the man that caused so much grief to the Realm. For a brief moment, anger surged in me and I considered striking him down but resisted that urge. A strong feeling of nausea reminded me of my bond with Gaea.

I felt my thread back to the farm shudder, and I realised that I was very exposed. Erebus must have sensed it at the same time as me. He lurched forward, and I pulled back. Erebus scowled as I exited the chambers. I wasted no time and pulled hard on the strand of life that connected me back to myself on the farm. The world blurred past at blinding speed. I felt the relief and joy in the draoi as I approached. My draoi guided me and eased me back into my body. I opened my eyes to find myself laying on my back on the kitchen table. Nadine held my hand and Steve looked down at me with worry etched on his face.

"Love, love, you're back. You're back," she collapsed on me before rearing back and thumping me on my chest. "Never do that again, you hear!" admonished my wife, and she continued to bang my chest with a weak fist until she collapsed again over my body. Weakly I held her. My limbs and body felt foreign and strange.

"What did you do, Will?" asked Steve.

"I-I went travelling," I lifted my head to look at him. "I went to Jergen and saw the Baron. He is sitting fat and happy in his mansion. He doesn't appear to be heading north yet."

"It's too soon, he has to train his people. He'll be there for another few weeks. What else?"

"I saw Brent and James. They were heading to Curachan with a small band of military men and women. They were driving hard, too hard. Their armour was mismatched and their weapons in poor quality. All of them were not well and looked like escaped prisoners. Except for Brent. He looked healthier than ever."

"Interesting. Do you know why they were heading to Curachan?"

I shook my head.

"Blast it. What's he up to, I wonder? Then what?"

"I went to Munsten. I saw the enemy." I turned my eyes to Nadine. "Erebus lives. He saw me. He is advising Healy. Disguised as someone from this eastern land."

Nadine gasped and covered her mouth. "We knew it didn't we? We now know for sure."

"There's more. I found the enemy in Munsten. They are not of the land, love. They're more like Seth. The ones I saw at least, and they could sense me."

Nadine looked defeated. "Sense you? That is unfortunate."

Steve looked back and forth between us. "What does that mean?"

I looked at Steve. "They are not of the land. The power of the draoi work only on the living. Erebus and this enemy—we cannot influence them. Our powers are nothing to them."

"Is there nothing you can do?"

"Yes, there is," I looked to Nadine. "I think we need to decide, love."

Nadine nodded. We reached out to the draoi and asked them what they thought. It was unanimous.

I looked at Steve and Franky. "We come with you to the North. The enemy of the land is our enemy. We will help."

"I guess we need not convince them anymore," muttered Franky.

Steve smiled and took my hand to pull me off the table and on to my feet.

Sixteen

On the Road to Munsten - North of Jergen - August 901 A.C.

THE CARTS SLOWED Baron Andrew Windthrop's combined army down to a crawl and he was becoming more and more agitated. The mix of Jergen battalion members with his own Turgany regulars had proven difficult. Just getting the officers to agree to call themselves the Turgany Army had taken days. *How hard can it be to march on a road or swing a sword?* The Baron scowled at his newly promoted Turgany Army Commander, Colonel Robert Sibbald, as he rode up to join him. He had distinguished himself during the fighting in Jergen and the Admiral saw fit to promote him. The Admiral insisted he be absolved of his oath to Turgany in order to swear an oath to the Realm. *I shouldn't have agreed. That man could be doing more*, he thought. *Instead, he spends all his time riding up and down the line.*

The long train of soldiers, archers, cavalry, carts and horses went back beyond two miles. They had left Jergen two days ago and had only made it five miles to the north. *It was a disaster*, thought the Baron. *We'll never make Munsten at this rate.* The stops and starts had frustrated the Baron so much that he had ordered a small tent be established whenever they stopped so he could get a break from the sun. The Colonel had tried to talk him out of it but he had refused. *Serves them all right. Why can't they just keep moving? Steve would have had this lot moving by now.*

The Colonel cleared his throat, but the Baron chose to ignore him. *He needs to speak up. He'll want to talk about logistics again, and by the Word, I am sick of this. And my ass hurts on this saddle. Why must the horse rock so much?*

"Sir?" asked the Colonel in his soft, high-pitched voice. *Too high for a man to have*, thought the Baron. He hated it.

The Baron immediately thought of the Admiral. Their parting had been horrible, and he winced remembering it. He had been anxious to get on the road to claim his throne. The Admiral had urged caution and told him to listen to his officers. They had then argued and in a fit of pique, the Baron had slapped the Admiral. He had stunned himself with the act and had stood there staring at the Admiral. The last he saw of his lover was him rowing as fast as he could toward his ship-of-the-line. *I was right though, I am the head of my Army, what I say goes. This is not a democracy.*

"Sir?" probed the Colonel a little more forcefully.

The Baron gave a drawn-out sigh and turned his head toward the Colonel. "Yes, what is it this time?"

"We seem to have resolved some kinks in the formation, sir. We've sorted out the pulling horses and paired them better. We should make better time now, sir."

"You're blaming the horses?"

The Colonel opened his mouth and then closed it. The Baron raised an eyebrow at him. "Sir? No, of course not."

"It sounded exactly like that. I need this army moving faster, Colonel. Am I being clear?"

"Yes, sir, very clear. We are doing our best. The soldiers are a mix of experiences, sir. The men and women from the battalion are not used to marching like this. Garrison work is much more sedentary. Also, if I may speak freely, the garrison men and women are not always open to responding to my orders. This is causing problems."

The Baron ground his teeth. He couldn't hide his anger and he drew satisfaction seeing the glint of fear in the Colonel's eyes. "Then Colonel, I suggest you find a way to become the leader you have been promoted to. I can't say I am surprised to hear the men and women are struggling. They could barely hold their own against those invaders. Plus, women shouldn't be allowed in the army. They slow everything down."

The Colonel's face flashed with an expression that the Baron was sure was disgust and he glared at him. The Colonel mashed his lips together and said nothing for a moment. "Sir, as you say. You might be interested to know the garrison women are helping share the load off the backs of our own men. Now sir, I must go back and make sure this train stays steady. I beg your leave."

The Baron's face flushed crimson. He opened his mouth to yell at the insolence and then shut it. He thought for a moment and then smiled. "Better yet, call a halt. Have my tent set up over at that lovely meadow. We'll start moving again in an hour."

The Colonel stared back at the Baron with a blank face. The Baron could see the muscles at his jaw flex and twist and he grinned wider.

"Have I made my wishes clear, Colonel?"

"Yes, sir."

"Then carry them out."

The Colonel saluted and then yelled out for the train to halt.

Two hours later the train was moving again. The Colonel was pleased to see that it was moving at a brisker rate. His officers were moving through the garrison soldiers and correcting everything from how to wear a backpack to how to properly wear a sword when marching. He was very concerned about their future. He knew they were marching toward Munsten and would see battle against the army of the Realm. He had expressed concern with the Admiral before they had left Jergen.

"This is suicide, Admiral."

"Yes, perhaps."

"And?"

The Admiral had laughed, surprising the Colonel. "And? Why then we win, of course! What other option do we have?" The Admiral had sobered then and laid a hand on Robert's shoulder. "You're a good man, Robert. This is a shitty time to be in the military but what other options do we have? The Realm is in ruin. What you may not be hearing is that the towns and villages in the north and south are starting to rise. The same fear that struck our people during the Revolution is rising again. This time the swing is to the Church. Fear needs something to bring it back down. Across the land people are turning to the Church for answers and getting answers that will see us descend into anarchy.

"You say suicide, I say we fight to do our duty. We swore oaths to the Realm. I mean to uphold mine. It is on our shoulders that the future lives of everyday citizens depend. So, we fight. We do our best. I expect every man and woman to do his or her part.

"I understand your fear and share it. You march with a man I love but know in my heart is a fool. He will need your leadership in the end. Mark my words.

You are not his to command. Remember I tell you this: I am the senior officer in the Realm who sees the threat for what and where it is. I order you to get this band of unlikely soldiers working together.

"This is a difficult task. You will need to do this despite the Baron. Do you understand?"

Robert nodded. "I do, sir. Thank you."

The Admiral looked sad then. "You're welcome, Robert. I'll leave you with a little information that might give you hope. Steve Comlin should join you, I hope. I am certain he is off to convince a group of people that Comlin says will change the tide of this war. He's a brilliant man. Expert military man and tactician. He gives me hope. I hope he does for you, too."

Robert smiled at the news. "I liked that fellow. And his second, that one-armed woman Franky. It was his crew that turned the tide in Jergen. We would have lost many more men." Robert hesitated a moment. "And your guns, of course, sir."

"Ah, my guns. The secret will be out soon. Then everyone will have them. Frightening things. Devastating. I almost threw up when we first hit that ship. A lot of my crew did, too. It's too powerful. No honour. Still, it made a difference." The Admiral took stock of Robert. He looked him up and down. "You'll be fine, Robert. Stay strong. Hold your tongue around the Baron. He's a child and spiteful. He likes to make peoples' lives difficult."

"Thank you, sir. I appreciate the honesty and the trust."

"Cheers, Robert, safe travels."

Robert shifted his focus back to the present and directed his horse alongside Major William Crenshaw. He was the only officer to survive the garrison slaughter in the parade square. They had developed a friendship of sorts. Recently having been a major, Robert understood the role the man had to play and was counting on him to rectify some of the more difficult soldiers they had. "Morning, Bill," he said as a way of greeting. The man responded better to informal chatter.

"Robert," he replied and smiled. "Looks like another good day to be heading north, eh?"

Robert made a show of scanning the skies. "True. Not much cloud. Just blue sky."

Bill smiled and looked forward. They were in the middle of the train and up ahead it bent sharply to the left with the road. They were making good speed. Already four miles had passed since the morning late start. Bill stayed with the food carts as directed by Robert. They had the heaviest load and needed a constant eye to make sure the drivers were paying attention to the road.

Robert watched one of the horses pulling the cart next to him reach over and try to bite the horse next to him. The driver gave a quick whip, and the horse turned his head back to the road. "I want to introduce some night training."

Bill looked over at Robert in surprise. "Night training? What do you mean?"

"After the evening meal, while there is still light, I want the soldiers practising with their weapons."

"Bow, too?"

"Yes, and shield work. We need to get your garrison working seamlessly with my men. That means formations. Defensive positions. The works. We're too different."

Bill rode in silence for a long moment before he spoke again. "I understand. I'll make it happen. Leave it to me."

Robert tried to hide his surprise and Bill saw his face and chuckled a little. "Robert, Steve Comlin would have had much stronger words with me than that. At least you respect me a little. Thanks. I understand what you want and why. I'll speak with the others and make them understand. You would think we were just off for an exercise, eh? Marching up the road for a lark. I can see your concern and share it. If we're not ready, we die. Time to get ready."

Robert felt his respect for Bill rise at that moment. A stirring of hope spun round in his stomach somewhere in the middle and a knot loosened just a little and he smiled at Bill. "Good man, Bill. Thanks."

"My pleasure. Sir."

Robert's head tilted back a little at the honorific.

"Haha!" said Bill. "I respect you, Robert. I'll give you a *sir* now and then."

"Ha," chuckled Robert. "Good man. Tonight, okay? We start tonight. At this rate, we should get a good month's worth of training in. One last thing, this is your idea, alright? You and Major Tibert."

Bill looked up forward to where the Baron was likely plodding along on his wide piebald. Easily his horse was the slowest of the lot. Somewhere in that dust cloud the Baron was mopping his brow and complaining about his ass. Everyone could see he hated the Colonel and no one could figure out why. He looked at Robert and nodded. "Okay."

Two weeks later, the Turgany Army approached the Crossroads. To anyone who might have observed the soldiers leaving Jergen, they would not have recognised the troops before them now. They were cohesive and professional.

Even the Baron up front seemed to sit taller in his saddle. Colonel Sibbald was pleased with the Majors Crenshaw and Tibert. They had pulled the men and women together. Friendships amongst the soldiers had blossomed, and they had bonded. They were brothers and sisters at arms. Robert knew they were far from perfect, but they were as good as they would get. *And hopefully, that will be good enough*, he thought.

The Crossroads was a hamlet of sorts pulled together by the commerce that tracked along the two major roads that crossed the area. The northern road led to Munsten and fed the trade from the southern Turgany County and Portsmouth. The eastern road pulled in the goods from Curachan and the western road the goods from Salt Lake City and beyond.

Inns and pubs lined the roads one deep. Craftsmen sold their wares and a traveller could get any manner of trade work done; from blacksmithing to barrel repair. They would likely leave the Crossroads with women trailing behind, looking to earn coin during the evenings. His officers would turn a blind eye and allow it. Better the pleasures of life than just the prospect of a grim death. Robert shook the gloom from his thoughts and urged his horse forward to be with the Baron as they entered the area.

The Baron turned his torso toward him as he approached. "Ah, Colonel. Timely. The scouts have reported favourably?"

"Yes, my Lord. The crossroads are clear of the enemy troops. No sign."

"Good, I wish to spend two days here."

Robert had been told this three times in the past two days. "Yes, my Lord. Two days."

"Give the men... and women... time off."

"Liberty, aye, sir."

"Don't correct me."

"Sorry, sir."

'Two days."

"Yes, sir. Where will you be?" The Baron started to look angry and Robert continued. "Sir, in case we need to hurry out of the Crossroads. It would help to know your whereabouts."

"Yes, well. Ask my major. You know who."

"Tibert, sir."

"Yes, Tibert. If you need me, see Tibert, he'll find me."

Colonel Sibbald drew his horse a little closer to the Baron so he could speak quietly. "No sir, that's not how this works. I am the senior officer of this army. You will tell me where you are so I can plan accordingly. I will not report to a major." Although he kept his voice low, a few of the soldiers nearby heard the words and heard the chill in them. They grinned at one another and prodded each other to pay attention.

"Colonel Sibbald! You will speak to me with respect!"

"My Lord, I am speaking to you as the master of military matters. The time is coming when this army will face great odds. Where you are at the Crossroads must be clear with me at all times."

The Baron had turned crimson. He looked around to see if anyone had been listening and saw only a few faces turned aside. "Colonel Sibbald, you've gone too far. Your insolence and insubordination are too much!" The Baron yelled out for Major Crenshaw and yelped when his horse pulled up on the other side of him.

"My Lord, you called?"

The Baron sputtered. "Yes, I did! Congratulations, Major Crenshaw, you are now Colonel Crenshaw. Colonel Sibbald, you are no longer required. You are dismissed."

Bill looked at Robert. He shrugged in return and smiled. "Sir, thank you. Where can I find you at the Crossroads?"

"The Inn of the Spiked Wyvern."

"Thank you, sir." Bill looked over at Robert.

"Excellent, Colonel," replied Robert.

The Baron sputtered again. His cheekbones turned a deep crimson and his cheeks were spotted with broad white blotches. "You are dismissed, Colonel Sibbald!"

"Yes, sir, so you said."

"Leave!"

"I'm afraid I can't do that, sir. I was placed in charge of this Army by the Admiral. He told me the only person who can remove me from my duty is the Admiral himself. My oath is to the Realm, sir."

"That's preposterous! This is my army! Mine! If I decide to send your sorry ass packing, I will!"

"Begging your pardon, sir. Again, that's not correct. I am the head of the army that left Jergen. You agreed with the Admiral to merge our army with the garrison. The Admiral promoted me and placed me in charge and in command. You are not in authority and cannot dismiss me, sir."

The Baron erupted into a long diatribe of expletives that had the army hiding their laughter along the entire train. He finally became too winded to continue and heaved great gulps of air and wheezed.

Major Crenshaw waited until the silence stretched out and for the Baron to breathe a little easier. "Begging your pardon, sir. It wouldn't do to have two Colonels. Can I wait for my promotion until after the war before I accept?"

The next day, Colonel Sibbald and Major Crenshaw met over at the camp entrance. The army was spread out in a military square, tents arranged in order, horses off to one side, and the ablutions downwind. It was a standard military setup, and the army was adept now at setting it up and striking it down. They had positioned the camp blocking the north road out of the crossroads. They were stopping all traffic heading north from warning the city of Munsten. Scouts ranged well outside the camp to search for spies and so far, had reported seeing nothing.

The Colonel had agreed to cycle through their people for liberty and gave the task over to the junior officers to manage. A small desk was set up in a tent and a small line formed of those lucky to be next to head into the pubs for a drink or two. The sergeants were in the pubs watching the soldiers and making sure order was maintained. It was a smooth operation and Robert was impressed.

"They're looking good, Bill."

"Thank you, sir. You were right about the shield drill, by the way. I think we've corrected the surge in the centre. We should be able to hold the line solid now." Bill looked around the camp. Soldiers milled about fulfilling tasks or sitting relaxed off-duty drinking tea or water. It was orderly and made Bill proud to see. It was a combined effort, but the main effort had been his. He felt professional pride for the first time and had Robert Sibbald to thank for it.

"Are you heading into the pubs?" asked Robert.

"No, sir. I thought I would stay sober and keep an eye on a couple of the young lance corporals. They have a reputation for losing their control after long exercises. They see beer and decide to swim in it. Then they find fights or create them. I've tagged them with two of our more stable corporals to watch over them."

"Good idea, we don't want trouble here. What about the other thing?"

"Done. We're watching the Baron. Major Tibert's on him all the time. Pardon the expression."

"Hmm. Good."

"You've likely noticed by now: my soldiers and yours are as thick as thieves."

"Yes, good to see that. Nothing better than knowing the soldier beside you has your back. We're in a better place now than we once were. You and Major Tibert have everything running smoothly."

"Yes, sir. Makes me proud to see the men and women working so well together."

"You should be, Bill. It's your leadership. You've earned the right to brag about this."

Bill looked away a little embarrassed. He looked up to the Colonel. Not that long ago they were the same rank, but he could see the leader he now was, and he was a man worth following. He couldn't think of a better man to lead this army. He wasn't alone in that. The soldiers of this piecemeal army trusted him. They watched him all day long moving up and down the line never tiring. He knew most by name and could share a joke and remember a tale a soldier might risk telling him. Many were comparing him to the Bairstow brothers, and that was heavy praise. He knew Robert pretended not to hear. Bill had met Brent Bairstow a few years back at a military symposium in Munsten. The man sweated confidence. He filled a room with his presence and heads turned to follow him and ears soaked up his every word.

Just then there was a cry from someone in the camp and many pointed up to the north. Both men turned to the sound. A cloud was kicked up and drifting eastward with the winds. Bill looked to the duty officer and he could hear him already calling out orders and bringing the camp to alert. The duty watch quickly formed up and moved to the road. Shields and pikes bristled as they form a phalanx.

The soldiers in the camp quickly grabbed weapons and shields and formed up in similar phalanxes beside the first. Robert and Bill stood to the side and watched the cloud get closer. The captains in the centres of the phalanxes called out orders, and the shields braced and locked together with a solid single sound.

"What do you think, sir?" asked Bill to Robert.

"I'm not sure, it's too small a cloud to be not much more than a hundred men. That many men on horseback mean they're an army for sure but too small to be from the President. Unless he means to parley. This does not bode well, I think we are about to test out the troops."

"Yes, sir."

"Dammit, the scouts should have picked this band up."

Bill grunted.

Tension filled the air. The army knew this was no exercise. They had fought in Jergen and been bloodied but this would be the first test of their new fighting prowess. Robert felt a trickle of sweat go down his spine. The cloud grew larger and the sound of hooves thundered in the still late-summer air.

"Steady!" cried out the captain in the phalanxes.

The army as one responded with the battle cry "For the Realm!"

Ahead the approaching horses split and slowed. They spread out into two rows. In the centre, four riders continued forward at a trot. The two centre figures rode tall in the saddle and with practised ease. Behind him struggled a figure on a horse who was having difficulty with the horse at speed. To Robert, he looked like clergy. Next to him was a chirurgeon dressed in black. One of the men in front seemed to shine in the afternoon sun. He approached a massive display of military might with a calm Robert hardly expected.

The man stopped about fifty yards beyond the closest phalanx. The vicar behind him stopped as well and moped his brow with a white cloth and then waved it weakly. Robert watched the man reach over and steal the small cloth away and then wave it above his head in a slow circle.

"It can't be," murmured Robert.

"Who is that?" muttered Bill.

"He looks familiar. Come, let's go talk to him," replied Robert.

"Both of us?"

"Yes, come on. I've a good feeling about this."

They called for horses and two were brought forward with a white parley flag attached to a pole. Bill held it aloft and the white pennant fluttered brightly in the light wind. They broke the horses into a trot and closed the lead figure. As they drew closer Robert could make out the features and recognised at last who it was. A grin broke across his face and he rose up in his stirrups.

"General Bairstow! By the Word! General Bairstow!"

Brent flashed his teeth and waved. "Just Brent Bairstow now, I'm afraid, Colonel. Sibbald, isn't it? You used to be a major, congratulations. What brings you out to the Crossroads?"

Seventeen

Munsten – Privy Council Chambers – end-August 901 A.C.

AFTER A LIGHT lunch in his chambers, President Healy continued the conversation at the long table that filled the Privy Council conference room. Seated at the table were Mushir Adham, Kamal Sherwami and the newly promoted General Ben Miller. They were dressed in contrast: the sand colour of Adham, the black cloth of Kamal, and the shining half-plate of Miller. The remnants of their lunch lay strewn across the table on platters and truncheons. Healy sat at one end with the others all seated to one side, placing the large windows overlooking the city of Munsten behind them. Fresh wine had been brought in and they resumed their conversation. They had been discussing the series of failures that had Healy furious over the past months. He was only now able to talk about it calmly.

"Despite your assurances that losing Jergen is not a significant setback and your willingness to lose half your army, I am worried, Mushir. This army of Turgany was to be no match for your men and yet they wiped them out in mere moments."

Mushir Adham kept his face impassive and waited until Kamal translated the words to him. He then spoke in his speech for a time. Kamal turned to Healy. "Mushir Adham says his men were ambushed at sea. The cannons of your Navy gave them no chance. But he also says it changes nothing. His main strength comes from here in Munsten. His army with yours will be unstoppable."

Healy shook his head. "That is what you said about the army entering Jergen. They were to be unstoppable. You are not giving me a sense of comfort here. I need assurances that our efforts will be successful."

"And you have them, President Healy. The army of Mushir Adham is formidable. It has crossed the entire breadth of his continent and was never beaten. The entire land is his. Once your army finishes their training and learns to fight with his men, you will see their strength." Kamal turned to Adham and said something quickly. Adham nodded and remained silent.

"This language barrier is proving to be tiring," said Healy. The pauses in the conversation were irritating and it was getting harder to stay calm.

Kamal smiled. "Yes, it is, but nothing can be done for it. There are things even I cannot do anything about."

Ben Miller leaned forward to speak. "Sir, what Mushir Adham says is correct. The army of y-Mushir Hassim was laid waste by cannon fire from the Admiral's ship-of-the-line and two other ships. It was the first time used in anger. The results were devastating. Reports are that over half his army was wiped out just approaching the harbour and all the ships sunk or damaged beyond repair. The Admiral is a potent adversary. With these new weapons, any ships—or an army too close to shore—are going to be hurt badly. We heard y-Mushir himself was killed by the guns. If I can find a way to mobilise the guns for use with my Army, I could take the entire realm in mere weeks.

"Thankfully, y-Mushir Hassim was able to burn two of the Admiral's ships to the waterline. Oil and flaming arrows. That leaves the Admiral with three ships. Only one with cannon. The other two remain at Portsmouth stopping the rest of the Fleet from leaving.

"Intelligence reports from Jergen tell us that the Baron Windthrop had outside assistance. Tough and capable fighters that no one had seen before. Well-armed trained and working too well as a team. Friendly to the Baron and guided the action in Jergen. They pushed the men of y-Mushir into the harbour and back into the maw of the Admiral's guns. The Baron has help. He has subsumed the garrison and increased his numbers. They trained together before leaving the city for the Crossroads. The threat is increased, and I do not recommend we take this army lightly.

"Speaking of which, as it is, we train every day to keep our readiness levels. But I do not have good news. My army is not learning to fight with your men, Kamal, begging your pardon. They are learning to fight alongside your men, but quite frankly their methods are too foreign to us and they show no sign of trying to adapt to our methods. We will need to remain in our own formations. The efforts in the field have been eye-opening, to say the least. I've ordered the men separated back into their formations. The men are now working better together by staying isolated. Discipline remains my main concern. There is a lot of discontent within the Army. They don't trust these men of yours, Kamal. Fights are springing up everywhere."

"The men of Mushir Adham, not mine," corrected Kamal with a slight bow of his head. Miller frowned confused and looked at Healy.

President Healy cleared his throat. "Nonetheless Kamal, my army must work alongside the army of Mushir Adham if we are to be successful. The threat from the south cannot be ignored especially if the Baron has help. You are forgetting that Bairstow and those loyal to him are now free and heading south to join Turgany."

"Yes, sir," said Miller. "They number close to one hundred and fifty. Bairstow is a sound tactician, not as good as Frederick was, but still a threat. His addition to the Turgany army is significant."

"I still find it unfathomable that he could escape the city so easily."

"It was Gillespie himself that brought them out. No one would question him. His temper was legendary and his punishments severe. Those on duty never had the mind to question him leaving the city with a large number of men and women soldiers, unarmed as they were. He was an ass and to be honest, the troops would rather see him fail than support him. I've taken the two sergeants he hung around with and moved them out of the city up to Cala. I never trusted them. Violent men and abusive. Just like Gillespie."

"Have you found Gillespie?"

"Yes, sir. It's one of the things I need to update you about. We tracked Bairstow to the old manse Redgrave owned some miles south of the city near the coast. Bairstow stopped there for a couple of nights and then headed south to Curachan. He resupplied his people and then continued south to join the Baron at the Crossroads. We found Gillespie lying by a small creek behind the ruins. His throat was sliced open right through to the spine. Whoever killed him hated that man more than most. I would wager Bairstow did the deed."

Healy drummed the table with the fingers of his right hand and then grunted. "So, Gillespie's dead. No loss to the world, I admit. The man was an idiot. I still fail to understand why you wanted to give that man so much responsibility." This last statement was directed to Kamal. Miller frowned at the words and looked over at Kamal, but the man merely shrugged. Healy scowled and looked back to Miller. "Rest assured Ben, you were chosen by me. Should have been you all along. Politics interfered with that. But Redgrave's manse? Why would they go there?" He looked at Kamal, but the man merely looked back at him.

"No idea, sir," answered Ben. "As I've said, Brent's met up with the Baron of Turgany and his army at the Crossroads. They've been there ever since training and exercising. The good news is the Baron has shown no sign he intends to move toward Munsten. The bad news is our estimates place the total number of enemy soldiers at the Crossroads at a thousand strong."

Healy drummed the table again and then sat up straighter and reached for his wine goblet. He swirled the fine wine and then set the goblet back down, untouched. "That vicar Martin surprised me. He seemed so craven. And yet he released all those prisoners and Brent. Surprising, all said and done. Who knew he had such depth?"

"Yes, sir. The turnkey has been executed as per your orders."

"Good. I cannot suffer those disloyal to the Realm."

"The escape has been kept quiet. No one knows."

"I find that unlikely, still, better to try to contain these kinds of things. I remember when..."

A soft tap at the conference room door interrupted President Healy, and they all looked toward the door. "Enter," he ordered, and the door swung inward to reveal the guard captain on duty outside the room.

"Sir, a message for you arrived moments ago along with a small sealed sack," announced the man and he strode forward with a silver tray held in both hands. He placed the tray on the table in front of Healy. On the tray were a scrolled missive and a small leather sack, tied tight with wire and sealed with wax. Healy thanked the man, who saluted and backed out of the chamber. The door closed quietly and Healy looked at the others.

"How strange," he said to them and then examined and broke the Turgany seal on the missive and unrolled it. "It's from Windthrop." He started reading and his eyes grew wider, and he stood up. "What is this? A jest?"

"What is it, President Healy?" asked Ben Miller. He rose from his seat and came around to stand beside Healy. Healy finished reading the message and handed it over to the General. Miller scanned the words and then read aloud to the others.

President Healy, the Army of Turgany demands parley at the Crossroads on First Mabon at midday. The subject of your tyranny and the open admission of enemy forces into Belkin requires resolution. The time has come to end your unlawful rule and return the realm to order.

It is expected you will refuse. We offer an incentive. A taste of that which you have sought for so many years from Bill Redgrave.

Signed Lord Andrew Windthrop, Baron of Turgany.

Healy grabbed the leather sack and broke the wax seal and pulled at the wire securing it. A soft metallic clink could be heard, and Healy emptied the sack onto the silver tray. Gold crown coins spilt noisily onto the tray. They glinted in the sunlight coming through the chamber windows. Healy gasped and reached out to snatch a coin. He held it close to his face and looked at both sides. They were old coins but real. Healy sat heavily into his chair and stared at the gold in silence. Mushir Adham stood up and spoke rapidly to Kamal.

Miller picked up a coin and examined it a moment. He dropped it back on the tray and picked up the small sack. He peered inside and then reached in and pulled out a small piece of paper. Healy looked up and Miller read it.

There are over five thousand more coins in my possession. Redgrave hid them in the ruins of his old manse. Come get them.

Signed General Brent Bairstow.

He handed the note to Healy who read it once and tossed the note and coin on the tray.

"The bastard," he said.

"Who?" asked Miller.

"Redgrave. He stole that gold right out from under me all those many years ago. I never knew who had taken it until he was found alive sitting fat and stupid in a small town in Turgany. We searched everywhere for years. Never found a trace. Never figured out how he got the gold out of the treasury." Healy grew quiet and then smashed the table with a fist. The silver tray and coins jumped. "The bastard! All those years he hid the gold under the ashes of his family's grave."

Mushir Adham spoke again in a rapid manner and pointed at the coins. Kamal frowned and turned to Healy. "Adham asks if this is part of the gold you promised him and have yet to deliver?"

Healy sighed.

"What now, my Lord?" inquired Miller after Healy sat fuming for a long time without answering.

"We march to the Crossroads."

Miller sat down in the chair next to Healy. "Sir, I cannot recommend that course of action. We are strong and secure here in Munsten. Let them come to us where we control the outcome. They will beat against our walls until nothing remains of the treasonous lot."

Healy appeared not to have heard and Miller swung in his seat to look to the Mushir for support. The Mushir frowned and turned to Kamal. Miller was surprised to see a small smile appear on Kamal's dark face.

"I think that will be showing weakness, General Miller. We should march to these crossroads and show the Realm we are not afraid to defend the land from those who would seek to usurp the rightful ruler. Long has Redgrave taunted the rule of President Healy. Your president is correct in what he means to do. With the army of Mushir Adham, you cannot lose. We must march to the Crossroads."

"That is madness!" said Miller. He turned back to Healy. "Sir, please, listen to me as your General. Give me time to pull in more troops. I need more longbow archers from Cala. They won't be here until October at the earliest. The Crossroads is a bad place to fight. It is nothing more than a vast plain. We give up all our advantages."

Healy blinked and focused on Miller. "Kamal is correct. We march to the Crossroads. Get started. Dismissed."

Miller sat back in his chair and stared at Healy for a moment. He glanced at Kamal and was aghast to see him openly smiling at him. He scowled and rose from the table. "Yes, sir. For the record, I am against this course of action."

"Noted. You are dismissed," repeated Healy.

"Aye, sir," replied Miller. He came to attention and saluted and quickly left the chambers.

Kamal smiled a little broader. "It has begun."

Healy nodded, continuing to stare at the gold on the silver tray.

Eighteen

The Crossroads – Day after September 21st, 901 A.C.

DAWN BROKE TO the east on First Mabon sending swaths of bright crimson bursting along the long line of distant clouds on the horizon. North of the Crossroads lay the combined Turgany Army in neat order. Nearly one thousand men and women were lined up and turned to the north where a half-mile away twelve hundred members of the combined army of the President stood in opposition. On closer inspection, the Turgany Army could be seen sweating despite the abnormally cold morning for September. The cool air with the warm, dew-covered grass had lifted a thin fog that drifted across the field. Rains had held off for a week and the field between the armies was dry with grass, full of seed, no higher than the knees.

Behind the Turgany Army, the leaders sat astride their destriers. The flags of Turgany and the Baron flapped lazily in the slight wind. The Baron sat ramrod straight in the saddle trying to strike a pose that would instil courage in the men and women fighting for him. Beside him was General Brent Bairstow, his rank restored by the Baron when Colonel Sibbald insisted and the men and women nearby cheered until he agreed. Beside Brent was Major James Dixon, his rank restored and then promoted by Brent.

The army of the President lined up across the field, led by General Ben Miller. Cavalry, archers and pikemen stood hazy in the foggy air. On the flanks were the strange men from the East. Some were on horseback, but most remained on foot. They were in constant motion—circling and jeering. The result was a considerable noise from the field. Men and women conversed, and the noise only grew louder.

Miller had arrived the day before and spent the time setting up his camp and moving back and forth across the line. Brent had formed up yesterday to keep an eye on Miller. It had been a long day. Nearby, the Crossroads had emptied on sighting Miller's army. The owners of the shops and taverns had vacated and moved well to the south. Sensing a feast, crows circled above riding the currents.

Brent turned his head to look behind him as Vicar Martin came hustling up to speak to him.

"Th-*huff*-the chirurgeons tents are set up as directed, General Bairstow."

"Very good, Vicar Martin."

"If you please, I would like to remain here and help where I can," said Martin out of breath.

Baron Windthrop snorted. "What are you going to do to help?"

Vicar Martin looked first to Brent and then to the Baron in some surprise. "Why, Lord Windthrop, I will attend to the men and women of your army and see to their spiritual needs. Especially when close to death. Many will need the comfort of prayer and the words of God."

The Baron looked awry and said nothing.

Brent smiled at Martin. "That would be most welcome, Vicar Martin. Please be careful. I can't spare anyone to watch over you."

"I place my safety in the hands of God."

Brent nodded.

James leaned over. "Tell me, Vicar, is Edward with the chirurgeons?"

"He rather insisted on it. He has already caused quite an uproar with them. They had to be reminded that he is the heir to the throne. Now he has them boiling water and bandages."

The Baron grunted. He had not taken the news that he was no longer the next in line for the throne well. He had disputed Edward Hitchens claim until the man had lowered his hood and shown what he looked like. There could be no doubt in anyone's mind: he was the son of the late King. Despite the evidence, the Baron continued to dispute the claim. Brent had suggested the druids confirm it. The Baron stopped arguing and instead became even more ornery.

"Daft lot those chirurgeons. Wish we had Will here," muttered James.

The Baron looked sharply at James. "Major Dixon, that's enough of that."

"Yes, my Lord," came the meek reply, but James winked at Brent.

The Baron looked around in annoyance. "I still fail to understand the need to be standing here for hours waiting for midday."

James remained silent but widened his eyes toward Brent.

Brent chewed the insides of his cheeks. "With me, James." Brent gave his horse his head and moved at a slow walk down toward the front line of soldiers. James fell in beside him. The Baron watched and then rolled his eyes.

"Where are they going?" complained the Baron out loud.

"I suspect they are going to talk to the men and women who fight for your cause, your Lordship," answered Martin. "And give them courage."

As the sun reached its zenith, the Baron ordered the white flag unfurled. His flagman held it aloft and rotated it in slow arcs above his head. In response, a similar white flag was raised by the other army.

"Your Lordship, the parley has been accepted. If you would?" Brent beckoned ahead of him with his arm.

The Baron swallowed and nodded his head. He gave a sharp kick to his horse and then reined it back to a brisk walk. Brent and the flagmen carrying the flags for Turgany and the white parley rode in behind. Once together they broke into a trot and rode down through the opening in the ranks to emerge out into the open field. A small table with two chairs had already been placed in the centre of the field. They rode directly toward the table and watched as a similar band of horses broke through the ranks of the enemy and preceded to the same location. The man at the head was General Ben Miller. He was flanked by two of the men from the East. Behind him were two flagmen carrying the parley flag and the flag of Belkin.

Both groups stopped short of the table and all but the flagmen dismounted. Baron Windthrop walked over to the table and stood behind his chair and placed a hand on the back of it. Brent stepped close but stopped a few feet short. He watched as the General dismounted and walked over to stand behind his chair. The two figures from the East came over and stood behind him on either side. They were dressed somewhat the same except the one on the right wore black with a bright sash over his shoulder and the other wore a light brown colour. *The one on the left is Mushir Adham, and the other in black must be that Kamal fellow,* thought Brent.

Kamal seemed intent on Brent and stared hard at him. Adham seemed bored and looked about aimlessly. Both Kamal and Adham carried scimitars, but they were sheathed, and their hands were kept well clear. Brent turned and nodded to the parley flag bearer. The man dismounted and came forward and placed the flagpole into a holder on the ground. Ben Miller's man did the same and soon both white flags fluttered in the midday sun.

"Shall we sit?" asked the Baron.

"I do not sit with criminals. You and Bairstow are under arrest for treason to the Realm. I suggest you surrender yourselves forthwith and retreat your armies from the field. This farce has gone on long enough."

The Baron opened his mouth to speak, but nothing came out. Brent cursed under his breath at the Baron. *Dammit, we spoke about this. We expected this line of discussion.*

The Baron looked back at Brent with eyes pleading for assistance. Brent sighed inwardly and stepped forward and stopped. Ben Miller arched an eyebrow at Brent.

"If I may, the Baron is not used to this kind of discussion. He simply does not know when a completely stupid remark is made in his presence and how to respond. We are not criminals. We represent the return of order to a realm long held hostage by the acts of a tyrant. We speak of Lord Protector John Healy."

"President," replied Ben Miller.

"I don't care what he calls himself. Ben, you can't possibly be siding with that ass."

Ben smiled. "From where I stand I appear to be on the winning side, Brent."

"I prefer to be on the right side."

"As do I."

Brent laughed, startling the Baron. "So here we are. Me, standing with an army behind me that seeks to revert the realm back to normalcy, and you with an army seeking to keep the people ignorant while one man opens the realm to an invading army. That sound about right?"

"No, it does not. I see my army trying to push back an open rebellion that threatens the realm to the point where an ally was required to exert authority. Your efforts are weakening the land. This is futile, Bairstow. Surely you see that? You were never the fool."

"And you were always the officer looking to get ahead quickly by whatever means. Enough, do you mean to engage?"

Ben nodded sharply.

"Fine. You there," said Brent to Kamal. "Why are you here? What do you hope to gain? Dominion?"

Ben spoke before Kamal could. "They are our ally. The realm is in turmoil throughout. Villages and townships are rising up. The Church is gaining strength and the threat of a new revolution is becoming surer every day. Your efforts have stirred up discontent throughout the land. With my allies, we will strike you down and re-assert control over the realm. You are criminals, nothing more."

Ben jutted his chin at the Baron. "Lord Andrew Windthrop is an embarrassment and a freak. He is playing at thrones and has no empathy for the grief and pain he is causing—he thinks only of his own personal gain. He was to be arrested in Jergen. Resisting arrest is only one of his many crimes. You, Brent Bairstow, are guilty by association. Both of you are to be trialled and then executed."

Brent grew quiet. "Tell me, Ben Miller. Did my brother Frederick ever speak to you? Share with you the results of the investigation I once led and handed over to him? You were never on our list of those under the thumb of the Lord Protector. He would have approached you. Showed you just how corrupt Healy is. What did you do then, I wonder? I think I know the answer for here you are standing tall and wearing the uniform my brother once wore with pride and honour.

"What swayed you? You know the man has a heart as black as the deepest night. He is greed and hunger for power all wrapped up in delusion. You have joined forces with an army that seeks to wipe this realm from the face of the earth. They will salt the lands and leave no one behind alive."

Ben glowered. "Enough. This parley is over." Ben turned away and mounted his horse. Kamal paused for a moment to stare at Brent with a cold intensity. Brent felt a sudden stab of cold fear and fumbled for his amulet and pulled it free. Kamal eyed it and spun away and mounted his horse. Mushir Adham grinned at Brent and went to his horse.

Brent kept an eye on the three as they started to ride away. "Come, Lord Windthrop. They will attack as soon as they return to their ranks."

The Baron looked around confused. "What just happened?"

"Nothing happened. We are at war. Same as before. Come."

"What about the table and chairs? And the parley flags?"

"Leave them. It will all be kindling soon enough."

The battle began with the skirl of the bagpipes and the hard beat of the drum. It was the Baron who called the attack first. The combined Turgany Army had its soldiers in three lines of equal ranks to the army of the Realm's two ranks.

Behind them were the archers in the staggered lines of a chevron. The cavalries of both sides were held back, and reserves were pulled to the rear. Central to both armies were the protected leaders. Red chirurgeon tents lay far back from the lines. Messengers stood ready beside their leaders to relay orders.

The front lines of the soldiers bristled with pikes, throwing spears, and locking shields. The Turgany Army's archers closed behind the soldiers until they reached bow range. The drums changed the beat, and the sky filled with arrows. Cries rose, and shields were lifted overhead. The arrows fell and here and there an unlucky soldier would fall with a cry, pierced through. From behind, they would be replaced as others moved forward from the rear ranks to fill the holes. With twenty paces between the armies, the order to throw was given and throwing spears sped between the armies. The army of the Realm protected forward against spears as arrows rained down from on high.

Baron Windthrop gave a nod to General Brent Bairstow. "Excellent timing, General. The practice paid off."

Brent ignored the comment and kept his focus on the field. The Baron, Colonel Robert Sibbald and Major James Dixon were all that made up the field headquarters. All the other officers were down at the battle. They refused to remain apart from the soldiers. Brent could see them now yelling orders and riding back and forth behind the line deflecting arrows with a raised shield. Brent was proud of them.

"Arrows down to half," intoned Colonel Sibbald.

"Roger," replied Brent.

"Adham's men are behaving oddly," said James.

Brent had noticed. Adham's men were positioned on each flank of the Realm army. They walked almost nonchalantly, oblivious to the order of the Realm army. Many were struck by the arrows fired their way. They seemed to make a game of it, dodging and leaping to the side at the last possible moment.

"Here it comes," muttered James.

The armies clashed with a thundering crash. Brent winced at the sound. It was a sound like no other. Impossible to describe, but it could loosen the bowels of the stoutest individual. The crash was soon followed by the cries of pain and suffering from those struck on the field. The air above the soldiers filled with a fine red mist. The right flank wavered.

A change in the pipes from the enemy was heard and immediately the Calvary of the Realm wheeled in tight formation and surged toward the right flank. Brent opened his mouth to give an order but Sibbald beat him to it. The Turgany drums beat a quick staccato and the first Calvary of Turgany charged to the weakened flank. The enemy cavalry hit the flank but the Turgany soldiers were ready. They had trained for this and shields were set and pikes lowered in a descending line.

A moment later the enemy cavalry hit the line. It erupted with sod and earth and flying horses and men. Horses screamed in pain and terror and Brent held his breath. His soldiers seemed to bend backwards and then, miraculously held strong. For a moment, cheers were louder than the cries of pain and death. Half the cavalry lay broken on the line. But the line was weakened, and the soldiers struggled to right themselves against the enemy soldiers prodding for weakness.

"Reserves," ordered Brent.

The pipes blew a quick series of notes and the reserves, already anticipating the order, ran forward to bolster the weakened flank.

"Good job, Major Crenshaw," murmured Brent. He glanced to Sibbald. "Good choice putting Bill in charge of the reserve."

"Humph, it wasn't a hard choice."

Brent smiled and then scowled when he spotted the look on the Baron's face. The man was revelling in the mayhem in front of him. A look of lust filled his face and Brent caught James' eyes and tilted his chin toward the Baron.

James looked over and gave Brent a look of worry.

"Keep an eye on him," whispered Brent. James and Sibbald both nodded.

The reserve joined the line and quickly filled the ranks. The line wavered with the newcomers until a balance was found and then held. Along the line, the soldiers hacked at each other. The splintering sound of shields and the strike of metal on metal was high and piercing.

Men and women moved forward and pulled the wounded free where they could. The wounded who could walk would stagger out of the line to be replaced by soldiers from the second or third ranks. Elsewhere, chirurgeons would dart forward to drag individuals out from the line regardless of what wounds they had. Entrails and limbs often followed their effort. Chirurgeons would jump forward and apply tourniquets, point toward their tents, or simply shake their head and move on.

Steve Comlin had discussed how to use the chirurgeons with Brent one night at the Rigby farm. He mourned the loss of so many who could have been saved. "We need a way to get trained people up to the line to tend to the wounded. A great many simply bleed out who could be saved."

Brent had never forgotten the conversation and had discussed it with his officers. It was Crenshaw who suggested the chirurgeons take a more active role. He had seen the mayhem at Jergen first hand. "Have them move forward and pull out the wounded. Saves our own men doing it, or watching their friends bleed out beside them. We have enough. Mark them with white armbands. Hopefully, the enemy honours them and leaves them well enough alone."

The enemy appeared to be honouring them. Except for the Adham soldiers. They whirled and struck wherever they could. He feared they honoured little but themselves. Both flanks were hard pressed now against the superior numbers. Brent watched the Adham cavalry milling about across the field. They seemed to be readying for something.

"Send in the second cavalry. Have them strike the enemy's left flank," ordered Brent.

Brent heard Sibbald yell out to the pipers and drummers. The pipes changed their tune, and the drums beat out a complicated rhythm. The cavalry spewed up the grass and sped directly at the left flank. The left flank pushed hard once and then pulled back and split. The cavalry charged through the opening and plunged into the enemy flank. They burst through and a great cheer erupted across the field.

The Adham Calvary appeared confused for a moment and then charged at speed. Brent watched his cavalry reform and then charge the enemy cavalry. They were on the other side of the line and charging at a full gallop. Swords whirled and glinted in the sun. Horse met horse and the sound of hundreds of pounds of flesh impacting and bones shattering filled the air. Swords flashed, and bodies fell from horseback. Horses free of riders continued to run full speed in a straight line, some dragging their lifeless or wounded riders behind them.

The cavalries shattered. What remained wheeled and charged again. Soon only a few horses and riders remained, and they stopped beside each other and hacked at one another until only a dozen Adham riders remained.

"By God, what a waste," said Brent. "That was stupid."

"By the Word! That was tremendous!" cried out the Baron.

James caught Brent's eye. "A waste for certain, but they eliminated a threat. They did not die in vain."

Brent grimaced and then nodded. Sibbald looked shocked at the loss.

On the field, the armies of both sides were staggering in exhaustion. They could barely lift shield or sword. Those that did hit did little damage with no weight behind the swings.

"Call for a rest," ordered Brent.

The pipes soon called out a tune that any in the Realm would recognise.

Both armies slowed down and separated a little. The Adham soldiers hesitated and then stepped back. The army of the Realm looked back at their leaders and soon an answering tune was heard in return. A dull cheer rose from both sides. Men and women reached down and pulled the wounded free of the carnage and retreated across the field. Mercy was given to those who asked. Chirurgeons from both sides raced from wounded to wounded. Reserves came forward with water and food.

"Ask for an hour," stated Brent.

The pipes queried, and an agreement was returned.

The Baron did not look happy. Sibbald looked to speak to his Lordship, but Brent held up a hand and stopped him. "Let me," he said. "Baron, a word in your tent, if you please."

The hour passed all too quickly, and the lines reformed. The reserves were now gone and only half the cavalry remained. It looked much the same for the Army of the Realm except they continued to have greater numbers. The archers spent the hour crafting as many additional arrows as they could, but in an hour, it wasn't much.

The pipes called the attack, and the battle resumed. The arrows flew, shields blocked, some fell, and then the armies clashed again but with renewed energy. As suddenly as the clash was heard the enemy cavalry called a full charge and ran the centre of the line. As before the Turgany centre was not holding strong. Brent saw what was coming and called out, but it was too late. The enemy had reacted too quickly. The cavalry ran over their own people and drove hard into the middle of the line. The soldiers were not ready, and the cavalry burst through. Bodies flew left and right.

Crenshaw on the field ordered the cavalry to respond just as the pipes began to repeat Brent's orders. Brent gripped the pommel of his horse and leaned forward. The cavalries met and separated. *Too many*, though Brent. *Too many have fallen. We can't counter this.* He considered ordering the archers to fire, but the combat was too close. He would be killing his own people. He looked to Sibbald and saw a horror there that mirrored his own.

He heard cries from behind him and his stomach lurched. *They have flanked our rear. Somehow, they got behind us.* He turned, drawing his sword, to face his doom and cried out in alarm as he spied dozens of bears and wolves running through the camp. They ran past him and charged into the enemy cavalry. They leapt up to the throats of horses or took swings with massive claws. The eyes of the horses of the enemy turned white in fear and they reared and bolted. *Why are our horses not reacting?*

He heard the thundering of horses behind him and looked back to see Steve Comlin leading his crew toward the battle. Steve raised his sword in salute and Brent laughed and brandished his own. "About time!" yelled out Brent.

"Sorry," yelled back Steve as he thundered past a startled Baron. "Takes a while to round up bears and wolves..." and then he was gone and leading his crew toward the break in the line.

Nineteen

The Crossroads - September 901 A.C.

MY DRAOI AND I had drawn power heavily from the land to run the entire way to the Crossroads from the farm. We lent our strength to the horses of the crew and they surged ahead and made exceptional time. We followed on foot and ran with the wind. Nadine remained in constant communion with Gaea and relayed the details of the battle from the eyes of the crows flying high overhead. We knew we were late, but it couldn't be helped. In desperation, I had asked those with the greatest skill in working with the animals of the land to lend their aid.

It turned out Gaea had been ahead of us. Dozens of bears and wolves were already gathering and heading to join the fight. I was pleased and saddened. It was not only people who would fight for the Realm but the wildlife as well.

On hearing we would be late, Steve had asked the draoi riding with him for a burst of speed and we gave it to him. He leapt ahead, and Nadine reported he was now engaged on the front line and fighting to repair a break. I wasn't sure what that meant exactly and just nodded.

We reached the Crossroads soon after Steve and raced forward toward the sound of battle. We came through the camp and there we found Brent Bairstow wearing the rank of General yelling orders. The skirl of pipes filled the air with an annoying sound that nearly drowned out normal conversation. Nadine and I rushed up to Brent and looked up to see him smiling down at us from horseback.

"Well met, Will Arbor. Thanks for bringing Steve and his crew to us. But I suspect it is you who we will be needing the most. Have you come to heal the wounded?"

I glanced over at the Baron who was bringing his horse over. A deep frown on his face clear for everyone to see. "No. Well, sorry, yes, we are. But more, too."

"More?"

"Yes, we've come to fight. Join you. This is our fight, too. There's something you need to know…"

"About time you realised that young man!" interrupted the Baron with a bellow. "Where were you when I asked those many months ago, you coward?"

Nadine growled and made a motion with her hand. I have no idea why she always has to make motions when she uses Gaea's power. Yet she does. This time it marked the seizing of the Baron's jaw and tongue. The Baron choked and grabbed for his throat. "There, there," cooed Nadine. "You can breathe just fine… for now." Nadine turned to Brent and beamed a smile. The sun lit up her face and her heavily freckled cheeks and nose were there for all to see. I wouldn't let her remove them. I loved them. My heart lurched to see her so vibrant every time I looked at her. She skewed her eyes at me and glared and I turned my thoughts back to the here and now. "Brent Bairstow!" she cried. "Look at you all high and mighty now! When did you get to be so tall?"

"Cill Darae," replied Brent and bowed his head a moment. "Still as charming as ever. Glad to see you. Now would be a good time to do something about…" he waved a hand over the battle behind him. "You know, the battle?"

"Ah yes, we've already started, young man. Patience."

Brent blinked and looked back at the field. His men and women had found new reserves of energy. He could see them swinging harder and defending faster. The druids had formed a tight cluster near Brent and were holding hands with their eyes closed. A handful of them was running toward the chirurgeons tents. Brent looked around and counted my draoi. "Three dozen?" he asked.

"Yes. Our people are combining their strength and channelling Gaea's power to the men and women," I said as a way of explanation. "It takes focus of mind. Now, if you could excuse me? Nadine?"

"On my way," she said and ran off toward the healing tents.

I joined my draoi. Tara took my hand without looking and I closed my eyes and opened my sight and drew in the combined power of Gaea.

My *vision* flared with the life forces of the armies. I saw the life drain from those fallen and merge with Gaea. I saw the bright life forces of the men and women straining to vanquish each other and we pulled power and steeled arms and quickened muscles. Shields now raised with little effort to block blows and steel whistled faster through the air to strike down those in range. It was effortless to us. Gaea lent the draoi her strength and with our guidance, we became a finely tuned weapon of destruction.

My gut recoiled, and I expected the cost of doing harm to strike us. In a moment, when nothing came back to punish us, I realised we were correct in what we thought would happen. I smiled. We were not directly attacking the enemy. Instead, we merely strengthened those who would do the harm. It was a way to cheat the penalty, but one that worked for us. Gaea seemed not to mind.

I had never seen a battle, but I imagined this was no ordinary fight. Gaea had made it clear that this was important. We were not attacking an enemy so much as attacking a force whose only goal was the eradication of the Realm and the nature of the land. We could not afford to lose. The enemy we faced on the field was only a small part of the war that Gaea had been fighting for a millennium. The winner would be left to finish the fight. This was only the beginning.

I heard Brent cry out softly in triumph. The line was moving forward and pushing the enemy back. Here and there the line was bending. The enemy was breaking down into knots of defenders, surrounded by our strengthened soldiers. I watched Steve harry the cavalry and force them from the field. He moved his crew into the fight and they chopped down at the enemy lines. Here and there cries of elation broke from the soldiers and cries of "For the Realm!" could now be heard rising above the din. Even the annoying bagpipes seemed to reach a new louder volume.

The dead were stepped over and left behind and the enemy line was pushed back two feet, then four, then ten. My draoi were elated at being a force of change. They channelled their power through me. Tendrils fed the bears and wolves and enabled them to leap higher and reach further. I felt the first stirring of hope and pride surge through me. I also felt a fear grow inside me.

The power we wielded was unseen in this world. Never before had the druids come together for such a purpose. Without Gaea's guiding hand the power would be unstoppable. We could rule this land with ease. Take it for our own and force it to do our bidding. The power was intoxicating. *Was this my future?* I worried. *What horrors could I commit with this power?* As soon as I thought these words, I knew they came from the fear that had always lain within me. My doubts about Gaea lay open for me to examine them. And I knew them to be false. A sense of relief came over me and my draoi sensed it. Their joy and release gave me new strength.

Just as I began to smile I heard cries from the field. I opened my eyes and watched as the fallen, now behind the ranks, rose from the ground and attacked our army from the rear. Cries of fear rippled across the field from both sides. The Turgany Army turned to this new threat and the Army of the Realm broke and ran from the field. Their General rode forward screaming, and the enemy turned back to the field and closed the line.

I watched a lone figure walk toward the line from where the leaders of the Army of Turgany were clustered. He was a strange figure, covered in a black coloured tight-fitting attire with a sash across his shoulder. Here was the enemy I had seen with the President in Munsten. I watched as he pushed forward through his army. Erebus had joined the battle.

On the far ridge, I could still see the General of the Army of the Realm screaming at his soldiers and pointing to the battle line. Most had returned and realised the risen were fighting on their side. Chaos swirled across the field. The risen army hacked and slashed at the Turgany Army. The soldiers on the field screamed in terror and tried to flee, but the dead rose all around them. Former friends rose to fight against friend. Our Army was overwhelmed.

My attention was pulled back to Erebus. As I watched as his form shimmered and writhed. Suddenly Erebus revealed himself and strode forward, his body sucking in the light. A shadow lay all around him. Fear stabbed me. This was what I had wanted to warn Brent about. Here was the true enemy to the land.

My *sight* was blind to him just as it was with the risen army. My powers could do nothing to him or them. I watched as our army fought against the risen. They hacked off limbs and yet the risen continued to fight. Erebus continued to stride confidently forward and there was nothing we could do.

I heard a horse dig deep into the soil with its hooves behind me and Brent raced past me toward the line. He stood on his stirrups with his sword held high and was screaming in defiance.

"Begone creature of chaos!" cried Brent. He reached within his tunic and tore something free. He held it forward beside his sword. It was his amulet. It twisted in the wind of his passage. I saw Erebus stop and turn its head toward Brent. As one the risen stopped and spun in place until they faced Brent. In a moment, they ran at him in a strange loping gate. Brent continued to charge toward Erebus, heedless of the risen who closed in on him.

As I watched, the amulet froze against the wind and a piercing light burst from it and struck Erebus in the chest. The risen between Brent and Erebus were flung to the side and lay motionless. Erebus staggered to a knee and then righted himself. He held up his hands and pushed back on the light. I reached out desperate with my powers, but it flowed uselessly around Erebus like river water around a boulder.

A second flash of light appeared behind Erebus and Gaea stood there alone and vulnerable. Erebus turned toward her and the light from Brent struck him on the back. He staggered forward and then stopped. I could see Gaea say something to Erebus and he moved toward her.

"No!" I cried. I reached into my power and drew strength from the life all around us. I reached out to everything I could. I became a conduit and was soon surrounded by swirling energies expanding outwards from me like a flood. As the power touched the risen, I found to my surprise I could faintly sense them. It took so much power to do so. I seized the opportunity and focused on the nearest and fell into it with my *sight*. My draoi came with me. Much like I had done in Jaipers to cure the plague I now searched for answers within the body.

I dove deeper into the corpse and found motes similar to the ones from that small town. They were everywhere in the blood and flesh. Tiny motes that seemed to have their own will. The body was riddled with them. I then noticed that there were two kinds of motes. Throughout the body, I could see motes emptied of life and recognised I was seeing the remnants of a battle between Gaea and Erebus—only at a much smaller scale. Here in this body, Gaea had lost the fight with the life of the person and opened it to control by Erebus.

I reached out to a living soldier. In her blood and flesh, I observed the two kinds of motes but both in balance and fighting. I turned to one of my draoi and there I saw only one kind of mote. I turned to Brent and found both, but one in greater numbers.

I understood then and shared the knowledge with Nadine and my draoi. *Why didn't you tell us?* I asked Gaea.

It does not change anything, she replied. *It is what it is. This is the battle I have fought for my entire existence. Some long ago would have called it the battle between good and evil. It is not. It is a battle for dominance of the planet. Erebus is not any eviler than I am. We have our purpose. We fulfil it. I would argue he has lost his purpose, but he continues to disagree with me.*

Planet? I asked.

This world, she replied. *I fear my battle may soon be lost. I had hoped an open confrontation would result in a different outcome.*

I sensed Brent drawing closer to Erebus, his amulet still shining brightly. Nadine and the draoi listened to everything that was said and remained silent, but I felt their confusion at the words.

We all sensed a finality from Gaea that we could not accept. Time was almost up. Erebus continued to advance on Gaea, his back absorbing the power from Brent's amulet. It was in that moment I accepted fully I was the Freamhaigh. My draoi looked to me for direction.

With my *vision,* I could see the power coming out of the church symbol on one side. The other side, which bore the mark of the draoi, was dull. With inspiration, I focused and pushed all my power into the symbol of the Tree. My power was pulled like a nail to a lodestone through the amulet.

The light pouring from the amulet doubled in strength and continued to drive into Erebus. He froze for a moment and then lunged at Gaea and smashed her in the chest with both fists. Gaea staggered backwards and the light from the amulet winked out. Gaea was gone. My power was gone. My draoi staggered at the sudden loss.

Brent screamed in defiance and leapt from his horse and flew toward Erebus. He struck him from behind and drove him to the ground. Erebus reached behind him and threw Brent aside. In an explosive shout, he screamed at Brent. "It is over, can you not see that? I have won! This planet shall now return to what it must. The long wait is over."

I reached for the power of Gaea and found nothing. My draoi all reached out and grasped at nothing with each attempt. I refused to believe Gaea was gone. All around me was life. She could not be defeated by a simple blow. I watched as the bears and wolves fled the field in all directions. The risen stood and did nothing.

Brent got to his feet and recovered his sword. He held it out to one side and circled Erebus with the amulet held out with the other hand. Without my power, I could no longer hear what was being said, but it looked like Brent was taunting him. Erebus turned with him and then lunged at Brent. He sidestepped and swung at an outstretched arm and struck it. From the distance, it didn't look like it did any harm.

Gaea? I cried out. *Where are you?*

Brent and Erebus continued to circle one another. Erebus was laughing and beckoning Brent to come forward. I could see Brent looking at the amulet and saying something.

He's praying to his god, I realised. I had a sinking feeling. *Now's the time, Gaea. Wake up!*

Like the sun bursting through a hole in the clouds I felt a stutter in my power. I grabbed it and felt elation and the return of my strength. My draoi all looked up with joy and grabbed hands. I pulled power through them with no limitations. I reached out to the land of Belkin and pulled it all to me. I held it in my mind and then burst the power through Brent's amulet.

The beam of power from the amulet was as bright as a small sun. The full force of it struck Erebus in the chest and he burst into a cloud of a million black specks. The wind tore the cloud and lifted it clear and away to the east. The risen fell lifeless to the ground.

A blackness tore through my draoi and I. We had used too much power. The blackness reached up and pulled me down.

Brent blinked away the bright spot that filled his vision and swung wildly with his sword in case Erebus was still standing near him. He heard in the near distance the roar of Ben Miller ordering his men back to the battle. *It seems the battle is not over yet*, he thought. *And I'm on the wrong side of the line.*

He thought for a moment and stilled his sword swings. There were too many sounds around him, but he could hear the smashing of swords and yells that marked the line. He was blind and knew he had to get away. He whistled and called out for his horse. *It must still be around. Where would it go? Home? Hmm, perhaps. It was a smart horse.*

He heard the clop of hooves right near him and he turned and reached out and found his saddle. "Good girl!" he cried and reached up and pulled himself into the saddle and kicked the horse into a gallop. He rode toward the sound of his troops, blinking his eyes furiously but they refused to clear. All was white. *Probably burned them out of my head. I thought blindness would be black, not white.*

He heard a call ahead that sounded like his name. He urged his horse toward it.

"Brent, this way!" came the familiar voice of James.

Brent thanked God and drove his horse toward the direction of his friend's voice.

Franky parried a low strike and moved sideways around the man's shield and drove the point of her sword into the man's exposed armpit. He went down quickly, and she pulled her sword free before it was trapped. She sensed a strike from behind and turned to see Steve block a blow that would have easily killed her. She rolled forward and came up with her sword raking the woman's abdomen, splitting her leathers and cutting deep. The woman fell to the ground holding her guts. Franky stood up beside Steve and looked around. There was a lull in the surrounding fighting.

"Thanks, love," she managed to say between heavy breaths.

"No problem," replied Steve from atop his horse. "Would be easier if you had kept your horse."

"Be easier if it had managed to stay alive, poor thing." Franky looked around the battlefield. The armies were locked in combat once again. Without the draoi lending their power they were now losing. *Just when you think you are winning, you start losing. Pisses me off,* she grumbled to herself. "*Time to bug out* I would say back when we ruled the roads."

"Yup, except it's not. We are in this to the finish. You okay here?"

"Am now. Off you go, see to the others."

"Stay safe."

"Stay alive." She watched him leave and burned the image in her mind in case this was the last time she saw him alive. She had done that countless times in the past. She had been happiest when they were highwaymen. Life was simpler. Even the loss of her arm hadn't bothered as much as it should have because of the crew. They sympathised with her but never doubted her. *Least of all Steve. That kept me hopeful. I saw the concern and the love there that day. And I've chased it ever since. And now he's mine. All mine.*

Franky caught a strange motion in the corner of her eye and turned to see one of the eastern soldiers advancing on her position. He swirled and whirled with that sword dance they practised. Franky had seen many of them use it in Jergen. They were all dead. *Once you understood what they were doing, it was easy to see how to fight it.*

The man struck down one of the Baron's men and then looked over at Franky and smiled.

"What are you smiling at, you freak?" declared Franky.

The man noticed she was missing an arm, and the smile faltered. "No arm?" he asked. "Not much fight for a man such as me."

"Is that so? Who might you be?"

"I am Mushir Adham, leader of the Cian-Oirthear."

"You speak our language?"

"Yes, since a little boy. One of our house slaves was from your land. She taught me."

"She?"

"Yes, a wonderful slave. She gave me many pleasures."

Franky grinned at him. "Want one more?"

"Oh, what pleasure might that be?"

"Well, to be honest, it will please me more than you." Franky took a defensive stance.

Adham raised an eyebrow. "You wish to fight me? A one-armed woman? You throw your life away so easily?"

"Enough chatter, come at me, you sick bastard."

Adham scowled. He slowly started his dance with his sword and then sped up. He spun around Franky with a skill born of years of experience. Franky stayed still and only moved her eyes to follow him. She waited and then struck with a stunning speed. She landed one solid blow.

The head of Mushir Adham, last of a long line of Mushirs of the Cian-Oirthear dynasty, fell with a thud to the churned-up grass and rolled to end up facing the rear end of a fallen horse.

"Enjoy the view."

Steve Comlin spotted James Dixon riding with Brent Bairstow and wheeled away from the battle to join them. James was leading him back to the headquarters area where the Baron was arguing with Colonel Sibbald. He rode up beside them and noticed Brent blinking furiously.

"What's the matter with your eyes?"

"Blinded by the light."

"Saw that, thought you were dead, to be honest. Glad to see you're alive."

"How's the battle look? James isn't being honest with me, I think."

"Looks bloody awful. Without Will's druids, we are losing badly."

"What happened?"

James answered. "I'm not sure. That Gaea woman disappeared. Your light went out. Then it came back, stronger than ever. The draoi collapsed as soon as that black monster blew up into a cloud of smoke. We can't wake them."

"Steve, what do you think?" asked Brent.

"As the love of my life just told me, we need to bug out."

"Bug out? What's that mean?"

"Sorry, highway talk. Means retreat as fast as possible. We can save lives here. I think I have a way. Hold up, we're here and the Baron and the good Colonel are yelling at one another. Pretend you can see. Be easier. Trust me."

The sound of bickering grew louder until they rode up to the Baron. He stopped yelling at the Colonel and turned to Brent.

"General, you're back. Good. Tell the Colonel now is the time to push forward. Victory is at hand. He wants to retreat!"

"Good idea. Colonel, call the retreat," ordered Brent.

"What!? Are you insane? We have to win!"

"Yes, we do, on our terms. We were winning, now we aren't. The smart thing to do is run. Lick our wounds, regroup and strike again. Colonel, what are our loses?"

Steve could see the Colonel looked startled by the question. He raised a warning hand and shook his head ever so slightly. The Colonel closed his mouth and then turned to Brent. "Sir, we are suffering staggering losses. Two thirds dead or wounded. Sorry, but the count is not accurate. That is my best estimate. We should have enough to vacate the field provided the enemy allows us. It will be painful. We will lose many more. This needs to happen now, sir."

"Lose them by staying to fight!" yelled the Baron.

"Lord Windthrop. If we continue to fight, we lose all the men and women. If we retreat, we lose less and survive to fight another day. This is a simple matter. We must retreat, and we are."

"General Bairstow, I will have your head for this!"

"On whose order, Lord Windthrop? Enough, your ambition clouds your good judgement. Colonel, call the retreat. Steve, what's your plan?"

The Colonel yelled for the retreat and the bagpipes changed their tune. The Baron looked like he had apoplexy. Steve looked at the field and spotted Franky striking down another of the eastern soldiers. *She's taken a liking to fighting them.* "I'll harry them with my crew. Been doing this for years for the Baron. Fine time to start doing it for you, General. Start getting your people off the field. I'll give the soldiers something else to worry about. Could use your archers though. I need accurate shooters. People who can shoot near to us as they can and not hit us. Keep the pressure on the enemy. How much time will you need?"

Brent kept blinking his eyes and looking around. "That depends on the wounded." The Baron studied him trying to determine what the problem was.

Steve looked toward the red tents and saw the caregivers loading the wounded into carts. They weren't being soft about it. Steve could see the urgency. "I see the Colonel has already ordered emptying the red tents. Wounded are going into carts and wagons."

The Baron looked at the red tents being evacuated and frowned.

Colonel Sibbald snorted. "Seemed prudent."

Brent thought a moment. "Good man, Colonel. Hmm. Thirty minutes should see us moving south. Best guess I have."

James was nodding. "Sounds correct, Brent. Thirty minutes and we're moving south of the Crossroads."

"Fair enough," said Steve. "If you've archers fleet of foot, have them stay between you and the army and continue to rain down arrows when they can. It'll be helpful. We've wasted too much time already. People are dying."

"You'll have the archers, Steve. Thanks, and good luck."

Steve turned to the Colonel. "Get him to Will as soon as he wakes. He needs his eyes back."

Steve rode off to sounds of the Baron losing his mind once again and chuckled to himself.

Twenty

Rigby Farm - October 901 A.C.

WE MADE IT back to the farm three weeks later. The retreat from the Crossroads had only been possible with the help of Steve's crew. General Ben Miller had been unable to bring his army together to pursue the fleeing Army of Turgany with Steve's crew harrying them and keeping them scattered. The remnants of the Turgany Army were singing praises of his men and women. Franky had reached an exalted status with the tale of her beheading Mushir Adham. It was getting more elaborate by the day. We felt like heroes but in truth, we had suffered a tremendous loss.

The Baron had retreated to his manse in Turgany in the country. Before he left Brent had had a long discussion with him. Steve had joined them. The Baron would still be the figurehead of the rebellion, but no longer would he fight at the front.

Rebellion was a word Steve had come up with. We all liked it and it was spreading across the county. It was a much better word than Revolution. We already had one of those and it hadn't worked out well for anyone. We were in open rebellion and the Army of the Realm would soon come for us.

Brent, Vicar Martin, James, Steve, Franky and the crew, and the newcomer called Edward Hitchens, all returned to Rigby Farm. We were depressed and had a lot to talk about. We had remained silent most of the way remembering those who had fallen. My draoi moved through the army and consoled those who needed it. Vicar Martin had proven to be very good at helping others and many lit up just to see him come by to talk.

Many approached us cautiously and started to ask about the draoi and what we were. No one was frightened. At least not very much. They had seen the good we could do. Many talked about how it felt to swing a sword with such ease. Others pointed at areas of their body where they claimed to have been struck and then healed. With not a mark to show for their wounds, some were annoyed we had healed them so thoroughly. My draoi promised to leave scars the next time. It seemed we had been accepted.

Even Vicar Martin embraced us. He had seen both sides of the amulet and the light. I found out later that a light had come from me directly to the amulet. I hadn't seen that. He had and was thinking hard about it. He told me he was certain we weren't demons, and he had laughed such a deep and long laugh that Brent and the others had joined him.

When we arrived at the road leading to the farm Steve's crew and the draoi left the army and they carried on toward Jergen. We thought it best they winter there. The walls and harbour would protect them from President Healy. At least for a time. Colonel Sibbald, with Major Tibert and Crenshaw, were positive they could swell their numbers. We needed the army, but the future had yet to be discussed.

The draoi we had left behind on the farm told the others of our arrival. The farmhands greeted us and Dempster had prepared a feast for us. Of the sixty crew who had left the farm with the Baron, only thirty-six now remained. Twelve more had been killed at the Crossroads. Too many had died already in this stupid war. I wanted it over. There was too much death, and the crew were friends of ours.

We had a simple ceremony and a celebration of life at our farm cemetery. I looked at all the grave markers. There were so many. Most were empty, but the markers reminded us that we were paying a price and a heavy one.

My draoi were proven stocs and welcomed in this part of Belkin. We had recovered from the power drain with massive headaches and sore muscles. Use of our power was like heat on a burn. We avoided it for a time. We had woken on the run lying next to wounded in carts. Once we felt stronger, we went to work healing everyone. Forty stocs all working together can heal a staggering number of people. The chirurgeons had the good sense not to interfere. Edward Hitchens had made copious notes and observed our work. I found it hard to believe he was the rightful heir to the throne. Steve asked me quietly to check to see if it was true and I had laughed at him. The draoi were starting to have mystical powers now. When I told him I would need the father or mother to compare him to, Steve had stalked off. One thing was certain, the tale he told of his mother telling him he was the son of the mad King was truth to him. He believed it.

Of Gaea, we heard nothing from her. Nadine looked glum, but the fact that our powers were still with us gave us hope. We all heard what she had said on the field. This battle had been her plan all along. She had brought all this together and then failed.

The others all seemed so despondent and Nadine and I shared a look. The draoi had something we would share. We had hope for the future. We had learned life always finds a way, and we had life all around us. Nature was just as vibrant as always.

Once we were fed, and the horses cared for we retired to the dining room table in the main farmhouse. The crew were getting boisterously drunk in the outbuildings and Dempster was singing for them. He had a lovely tenor voice and knew a surprising number of dirty songs. All thanks for having owned the Woven Bail Inn in Jaipers.

Dempster had provided snacks and pulled out the very best wine for us. It all sat untouched, and we stared at one another. For some reason, I found myself at the head of the table in the same seat Ben Rigby had used. I felt small for the size of the chair and squirmed a little. Nadine smacked my leg and frowned at me.

"So, here we are," I began. Franky smirked and eyed Steve. Brent and James smiled a little. Vicar Martin was looking longingly at the pastries on the tray. Edward sat quietly and probably felt more uncertain than I.

"Here we are," agreed Brent. "Hope is not lost, everyone. We have an army made up of seasoned soldiers. They will train the new soldiers. We will be stronger than before. We know the effect of having draoi on our side. We will win this war and bring back the Realm to where it should be."

"And where is that exactly?" asked Steve.

Brent looked annoyed at the question.

"Now, now, hear me out. Where is it that the Realm has to be? Back to a King on the throne? We saw where that led us."

James leaned forward to speak. "In all fairness, we had one bad king in centuries of rule. You have to admit that the Realm under the Lord Protector..."

"President," interrupted Franky.

"President. Fine. Whatever. Anyway, it's been worse than the king before him. This can't continue. We need a better government. Why not start with a king? Maybe place rules on him this time. Govern him a little. No more 'his word is law' crap."

They bantered about government for a little until Nadine and I grew tired of it. It wasn't solving anything.

"Ladies and gentlemen, please!" I interrupted.

"Did he call me a lady?" asked Franky, faking insult.

"Hush," said Steve. "Let him speak. He's our boss now, remember?"

"Humph," said Franky and slouched lower in her chair.

"I'm no one's boss. I'm just the Freamhaigh of the draoi. A focal point. We decide as a group now. Just one of the many little changes we made, Nadine and I." Nadine made a small noise and when I looked she had her face expressionless. "Haha! This is serious. We need to speak about Gaea, Erebus and the amulet."

Brent leaned forward. "And God," he added. Vicar Martin nodded in agreement.

I looked at Nadine and she nodded. "And God. Sure. I discovered something remarkable on the battlefield. All my draoi know and we have talked about it. I want to share this with you. You all have a right to know. Steve, you remember Jaipers and the infection?"

Steve nodded.

"I cured the village. I saw within the villagers what I then called motes. Little things were in the blood of those infected. It caused the sickness. It attacked the body and spread itself. Duplicated."

Edward looked up, suddenly interested. "By the Word, motes, you say? I hypothesized that a year or so ago. Little organisms in the blood that cause sickness. You say you have seen them and can prove it?"

"Prove it? I suppose. I'm here to tell you it's the truth. What's more, at the Crossroads, I saw something else. All the draoi did. We shared the experience joined the way we were. I discovered two other kinds of motes. For a lack of a better way to explain it, I want to call one Gaea motes and the other Erebus motes. You all have them in your bodies."

I saw a look of concern cross everyone's faces, and I held up a hand. "Sorry, you do! But don't worry, they are in balance. Everyone has equal amounts of Gaea and Erebus motes. It's in the animals, too. It's everywhere. There are exceptions though.

"One, the draoi, we only have Gaea motes. I don't know why or how. But we have all checked each other. We all agree. No Erebus. Just Gaea. Brent, you have more Gaea than Erebus. Same as you, Vicar Martin. Everyone else, its equal proportions.

"I bring this to your attention because it brings things into focus. This is not a war between the President and the Realm. This is a war going on inside everyone and every animal. The results of which will mean that should we lose, Erebus will eradicate all life on earth. Gaea has been fighting him for thousands of years. She fights for us. If he wins, we all lose. Everyone and every living thing. Everyone has a war going on inside them

"The draoi were so confused for so long. Somewhere along the line this balance was what the draoi fought for. The draoi could have been doing so much more, I think. They didn't know, and Gaea said nothing. She's to blame for a lot of this. She says it didn't matter that we didn't know, but I don't believe her. I can't.

"So here we are. What we do know is that the President is under the sway of Erebus. We face an enemy of his making. We must fight the President and remove his influence on the land. It will give us a better position to fight from."

"Wait, what?" asked Brent. "Erebus is dead. We killed him. You all saw that."

"No, Brent," answered Nadine. "Only his corporal form was destroyed. He's in you right now. All of you. He is everywhere."

"You mean he can hear everything we are saying right now?"

"No, we don't think so. Gaea needs to focus herself to influence things directly. The day-to-day talk is ignored by her. We think it is the same for Erebus."

"You think?"

"We have no reason to believe otherwise, Brent Bairstow," responded Nadine glaring at him.

Vicar Martin patted Brent's arm to calm him. Brent leaned back in his seat. "It's important, Nadine. I ask because it is important to military planning. So, stop glaring at me. I'm not arguing with you, I'm asking questions that need to be answered."

Nadine opened her mouth to say something nasty, and I pinched her under the table. She yelped and turned on me. "Stop it, Nadine. He's right. We take things for granted and expect others to understand what we intimately know to be the truth. For others, we need to spell it out. Offer proof if need be."

Edward nodded at me.

"This is the challenge for the draoi. We need to make others understand what we are and why we are. Prove to them we are not a threat. We work for Gaea. Her soldiers, you might say. Time for us to get smarter."

"Great," said James. "Can we start that with wine and pastries in our stomachs?"

I couldn't help it. I laughed and soon the others joined in. Nadine found my hand under the table and squeezed it. We looked at each other and smiled.

We had hope.

Epilogue

Outside Cala, October 901 A.C.

KATHERINE RIGBY PULLED the rabbit out of the fire and tore it gingerly in two and then blew on her hands where the hot grease had burned them. Dog whined seated next to her and laid his head on her leg and forced it down a little to let her know he was there and hungry, too. He had watched the rabbit cook for the past thirty minutes, not letting it out of his sight once.

"Ya think I don't know you're hungry, Dog? I can feel it up here." She tapped her head for emphasis. "It's too hot and you know it. Be patient."

The past week had been spent gathering herbs in the area surrounding Cala. Having the sickle from Nadine made the job so easy. She almost respected Nadine when she had offered it to her. *I took it out of spite but now I love the feel of the black glass in my hand.* Dog thought of it as her little claw.

The nights were getting colder, and she had used the last of her herbs trading for warmer clothing and a thick wool blanket to sleep under. She and Dog curled up together every night now and shared the warmth. His coat was thick, and she loved lying next to him. She felt safe and warm. So did he.

Their relationship was a strange one, even she admitted it. They loved each other but not like Will and Nadine. It was a pure love but one that crossed species and had nothing of that gooey stuff Will and Nadine were always doing. They were companions of the heart, true and simple. She was finding it harder and harder to separate where she ended, and he began.

Adding to the mix was that Dog was becoming increasingly intelligent. They didn't speak but shared images as thoughts. She and he had become adept at understanding each other. She found it necessary to use words out loud if only for her own sanity. It kept her feeling human.

Dog had been a boon to her. When she had disappeared into her own despair and grief at the farm, it was Dog who reached down and pulled her up from the darkness. She owed her sanity and well-being to Dog. And she loved him all the more for it.

The journey to Cala had been long and arduous. Dog had an instinct for survival and had treated Katherine like a new cub for most of the journey. He always stayed close and steered her away from dangers only he could smell. They had avoided bears and wolves and stayed clear of other humans.

She couldn't stand being around people anymore. People reminded her of her other life. The one with mom and dad and the time before Will Arbor had shown up and destroyed all she had held dear. She didn't blame Will. He was her Freamhaigh and he could hide nothing from her. He was free of blame for what transpired. He felt guilt anyway. If anything, it was Gaea's fault. *Her, I hate.* And yet she loved her, too. It was complicated, and she hated complications.

Dog had it right. Stay away from bad things. Live a happy life chasing rabbits and eating rabbits and sleeping with a belly full of rabbits. That was life. That was all that was important.

But she was fooling herself and she knew it. She could sense the wrongness in the world and knew a terrible battle was occurring just beyond normal sight. A war that had likely been going on for a long time.

Katherine and Dog had spied Gaea from time to time. She would spy on her, always from a distance. It didn't bother Katherine. It gave her peace of mind. She was glad to know someone besides Dog was looking out for her.

Will had looked out for her. He had taken the time to show her how to survive out here. He had known somehow that she would be leaving. Sensed it and rather than dissuade her he had helped her. She admired that. He was a good man and she could see how Nadine had fallen for him.

She looked out with her senses and spied the thread that tied her to the other draoi. She could see the one that tied her to Will's and saw the white that was part of the link. Dog's bond, she could see, was thick and a bright solid white that pulsed with their shared heartbeat. She knew it wasn't normal, but she simply didn't care. It was what it was.

When she deemed the rabbit cool enough, she placed Dog's share down on the ground in front of him. He looked at her and when she took her first bite, he wolfed his down. Bones crunched and were swallowed, and in a matter of seconds, his rabbit was gone. She had barely swallowed two mouthfuls when he started eyeing hers.

"Hey, greedy guts. You want more, go hunt more. This is mine, doogie-doog."

Dog panted in laughter. It amused her that dogs really did pant in laughter. Their faces really did smile like humans, showing their teeth. Part of the bond between dogs and humans, she figured. They adapted to us. Poor things.

She finished her rabbit and gave the carcass to Dog. It was gone in seconds and Dog licked his chops in deep satisfaction. *Raw rabbit is good*, she thought, *but I like the cooked kind better.*

Katherine blinked and shot a look at Dog. It was happening again. Dog's thoughts became her own. "Stop that!" she admonished him. Dog looked guilty and then leaned forward and licked her greasy lips. "Yuck! Get off me, dog breath!" She pushed at him with one hand and wiped her mouth with the other. He playfully nipped at her fingers.

A small sound from just outside the campfire had them pause and look up. Dog didn't growl because they didn't smell anything. The wind was coming from that direction. *We don't smell anything. So it is nothing.*

Katherine and Dog looked back to the fire together.

"Can I come closer?" asked a familiar voice out of the darkness.

Katherine growled deep in her throat. Dog looked in the direction of the voice and panted a smile.

"I promise I won't stay long. We need to speak."

Katherine looked at Dog and he continued to pant happily.

She blew hair from her face. "Okay, come over to the fire."

Gaea stepped into the firelight and sat cross-legged on the ground across from Katherine and Dog.

"How was your rabbit?"

"Delicious. We would have saved you some if we had known you were coming," joked Katherine. Katherine kept her eyes away from Gaea. *It's easier to stay mad if we don't look at her.*

"I need to show you something."

Katherine glanced up and watched as Gaea opened her robe. Her chest and breasts were bruised a deep purple. Her whole chest was bruised. It looked terrible. Katherine stared in surprise.

"By the Word! What happened to you?"

"Erebus happened. One month ago, at the Crossroads. Do you know the Crossroads?"

Katherine nodded. *Of course, we know where the Crossroads are. Many smells of many people. We stayed away.*

"There was a battle. Against Erebus. You remember Erebus?"

Dog and Katherine growled.

"He struck me. The first time he has ever done that. It... it was unexpected. He has never attacked me directly. Not in that manner."

Katherine scratched the back of her ear. "Why?"

"We fight a different kind of battle. Always constant. I gambled and lost. I forced a direct confrontation. He was stronger. He always has been, but this was different."

"Different how?"

"I'm not sure, yet. I'm not sure I will ever figure it out."

Katherine stared at the bruise. In one month, it should have healed. Gaea should have healed it. She shrugged. "I'm not sure how we can help you."

Gaea closed her robes. "I think I know how, but it's drastic. Something someone a long time ago tried to convince me to do. I refused. Now, I don't see any other option."

"Who?"

"It doesn't matter. He was a good man. I miss him dearly."

Katherine picked at her pants a moment. "So, what do you want us to do?"

"Do you remember Seth?"

"Of course, I do! Why would you bring that monster up! He killed my mum and dad! Turned my dad into something horrible! He could never kill my mother, but he did! Seth did that!"

"Calm, Katherine. I don't mean to upset you. I just need you to understand what I am about to say. I think I have a way to defeat Erebus. I need you to become something not unlike what Seth was."

Katherine jumped to her feet and Dog raised his hackles and growled, teeth bared. "What!? Are you insane! I could never become what Seth was! An aos'si, one of the sluagh sidhe! How *dare* you ask that of us?"

"Calm, you two! Calm! It will not be like it was for Seth. I promise you that.

Seth was broken from me. Erebus used him then. I could not see him. Neither could Erebus. He was separated from the battle. Unseen by both of us. Erebus had gotten to him first. Moulded him into something he could use. I would do the same with you but with no deceit. I will be open and honest with you."

Katherine glared at Gaea for a moment and then slowly sat back down again. "You would separate me from your power?"

"Sort of. You would still have power. You would leach it from the world like Seth did. But I have to tell you, you would be separated from me and the other draoi. To them, it would appear that you died. But you would live. For a higher purpose."

"Wouldn't that do something to Dog and me?"

"Yes."

"Yes, what?"

"You would still have each other. I think it is that bond that will allow you to survive when for others it would drive them insane. Seth and the Archbishop lost their sanity over time. With Dog, that shouldn't happen."

"Shouldn't? You don't know?"

"No, I don't."

"What do you gain by this? Why would we agree to this?"

"Because you could single-handedly take down the greatest threat the world has ever known. You would eradicate Erebus."

"How?"

"You would infect him with what I am going to do to you."

"Infect him? How?"

"It's hard to explain. It is well beyond yours or anyone else's understanding. Much like a person gets infected and dies, you would become that infection. Except the infection would only target what Erebus is."

"And us? Would Dog and I get infected and die?"

"No, you would only be the carrier."

"Let me think on it."

"Fair enough. I'll be back tomorrow."

Katherine looked up and Gaea was gone.

Dog and Katherine sat in silence for a long time and the fire burned down to embers. She shivered in the cold night air and Dog moved up to lie against her. She grabbed his fur and laid her head on his back, and he laid his head on his front paws. They stayed that way for a time. The fire was almost gone, and the sky filled with stars.

"What do you think, Dog?"

Dog lifted his head and panted.

"Yeah, that's what I thought, too."

End of Volume Three

The New Druids Series continues with:

Freamhaigh: A New Druids Novel (Volume Four)

By Donald D. Allan

Acknowledgements

Along this journey I have been on for the past few years I have had a wealth of people who have supported me and encouraged me to continue writing. There's too many to thank you all personally. But, thank you all.

I've been recognised in Canadian Military magazines and had many interesting emails from fans of my stories. I've received a gold and bronze medal for Duilleog and Craobh (respectively) and that has helped me solidify my belief that I actually am an author. And getting better at this, I humbly submit. It's a wonderful feeling knowing that your work is appreciated.

I would like to thank my Friday night gaming friends, Ian and Steve (who crafted the maps). Thanks to Martin and Robert for the constructive criticism. Thanks to the Canadian Armed Forces and the Royal Canadian Navy for showing an interest in my writing.

Ciao!

Don
Ottawa, Canada, August 2017

World Details

Ranks and Hierarchies
Draoi (Druid) Ranks:
Freamhaigh (Root) – Head Druid

Cill Dara(e) – Druid Priest/Priestess (The Elevated Druid)

Stoc (Trunk) or informally just Draoi – Full Druid

Craobh (Branch) – Journeyman Druid

Duilleog (Leaf) – Apprentice Druid

The Church of the New Order Ranks:
King (in abeyance since Revolution)

Archbishop (acting head of the Church)

Bishop

Dean

Vicar

Army of the Realm Ranks:
Officers:

Knight General (former rank from before the Revolution)

General

Brigadier

Colonel

Lieutenant Colonel

Major

Captain

Lieutenant

Second Lieutenant

Enlisted:

Warrant Officer

Staff Sergeant

Sergeant

Corporal

Lance Corporal (appointment, not a rank)

Private

Recruit

Lord Protector's Guard Ranks:
The highest-ranking officer is General. Because the Lord Protector's Guard is a speciality occupation, the members come from the Army of the Realm, and occasionally from the Navy of the Realm. They share the same rank structure except that the lowest officer

rank is Captain and the lowest enlisted rank is Corporal; those being the earliest rank you can be selected or request service in the Lord Protector's Guard.

Navy of the Realm Ranks:
Officers:
> Fleet Admiral
> Admiral
> Commodore
> Captain (Navy)
> Commander
> Lieutenant-Commander
> Lieutenant (Navy)
> Ensign
> Midshipman

Enlisted:
> Chief Petty Officer
> Petty Officer
> Master Seaman
> Leading Seaman
> Able Seaman
> Ordinary Seaman

It should be noted that the General of the Realm is the head of the Army, the Navy, and the Lord Protector's Guard. The Lord Protector's Guard recruits from the Army of the Realm, and rarely, from the Navy. The Navy's top rank, the Fleet Admiral, is not equal to the General. In this world, the Navy is not the senior service.

Calendar and Seasons

The calendar is in the background of the world and not specifically referenced except where it occurs accidentally. We don't dwell on the calendar and neither do the folks in Turgany. In this world, the Celtic names for things have slipped and are rarely used. The common language is English.

Seasons:
Winter (Geimhreadh) – December, January, February (Nollaig, Eanair, Feabhra)
Spring (Earrach) – March, April, May (Marta, Aibrean, Bealtaine)
Summer (Samhraidh) – June, July, August (Meitheamh, Luil, Lunasa)
Autumn (Fomhar) – September, October, November (Mean Fomhair, Deirreadh Fomhair, Samhain)

Time Frames:
Day – dia

Night – nocht
Week – 8 days and nights—deug
Fortnight – 15 days and nights – cola-deug
Month – mios

Days of the Week:
Sunday – Domhnaich
Monday—Luain
Tuesday—Mairt
Wednesday—Ciadain
Pluday (Extra)—Durdaoin
Thursday—Ardaoin
Friday—Aoine
Saturday—Sathurna

Breakdown of a Year:
365 days in a calendar year for which only 360 are provided actual dates. The extra five days per year (see Solstices/Equinoxes) are used as celebration days and are known by their title rather than as a calendar date. It works like this: there is a December 24th, followed by Christmas Day, which is then followed by December 25th.
24 fortnights (24x15 days) per year
45 weeks per year
3 weeks and 6 days per month (totalling 30 days per month)

Solstices (longest/shortest day of the year)/Equinoxes:
Vernal Equinox is the day after March 19th (or Marta 19) and is celebrated for 1 day as Ostara Day (non-calendar day).
Estival Solstice (summer) is the day after June 20th (or Meitheamh 20) and is celebrated for 1 day as Litha Day (non-calendar day)
Autumnal Equinox is the day after September 21st (or Mean Fomhair 21) and is celebrated for 2 days as First Mabon Day (harvest) and Last Mabon Day (feast) (non-calendar days).
Hibernal Solstice (winter) is the day after December 20 (or Nollaig 20) and is celebrated for 1 day as Yule (non-calendar day).

Holidays:
Samhain. Nov 7 (Samhain 7). The midpoint between Autumn Equinox and Winter Solstice. Celebrates the last harvest, the cycle of life and gifts for passing spirits. Preparation to survive winter, confront the possibility of death. Colours: black, brown, reds, oranges. Opposite to Bealtaine.
Yule is the day after December 20 (Nollaig 20) and is a non-calendar day. Shortest day and longest night of the year. Celebrates the end of darkness, the return of light to the

earth. Herbs are at their least potent. Colours: green, red, white, silver, gold.

Imbolc. Feb 1 (Feabhra 1). The midpoint between Winter Solstice and Spring Equinox. Celebrates the quickening of spring, the end of winter, time of planning and hopes. Colours: red, orange, white.

Ostara Day is the day after March 19 (Marta 19) and is a non-calendar day. The first day of spring, the night and day stand equal. Celebrates the birth of spring, rebirth. Time of planting. Colours: red and yellow.

Bealtaine. May 6 (Bealtaine 6). The midpoint between Spring Equinox and Summer Solstice. Time of rebirth. Colours: blue, pink, yellow, green. Opposite to Samhain.

Litha Day is the day after June 20 (Meitheamh 20) and is a non-calendar day. Summer solstice, the first day of summer, longest day of the year. Celebrates the light and the sun without there would be no life. Time of strengths and accomplishments. Gather herbs as "herb night" is when they are at their most potent. Colours: blue, yellow, green.

Lammas. Aug 1 (Lunasa 1). The midpoint between Summer Solstice and the Autumn Equinox. First harvest festival. Celebrates the beginning of harvest season, the decline of summer to winter. Time to dismiss regrets, farewells, preparation for winter. Ceremonies involve bread, grains and corn dolls. Colours: oranges, greens, browns.

Mabon Days are the two days after September 21st (Mean Fomhair 21) and they are non-calendar days. Referred to as *First Mabon* and *Last Mabon*. Autumn Equinox, the first day of autumn. Celebrates harvest. First Mabon is harvesting time and Last Mabon is the feast. Time for thanks and learning, repairing all things. Colours: dark reds, yellows, browns.

Important Calendar Dates Summary:

February 1 (Feabhra 1)—Imbolc

March (Marta)—Ostara Day (Vernal Equinox) is the day after March 19th

May 6 (Bealtaine 6)—Bealtaine

June (Meitheamh)—Litha Day (Estival Solstice (summer)) is the day after June 20th

August 1 (Lunasa 1)—Lammas

September (Mean Fomhair)—First/Last Mabon Days (Autumnal Equinox) is the two days after September 21st

November 7 (Samhain 7)—Samhain

December (Nollaig)—Yule (Hibernal Solstice (winter)) is the day after December 20th

Currency

1 crown (large round gold coin) = 36 groats = 144 pence

1 half-crown (large round gold coin with a centre hole) = 18 groats = 72 pence

1 mark (small gold coin) = 9 groats = 36 pence

1 groat (silver rectangular coin) = 4 pence

1 tuppence (a small silver coin or large copper coin) = 2 pence

1 pence (copper coin) = 1 pence

1 half-pence (copper coin with a centre hole) = 1/2 pence

1 farthing (small rectangular copper coin) = 1/4 pence

Coins are measured by known weights under the Turgany Weights and Measures Act. For example, a full crown must weigh one royal ounce (28 gramme). A half-crown weighs a half ounce (14 gramme). And a mark weighs a quarter ounce (7 gramme) which means it is heavier than a Canadian quarter (25 cent piece) but sized about the same. A groat weighs the same as a mark (but is larger), and a tuppence weighs half that of a groat (hence if it is made of copper it will be larger). Typically, wealthy merchants will carry coin scales to verify that they are not being cheated with counterfeit coins. The habit of biting a gold coin was to prove that it was indeed gold—which is soft—and not some impostor.

Seven Tenets of Morality

1. Strive to act with compassion and empathy toward all creatures in accordance with reason.

2. The struggle for justice is an ongoing and necessary pursuit that should prevail over laws and institutions.

3. One's body is inviolable, subject to one's own will alone.

4. The freedoms of others should be respected, including the freedom to offend. To wilfully and unjustly encroach upon the freedoms of another is to forgo your own.

5. Beliefs should conform to our best scientific understanding of the world. We should take care never to distort scientific facts to fit our beliefs.

6. People are fallible. If we make a mistake, we should do our best to rectify it and resolve any harm that may have been caused.

7. Every tenet is a guiding principle designed to inspire nobility in action and thought. The spirit of compassion, wisdom, and justice should always prevail over the written or spoken word.

About the Author

DONALD D. ALLAN is an award-winning author for the New Druids epic fantasy series. He is best known for his knowledge of just about everything – just ask him, he'll tell you. He takes being a geek to massively huge geek levels – like level twelve. That's pretty high. Mostly, he's an introvert pretending to be an extrovert and so far, he's fooling everybody. Wine helps.

He loves lying around and planning his next activities, such as yard work, house repairs, cleaning, cooking, etc. He plans a lot, but never really completes it. But planning is everything. He does complete novels though, and that surprises most people. They say, "YOU wrote a book?"

Donald lives with his wife Marilyn, son James, daughter Katherine, and dog Woody, in Ottawa, Canada. Yup, he's Canadian. Respect.

Connect with Donald D. Allan:

BLOG: http://donalddallan.com
FACEBOOK: https://www.facebook.com/donalddallan
TWITTER: https://twitter.com/donalddallan/
EMAIL: donalddallan@gmail.com